TOMARE!

[STOP!]

You're going the wrong way!

Manga is a completely different type of reading experience.

To start at the *beginning*, go to the *end*!

That's right! Authentic manga is read the traditional Japanese way—from right to left. Exactly the *opposite* of how American books are read. It's easy to follow: Just go to the other end of the book, and read each page—and each panel—from right side to left side, starting at the top right. Now you're experiencing manga as it was meant to be!

CLAMP

TRANSLATED AND ADAPTED BY
Bill Flanagan

LETTERED BY
Dana Hayward

BALLANTINE BOOKS · NEW YORK

NEW HANOVER COUNTY PUBLIC LIBRARY
201 Chestnut Street
Wilmington, NC 28401

xxxHOLiC Volume 2 crosses over with *Tsubasa* Volume 1. Although it isn't necessary to read *Tsubasa* to understand the events in *xxxHOLiC,* you'll get to see the same events from different perspectives if you read both!

A Del Rey® Book
Published by The Random House Publishing Group
Copyright © 2004 CLAMP. All rights reserved.
First published in Japan in 2003 by Kodansha Ltd., Tokyo
This publication — rights arranged through Kodansha Ltd.

Published in the United States by Del Rey Books,
an imprint of The Random House Publishing Group,
a division of Random House, Inc., New York, and simultaneously
in Canada by Random House of Canada Limited, Toronto.

Del Rey is a registered trademark and the Del Rey colophon is a
trademark of Random House, Inc.

www.delreymanga.com

Library of Congress Control Number is available upon request
from the publisher.

ISBN 0-345-47119-9

Text design by Dana Hayward

Manufactured in the United States of America

First Edition: July 2004

12 13 14 15 16 17 18 19

Contents

Honorifics

Throughout the Del Rey Manga books, you will find Japanese honorifics left intact in the translations. For those not familiar with how the Japanese use honorifics, and more important, how they differ from American honorifics, we present this brief overview.

Politeness has always been a critical facet of Japanese culture. Ever since the feudal era, when Japan was a highly stratified society, use of honorifics—which can be defined as polite speech that indicates relationship or status—has played an essential role in the Japanese language. When addressing someone in Japanese, an honorific usually takes the form of a suffix attached to one's name (example: "Asuna-san"), or as a title at the end of one's name or in place of the name itself (example: "Negi-sensei," or simply "Sensei!").

Honorifics can be expressions of respect or endearment. In the context of manga and anime, honorifics give insight into the nature of the relationship between characters. Many translations into English leave out these important honorifics, and therefore distort the "feel" of the original Japanese. Because Japanese honorifics contain nuances that English honorifics lack, it is our policy at Del Rey not to translate them. Here, instead, is a guide to some of the honorifics you may encounter in Del Rey Manga.

-san: This is the most common honorific, and is equivalent to Mr., Miss, Ms., Mrs., etc. It is the all-purpose honorific and can be used in any situation where politeness is required.

-sama: This is one level higher than "-san." It is used to confer great respect.

-dono: This comes from the word "tono," which means "lord." It is an even higher level than "-sama," and confers utmost respect.

-kun: This suffix is used at the end of boys' names to express familiarity or endearment. It is also sometimes used by men among friends, or when addressing someone younger or of a lower station.

-chan: This is used to express endearment, mostly toward girls. It is also used for little boys, pets, and even among lovers. It gives a sense of childish cuteness.

Bozu: This is an informal way to refer to a boy, similar to the English term "kid" or "squirt".

Sempai: This title suggests that the addressee is one's "senior" in a group or organization. It is most often used in a school setting, where underclassmen refer to their upperclassmen as "sempai." It can also be used in the workplace, such as when a newer employee addresses an employee who has seniority in the company.

Kohai: This is the opposite of "-sempai," and is used toward underclassmen in school or newcomers in the workplace. It connotes that the addressee is of lower station.

Sensei: Literally meaning "one who has come before," this title is used for teachers, doctors, or masters of any profession or art.

[blank]: Usually forgotten in these lists, but perhaps the most significant difference between Japanese and English. The lack of honorific means that the speaker has permission to address the person in a very intimate way. Usually, only family, spouses, or very close friends have this kind of permission. Known as *yobisute,* it can be gratifying when someone who has earned the intimacy starts to call one by one's name without an honorific. But when that intimacy hasn't been earned, it can also be very insulting.

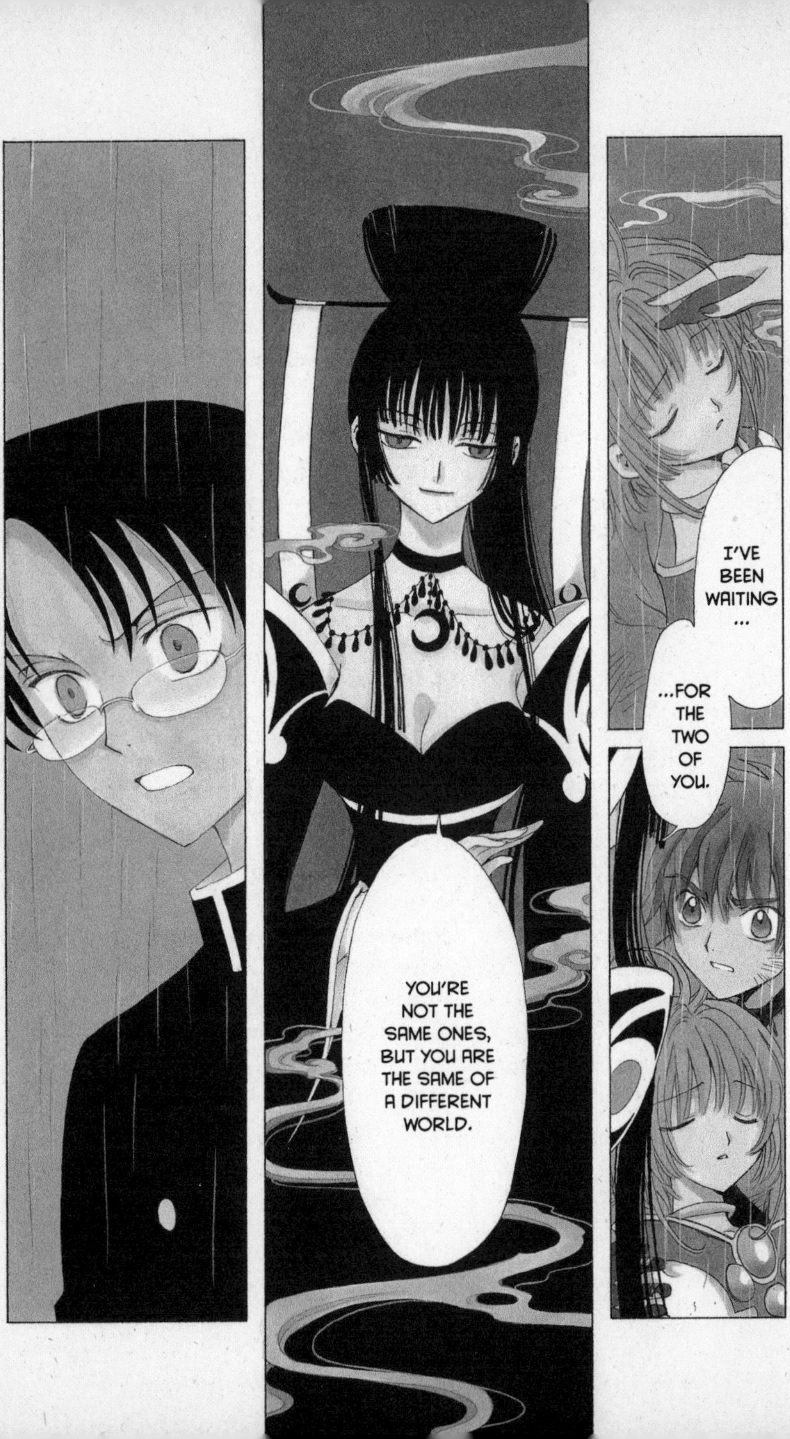
I'VE BEEN WAITING ...
...FOR THE TWO OF YOU.
YOU'RE NOT THE SAME ONES, BUT YOU ARE THE SAME OF A DIFFERENT WORLD.

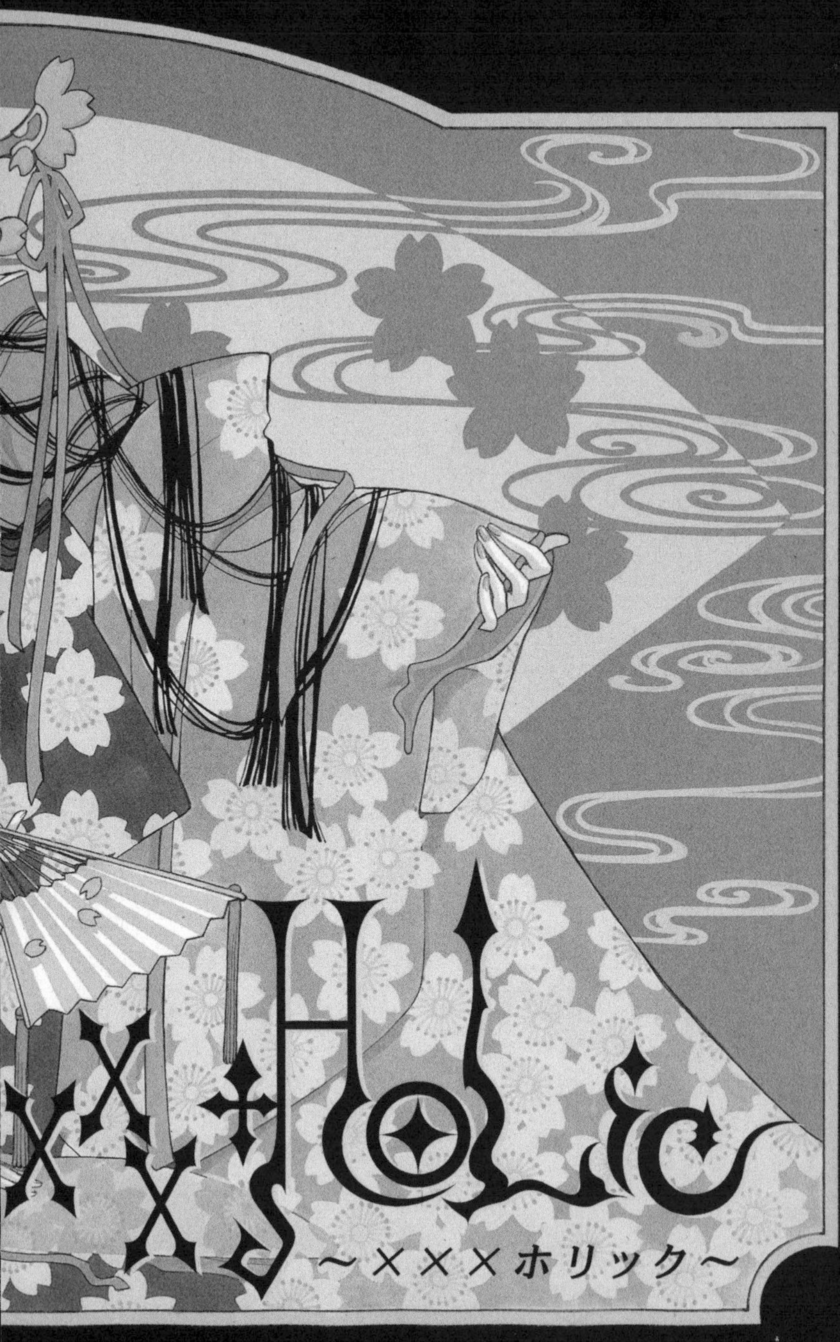
xxxHOLiC
〜×××ホリック〜

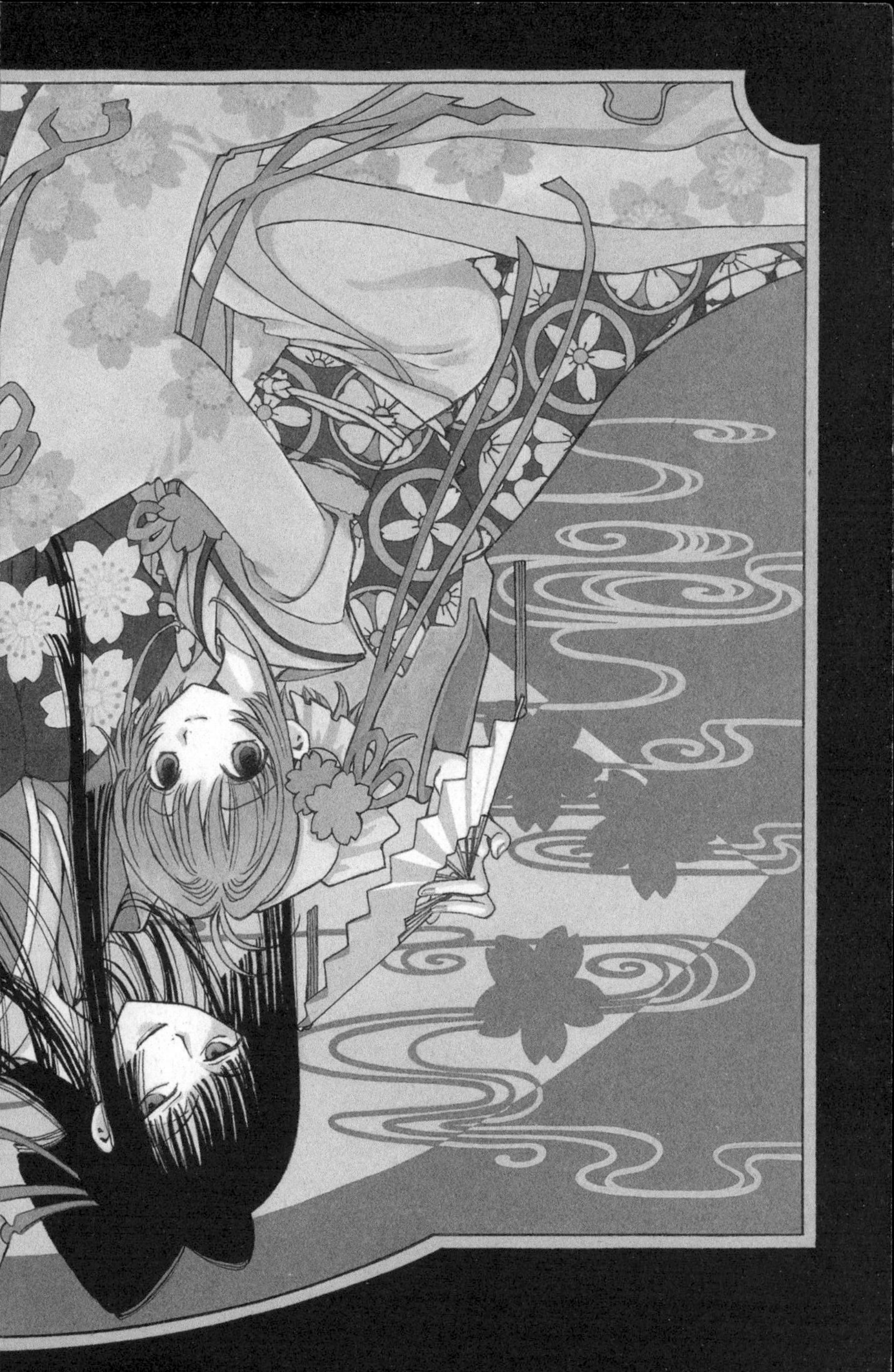

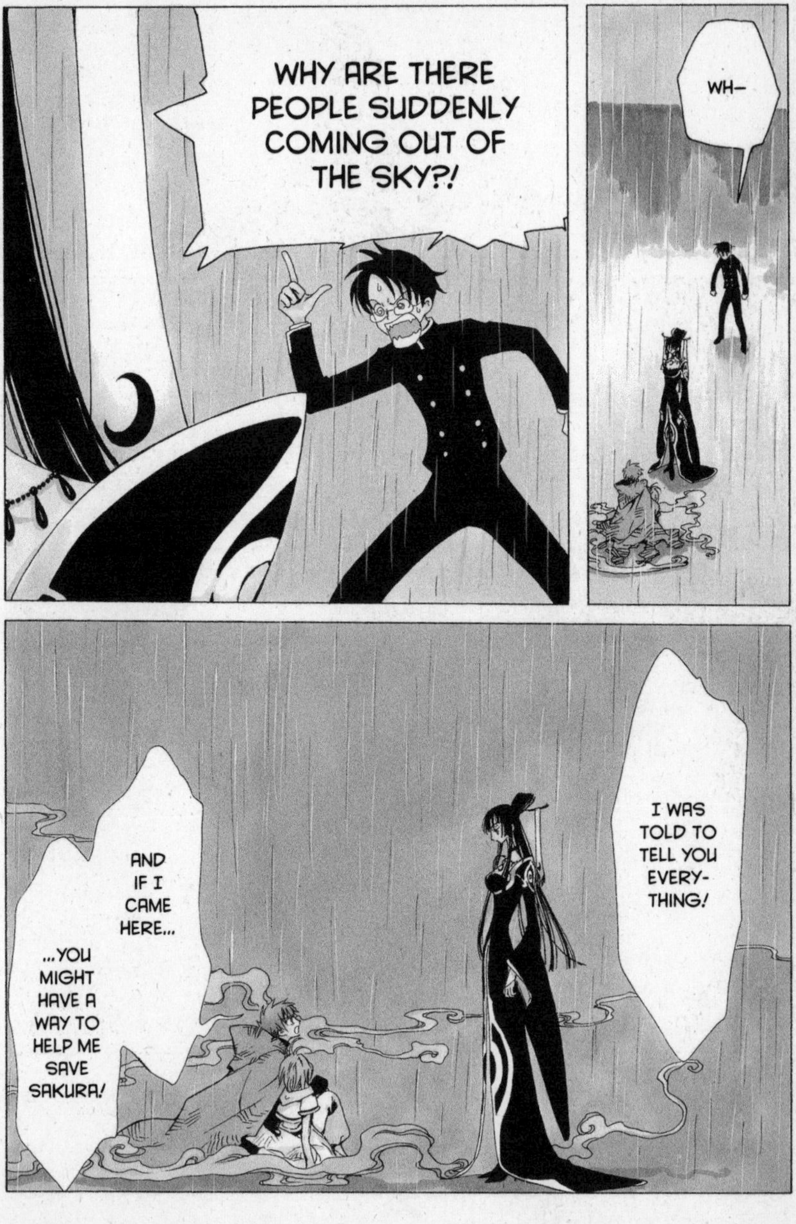
WH–
WHY ARE THERE PEOPLE SUDDENLY COMING OUT OF THE SKY?!
I WAS TOLD TO TELL YOU EVERY-THING!
AND IF I CAME HERE...
...YOU MIGHT HAVE A WAY TO HELP ME SAVE SAKURA!

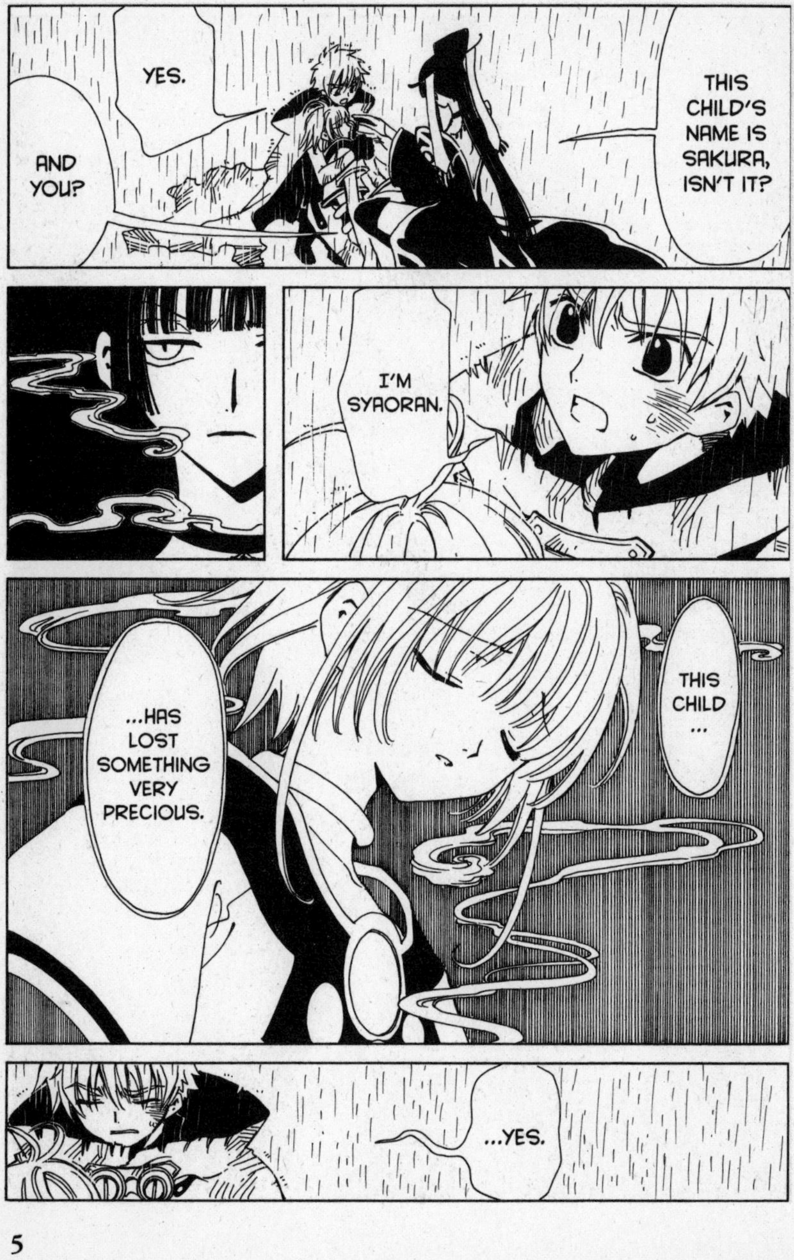
THIS CHILD'S NAME IS SAKURA, ISN'T IT?
YES.
AND YOU?
I'M SYAORAN.
THIS CHILD ...
...HAS LOST SOMETHING VERY PRECIOUS.
...YES.

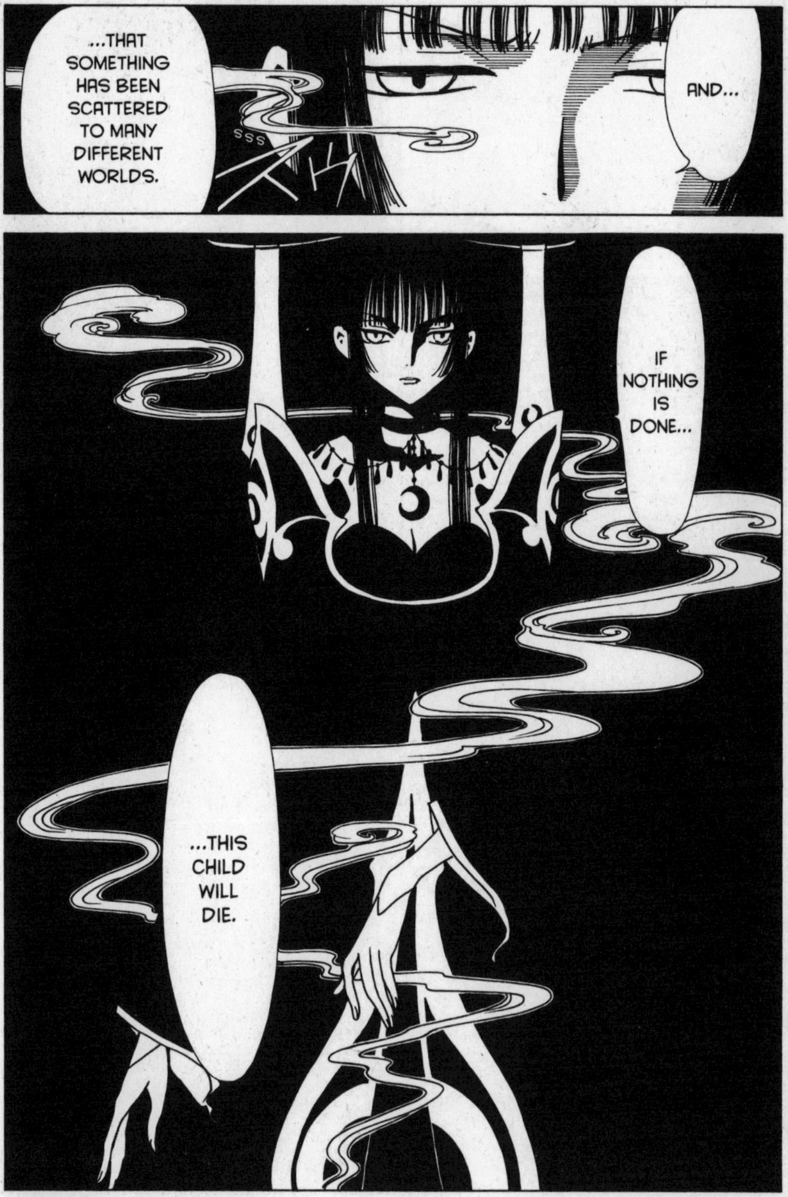
AND...
...THAT SOMETHING HAS BEEN SCATTERED TO MANY DIFFERENT WORLDS.
SSS
IF NOTHING IS DONE...
...THIS CHILD WILL DIE.

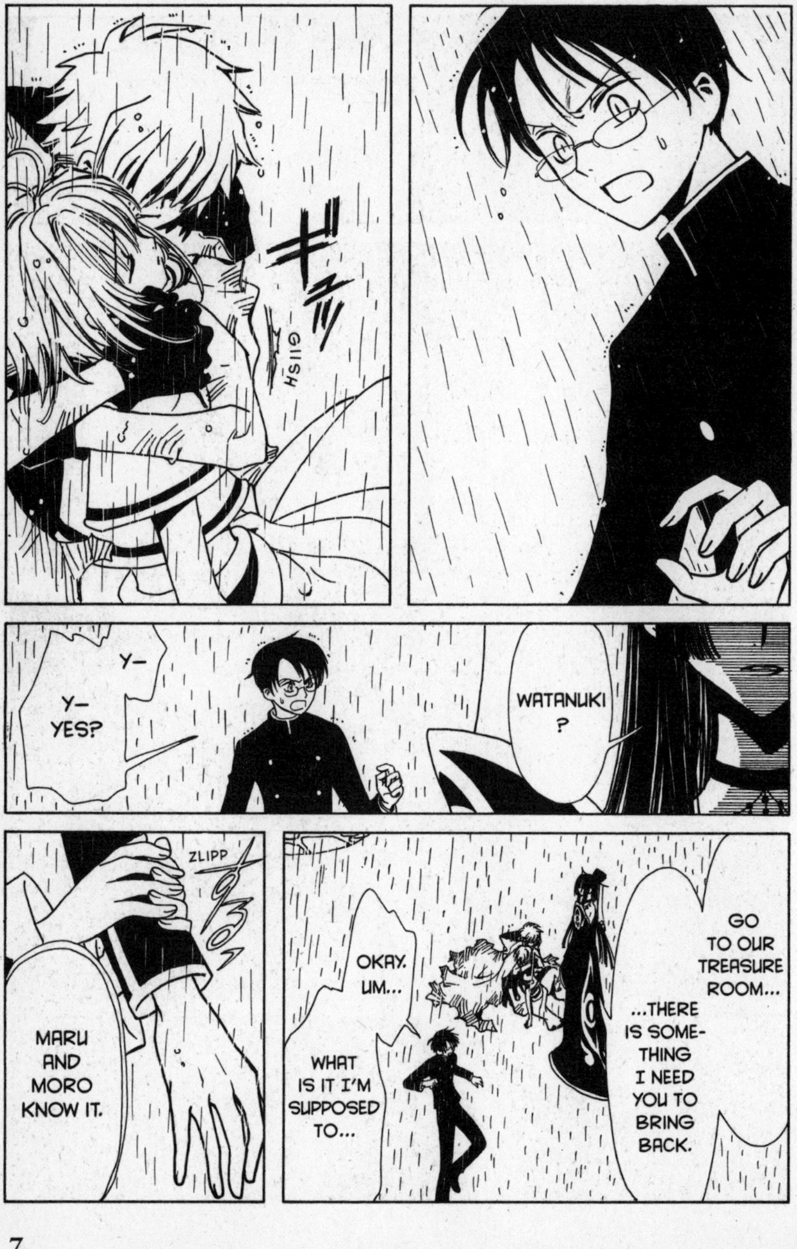
GIISH
WATANUKI ?
Y— Y— YES?
GO TO OUR TREASURE ROOM...
...THERE IS SOME-THING I NEED YOU TO BRING BACK.
OKAY. UM...
WHAT IS IT I'M SUPPOSED TO...
ZLIPP
MARU AND MORO KNOW IT.

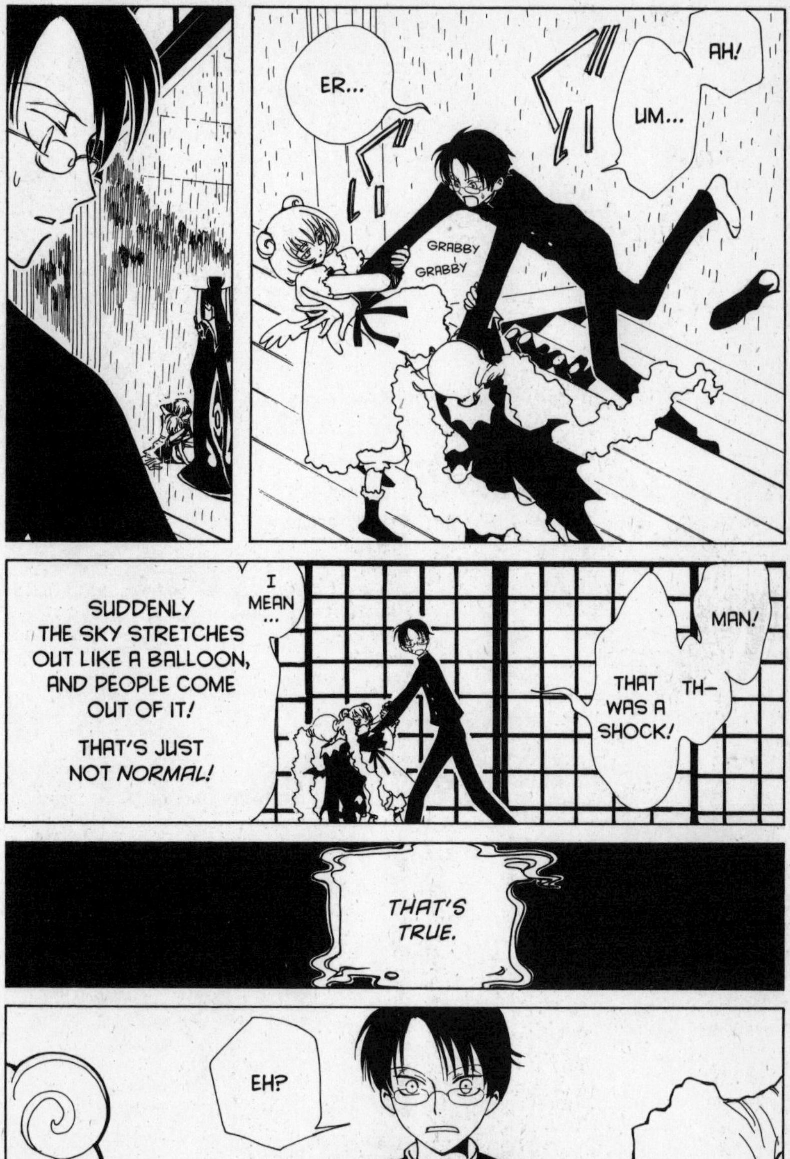
AH!
UM...
ER...
GRABBY GRABBY
TH—
THAT WAS A SHOCK!
MAN!
I MEAN ...
SUDDENLY THE SKY STRETCHES OUT LIKE A BALLOON, AND PEOPLE COME OUT OF IT!
THAT'S JUST NOT *NORMAL!*
THAT'S TRUE.
EH?

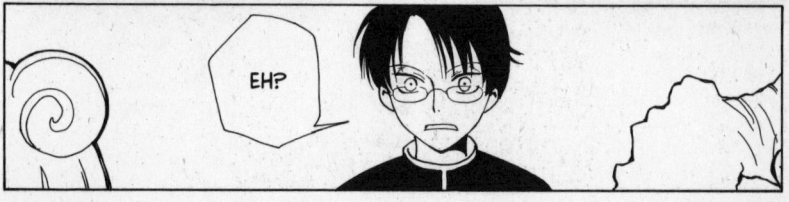

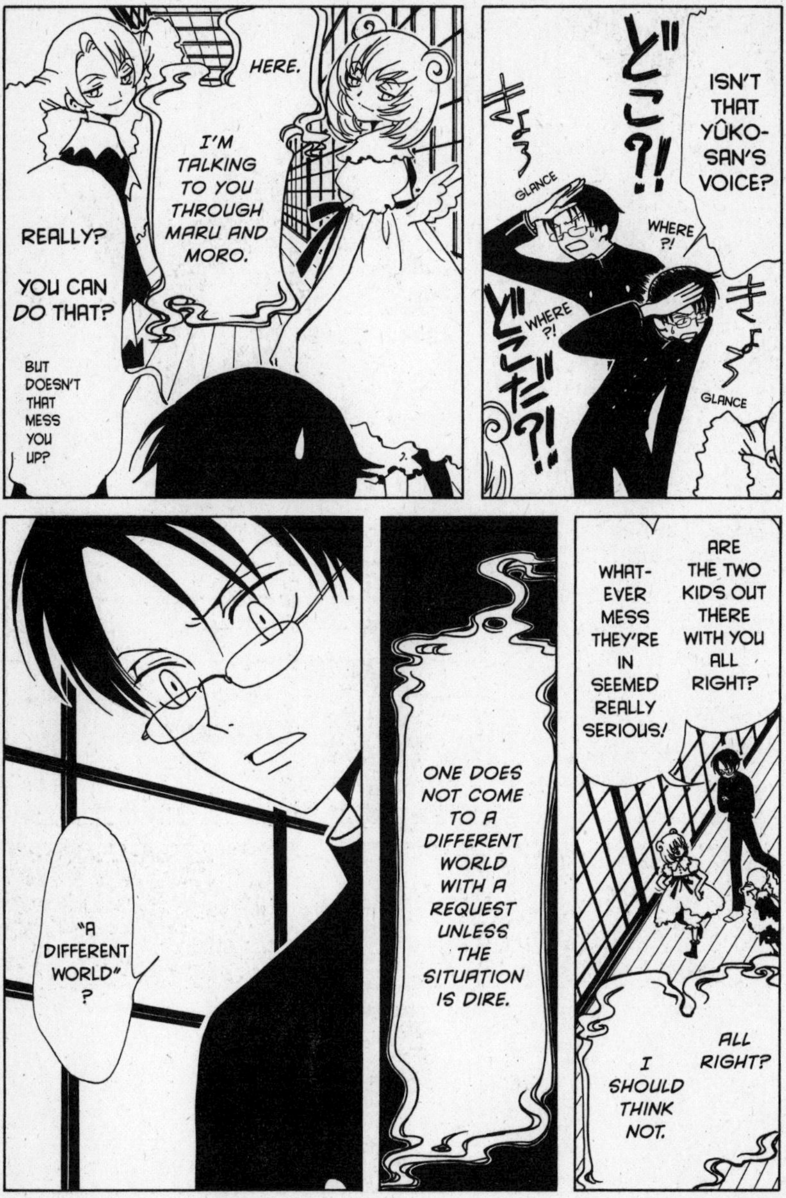
ISN'T THAT YÛKO-SAN'S VOICE?
どこ?!!
WHERE ?!
きょろ
GLANCE
きょろ
GLANCE
どこだ?!!
WHERE ?!
HERE.
I'M TALKING TO YOU THROUGH MARU AND MORO.
REALLY?
YOU CAN DO THAT?
BUT DOESN'T THAT MESS YOU UP?
ARE THE TWO KIDS OUT THERE WITH YOU ALL RIGHT?
WHAT-EVER MESS THEY'RE IN SEEMED REALLY SERIOUS!
ALL RIGHT?
I SHOULD THINK NOT.
ONE DOES NOT COME TO A DIFFERENT WORLD WITH A REQUEST UNLESS THE SITUATION IS DIRE.
"A DIFFERENT WORLD" ?

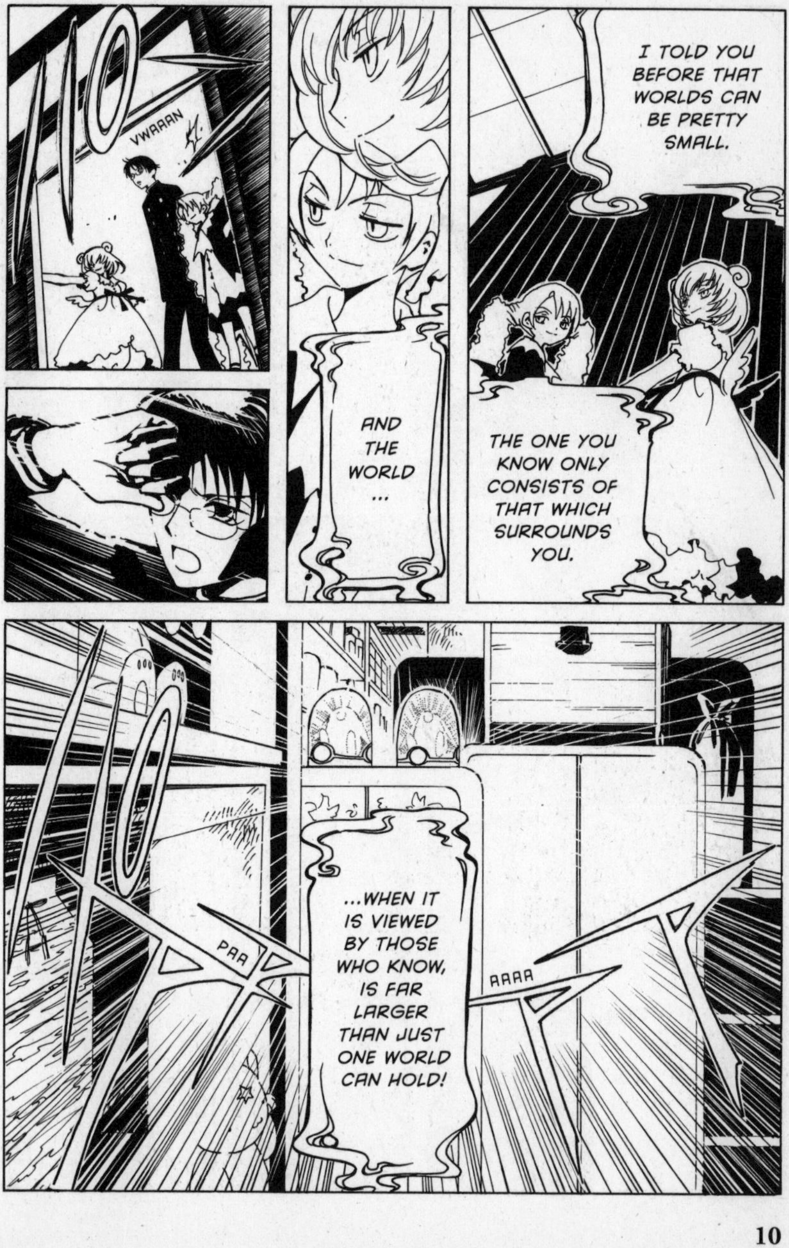
I TOLD YOU BEFORE THAT WORLDS CAN BE PRETTY SMALL.
THE ONE YOU KNOW ONLY CONSISTS OF THAT WHICH SURROUNDS YOU.
AND THE WORLD ...
VWAAAN
...WHEN IT IS VIEWED BY THOSE WHO KNOW, IS FAR LARGER THAN JUST ONE WORLD CAN HOLD!
AAAA
PAA

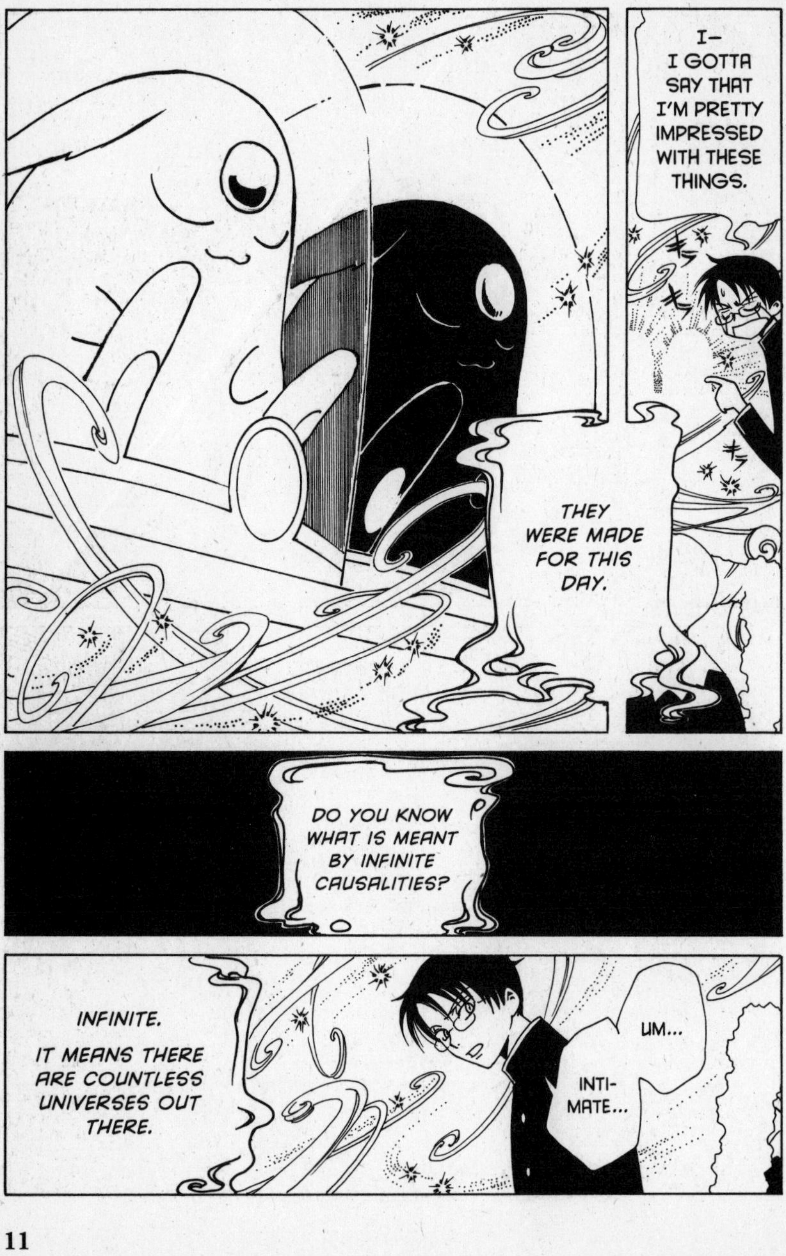
I— I GOTTA SAY THAT I'M PRETTY IMPRESSED WITH THESE THINGS.
THEY WERE MADE FOR THIS DAY.
DO YOU KNOW WHAT IS MEANT BY INFINITE CAUSALITIES?
UM...
INTI-MATE...
INFINITE.
IT MEANS THERE ARE COUNTLESS UNIVERSES OUT THERE.

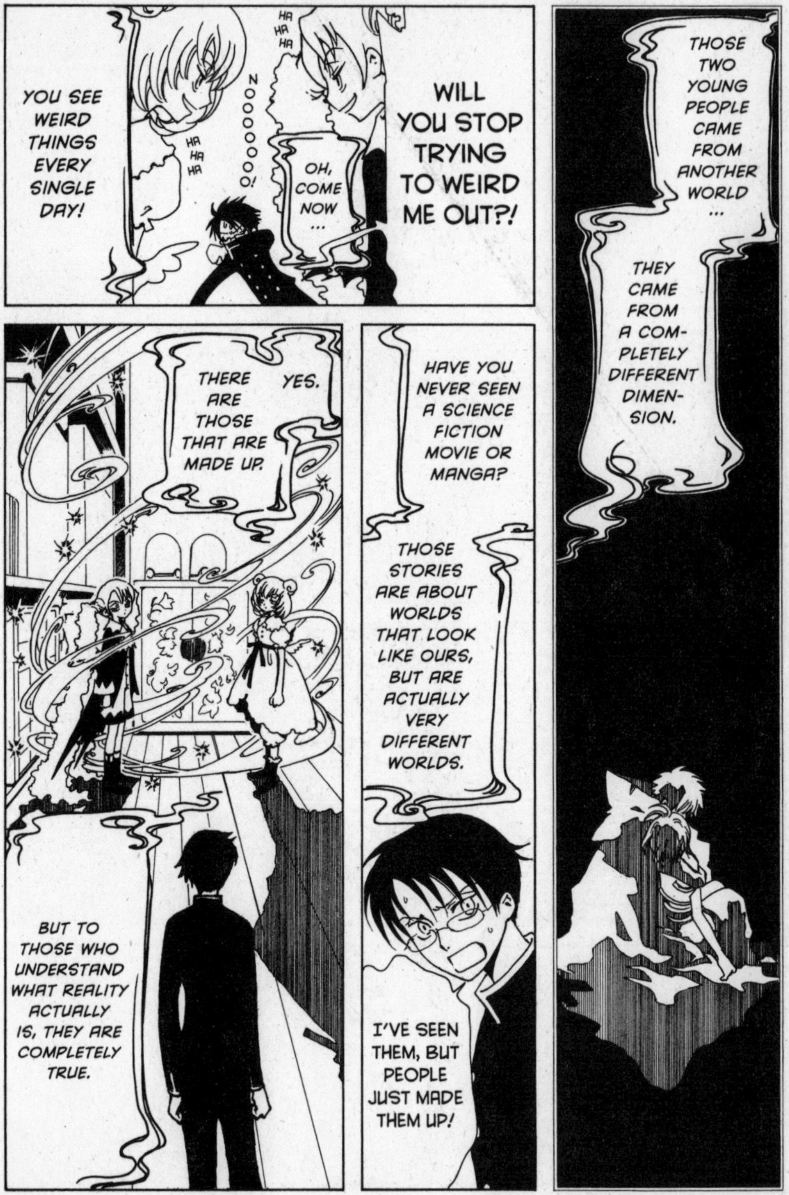
THOSE TWO YOUNG PEOPLE CAME FROM ANOTHER WORLD ...
THEY CAME FROM A COMPLETELY DIFFERENT DIMENSION.
WILL YOU STOP TRYING TO WEIRD ME OUT?!
OH, COME NOW ...
NOOOOOOO!
HA HA HA
HA HA HA
YOU SEE WEIRD THINGS EVERY SINGLE DAY!
HAVE YOU NEVER SEEN A SCIENCE FICTION MOVIE OR MANGA?
THOSE STORIES ARE ABOUT WORLDS THAT LOOK LIKE OURS, BUT ARE ACTUALLY VERY DIFFERENT WORLDS.
I'VE SEEN THEM, BUT PEOPLE JUST MADE THEM UP!
YES.
THERE ARE THOSE THAT ARE MADE UP.
BUT TO THOSE WHO UNDERSTAND WHAT REALITY ACTUALLY IS, THEY ARE COMPLETELY TRUE.

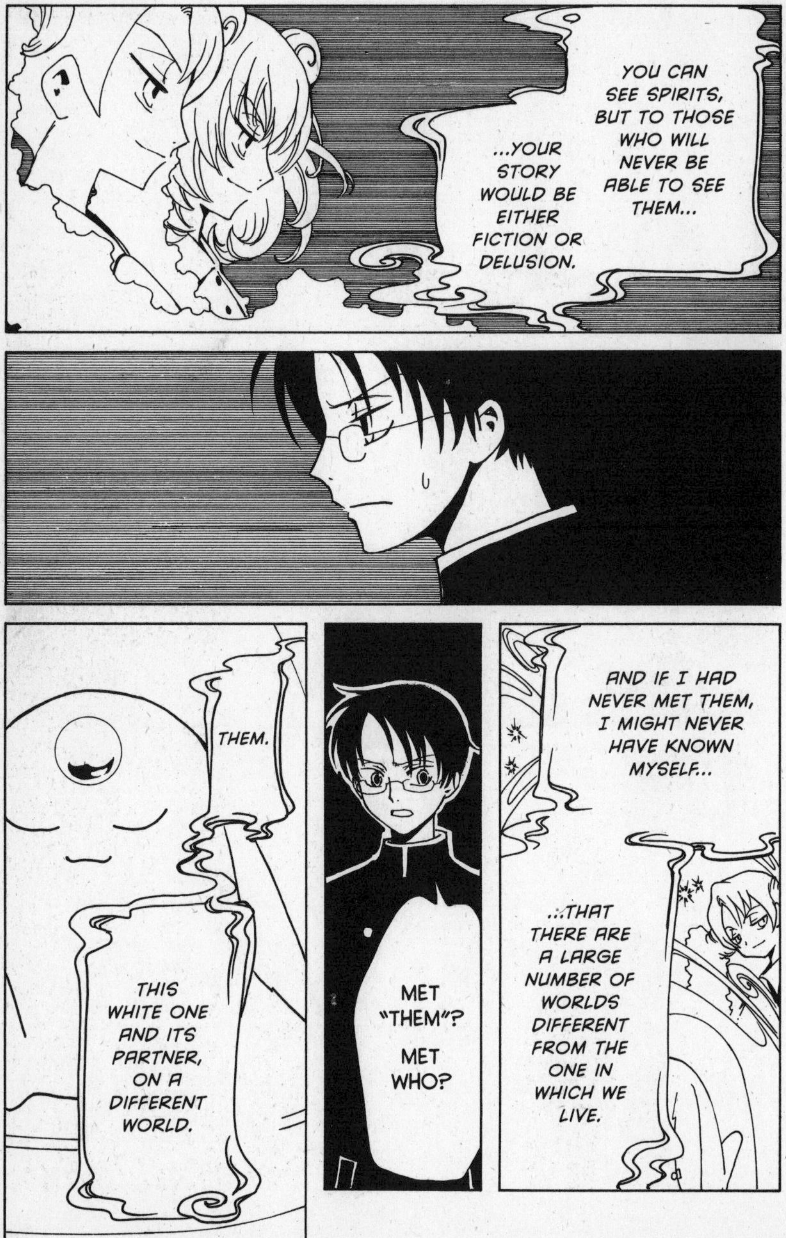
YOU CAN SEE SPIRITS, BUT TO THOSE WHO WILL NEVER BE ABLE TO SEE THEM...
...YOUR STORY WOULD BE EITHER FICTION OR DELUSION.
AND IF I HAD NEVER MET THEM, I MIGHT NEVER HAVE KNOWN MYSELF...
...THAT THERE ARE A LARGE NUMBER OF WORLDS DIFFERENT FROM THE ONE IN WHICH WE LIVE.
MET "THEM"?
MET WHO?
THEM.
THIS WHITE ONE AND ITS PARTNER, ON A DIFFERENT WORLD.

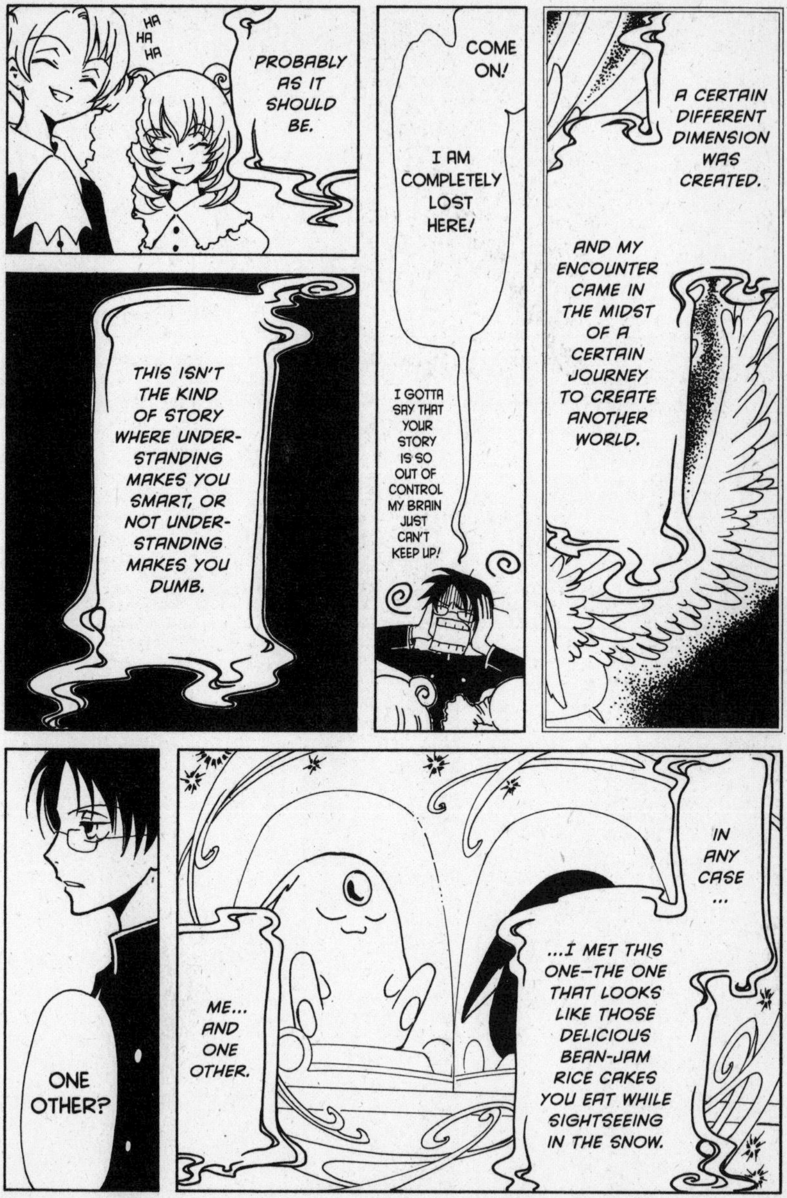
A CERTAIN DIFFERENT DIMENSION WAS CREATED.
AND MY ENCOUNTER CAME IN THE MIDST OF A CERTAIN JOURNEY TO CREATE ANOTHER WORLD.
COME ON!
I AM COMPLETELY LOST HERE!
I GOTTA SAY THAT YOUR STORY IS SO OUT OF CONTROL MY BRAIN JUST CAN'T KEEP UP!
PROBABLY AS IT SHOULD BE.
HA HA HA
THIS ISN'T THE KIND OF STORY WHERE UNDER-STANDING MAKES YOU SMART, OR NOT UNDER-STANDING MAKES YOU DUMB.
IN ANY CASE ...
...I MET THIS ONE—THE ONE THAT LOOKS LIKE THOSE DELICIOUS BEAN-JAM RICE CAKES YOU EAT WHILE SIGHTSEEING IN THE SNOW.
ME... AND ONE OTHER.
ONE OTHER?

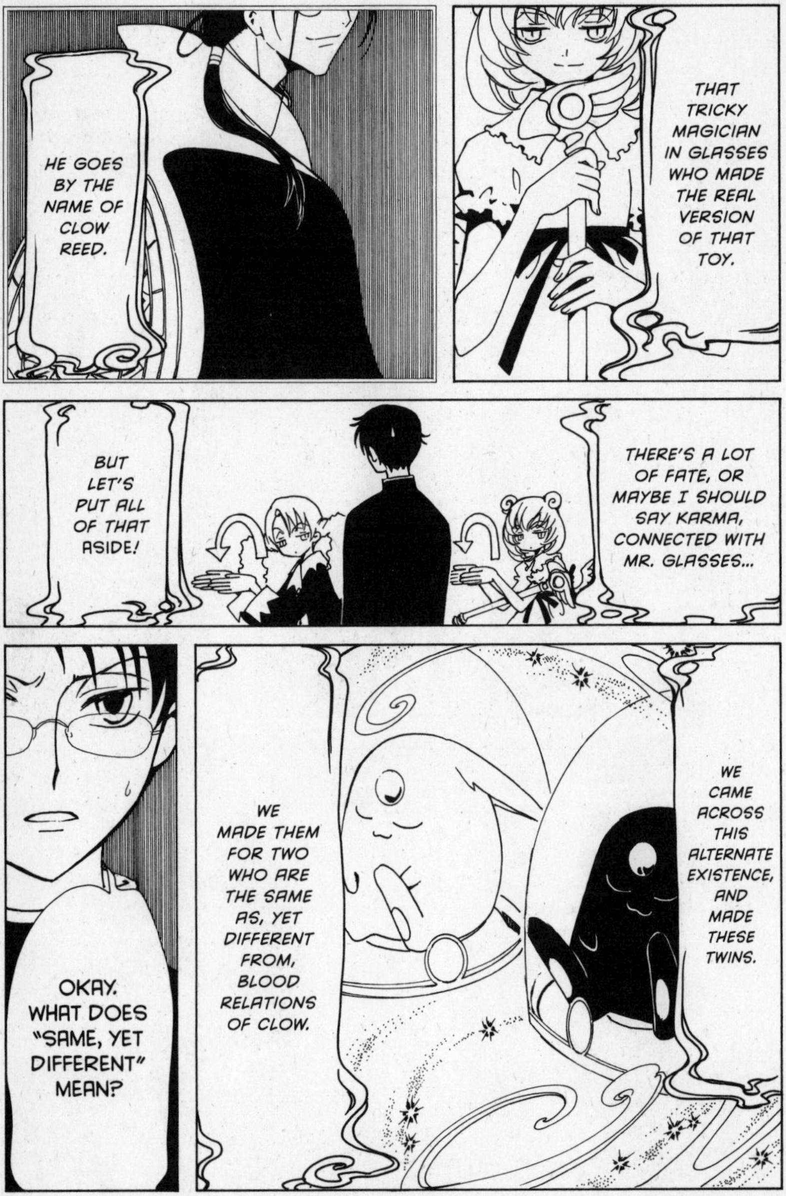
THAT TRICKY MAGICIAN IN GLASSES WHO MADE THE REAL VERSION OF THAT TOY.
HE GOES BY THE NAME OF CLOW REED.
THERE'S A LOT OF FATE, OR MAYBE I SHOULD SAY KARMA, CONNECTED WITH MR. GLASSES...
BUT LET'S PUT ALL OF THAT ASIDE!
WE CAME ACROSS THIS ALTERNATE EXISTENCE, AND MADE THESE TWINS.
WE MADE THEM FOR TWO WHO ARE THE SAME AS, YET DIFFERENT FROM, BLOOD RELATIONS OF CLOW.
OKAY. WHAT DOES "SAME, YET DIFFERENT" MEAN?

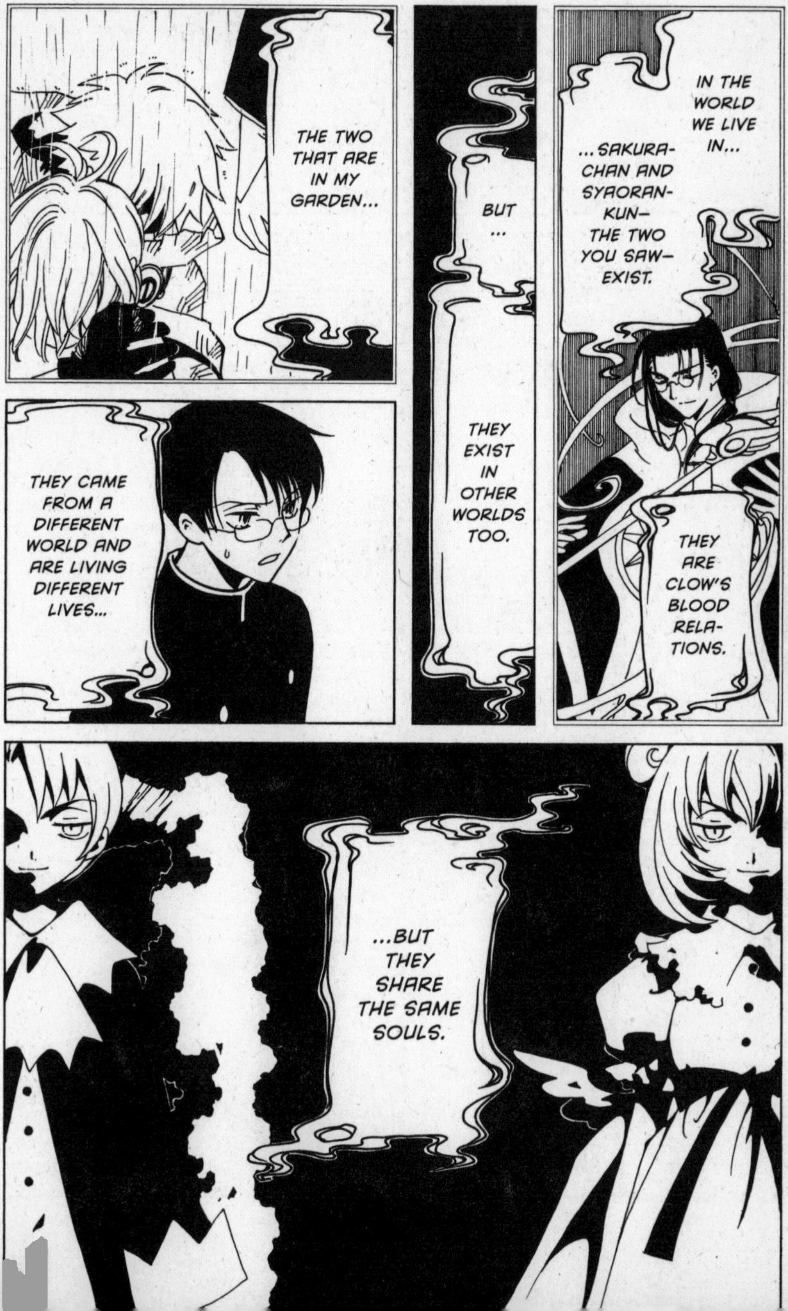
IN THE WORLD WE LIVE IN...
...SAKURA-CHAN AND SYAORAN-KUN—THE TWO YOU SAW—EXIST.
THEY ARE CLOW'S BLOOD RELATIONS.
BUT ...
THEY EXIST IN OTHER WORLDS TOO.
THE TWO THAT ARE IN MY GARDEN...
THEY CAME FROM A DIFFERENT WORLD AND ARE LIVING DIFFERENT LIVES...
...BUT THEY SHARE THE SAME SOULS.

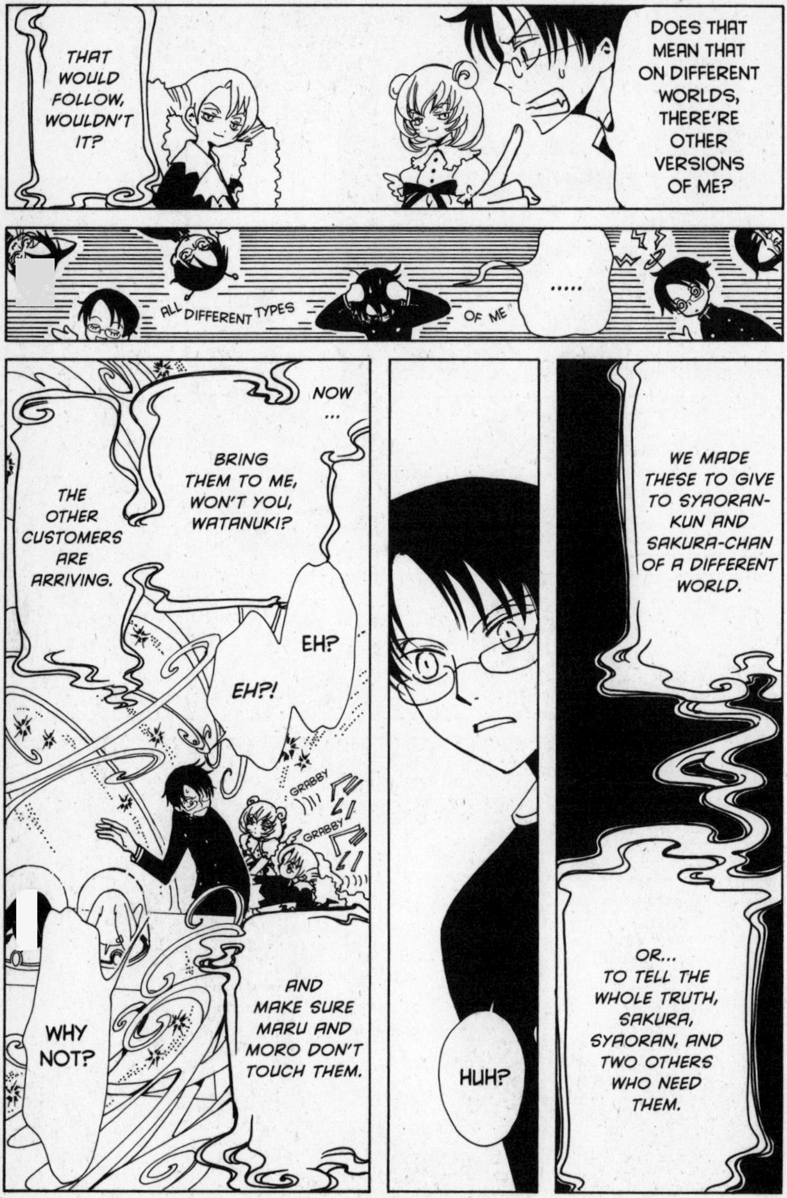
DOES THAT MEAN THAT ON DIFFERENT WORLDS, THERE'RE OTHER VERSIONS OF ME?
THAT WOULD FOLLOW, WOULDN'T IT?
.....
ALL DIFFERENT TYPES OF ME
WE MADE THESE TO GIVE TO SYAORAN-KUN AND SAKURA-CHAN OF A DIFFERENT WORLD.
OR... TO TELL THE WHOLE TRUTH, SAKURA, SYAORAN, AND TWO OTHERS WHO NEED THEM.
HUH?
NOW ...
BRING THEM TO ME, WON'T YOU, WATANUKI?
THE OTHER CUSTOMERS ARE ARRIVING.
EH?
EH?!
GRABBY
GRABBY
AND MAKE SURE MARU AND MORO DON'T TOUCH THEM.
WHY NOT?

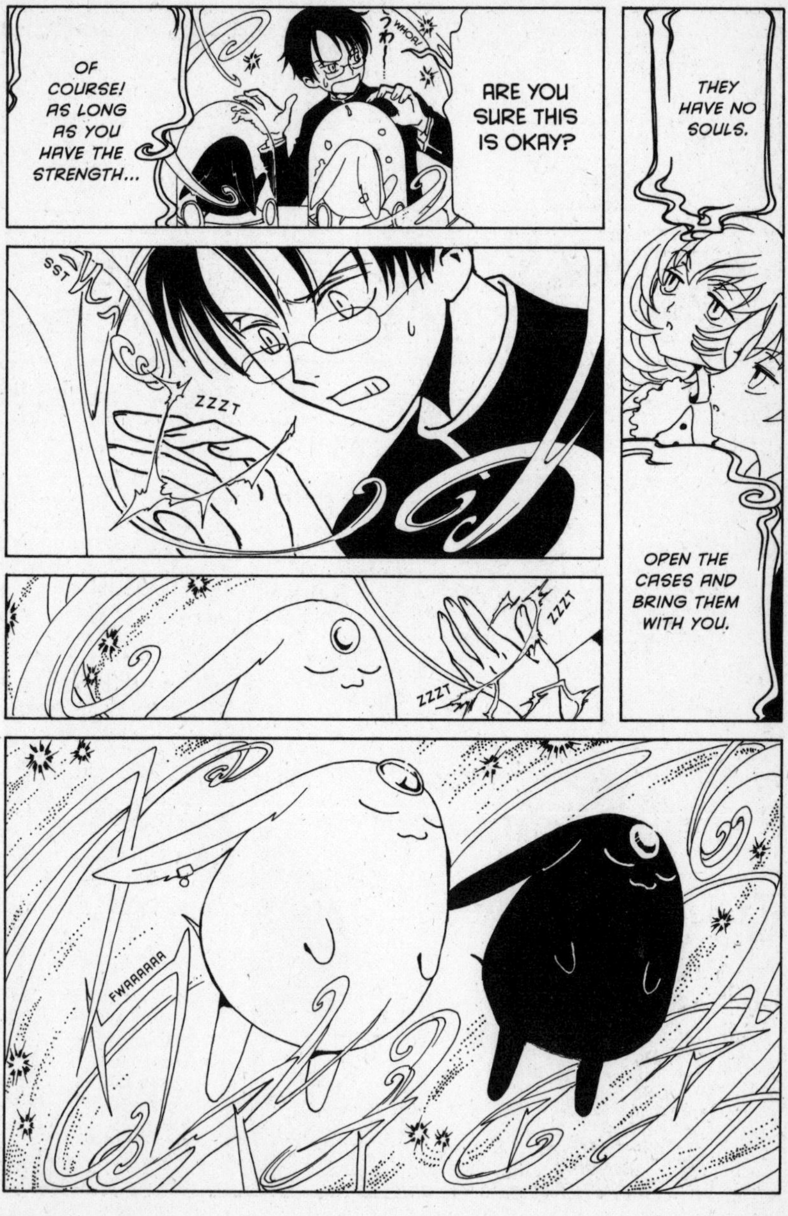
THEY HAVE NO SOULS.
OPEN THE CASES AND BRING THEM WITH YOU.
ARE YOU SURE THIS IS OKAY?
うわー WHOA!
OF COURSE! AS LONG AS YOU HAVE THE STRENGTH...
SST
ZZZT
ZZZT
ZZZT
FWARARARA

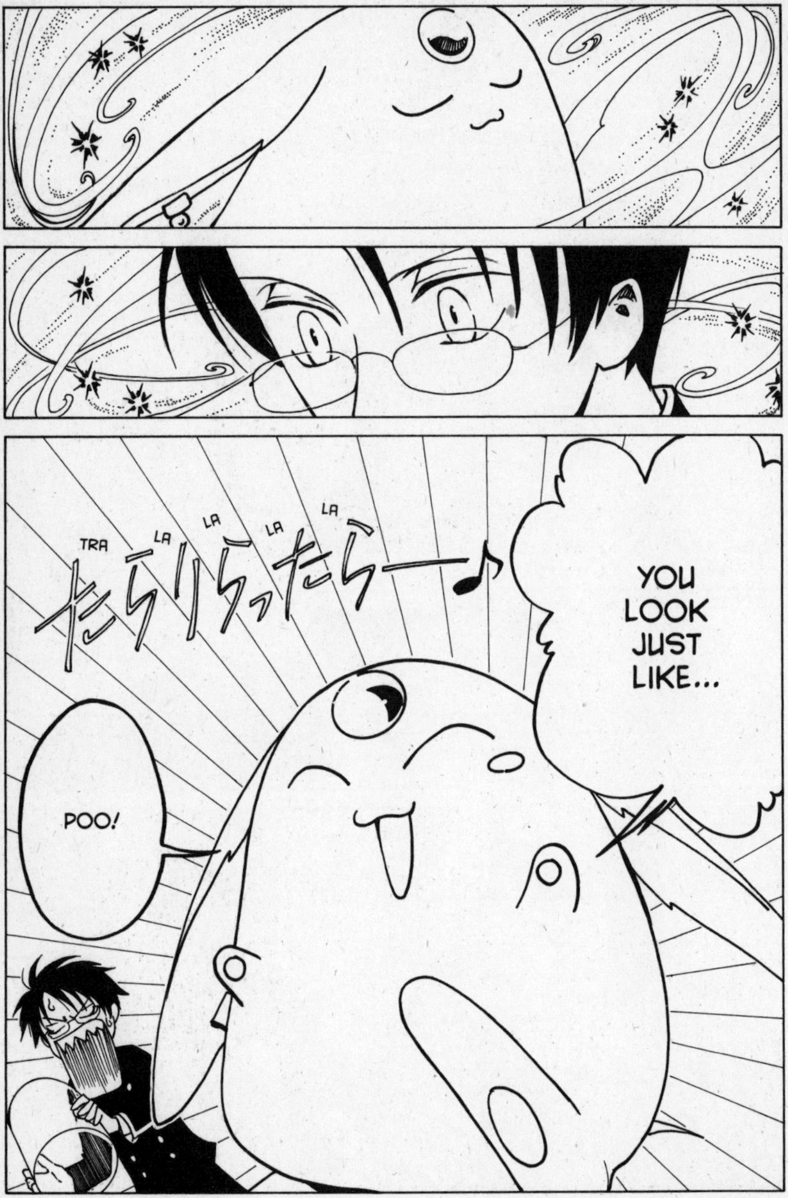
YOU LOOK JUST LIKE...
TRA LA LA LA LA
たらりらったらー♪
POO!

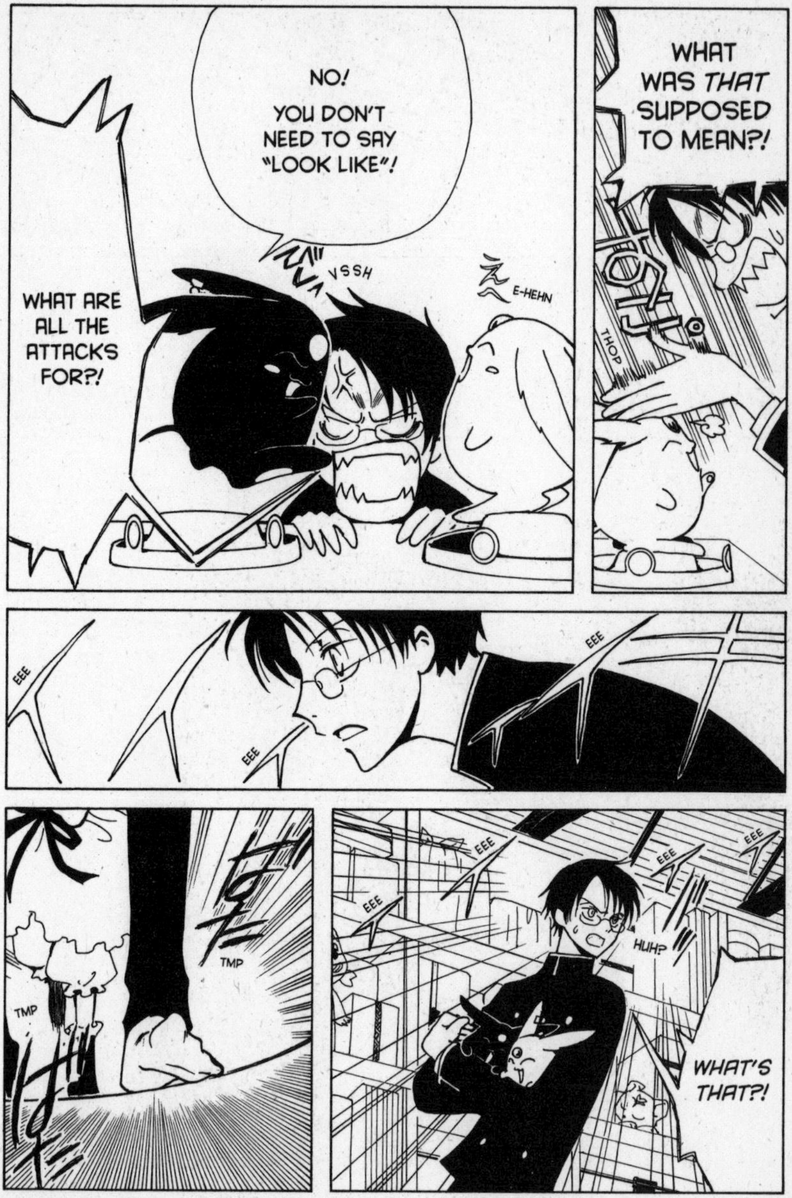
WHAT WAS THAT SUPPOSED TO MEAN?!
THOP
NO!
YOU DON'T NEED TO SAY "LOOK LIKE"!
E-HEHN
VSSH
WHAT ARE ALL THE ATTACKS FOR?!
EEE
EEE
EEE
EEE
EEE
EEE
EEE
HUH?
WHAT'S THAT?!
TMP
TMP

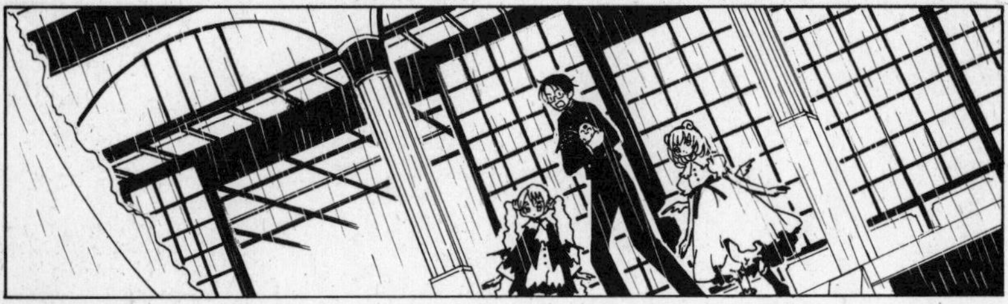
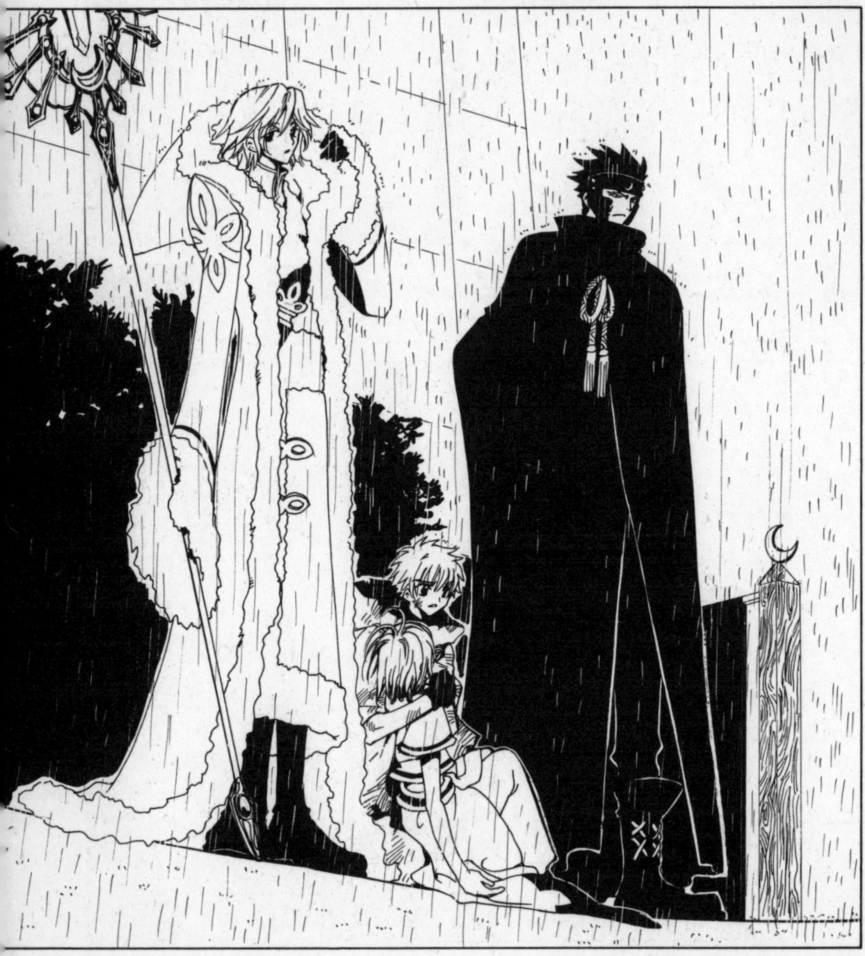

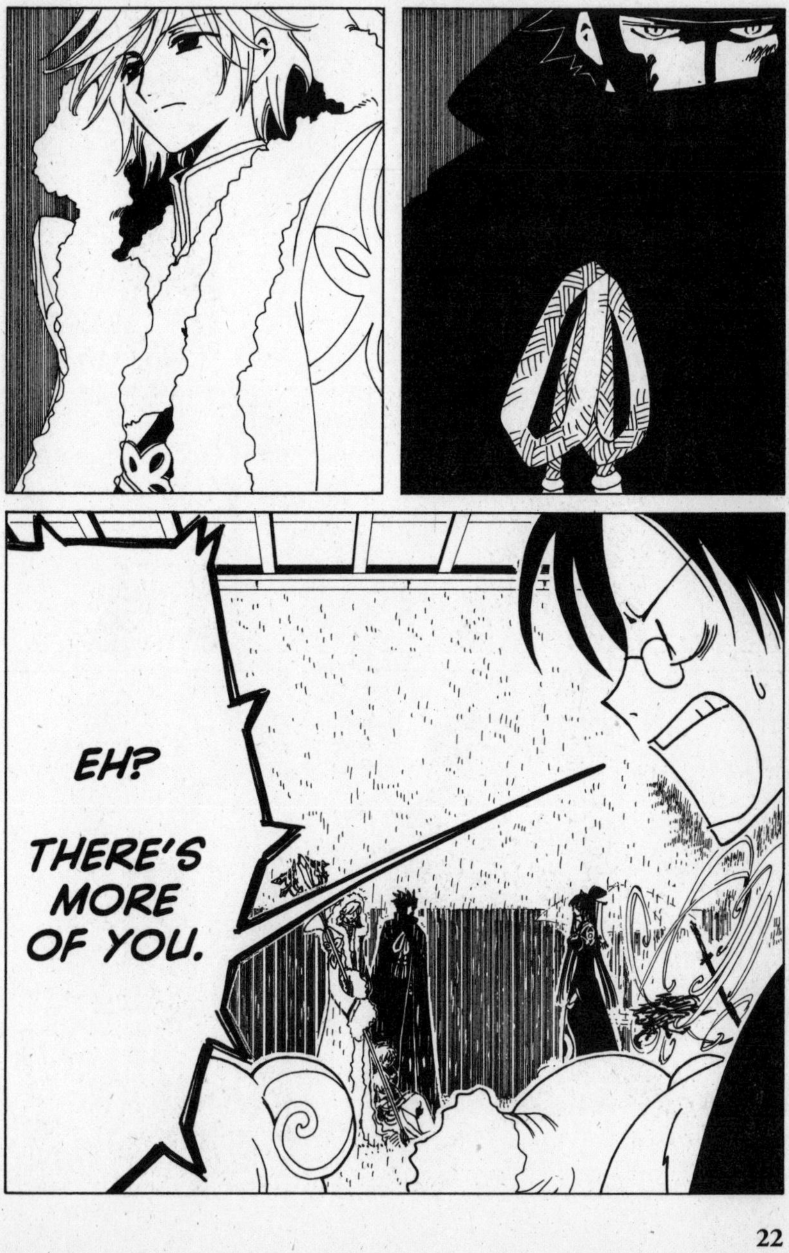
EH?
THERE'S MORE OF YOU.

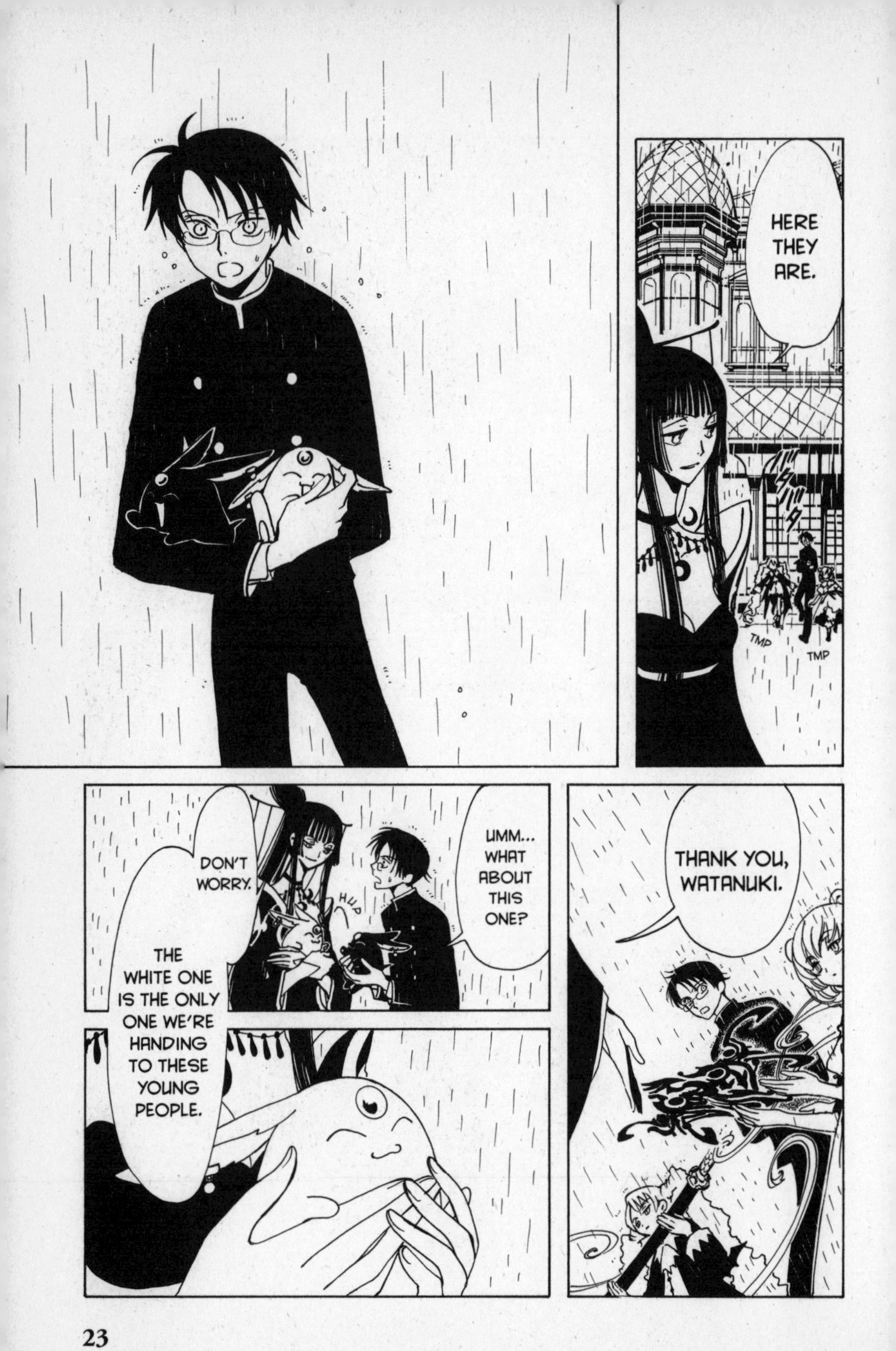
HERE THEY ARE.
TMP
TMP
THANK YOU, WATANUKI.
UMM... WHAT ABOUT THIS ONE?
HUP
DON'T WORRY.
THE WHITE ONE IS THE ONLY ONE WE'RE HANDING TO THESE YOUNG PEOPLE.

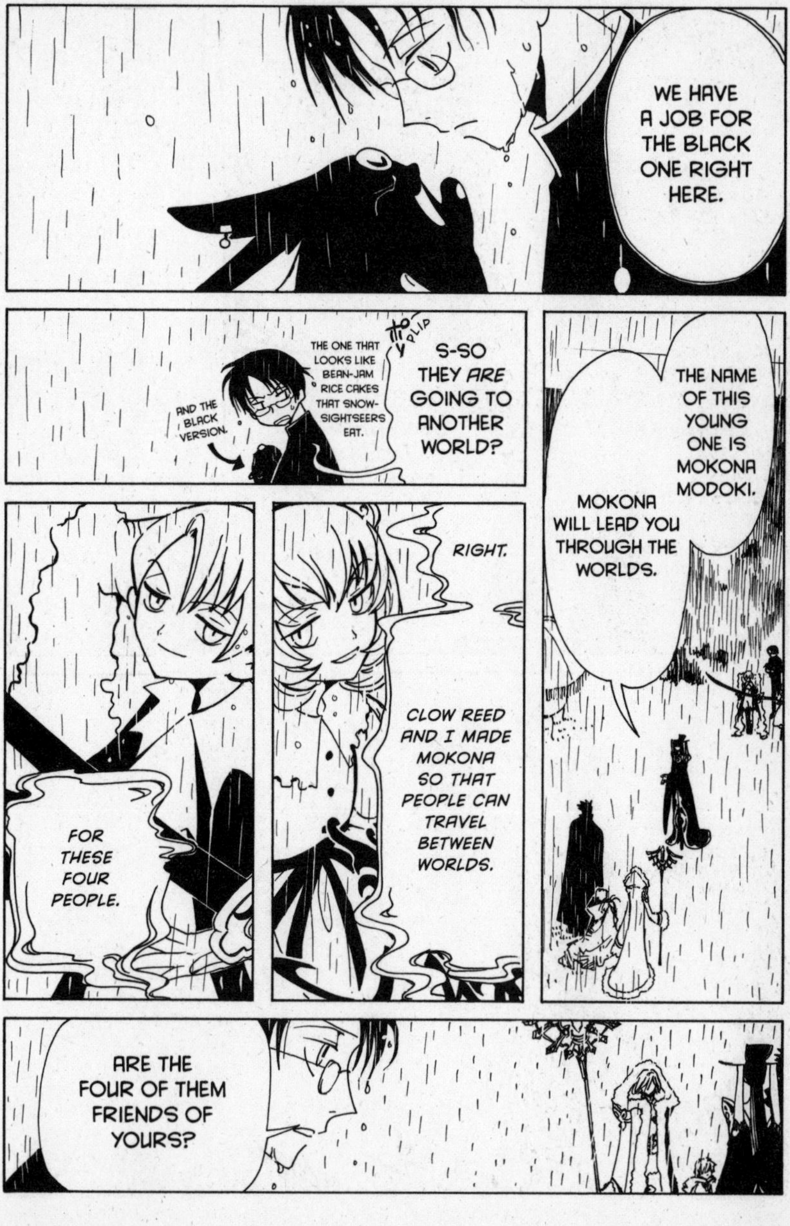
WE HAVE A JOB FOR THE BLACK ONE RIGHT HERE.
THE NAME OF THIS YOUNG ONE IS MOKONA MODOKI.
MOKONA WILL LEAD YOU THROUGH THE WORLDS.
S-SO THEY ARE GOING TO ANOTHER WORLD?
PLIP
THE ONE THAT LOOKS LIKE BEAN-JAM RICE CAKES THAT SNOW-SIGHTSEERS EAT.
AND THE BLACK VERSION.
RIGHT.
CLOW REED AND I MADE MOKONA SO THAT PEOPLE CAN TRAVEL BETWEEN WORLDS.
FOR THESE FOUR PEOPLE.
ARE THE FOUR OF THEM FRIENDS OF YOURS?

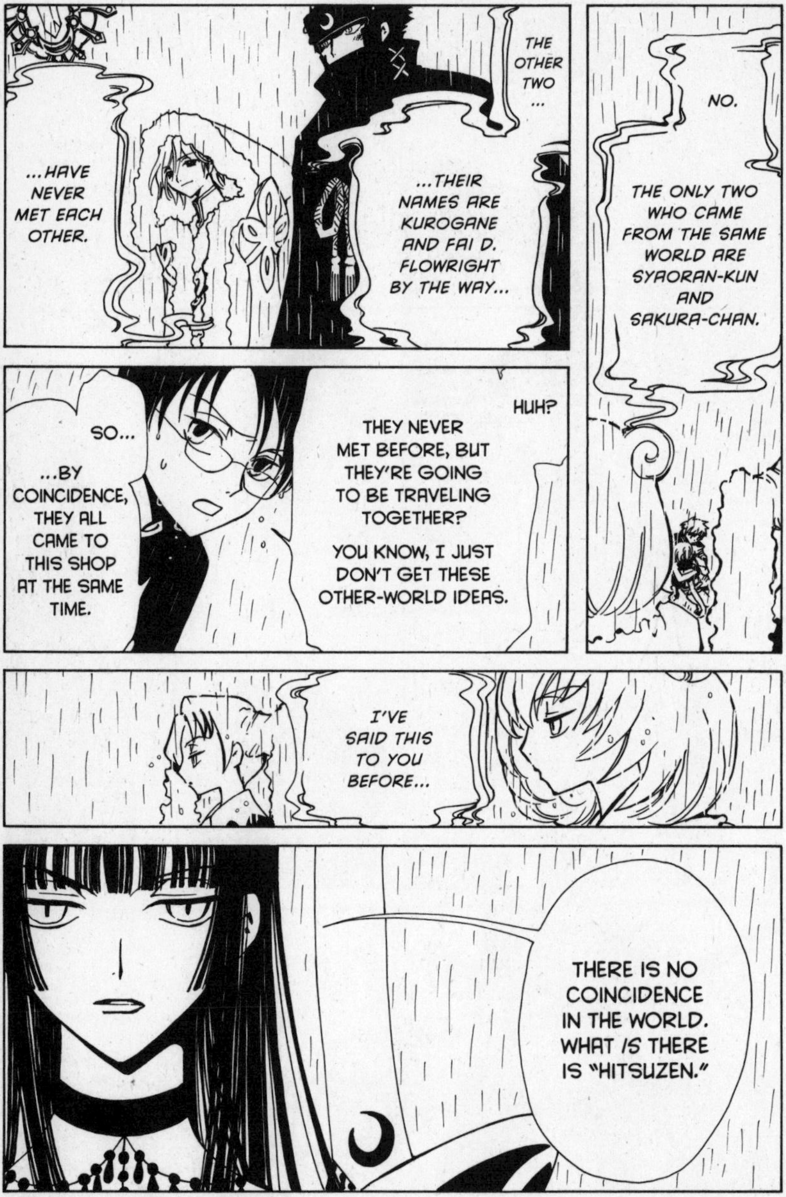
NO.
THE ONLY TWO WHO CAME FROM THE SAME WORLD ARE SYAORAN-KUN AND SAKURA-CHAN.
THE OTHER TWO ...
...THEIR NAMES ARE KUROGANE AND FAI D. FLOWRIGHT BY THE WAY...
...HAVE NEVER MET EACH OTHER.
HUH?
THEY NEVER MET BEFORE, BUT THEY'RE GOING TO BE TRAVELING TOGETHER?
YOU KNOW, I JUST DON'T GET THESE OTHER-WORLD IDEAS.
SO...
...BY COINCIDENCE, THEY ALL CAME TO THIS SHOP AT THE SAME TIME.
I'VE SAID THIS TO YOU BEFORE...
THERE IS NO COINCIDENCE IN THE WORLD. WHAT IS THERE IS "HITSUZEN."

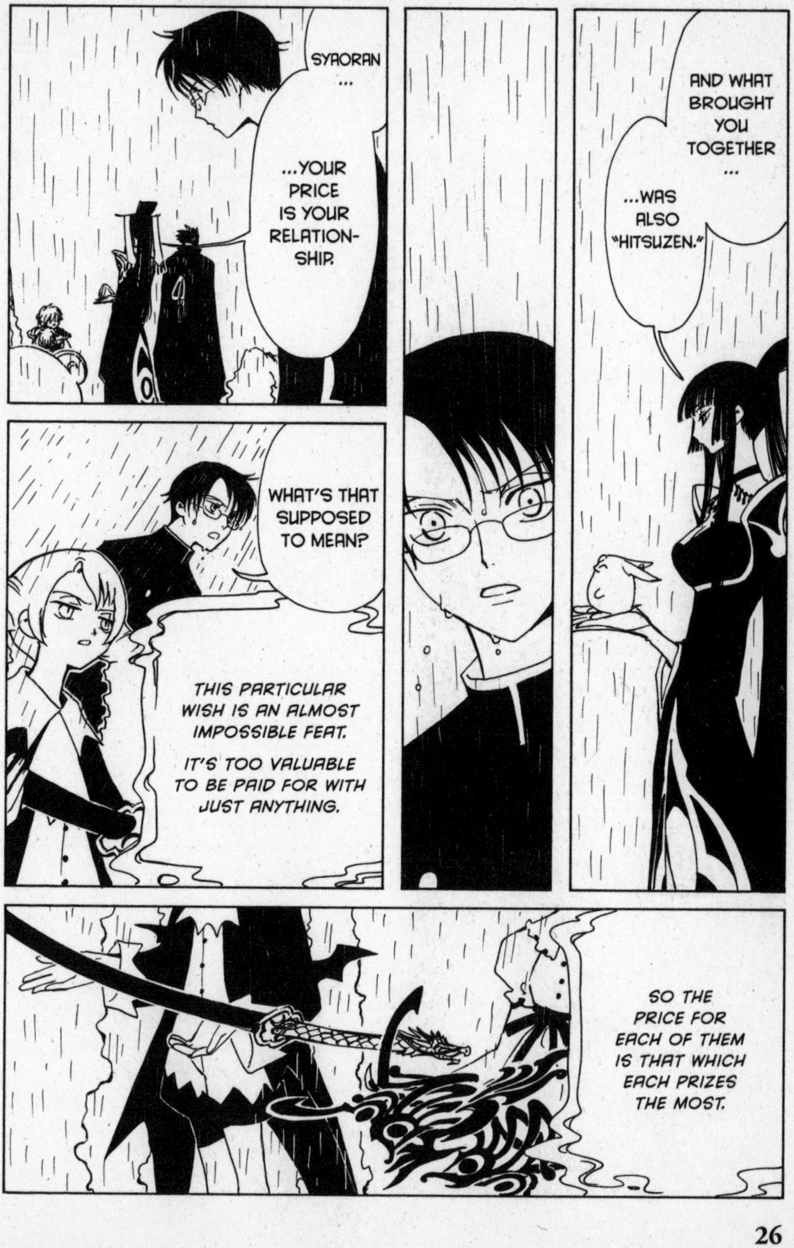
AND WHAT BROUGHT YOU TOGETHER ...
...WAS ALSO "HITSUZEN."
SYAORAN ...
...YOUR PRICE IS YOUR RELATION-SHIP.
WHAT'S THAT SUPPOSED TO MEAN?
THIS PARTICULAR WISH IS AN ALMOST IMPOSSIBLE FEAT.
IT'S TOO VALUABLE TO BE PAID FOR WITH JUST ANYTHING.
SO THE PRICE FOR EACH OF THEM IS THAT WHICH EACH PRIZES THE MOST.

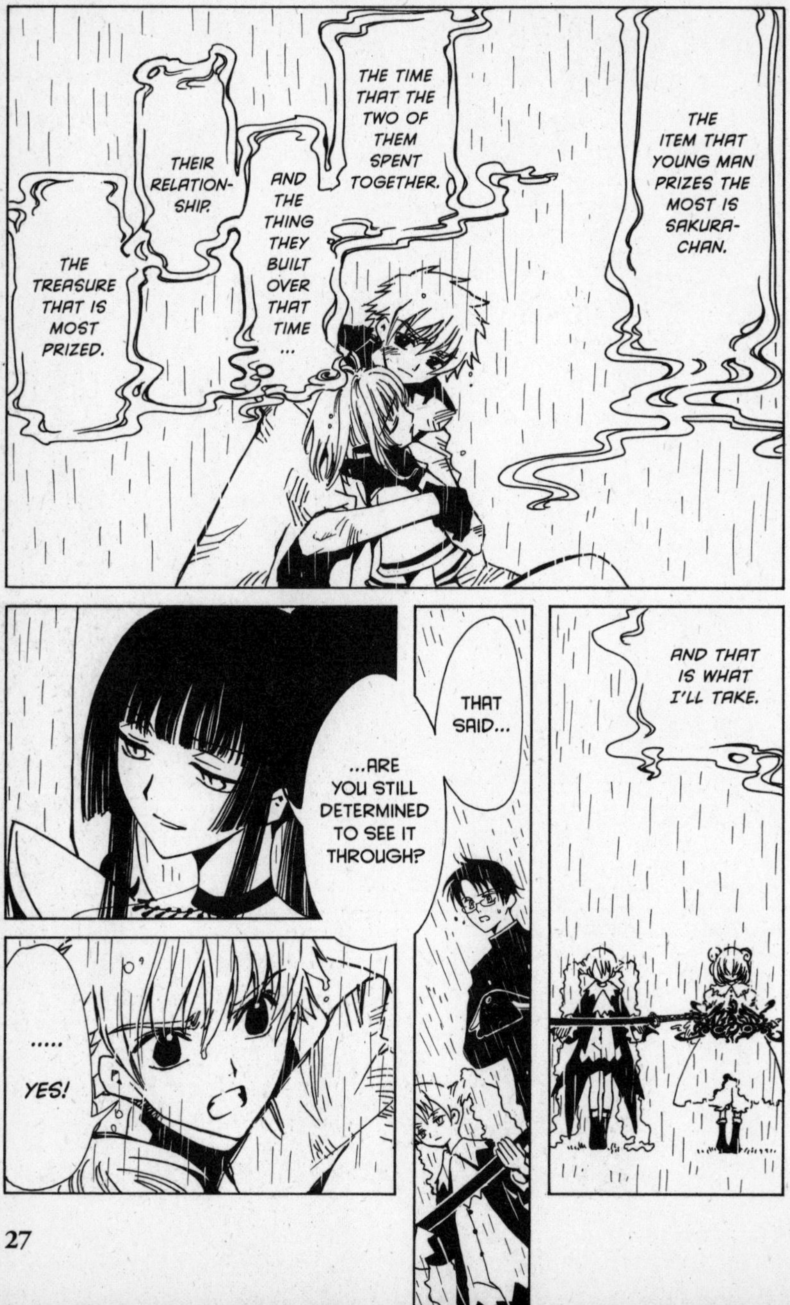
THE ITEM THAT YOUNG MAN PRIZES THE MOST IS SAKURA-CHAN.
THE TIME THAT THE TWO OF THEM SPENT TOGETHER.
AND THE THING THEY BUILT OVER THAT TIME ...
THEIR RELATION-SHIP.
THE TREASURE THAT IS MOST PRIZED.
AND THAT IS WHAT I'LL TAKE.
THAT SAID...
...ARE YOU STILL DETERMINED TO SEE IT THROUGH?
.....
YES!

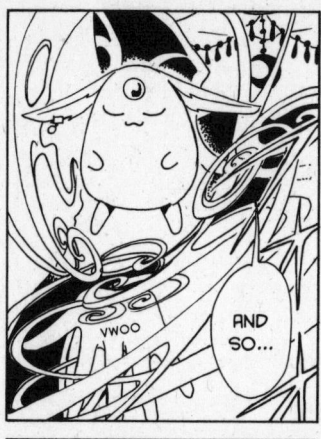

VWOO

AND SO...

SINCERITY AND DETERMINATION...

NO MATTER WHAT A PERSON WANTS TO ATTEMPT, THOSE ARE NEEDED. AND IT SEEMS THAT YOU ARE WELL PROVIDED WITH BOTH.

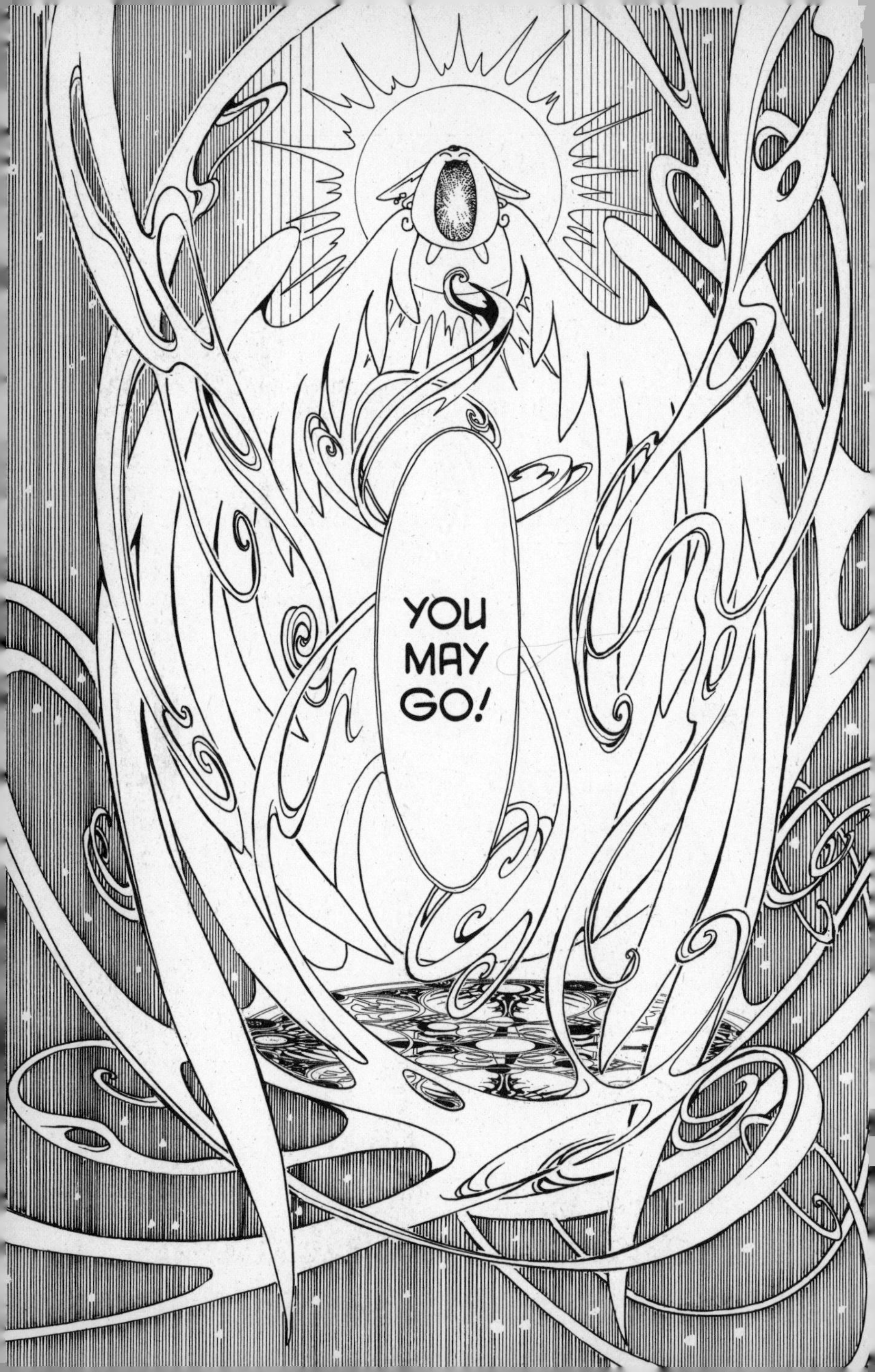
YOU MAY GO!

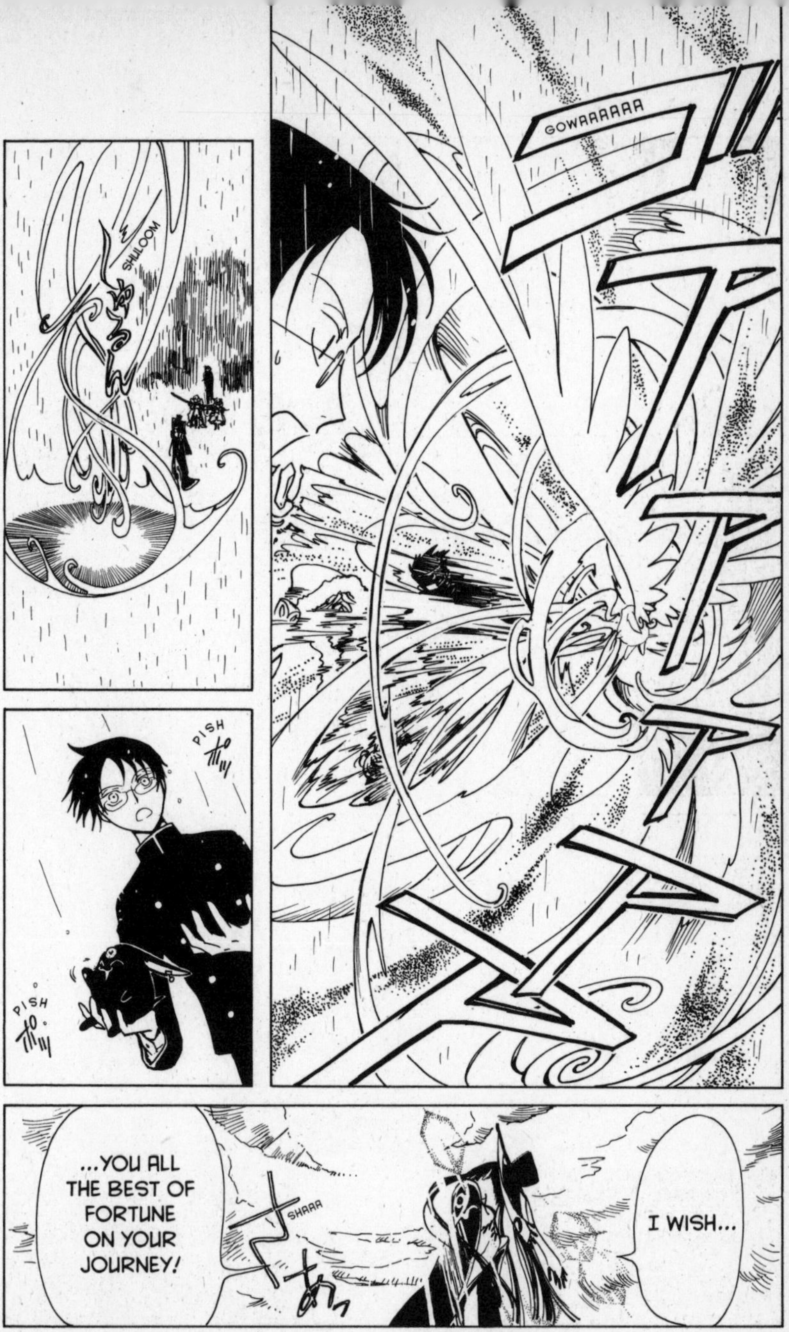
GOWAAAAAA
SHULOOM
PISH
PISH
I WISH...
...YOU ALL THE BEST OF FORTUNE ON YOUR JOURNEY!
SHARA

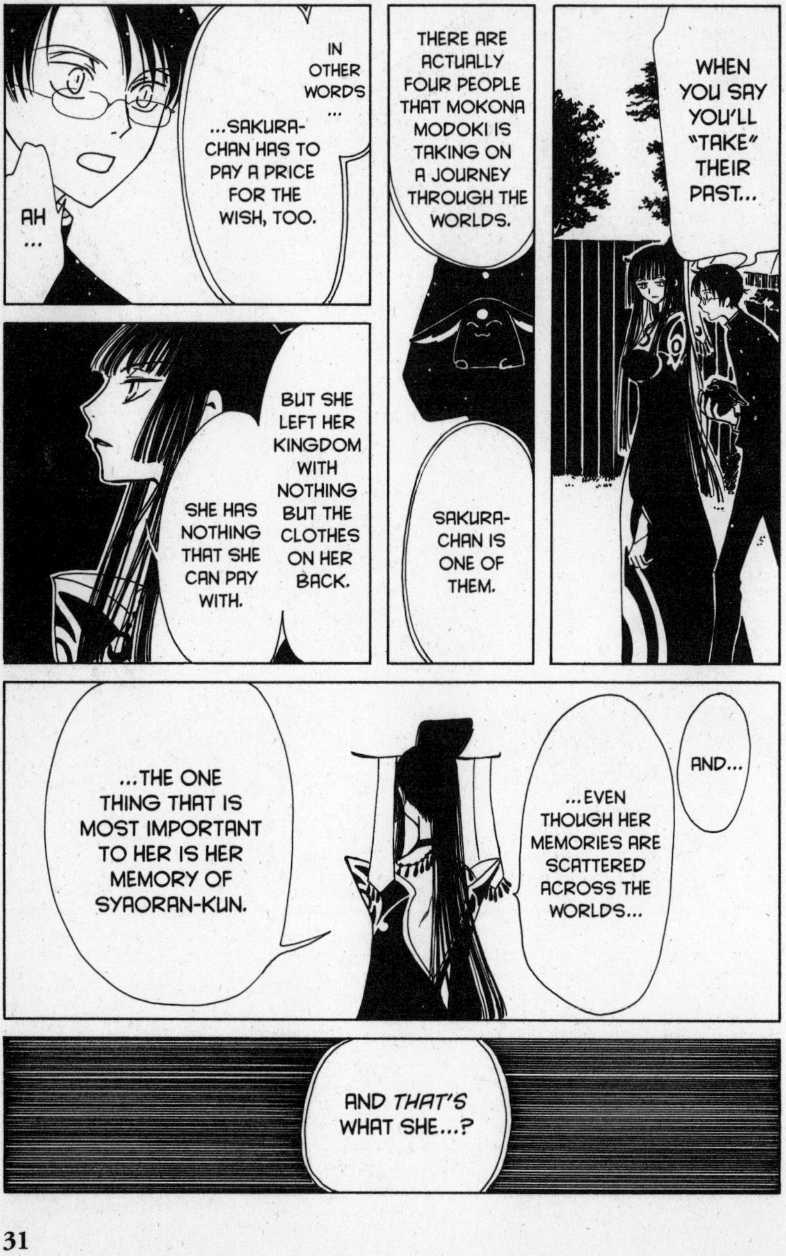
WHEN YOU SAY YOU'LL "TAKE" THEIR PAST...
THERE ARE ACTUALLY FOUR PEOPLE THAT MOKONA MODOKI IS TAKING ON A JOURNEY THROUGH THE WORLDS.
SAKURA-CHAN IS ONE OF THEM.
IN OTHER WORDS ...
...SAKURA-CHAN HAS TO PAY A PRICE FOR THE WISH, TOO.
AH ...
BUT SHE LEFT HER KINGDOM WITH NOTHING BUT THE CLOTHES ON HER BACK.
SHE HAS NOTHING THAT SHE CAN PAY WITH.
AND...
...EVEN THOUGH HER MEMORIES ARE SCATTERED ACROSS THE WORLDS...
...THE ONE THING THAT IS MOST IMPORTANT TO HER IS HER MEMORY OF SYAORAN-KUN.
AND *THAT'S* WHAT SHE...?

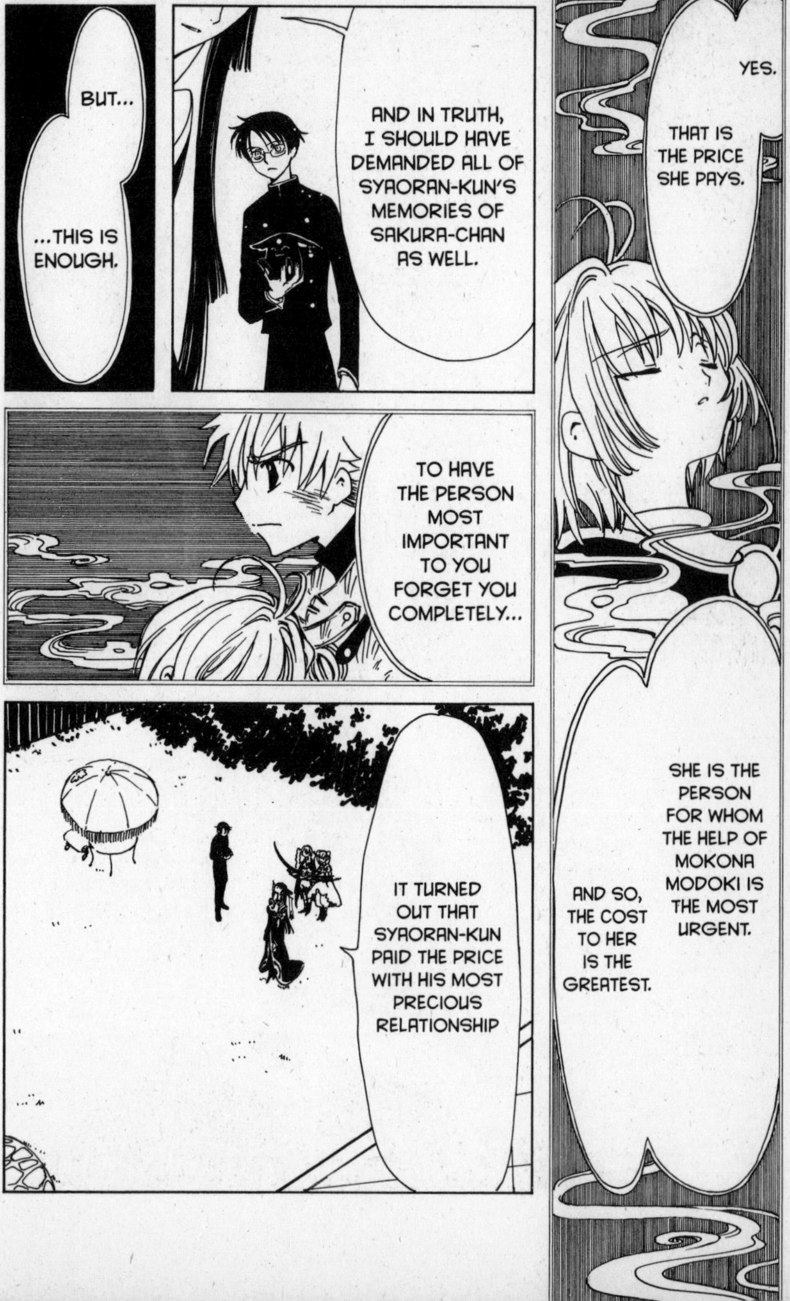
YES.
THAT IS THE PRICE SHE PAYS.
SHE IS THE PERSON FOR WHOM THE HELP OF MOKONA MODOKI IS THE MOST URGENT.
AND SO, THE COST TO HER IS THE GREATEST.
AND IN TRUTH, I SHOULD HAVE DEMANDED ALL OF SYAORAN-KUN'S MEMORIES OF SAKURA-CHAN AS WELL.
BUT...
...THIS IS ENOUGH.
TO HAVE THE PERSON MOST IMPORTANT TO YOU FORGET YOU COMPLETELY...
IT TURNED OUT THAT SYAORAN-KUN PAID THE PRICE WITH HIS MOST PRECIOUS RELATIONSHIP

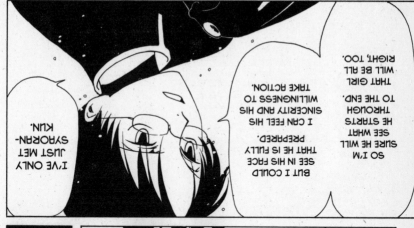

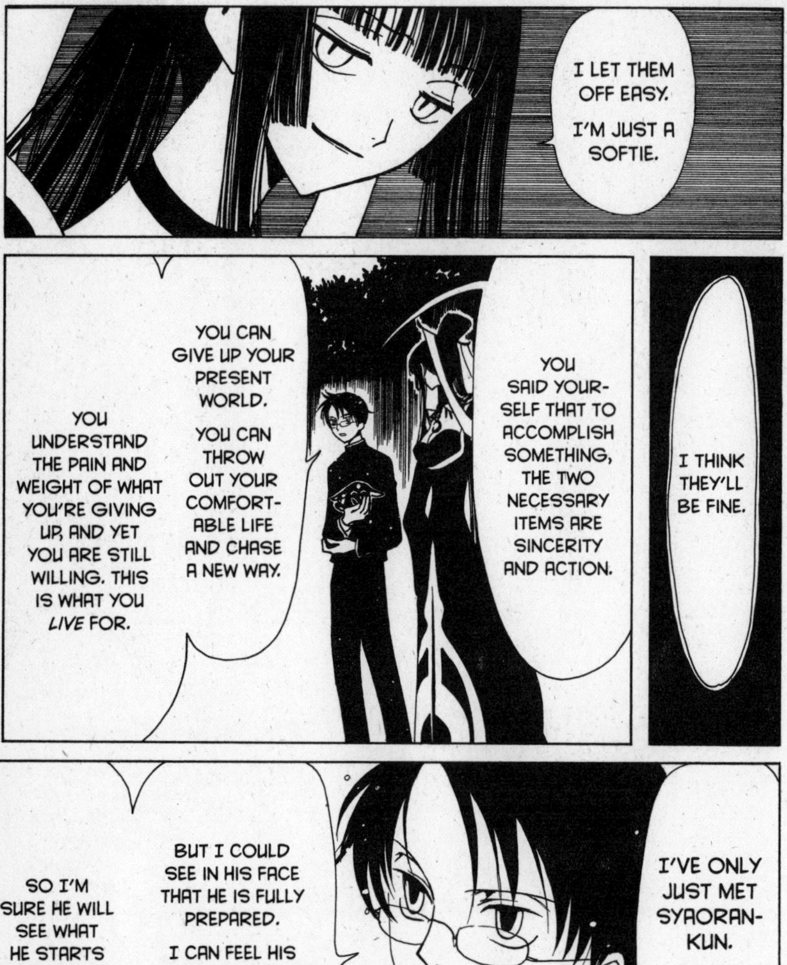
I LET THEM OFF EASY.
I'M JUST A SOFTIE.
I THINK THEY'LL BE FINE.
YOU SAID YOURSELF THAT TO ACCOMPLISH SOMETHING, THE TWO NECESSARY ITEMS ARE SINCERITY AND ACTION.
YOU CAN GIVE UP YOUR PRESENT WORLD.
YOU CAN THROW OUT YOUR COMFORTABLE LIFE AND CHASE A NEW WAY.
YOU UNDERSTAND THE PAIN AND WEIGHT OF WHAT YOU'RE GIVING UP, AND YET YOU ARE STILL WILLING. THIS IS WHAT YOU *LIVE* FOR.
I'VE ONLY JUST MET SYAORAN-KUN.
BUT I COULD SEE IN HIS FACE THAT HE IS FULLY PREPARED.
I CAN FEEL HIS SINCERITY AND HIS WILLINGNESS TO TAKE ACTION.
SO I'M SURE HE WILL SEE WHAT HE STARTS THROUGH TO THE END.
THAT GIRL WILL BE ALL RIGHT, TOO.

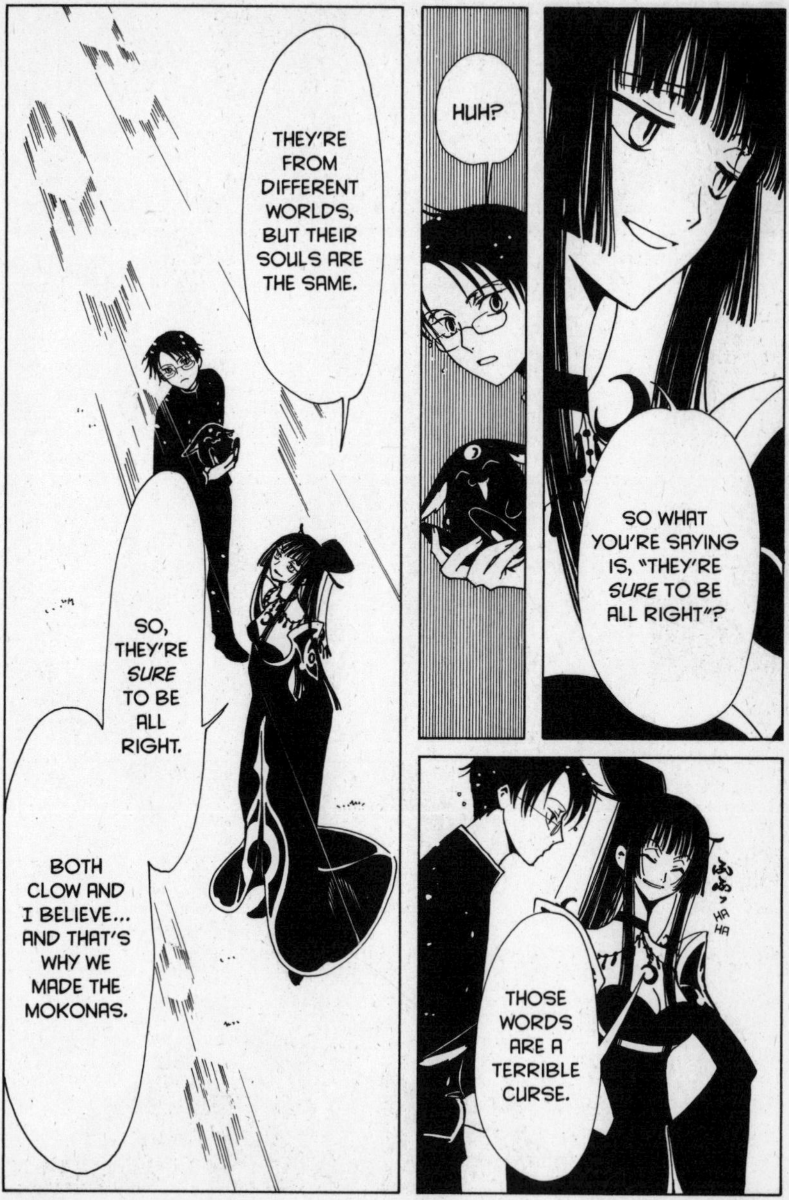
SO WHAT YOU'RE SAYING IS, "THEY'RE *SURE* TO BE ALL RIGHT"?
HUH?
THOSE WORDS ARE A TERRIBLE CURSE.
HA HA
THEY'RE FROM DIFFERENT WORLDS, BUT THEIR SOULS ARE THE SAME.
SO, THEY'RE *SURE* TO BE ALL RIGHT.
BOTH CLOW AND I BELIEVE... AND THAT'S WHY WE MADE THE MOKONAS.

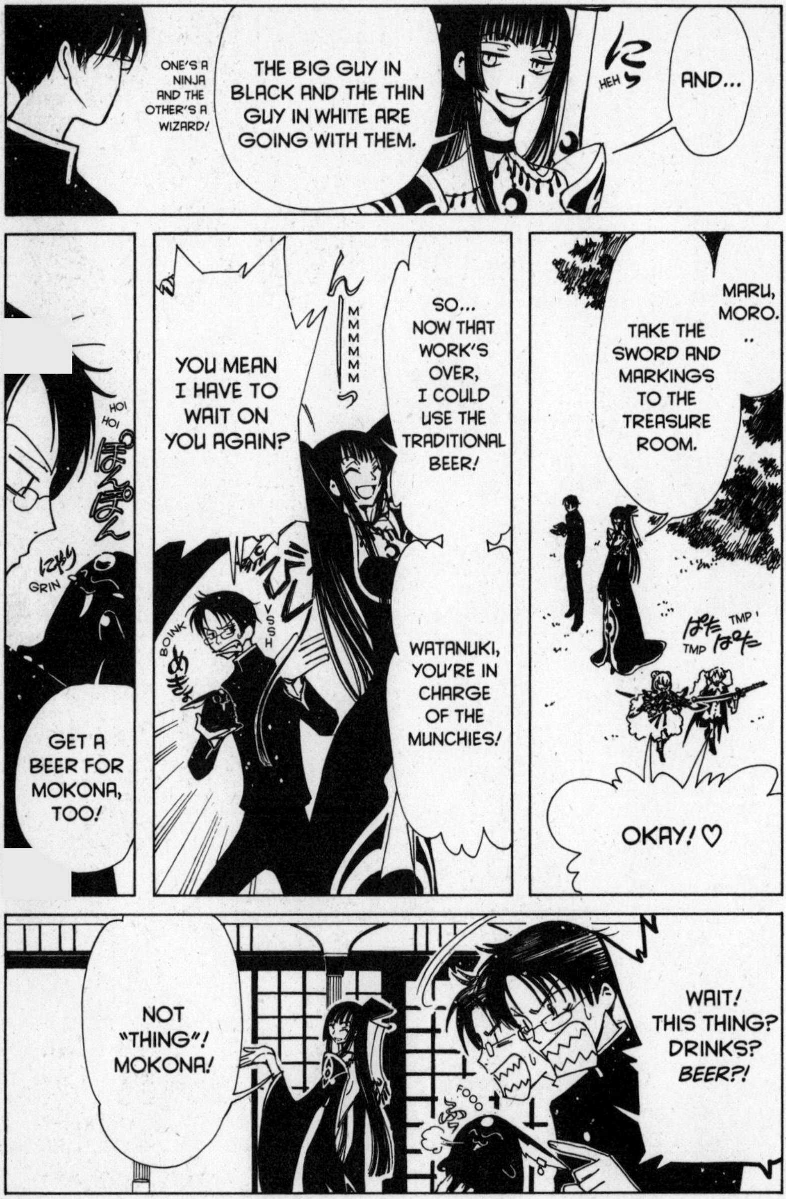
AND...
HEH
THE BIG GUY IN BLACK AND THE THIN GUY IN WHITE ARE GOING WITH THEM.
ONE'S A NINJA AND THE OTHER'S A WIZARD!
MARU, MORO. ..
TAKE THE SWORD AND MARKINGS TO THE TREASURE ROOM.
TMP TMP
OKAY! ♡
SO... NOW THAT WORK'S OVER, I COULD USE THE TRADITIONAL BEER!
MMMMMM
YOU MEAN I HAVE TO WAIT ON YOU AGAIN?
VSSH
BOINK
WATANUKI, YOU'RE IN CHARGE OF THE MUNCHIES!
HOI HOI
GRIN
GET A BEER FOR MOKONA, TOO!
WAIT! THIS THING? DRINKS? BEER?!
FOOO
NOT "THING"! MOKONA!

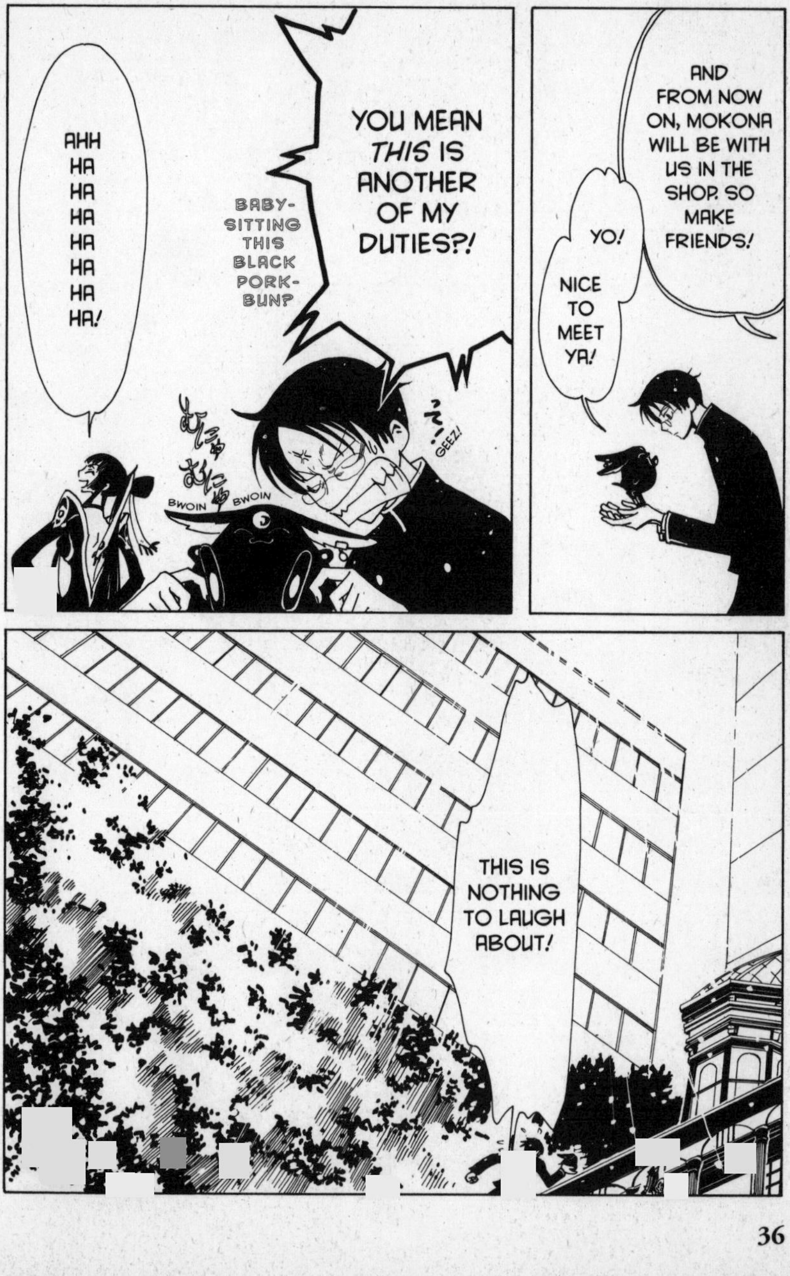
AND FROM NOW ON, MOKONA WILL BE WITH US IN THE SHOP. SO MAKE FRIENDS!
YO!
NICE TO MEET YA!
YOU MEAN *THIS* IS ANOTHER OF MY DUTIES?!
BABY-SITTING THIS BLACK PORK-BUN?
GEEZ!
BWOIN BWOIN
AHH HA HA HA HA HA HA HA!
THIS IS NOTHING TO LAUGH ABOUT!

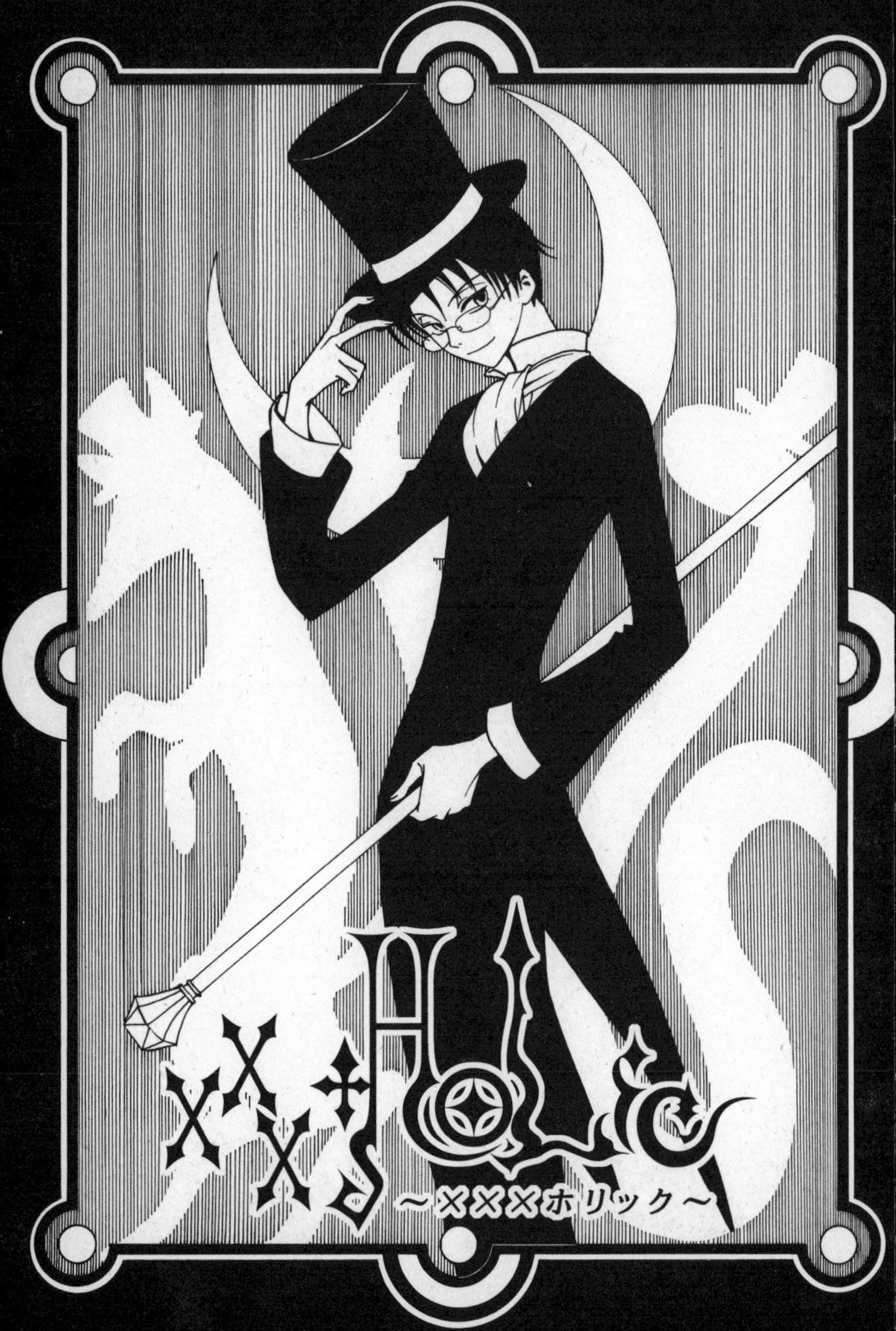
xxxHOLiC
~×××ホリック~

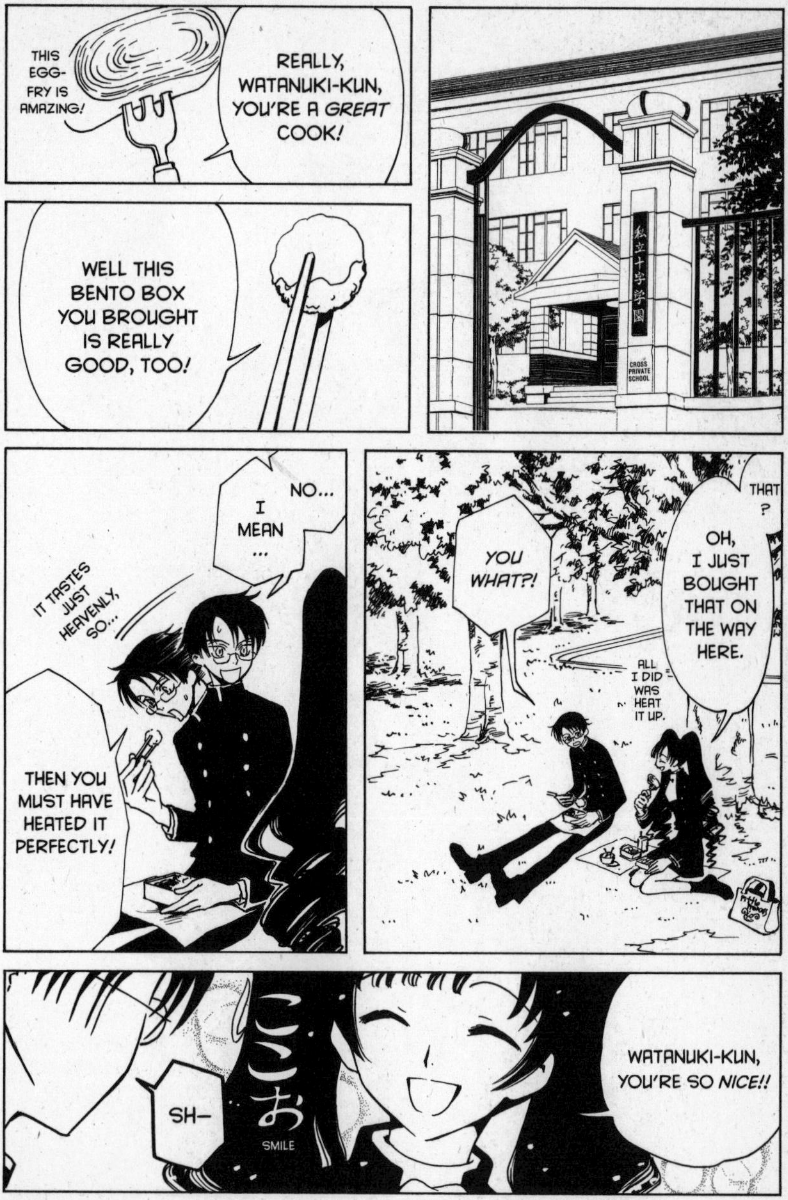
私立十字學園
CROSS PRIVATE SCHOOL
THIS EGG-FRY IS AMAZING!
REALLY, WATANUKI-KUN, YOU'RE A GREAT COOK!
WELL THIS BENTO BOX YOU BROUGHT IS REALLY GOOD, TOO!
THAT?
OH, I JUST BOUGHT THAT ON THE WAY HERE.
YOU WHAT?!
ALL I DID WAS HEAT IT UP.
NO... I MEAN ...
IT TASTES JUST HEAVENLY, SO...
THEN YOU MUST HAVE HEATED IT PERFECTLY!
WATANUKI-KUN, YOU'RE SO NICE!!
SMILE
SH-

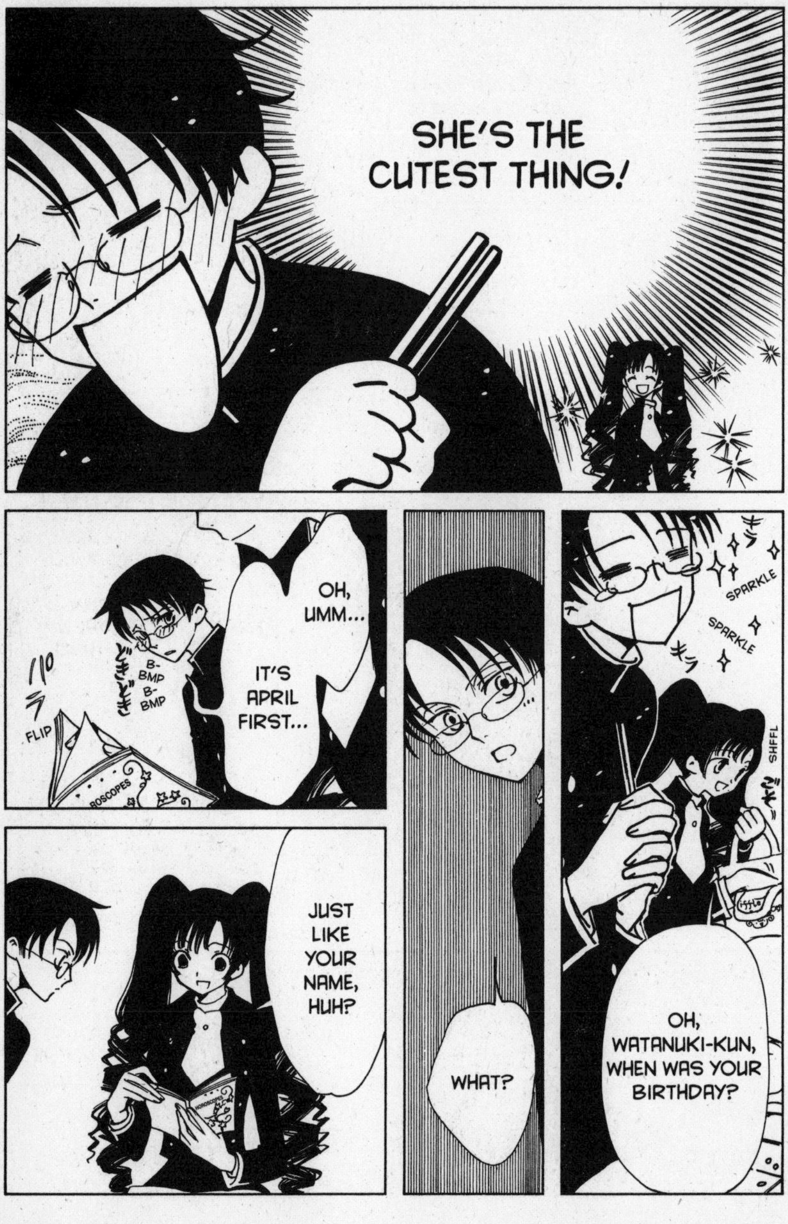
SHE'S THE CUTEST THING!
SPARKLE
SPARKLE
SHFFL
OH, WATANUKI-KUN, WHEN WAS YOUR BIRTHDAY?
WHAT?
OH, UMM...
IT'S APRIL FIRST...
B-BMP B-BMP
FLIP
ROSCOPES
JUST LIKE YOUR NAME, HUH?
HOROSCOPES

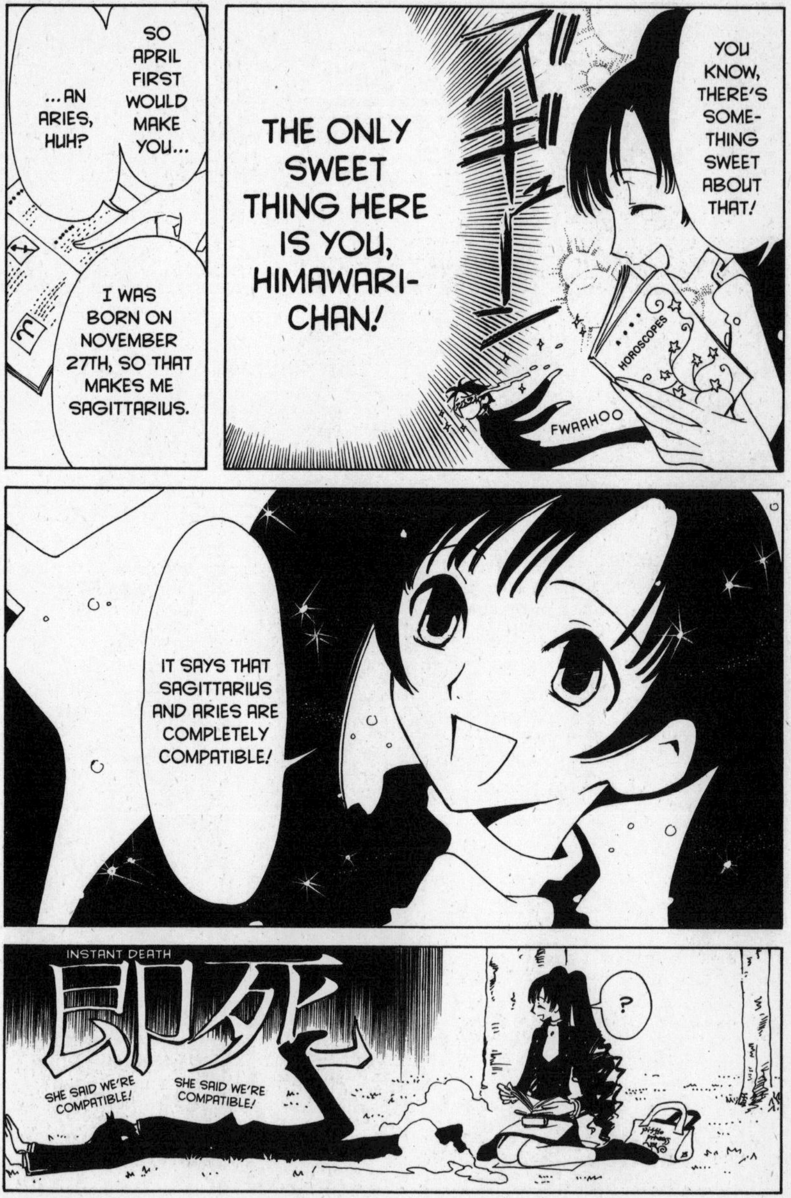
YOU KNOW, THERE'S SOME-THING SWEET ABOUT THAT!
THE ONLY SWEET THING HERE IS YOU, HIMAWARI-CHAN!
FWAAHOO
HOROSCOPES
SO APRIL FIRST WOULD MAKE YOU...
...AN ARIES, HUH?
I WAS BORN ON NOVEMBER 27TH, SO THAT MAKES ME SAGITTARIUS.
IT SAYS THAT SAGITTARIUS AND ARIES ARE COMPLETELY COMPATIBLE!
?
INSTANT DEATH
SHE SAID WE'RE COMPATIBLE!
SHE SAID WE'RE COMPATIBLE!

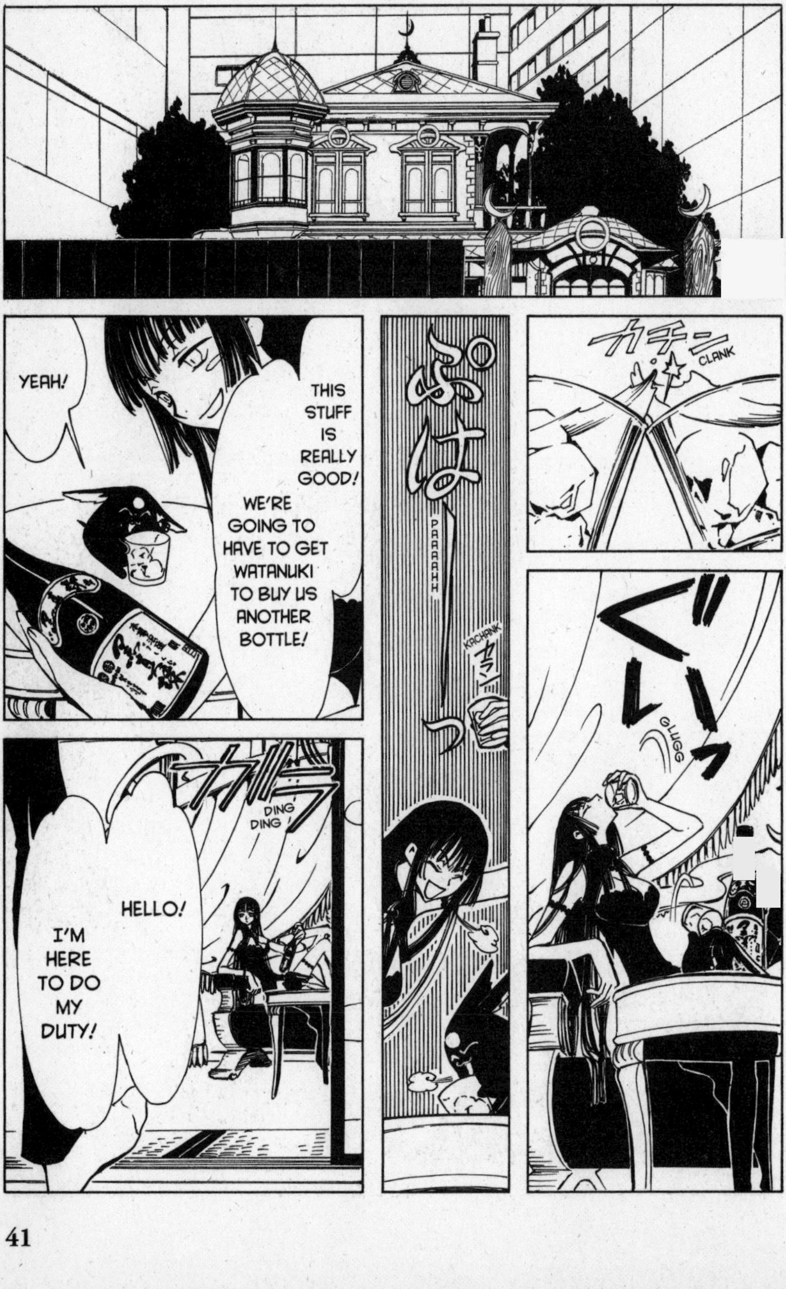
CLANK
GLUGG
PAAAAAHH
KACHANK
THIS STUFF IS REALLY GOOD!
YEAH!
WE'RE GOING TO HAVE TO GET WATANUKI TO BUY US ANOTHER BOTTLE!
DING DING
HELLO!
I'M HERE TO DO MY DUTY!

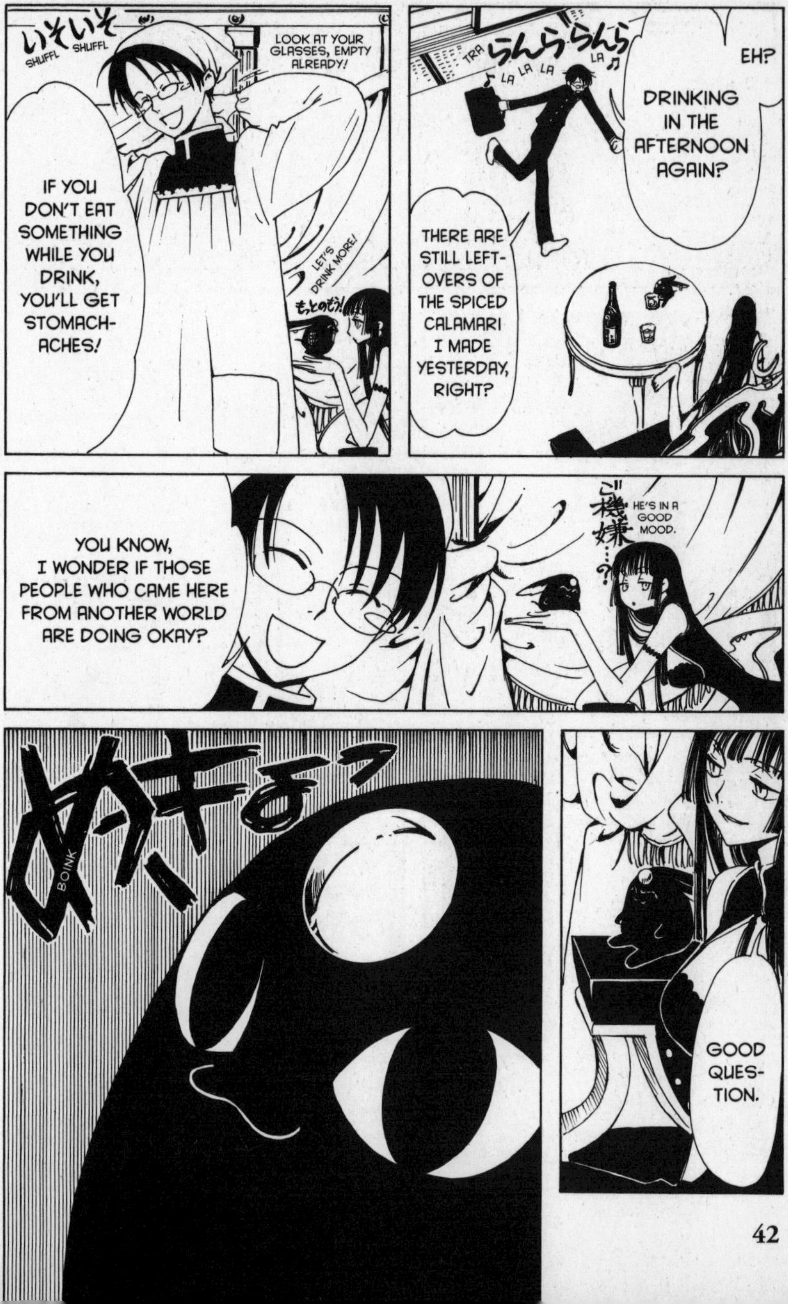
EH?
DRINKING IN THE AFTERNOON AGAIN?
らんらんら
TRA LA LA LA LA
THERE ARE STILL LEFT-OVERS OF THE SPICED CALAMARI I MADE YESTERDAY, RIGHT?
いそいそ
SHUFFL SHUFFL
LOOK AT YOUR GLASSES, EMPTY ALREADY!
IF YOU DON'T EAT SOMETHING WHILE YOU DRINK, YOU'LL GET STOMACH-ACHES!
もっとのむぞ!
LET'S DRINK MORE!
ご機嫌…?
HE'S IN A GOOD MOOD.
YOU KNOW, I WONDER IF THOSE PEOPLE WHO CAME HERE FROM ANOTHER WORLD ARE DOING OKAY?
GOOD QUES-TION.
めきょっ
BOINK

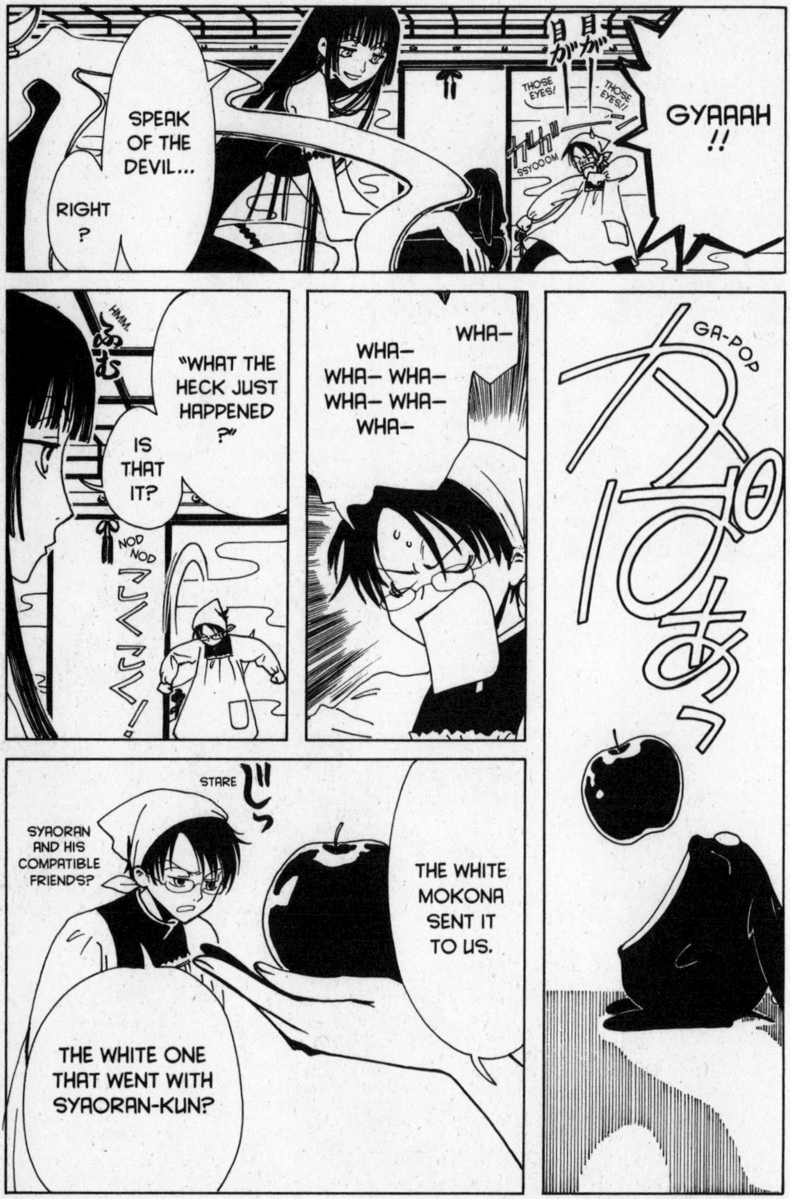
GYAAAH !!
THOSE EYES!!
THOSE EYES!
SSYOOOM
SPEAK OF THE DEVIL...
RIGHT ?
GA-POP
WHA-
WHA- WHA- WHA- WHA- WHA- WHA-
"WHAT THE HECK JUST HAPPENED ?"
IS THAT IT?
HMM.
NOD NOD
STARE
THE WHITE MOKONA SENT IT TO US.
SYAORAN AND HIS COMPATIBLE FRIENDS?
THE WHITE ONE THAT WENT WITH SYAORAN-KUN?

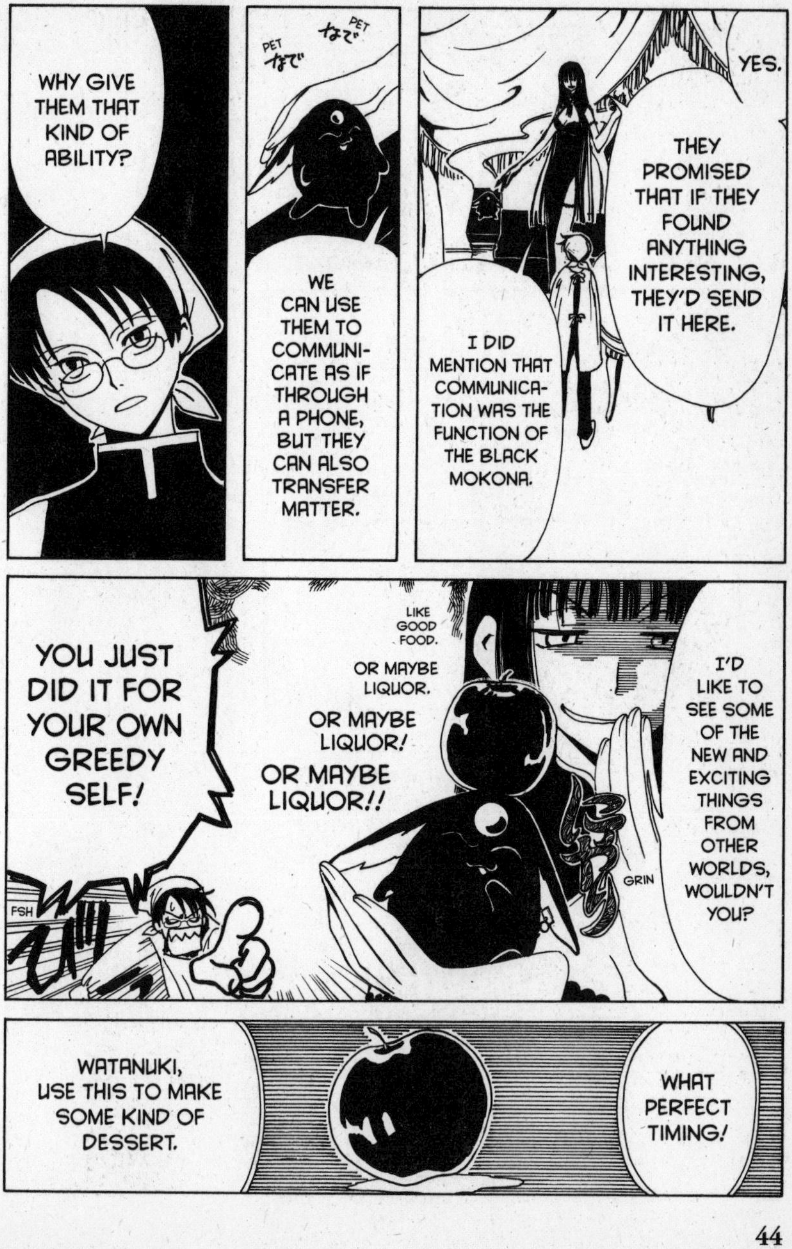
YES.
THEY PROMISED THAT IF THEY FOUND ANYTHING INTERESTING, THEY'D SEND IT HERE.
I DID MENTION THAT COMMUNICATION WAS THE FUNCTION OF THE BLACK MOKONA.
PET なで
PET なで
WE CAN USE THEM TO COMMUNICATE AS IF THROUGH A PHONE, BUT THEY CAN ALSO TRANSFER MATTER.
WHY GIVE THEM THAT KIND OF ABILITY?
I'D LIKE TO SEE SOME OF THE NEW AND EXCITING THINGS FROM OTHER WORLDS, WOULDN'T YOU?
GRIN
LIKE GOOD FOOD.
OR MAYBE LIQUOR.
OR MAYBE LIQUOR!
OR MAYBE LIQUOR!!
YOU JUST DID IT FOR YOUR OWN GREEDY SELF!
FSH
WHAT PERFECT TIMING!
WATANUKI, USE THIS TO MAKE SOME KIND OF DESSERT.

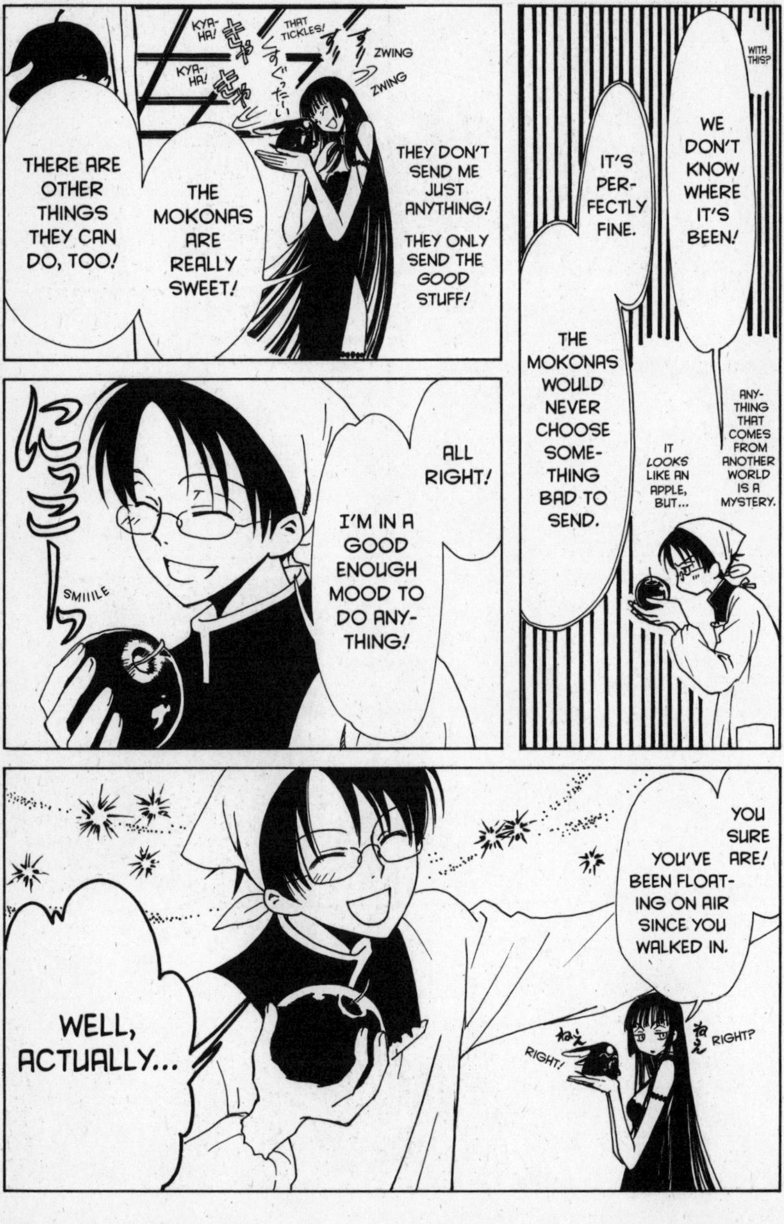
WITH THIS?
WE DON'T KNOW WHERE IT'S BEEN!
ANY-THING THAT COMES FROM ANOTHER WORLD IS A MYSTERY.
IT'S PER-FECTLY FINE.
IT LOOKS LIKE AN APPLE, BUT...
THE MOKONAS WOULD NEVER CHOOSE SOME-THING BAD TO SEND.
THAT TICKLES!
ZWING
ZWING
KYA-HA!
KYA-HA!
THEY DON'T SEND ME JUST ANYTHING!
THEY ONLY SEND THE GOOD STUFF!
THE MOKONAS ARE REALLY SWEET!
THERE ARE OTHER THINGS THEY CAN DO, TOO!
ALL RIGHT!
I'M IN A GOOD ENOUGH MOOD TO DO ANY-THING!
SMIIILE
YOU SURE ARE!
YOU'VE BEEN FLOAT-ING ON AIR SINCE YOU WALKED IN.
RIGHT?
RIGHT!
WELL, ACTUALLY...

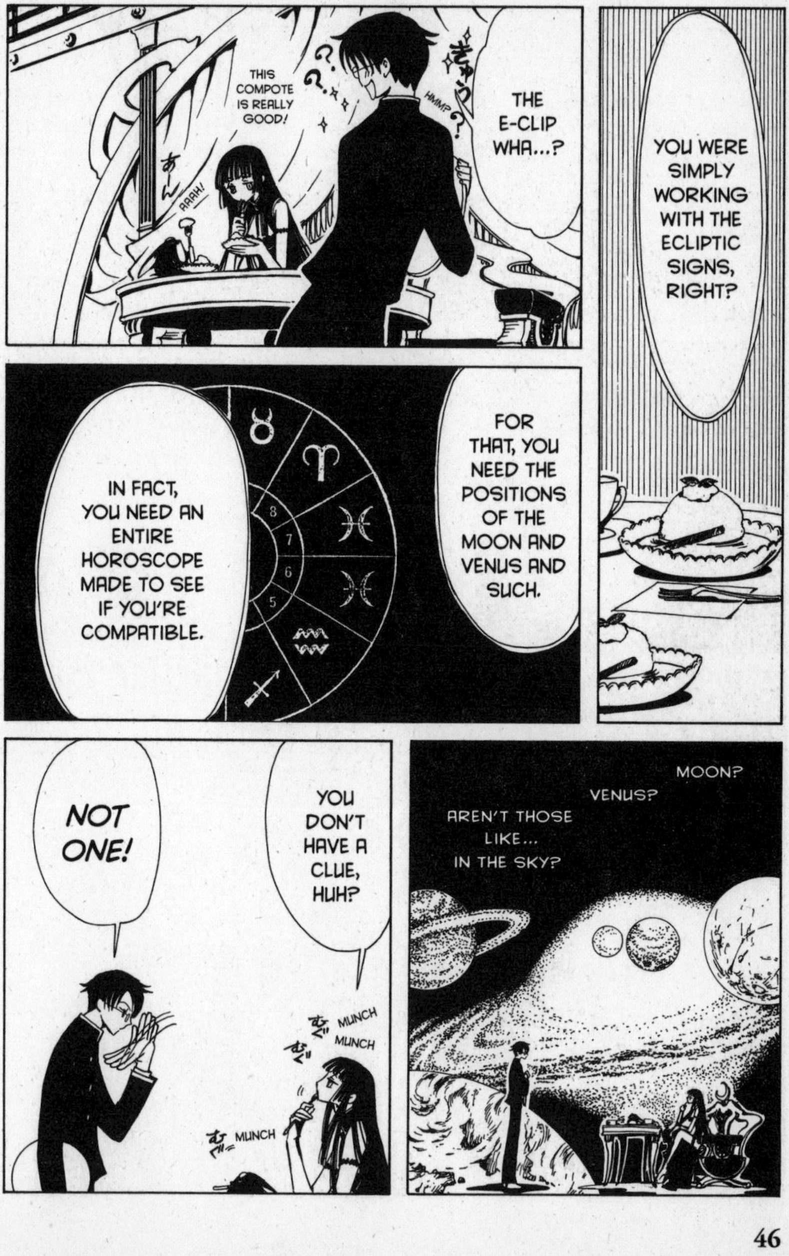
YOU WERE SIMPLY WORKING WITH THE ECLIPTIC SIGNS, RIGHT?
THE E-CLIP WHA...?
HMMP?
THIS COMPOTE IS REALLY GOOD!
AAAH!
FOR THAT, YOU NEED THE POSITIONS OF THE MOON AND VENUS AND SUCH.
IN FACT, YOU NEED AN ENTIRE HOROSCOPE MADE TO SEE IF YOU'RE COMPATIBLE.
MOON?
VENUS?
AREN'T THOSE LIKE... IN THE SKY?
YOU DON'T HAVE A CLUE, HUH?
NOT ONE!
MUNCH
MUNCH
MUNCH

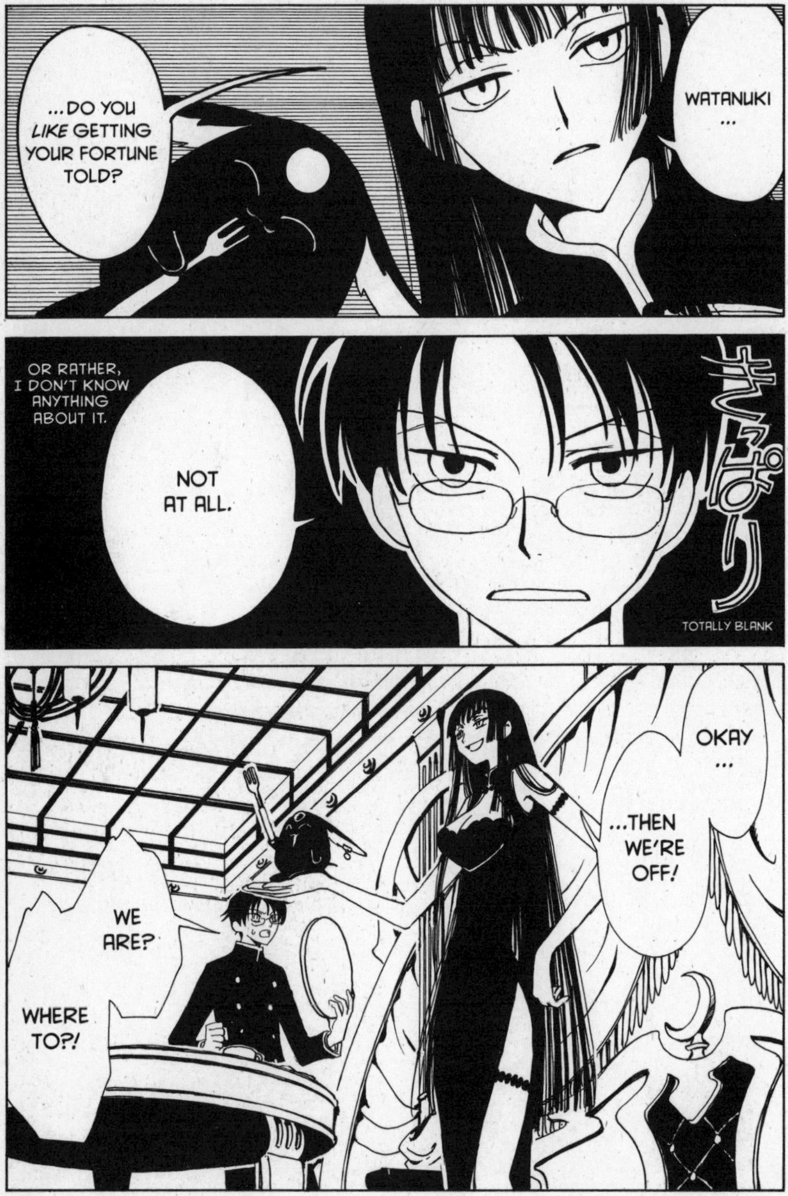
WATANUKI ...
...DO YOU *LIKE* GETTING YOUR FORTUNE TOLD?
きっぱり
TOTALLY BLANK
NOT AT ALL.
OR RATHER, I DON'T KNOW ANYTHING ABOUT IT.
OKAY ...
...THEN WE'RE OFF!
WE ARE?
WHERE TO?!

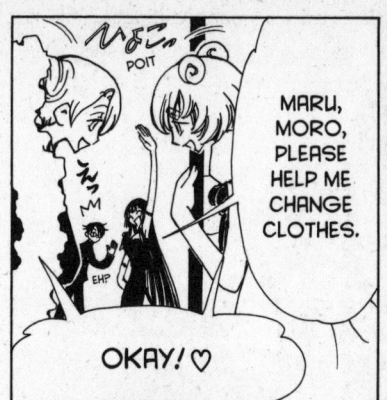

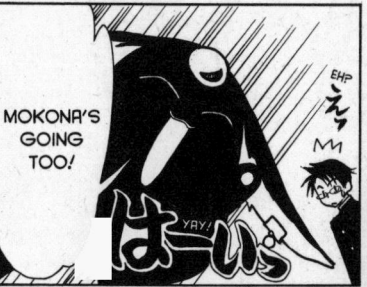

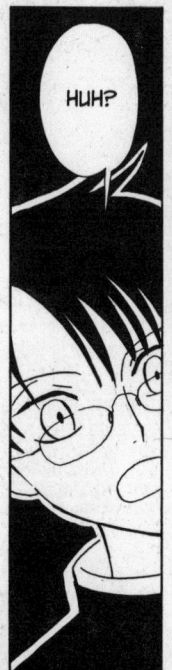

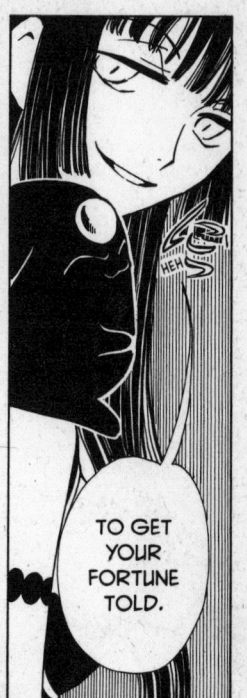

TO GET YOUR FORTUNE TOLD.
HEH
HUH?
MARU, MORO, PLEASE HELP ME CHANGE CLOTHES.
POIT
EHP
OKAY! ♡
MOKONA'S GOING TOO!
YAY!
EHP
WHY DOES THIS HAPPEN TO ME!!
I DON'T GET ANY OF THIS!!
WE'RE OFF! WE'RE OFF!

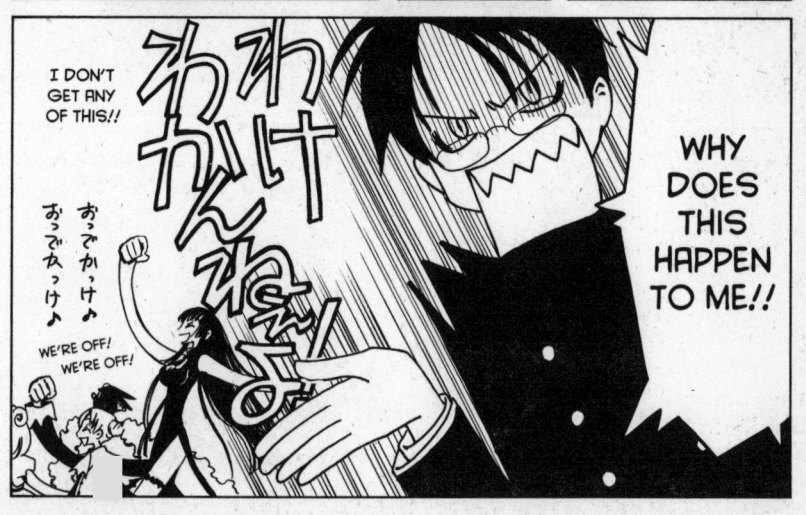

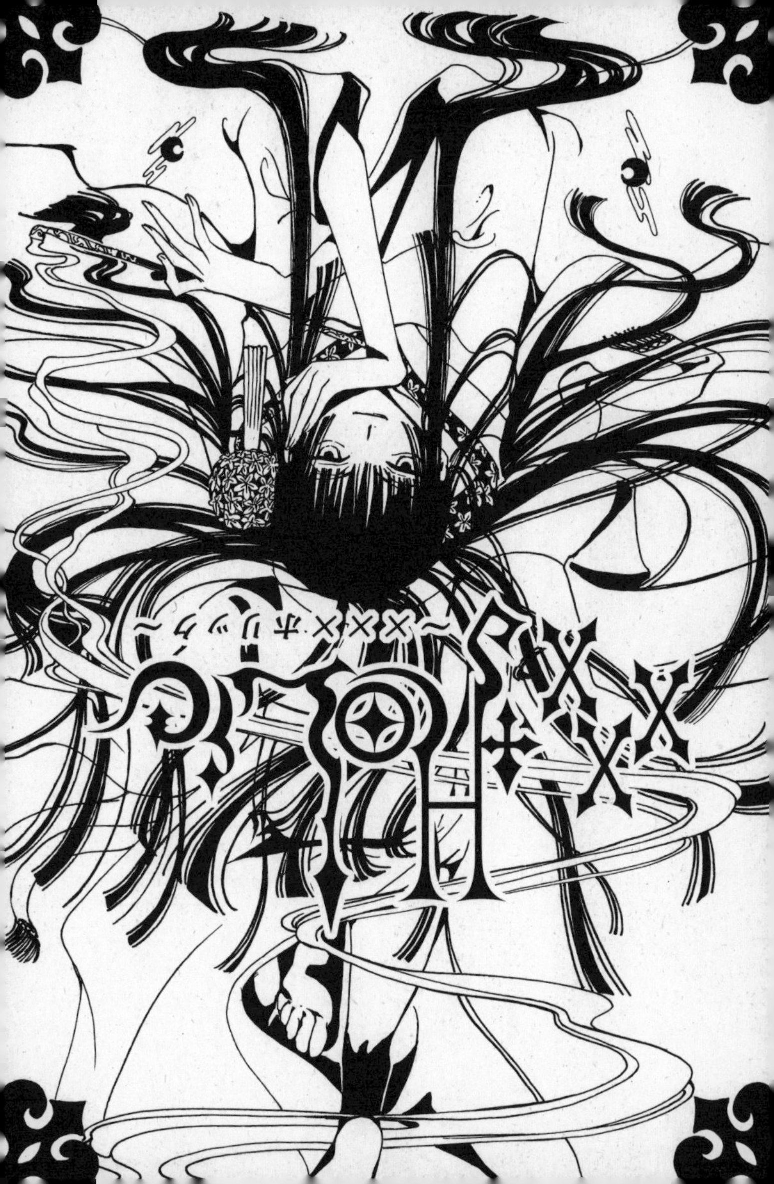
〜×××ホリック〜
xxxHOLiC

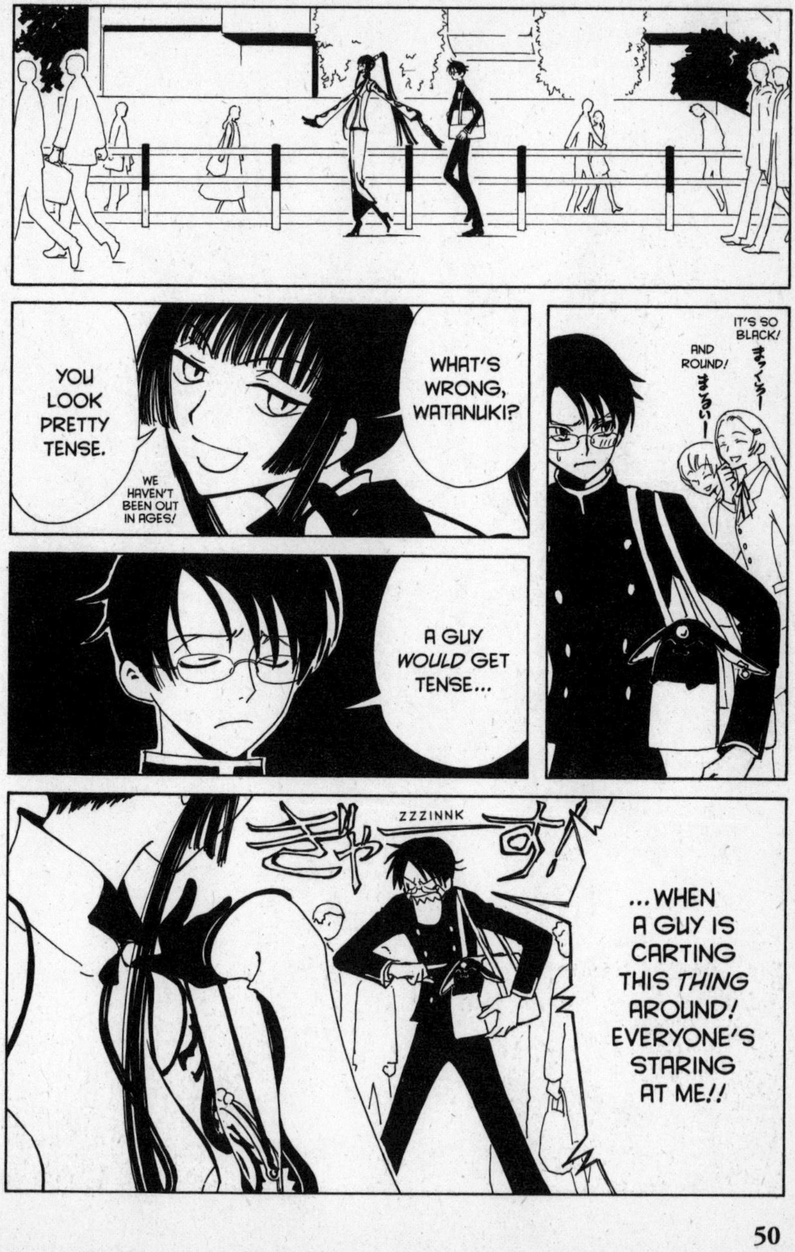
IT'S SO BLACK!
まっくろー
AND ROUND!
まるいー
WHAT'S WRONG, WATANUKI?
YOU LOOK PRETTY TENSE.
WE HAVEN'T BEEN OUT IN AGES!
A GUY *WOULD* GET TENSE...
ZZZINNK
きゃーっ!
...WHEN A GUY IS CARTING THIS *THING* AROUND! EVERYONE'S STARING AT ME!!

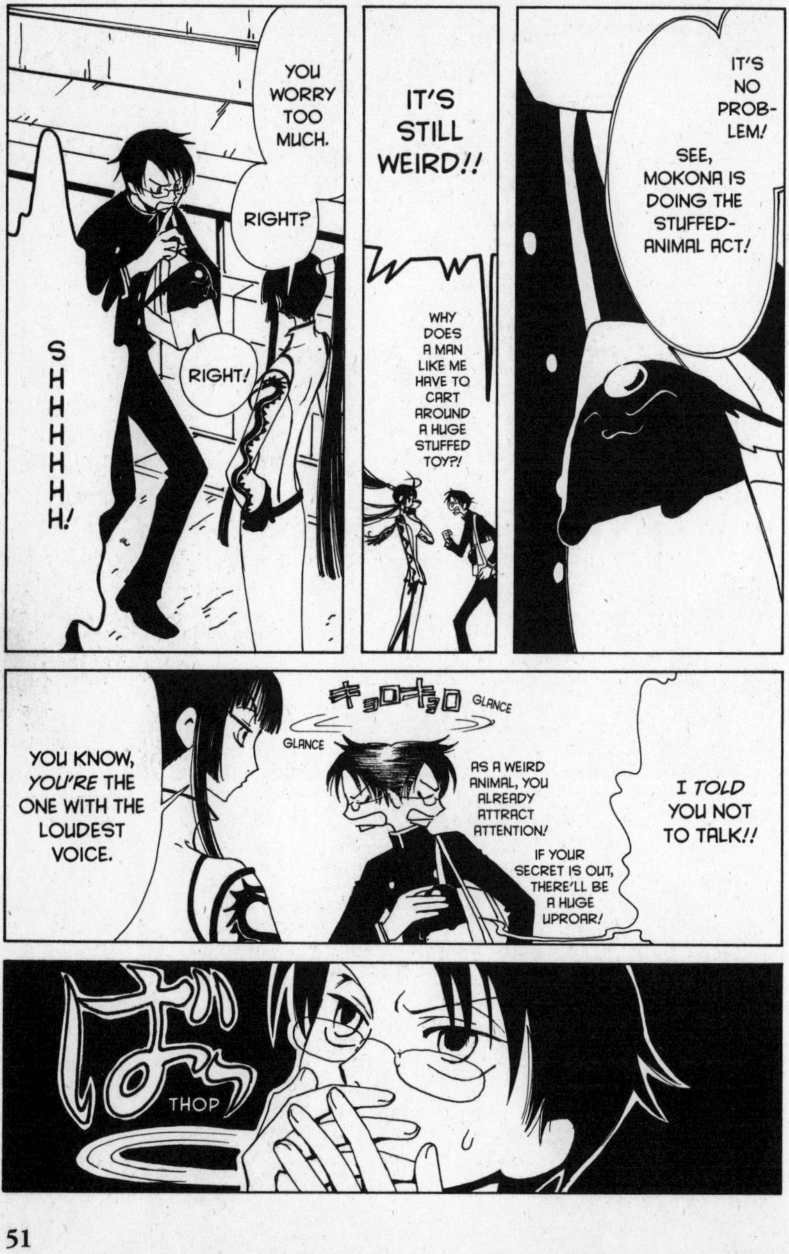
IT'S NO PROB-LEM!
SEE, MOKONA IS DOING THE STUFFED-ANIMAL ACT!
IT'S STILL WEIRD!!
WHY DOES A MAN LIKE ME HAVE TO CART AROUND A HUGE STUFFED TOY?!
YOU WORRY TOO MUCH.
RIGHT?
RIGHT!
SHHHHHH!
I TOLD YOU NOT TO TALK!!
IF YOUR SECRET IS OUT, THERE'LL BE A HUGE UPROAR!
GLANCE
GLANCE
AS A WEIRD ANIMAL, YOU ALREADY ATTRACT ATTENTION!
YOU KNOW, YOU'RE THE ONE WITH THE LOUDEST VOICE.
THOP

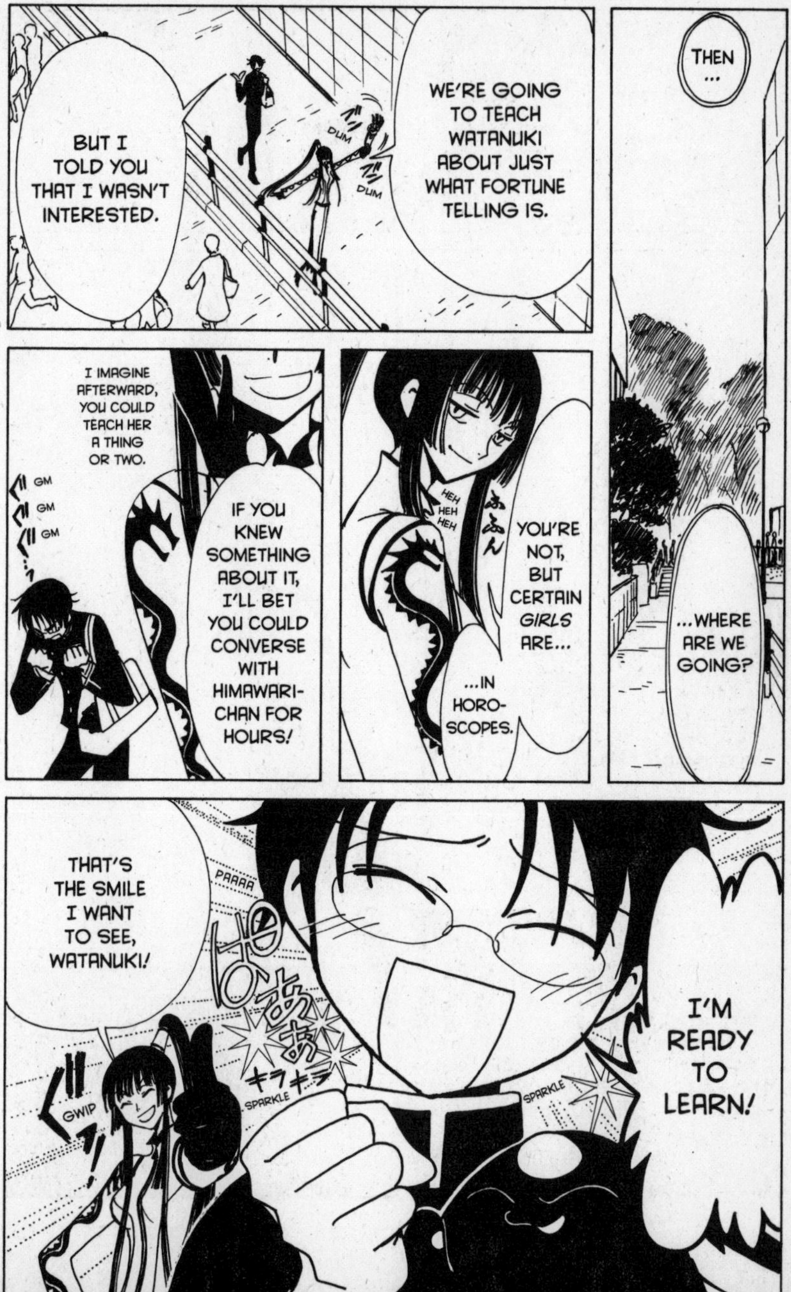
THEN ...
...WHERE ARE WE GOING?
WE'RE GOING TO TEACH WATANUKI ABOUT JUST WHAT FORTUNE TELLING IS.
DUM
DUM
BUT I TOLD YOU THAT I WASN'T INTERESTED.
YOU'RE NOT, BUT CERTAIN *GIRLS* ARE...
HEH HEH HEH
...IN HORO-SCOPES.
IF YOU KNEW SOMETHING ABOUT IT, I'LL BET YOU COULD CONVERSE WITH HIMAWARI-CHAN FOR HOURS!
I IMAGINE AFTERWARD, YOU COULD TEACH HER A THING OR TWO.
GM
GM
GM
I'M READY TO LEARN!
SPARKLE
PARRRA
SPARKLE
THAT'S THE SMILE I WANT TO SEE, WATANUKI!
GWIP

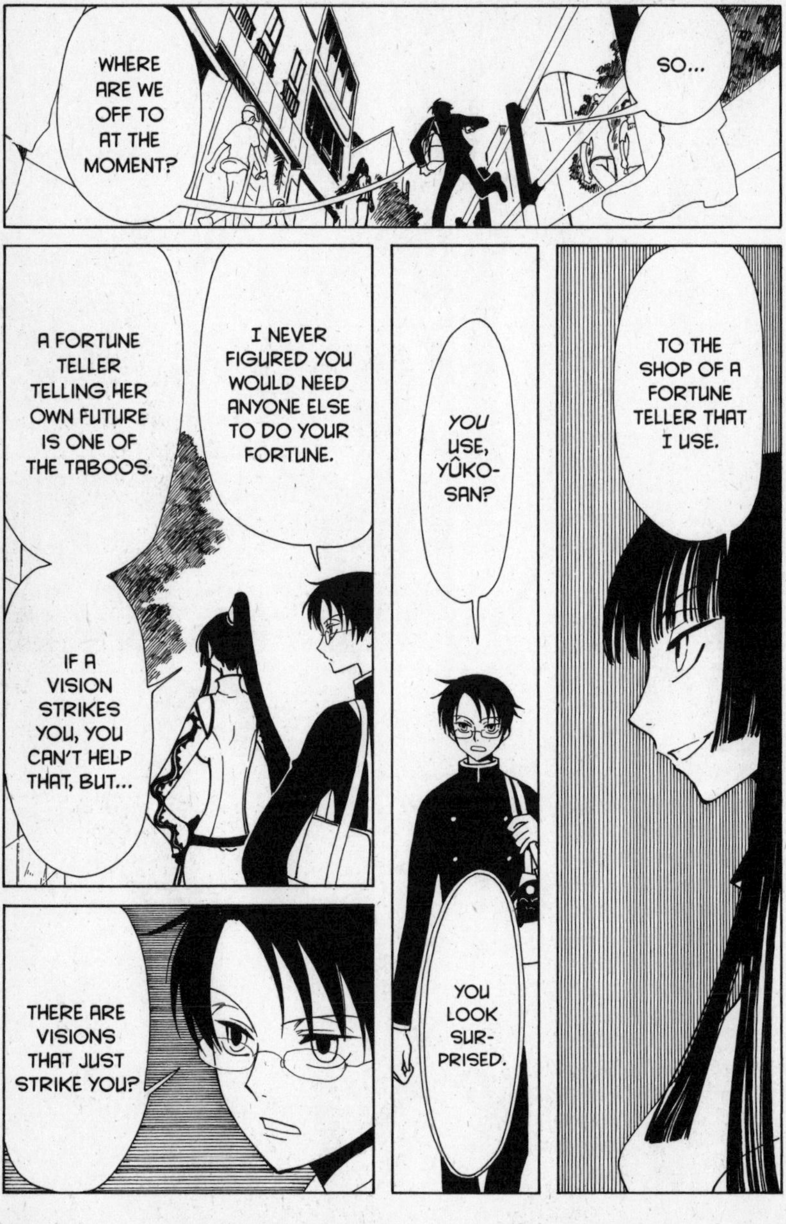
SO...
WHERE ARE WE OFF TO AT THE MOMENT?
TO THE SHOP OF A FORTUNE TELLER THAT I USE.
YOU USE, YÛKO-SAN?
YOU LOOK SUR-PRISED.
I NEVER FIGURED YOU WOULD NEED ANYONE ELSE TO DO YOUR FORTUNE.
A FORTUNE TELLER TELLING HER OWN FUTURE IS ONE OF THE TABOOS.
IF A VISION STRIKES YOU, YOU CAN'T HELP THAT, BUT...
THERE ARE VISIONS THAT JUST STRIKE YOU?

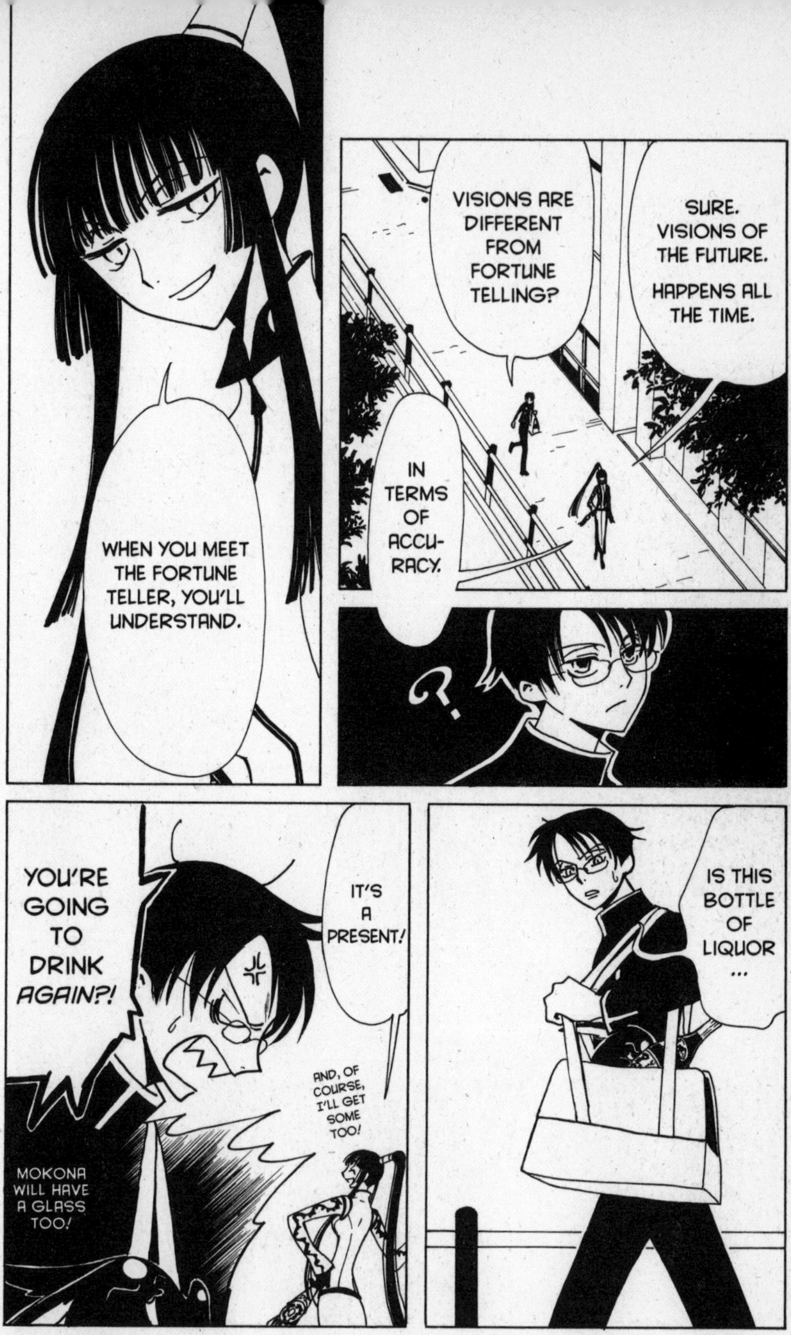
SURE. VISIONS OF THE FUTURE.
HAPPENS ALL THE TIME.
VISIONS ARE DIFFERENT FROM FORTUNE TELLING?
IN TERMS OF ACCU-RACY.
WHEN YOU MEET THE FORTUNE TELLER, YOU'LL UNDERSTAND.
IS THIS BOTTLE OF LIQUOR ...
IT'S A PRESENT!
AND, OF COURSE, I'LL GET SOME TOO!
YOU'RE GOING TO DRINK AGAIN?!
MOKONA WILL HAVE A GLASS TOO!

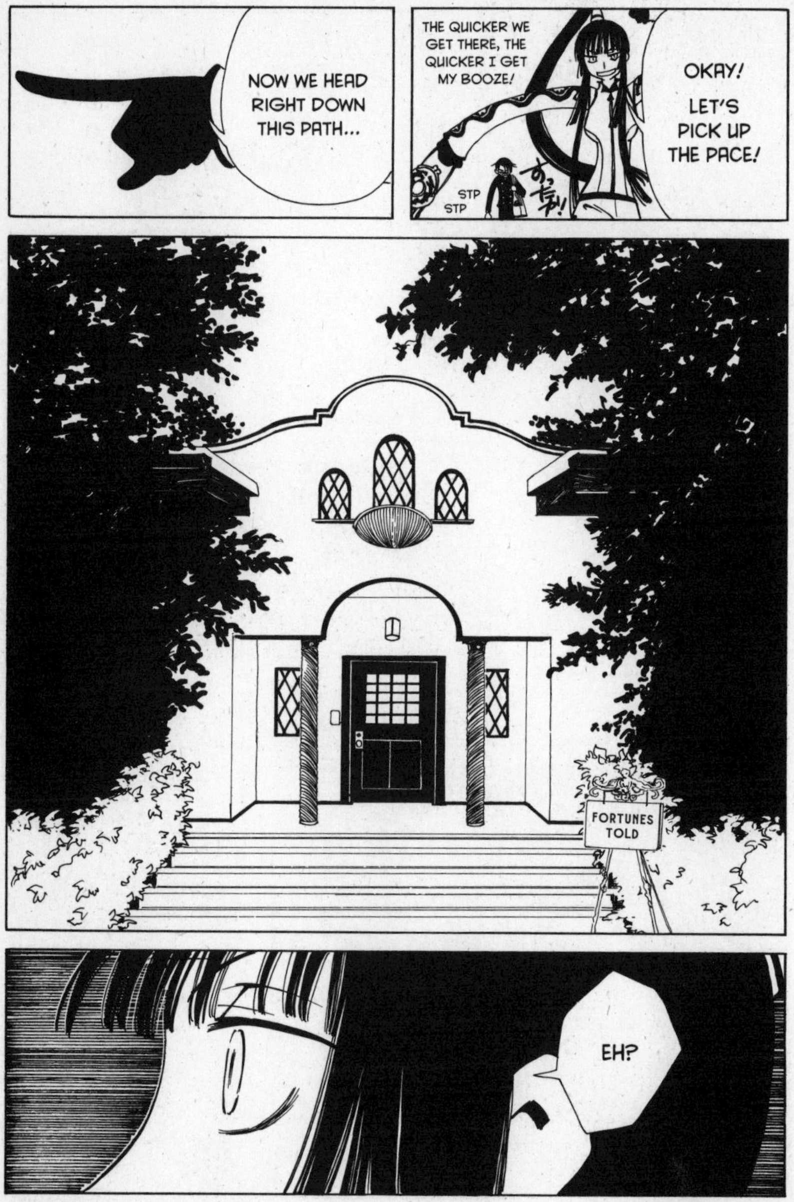
OKAY!
LET'S PICK UP THE PACE!
THE QUICKER WE GET THERE, THE QUICKER I GET MY BOOZE!
STP
STP
NOW WE HEAD RIGHT DOWN THIS PATH...
FORTUNES TOLD
EH?

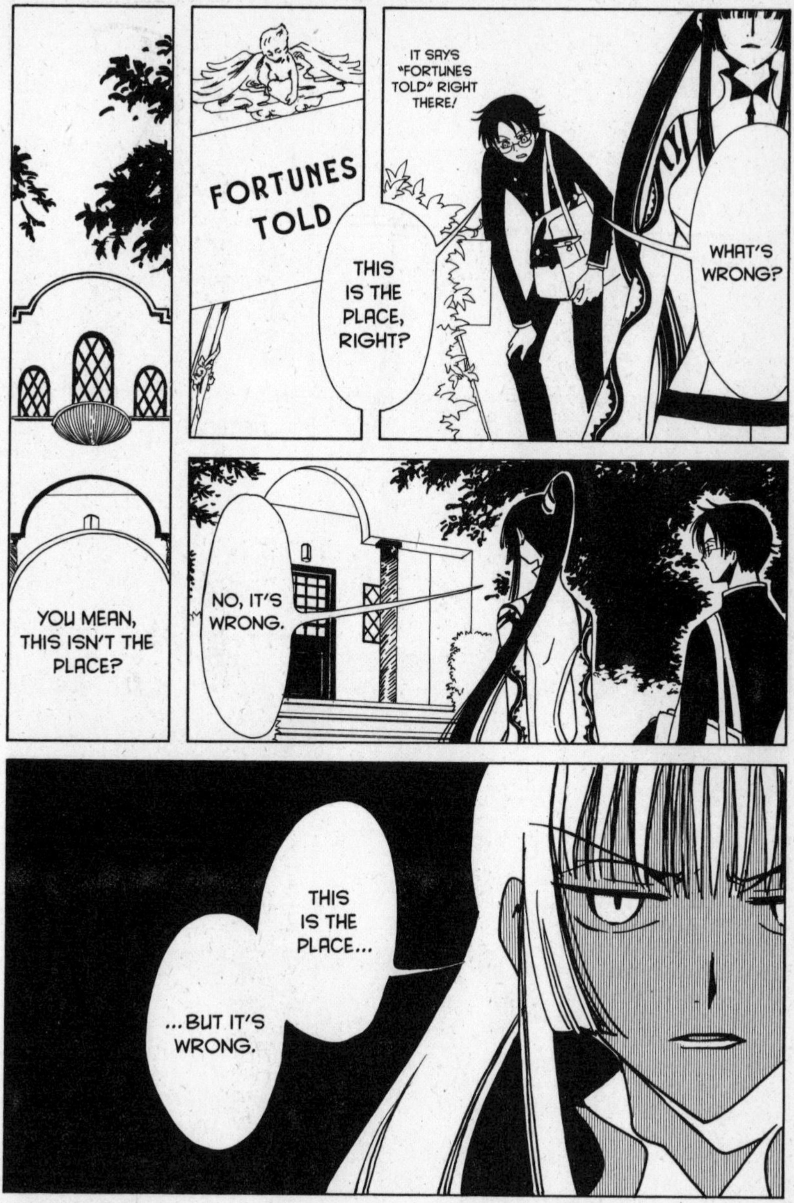
WHAT'S WRONG?
IT SAYS "FORTUNES TOLD" RIGHT THERE!
FORTUNES TOLD
THIS IS THE PLACE, RIGHT?
NO, IT'S WRONG.
YOU MEAN, THIS ISN'T THE PLACE?
THIS IS THE PLACE...
...BUT IT'S WRONG.

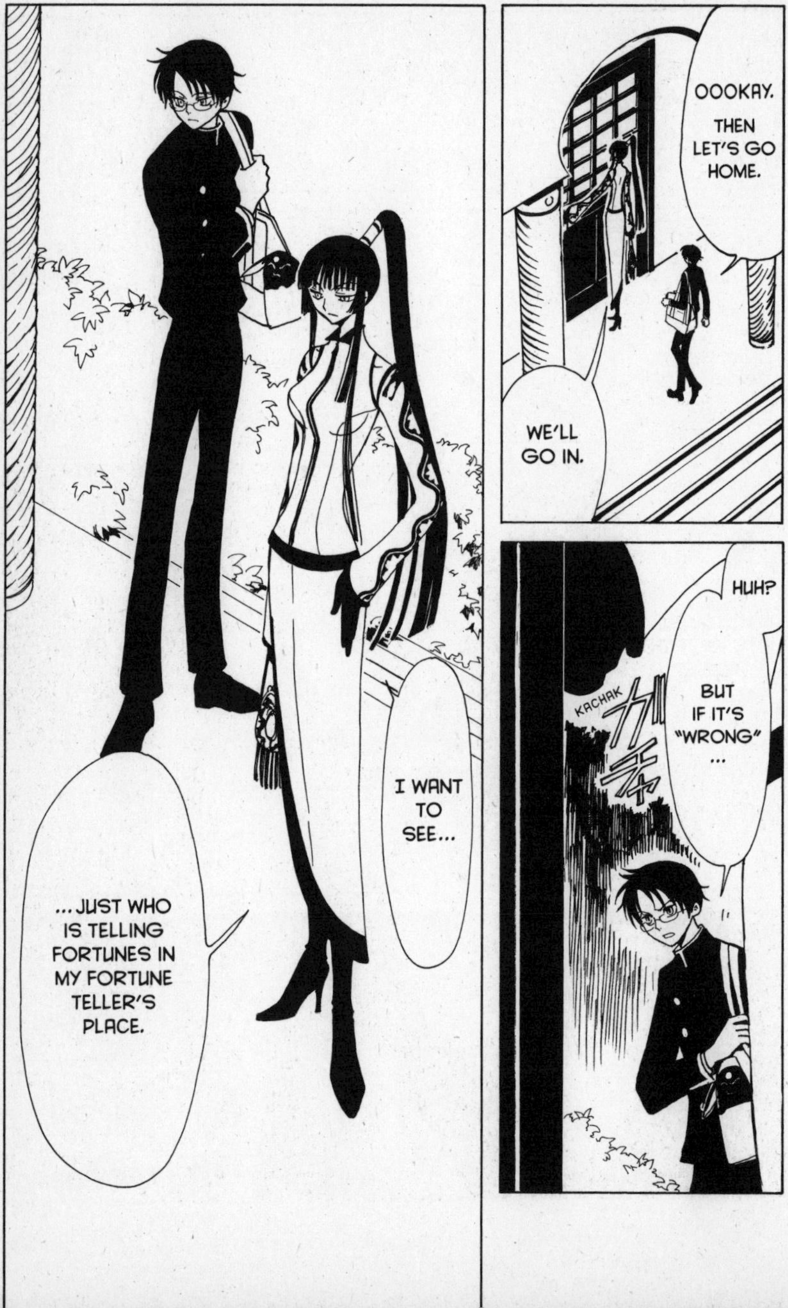
OOOKAY.
THEN LET'S GO HOME.
WE'LL GO IN.
HUH?
BUT IF IT'S "WRONG"...
KACHAK
I WANT TO SEE...
...JUST WHO IS TELLING FORTUNES IN MY FORTUNE TELLER'S PLACE.

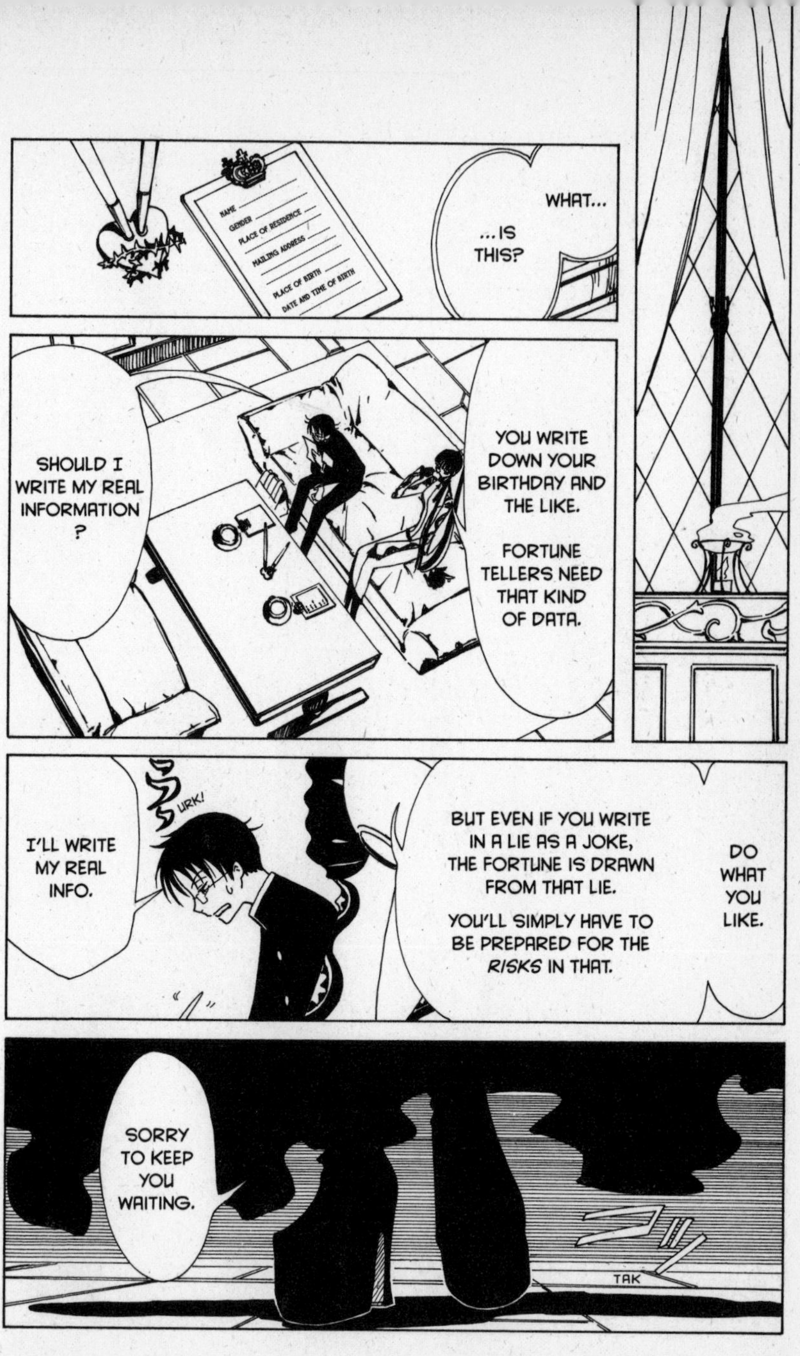
WHAT...
...IS THIS?
NAME
GENDER
PLACE OF RESIDENCE
MAILING ADDRESS
PLACE OF BIRTH
DATE AND TIME OF BIRTH
YOU WRITE DOWN YOUR BIRTHDAY AND THE LIKE.
FORTUNE TELLERS NEED THAT KIND OF DATA.
SHOULD I WRITE MY REAL INFORMATION ?
DO WHAT YOU LIKE.
BUT EVEN IF YOU WRITE IN A LIE AS A JOKE, THE FORTUNE IS DRAWN FROM THAT LIE.
YOU'LL SIMPLY HAVE TO BE PREPARED FOR THE *RISKS* IN THAT.
URK!
I'LL WRITE MY REAL INFO.
SORRY TO KEEP YOU WAITING.
TAK

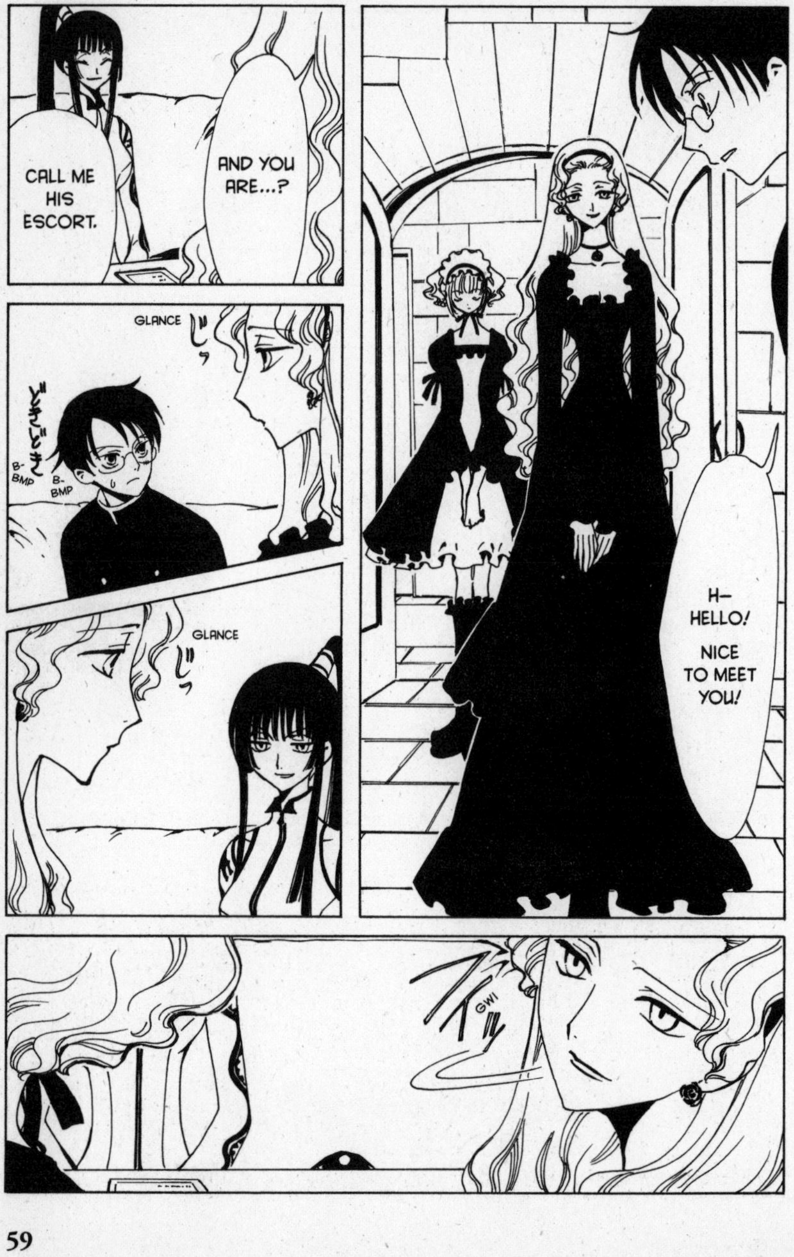
H— HELLO! NICE TO MEET YOU!
AND YOU ARE...?
CALL ME HIS ESCORT.
じっ
GLANCE
どきどき
B-BMP B-BMP
じっ
GLANCE
GWI

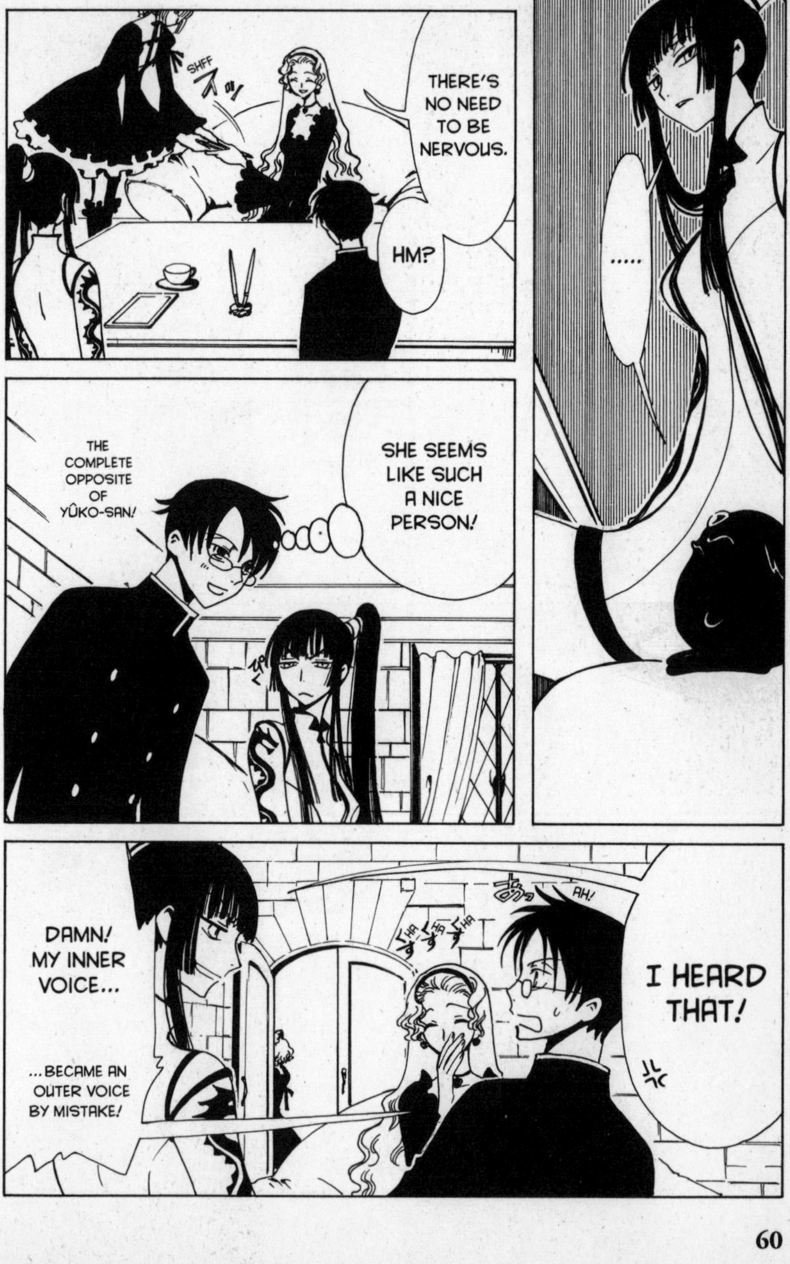
.....
HM?
THERE'S NO NEED TO BE NERVOUS.
SHFF
SHE SEEMS LIKE SUCH A NICE PERSON!
THE COMPLETE OPPOSITE OF YÛKO-SAN!
I HEARD THAT!
AH!
HA HA HA
DAMN! MY INNER VOICE...
...BECAME AN OUTER VOICE BY MISTAKE!

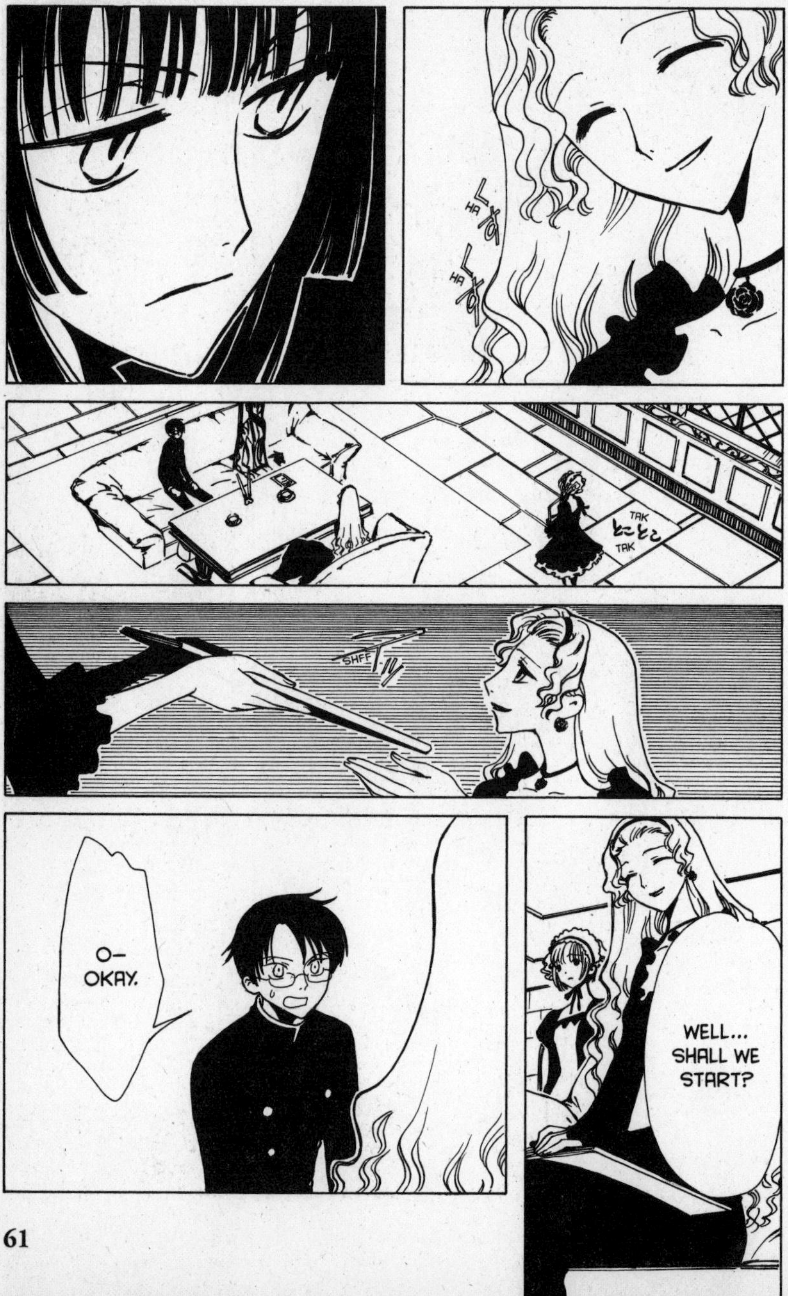

HA
HA
TAK とことこ TAK
SHFF
WELL... SHALL WE START?
O— OKAY.

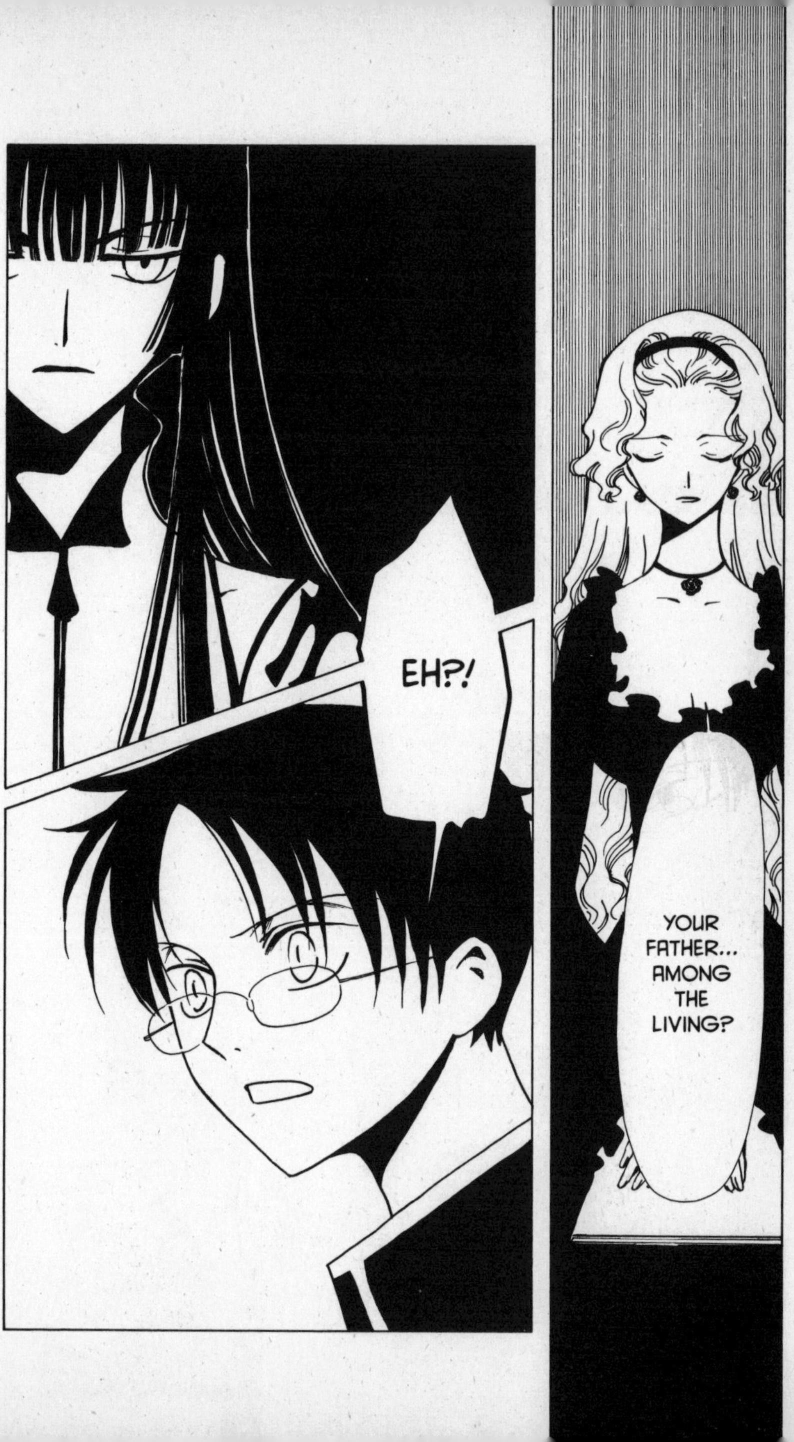
YOUR FATHER... AMONG THE LIVING?
EH?!

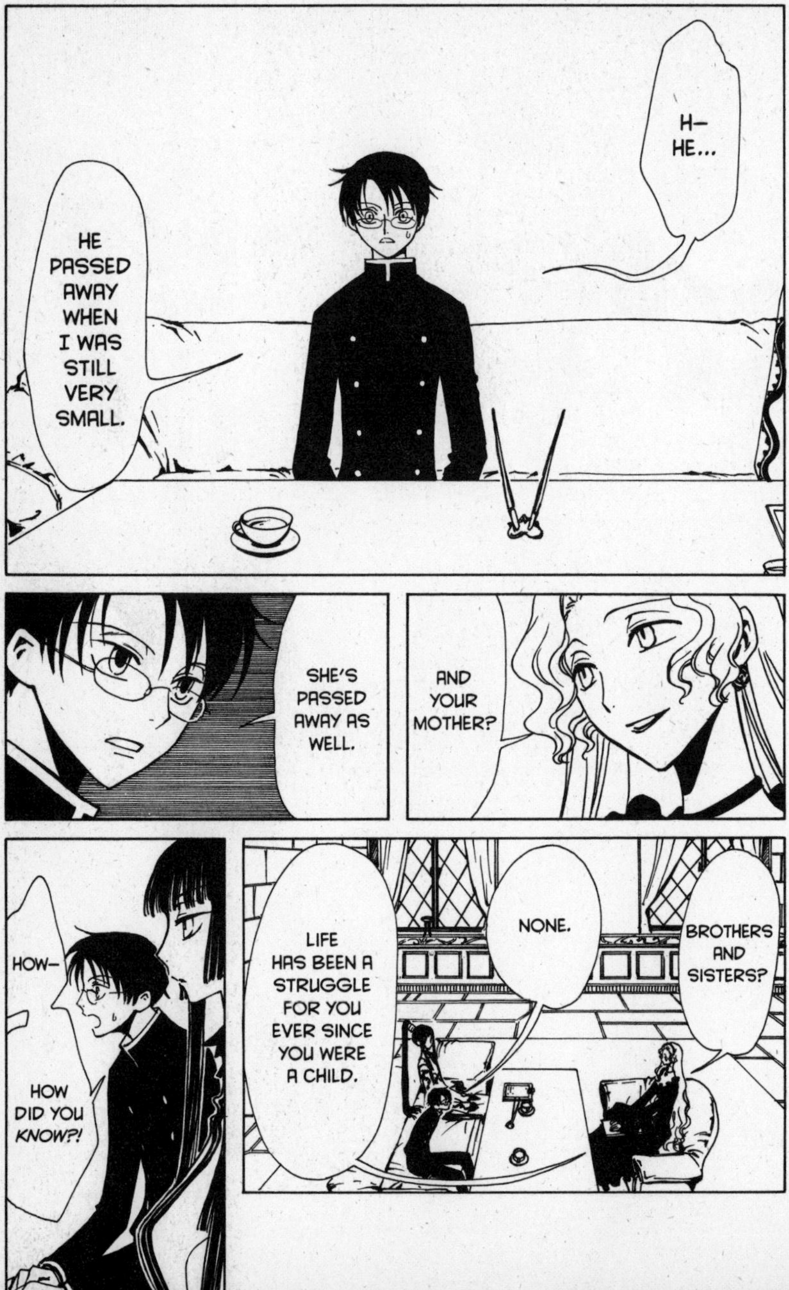
H— HE...
HE PASSED AWAY WHEN I WAS STILL VERY SMALL.
AND YOUR MOTHER?
SHE'S PASSED AWAY AS WELL.
BROTHERS AND SISTERS?
NONE.
LIFE HAS BEEN A STRUGGLE FOR YOU EVER SINCE YOU WERE A CHILD.
HOW—
HOW DID YOU KNOW?!

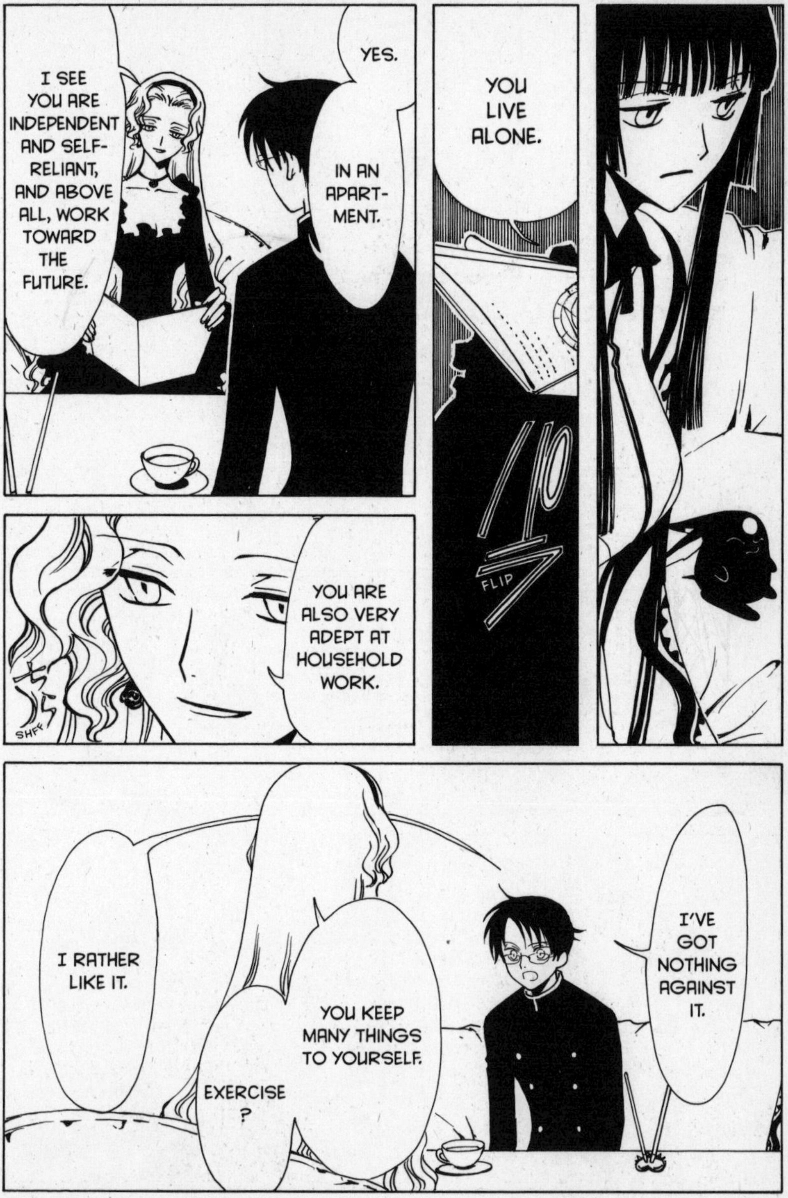
YOU LIVE ALONE.
FLIP
YES.
IN AN APART-MENT.
I SEE YOU ARE INDEPENDENT AND SELF-RELIANT, AND ABOVE ALL, WORK TOWARD THE FUTURE.
YOU ARE ALSO VERY ADEPT AT HOUSEHOLD WORK.
SHFF
I'VE GOT NOTHING AGAINST IT.
YOU KEEP MANY THINGS TO YOURSELF.
EXERCISE ?
I RATHER LIKE IT.

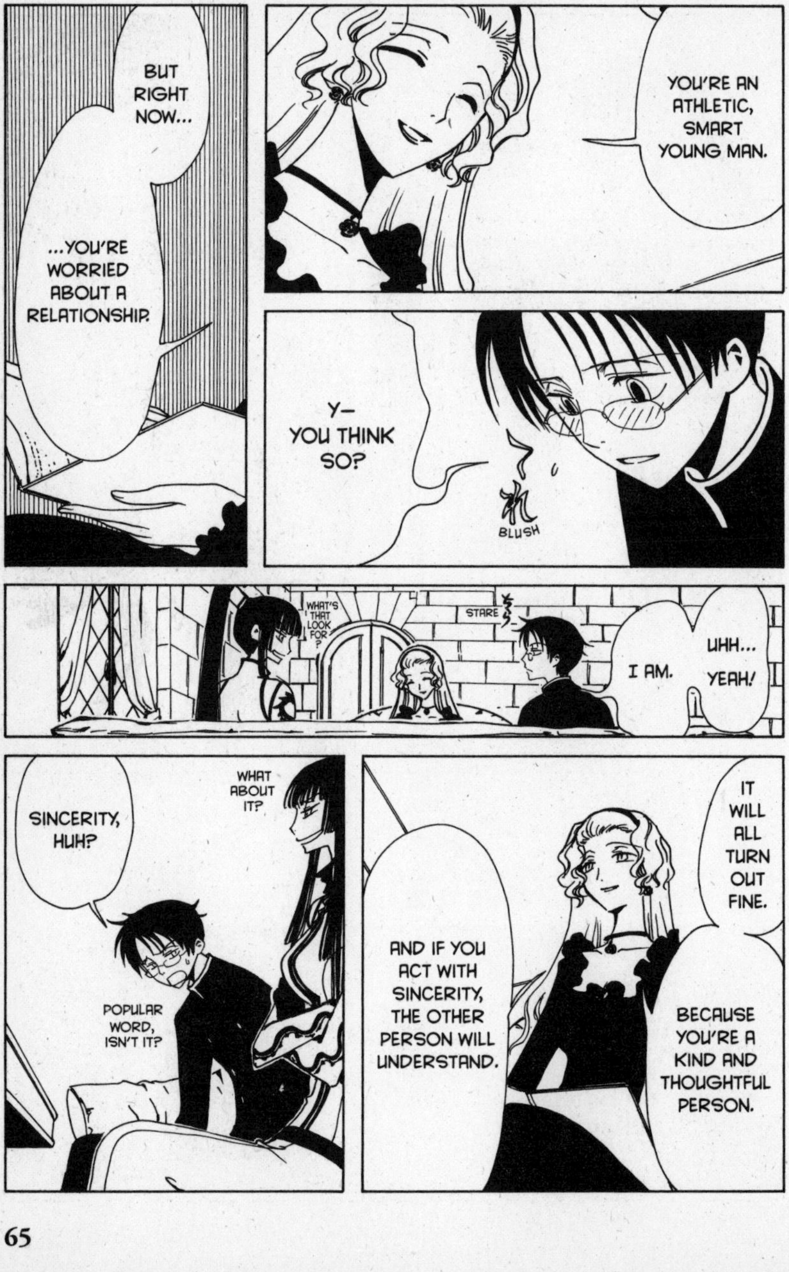
YOU'RE AN ATHLETIC, SMART YOUNG MAN.
BUT RIGHT NOW...
...YOU'RE WORRIED ABOUT A RELATIONSHIP.
Y— YOU THINK SO?
BLUSH
UHH... YEAH!
I AM.
STARE
WHAT'S THAT LOOK FOR?
IT WILL ALL TURN OUT FINE.
BECAUSE YOU'RE A KIND AND THOUGHTFUL PERSON.
AND IF YOU ACT WITH SINCERITY, THE OTHER PERSON WILL UNDERSTAND.
WHAT ABOUT IT?
SINCERITY, HUH?
POPULAR WORD, ISN'T IT?

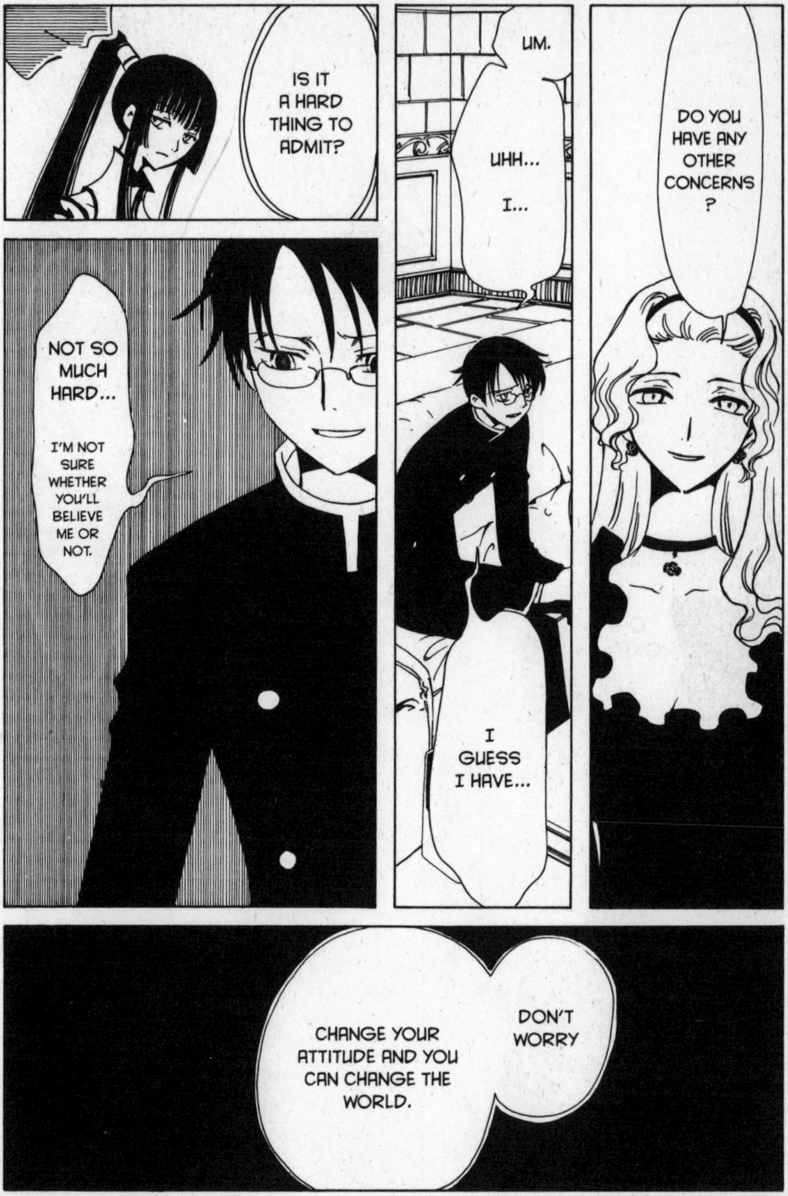
DO YOU HAVE ANY OTHER CONCERNS ?
UM.
UHH... I...
I GUESS I HAVE...
IS IT A HARD THING TO ADMIT?
NOT SO MUCH HARD...
I'M NOT SURE WHETHER YOU'LL BELIEVE ME OR NOT.
DON'T WORRY
CHANGE YOUR ATTITUDE AND YOU CAN CHANGE THE WORLD.

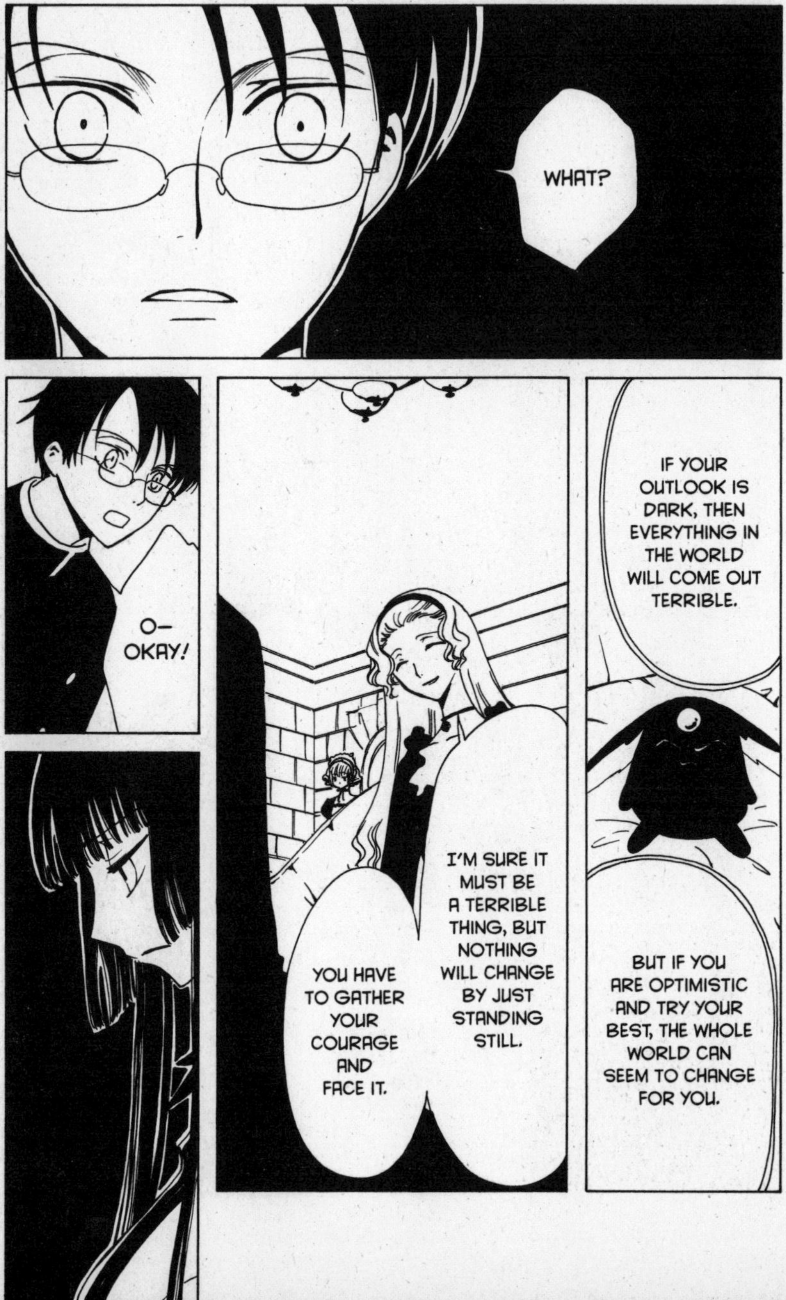
WHAT?
IF YOUR OUTLOOK IS DARK, THEN EVERYTHING IN THE WORLD WILL COME OUT TERRIBLE.
BUT IF YOU ARE OPTIMISTIC AND TRY YOUR BEST, THE WHOLE WORLD CAN SEEM TO CHANGE FOR YOU.
I'M SURE IT MUST BE A TERRIBLE THING, BUT NOTHING WILL CHANGE BY JUST STANDING STILL.
YOU HAVE TO GATHER YOUR COURAGE AND FACE IT.
O-OKAY!

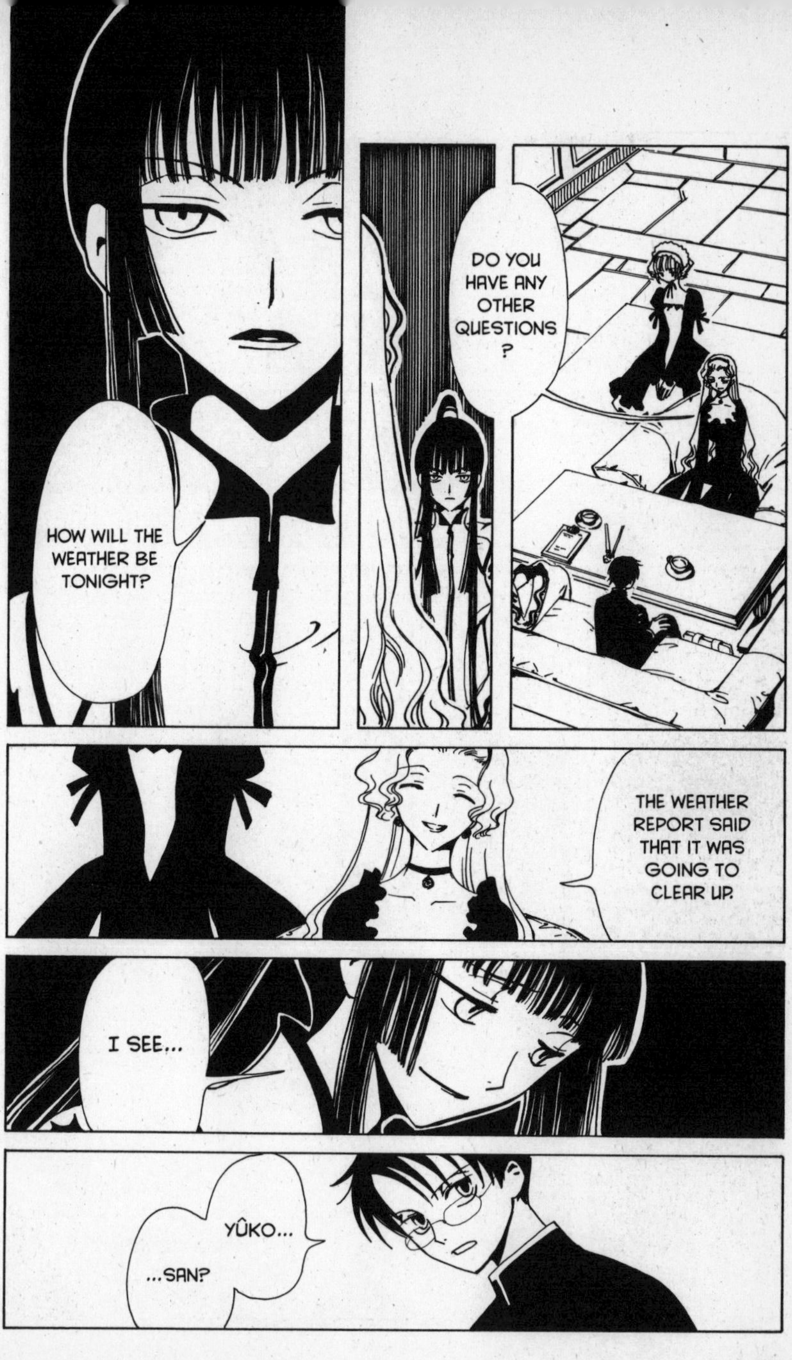
DO YOU HAVE ANY OTHER QUESTIONS ?
HOW WILL THE WEATHER BE TONIGHT?
THE WEATHER REPORT SAID THAT IT WAS GOING TO CLEAR UP.
I SEE...
YÛKO...
...SAN?

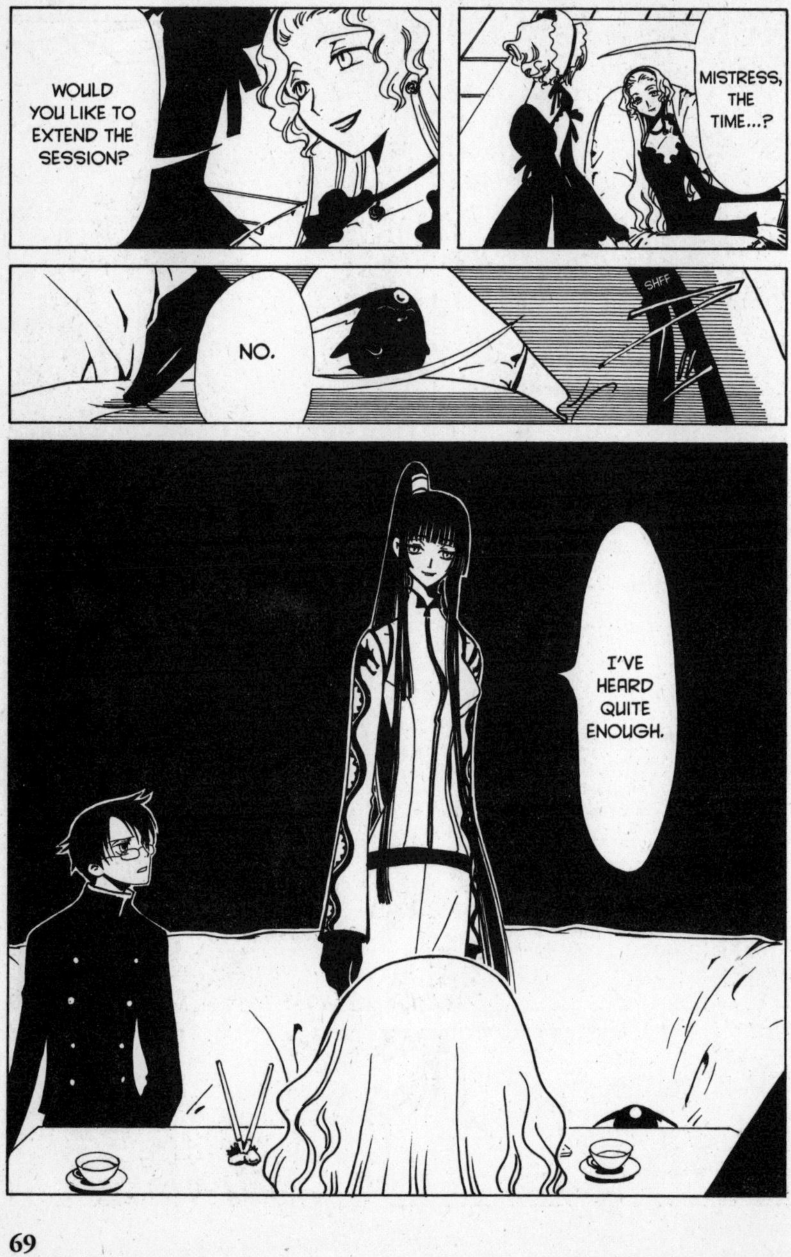
MISTRESS, THE TIME...?
WOULD YOU LIKE TO EXTEND THE SESSION?
SHFF
NO.
I'VE HEARD QUITE ENOUGH.

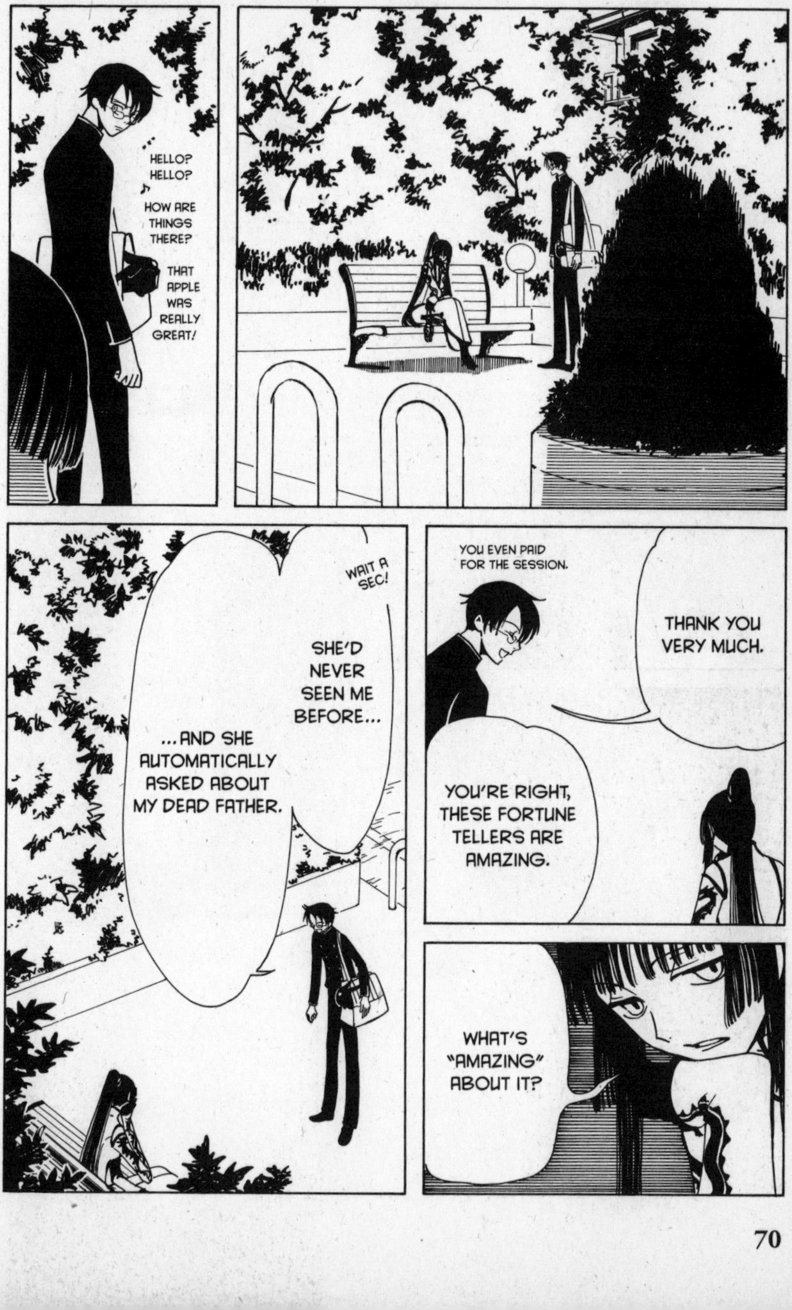
HELLO? HELLO? ♪
HOW ARE THINGS THERE?
THAT APPLE WAS REALLY GREAT!
YOU EVEN PAID FOR THE SESSION.
THANK YOU VERY MUCH.
YOU'RE RIGHT, THESE FORTUNE TELLERS ARE AMAZING.
WHAT'S "AMAZING" ABOUT IT?
WAIT A SEC!
SHE'D NEVER SEEN ME BEFORE...
...AND SHE AUTOMATICALLY ASKED ABOUT MY DEAD FATHER.

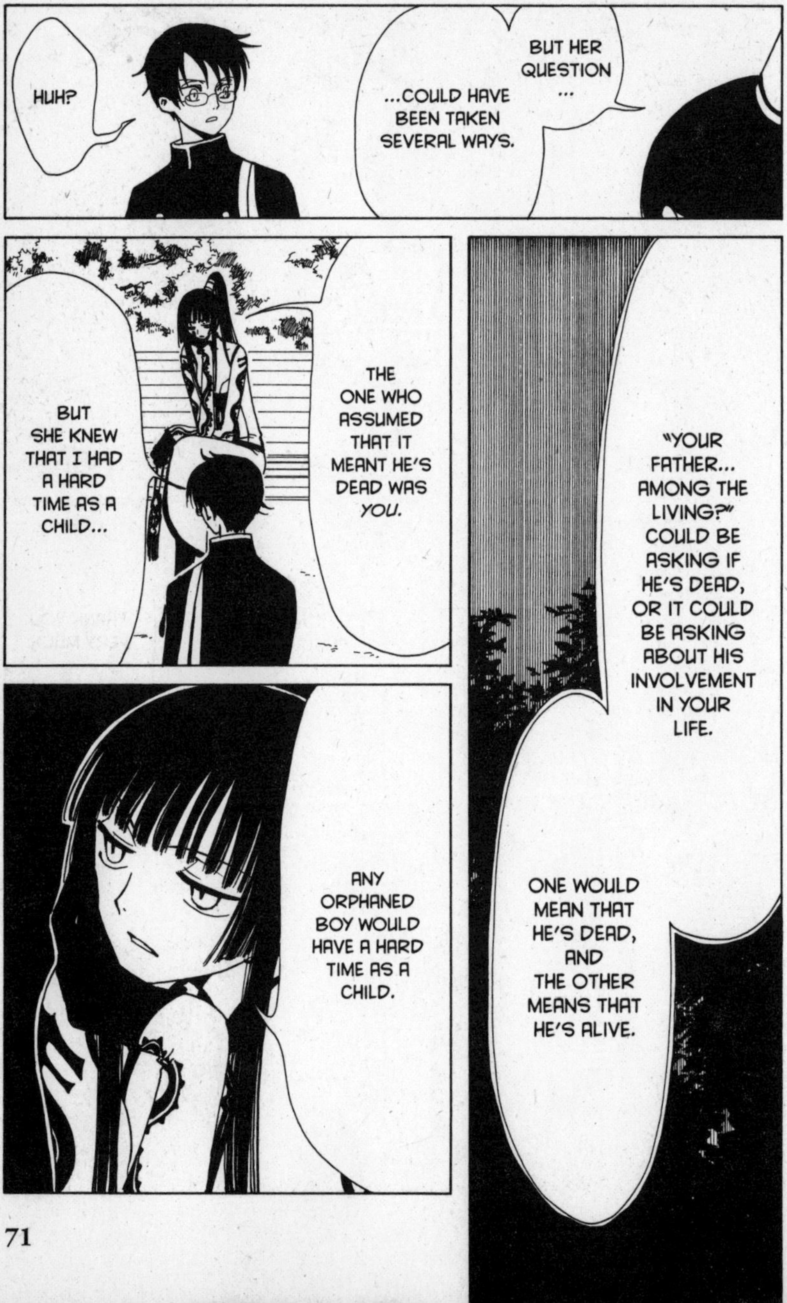
BUT HER QUESTION ...
...COULD HAVE BEEN TAKEN SEVERAL WAYS.
HUH?
"YOUR FATHER... AMONG THE LIVING?" COULD BE ASKING IF HE'S DEAD, OR IT COULD BE ASKING ABOUT HIS INVOLVEMENT IN YOUR LIFE.
ONE WOULD MEAN THAT HE'S DEAD, AND THE OTHER MEANS THAT HE'S ALIVE.
THE ONE WHO ASSUMED THAT IT MEANT HE'S DEAD WAS *YOU.*
BUT SHE KNEW THAT I HAD A HARD TIME AS A CHILD...
ANY ORPHANED BOY WOULD HAVE A HARD TIME AS A CHILD.

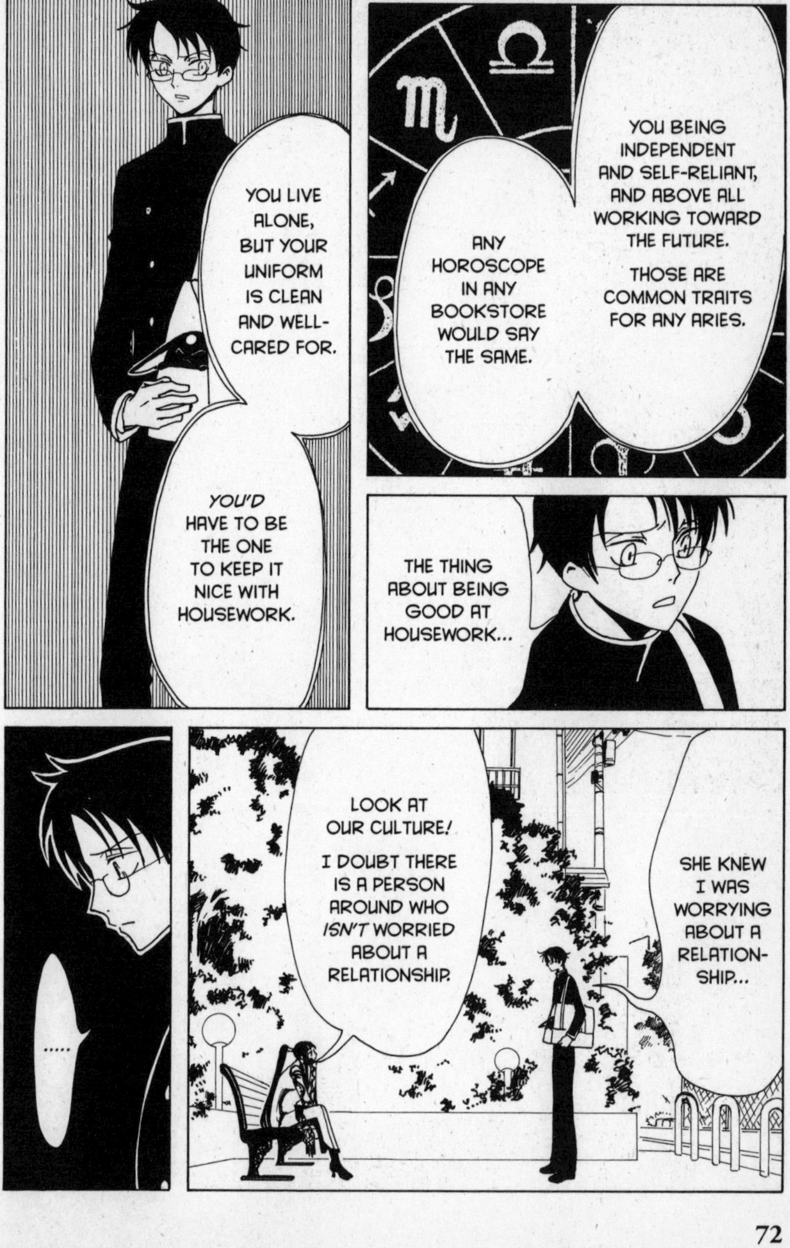
YOU BEING INDEPENDENT AND SELF-RELIANT, AND ABOVE ALL WORKING TOWARD THE FUTURE.
THOSE ARE COMMON TRAITS FOR ANY ARIES.
ANY HOROSCOPE IN ANY BOOKSTORE WOULD SAY THE SAME.
THE THING ABOUT BEING GOOD AT HOUSEWORK...
YOU LIVE ALONE, BUT YOUR UNIFORM IS CLEAN AND WELL-CARED FOR.
YOU'D HAVE TO BE THE ONE TO KEEP IT NICE WITH HOUSEWORK.
SHE KNEW I WAS WORRYING ABOUT A RELATION-SHIP...
LOOK AT OUR CULTURE!
I DOUBT THERE IS A PERSON AROUND WHO *ISN'T* WORRIED ABOUT A RELATIONSHIP.
.....

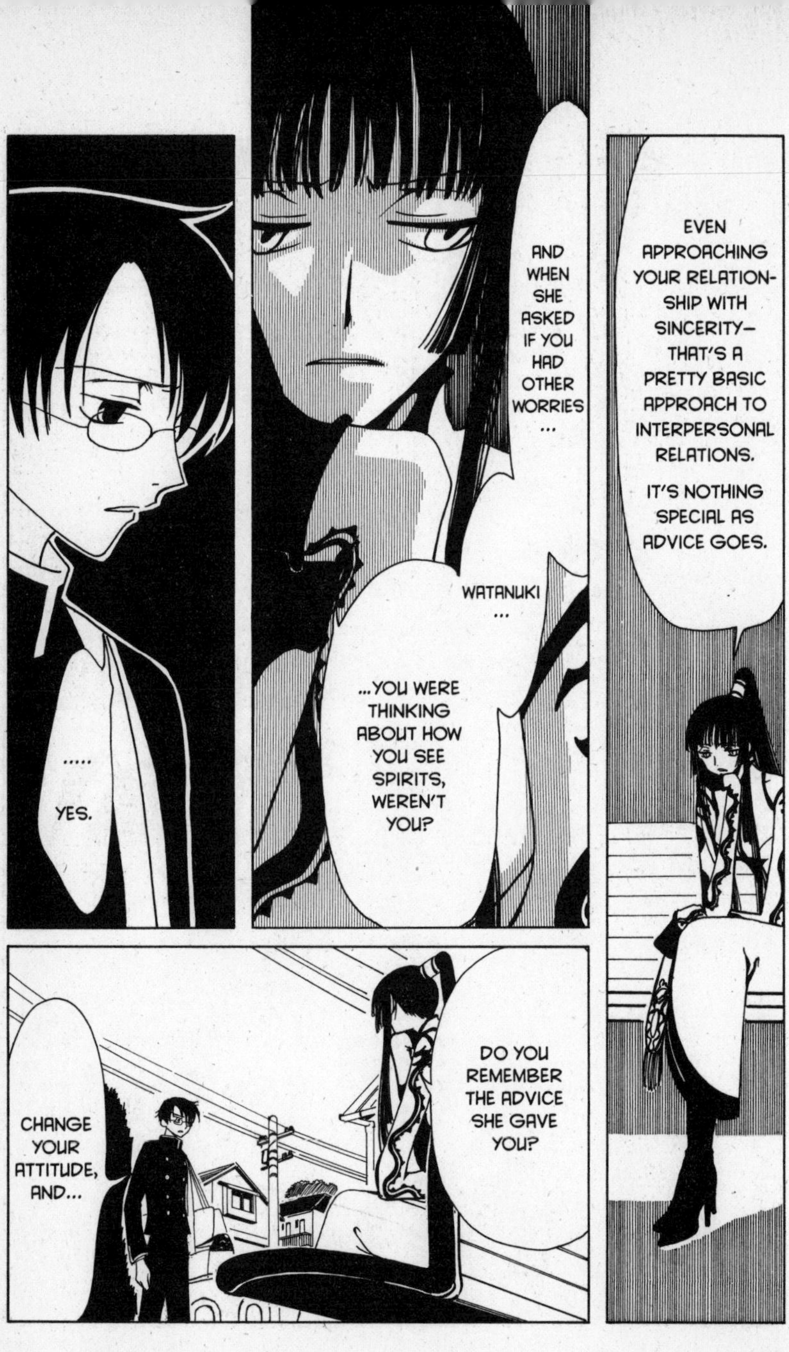
EVEN APPROACHING YOUR RELATIONSHIP WITH SINCERITY—THAT'S A PRETTY BASIC APPROACH TO INTERPERSONAL RELATIONS.
IT'S NOTHING SPECIAL AS ADVICE GOES.
AND WHEN SHE ASKED IF YOU HAD OTHER WORRIES...
WATANUKI...
...YOU WERE THINKING ABOUT HOW YOU SEE SPIRITS, WEREN'T YOU?
.....
YES.
DO YOU REMEMBER THE ADVICE SHE GAVE YOU?
CHANGE YOUR ATTITUDE, AND...

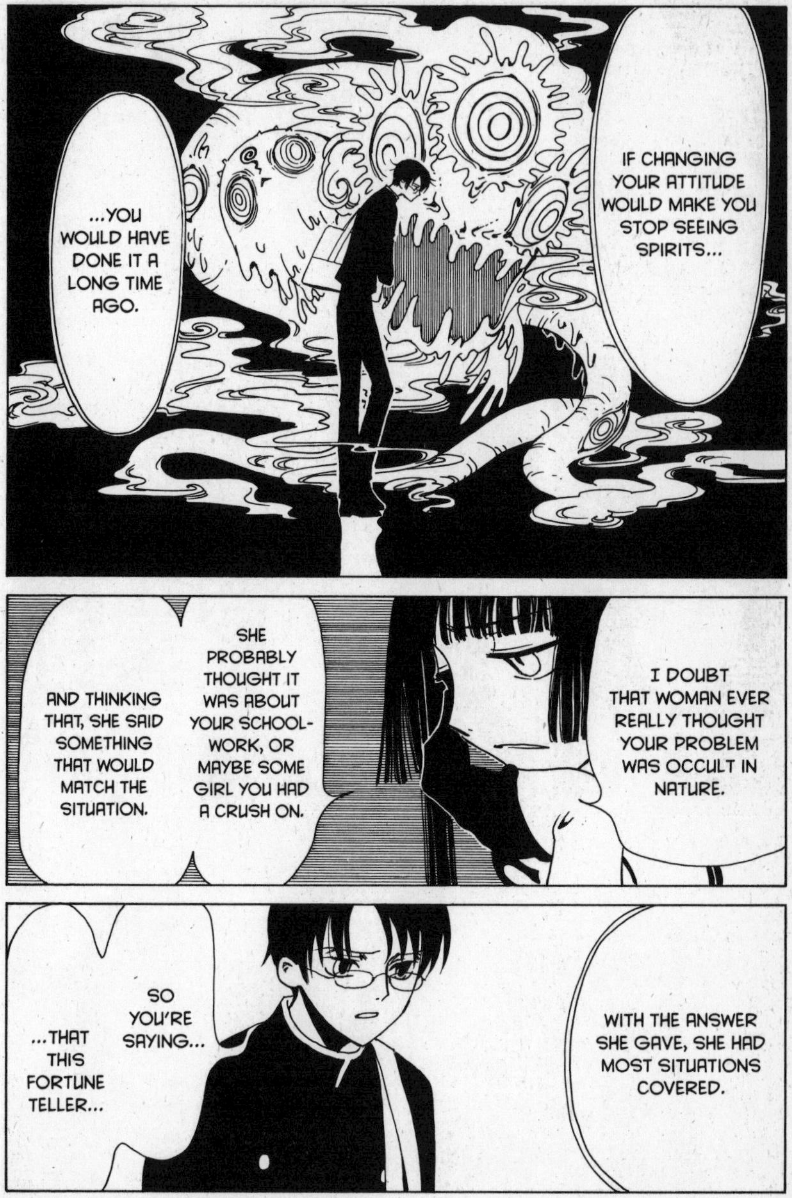
IF CHANGING YOUR ATTITUDE WOULD MAKE YOU STOP SEEING SPIRITS...
...YOU WOULD HAVE DONE IT A LONG TIME AGO.
I DOUBT THAT WOMAN EVER REALLY THOUGHT YOUR PROBLEM WAS OCCULT IN NATURE.
SHE PROBABLY THOUGHT IT WAS ABOUT YOUR SCHOOL-WORK, OR MAYBE SOME GIRL YOU HAD A CRUSH ON.
AND THINKING THAT, SHE SAID SOMETHING THAT WOULD MATCH THE SITUATION.
WITH THE ANSWER SHE GAVE, SHE HAD MOST SITUATIONS COVERED.
SO YOU'RE SAYING...
...THAT THIS FORTUNE TELLER...

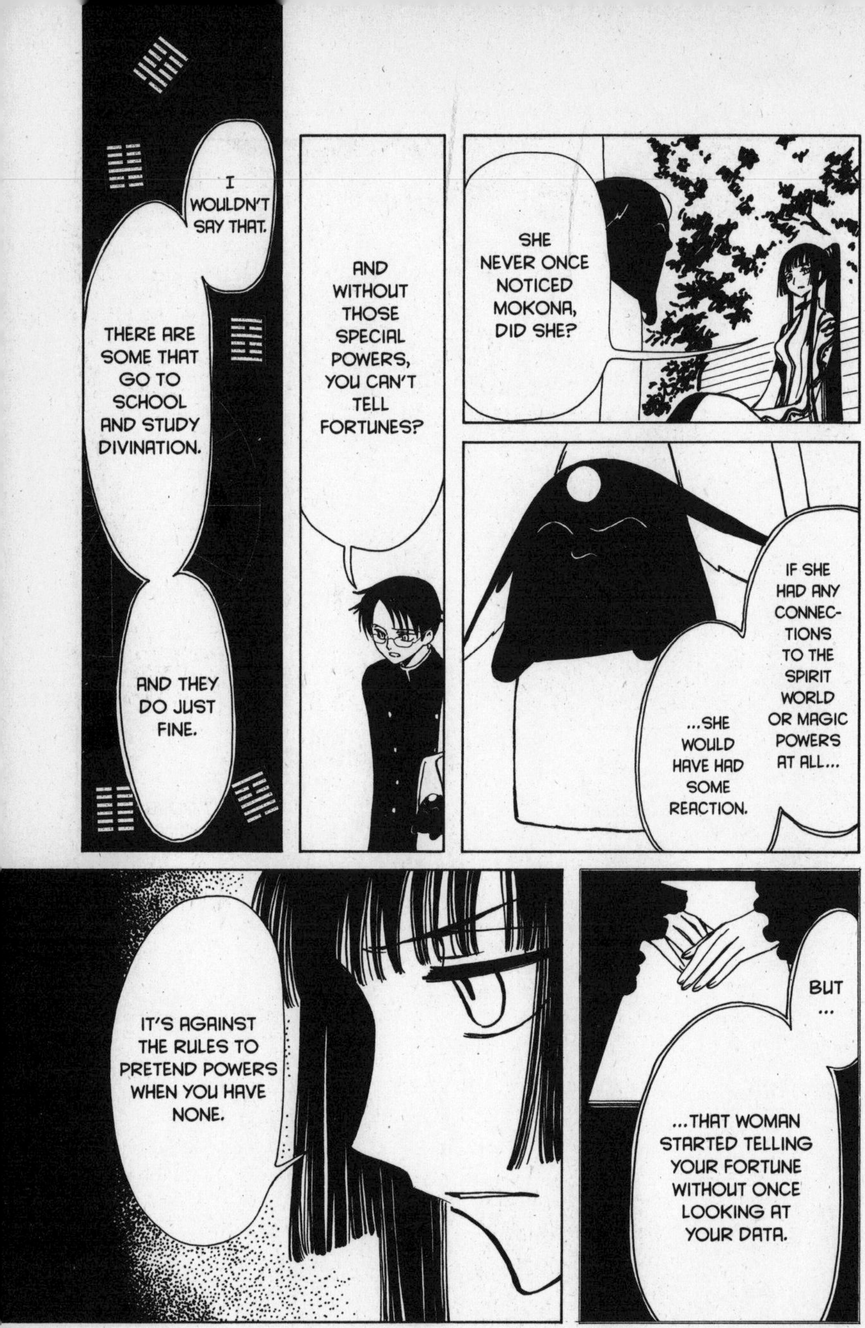
SHE NEVER ONCE NOTICED MOKONA, DID SHE?
IF SHE HAD ANY CONNEC-TIONS TO THE SPIRIT WORLD OR MAGIC POWERS AT ALL...
...SHE WOULD HAVE HAD SOME REACTION.
AND WITHOUT THOSE SPECIAL POWERS, YOU CAN'T TELL FORTUNES?
I WOULDN'T SAY THAT.
THERE ARE SOME THAT GO TO SCHOOL AND STUDY DIVINATION.
AND THEY DO JUST FINE.
BUT ...
...THAT WOMAN STARTED TELLING YOUR FORTUNE WITHOUT ONCE LOOKING AT YOUR DATA.
IT'S AGAINST THE RULES TO PRETEND POWERS WHEN YOU HAVE NONE.

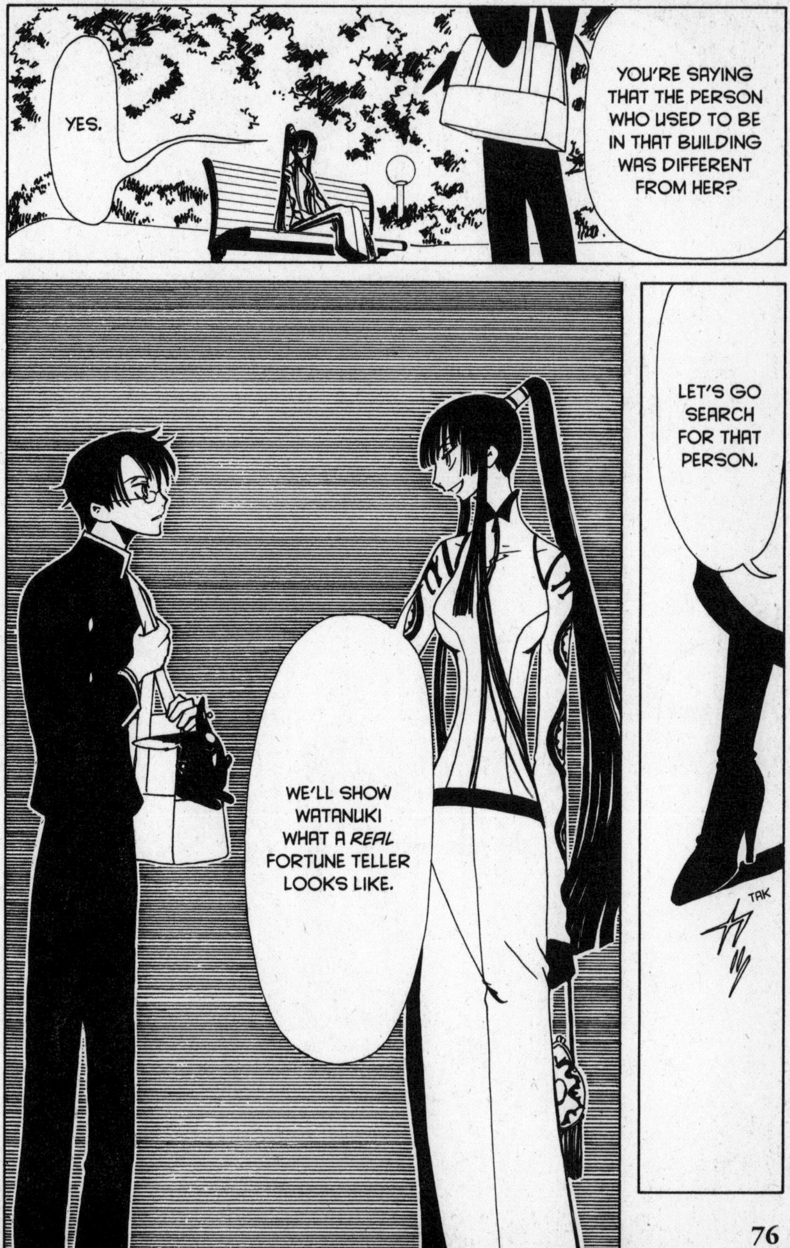
YOU'RE SAYING THAT THE PERSON WHO USED TO BE IN THAT BUILDING WAS DIFFERENT FROM HER?
YES.
LET'S GO SEARCH FOR THAT PERSON.
TAK
WE'LL SHOW WATANUKI WHAT A *REAL* FORTUNE TELLER LOOKS LIKE.

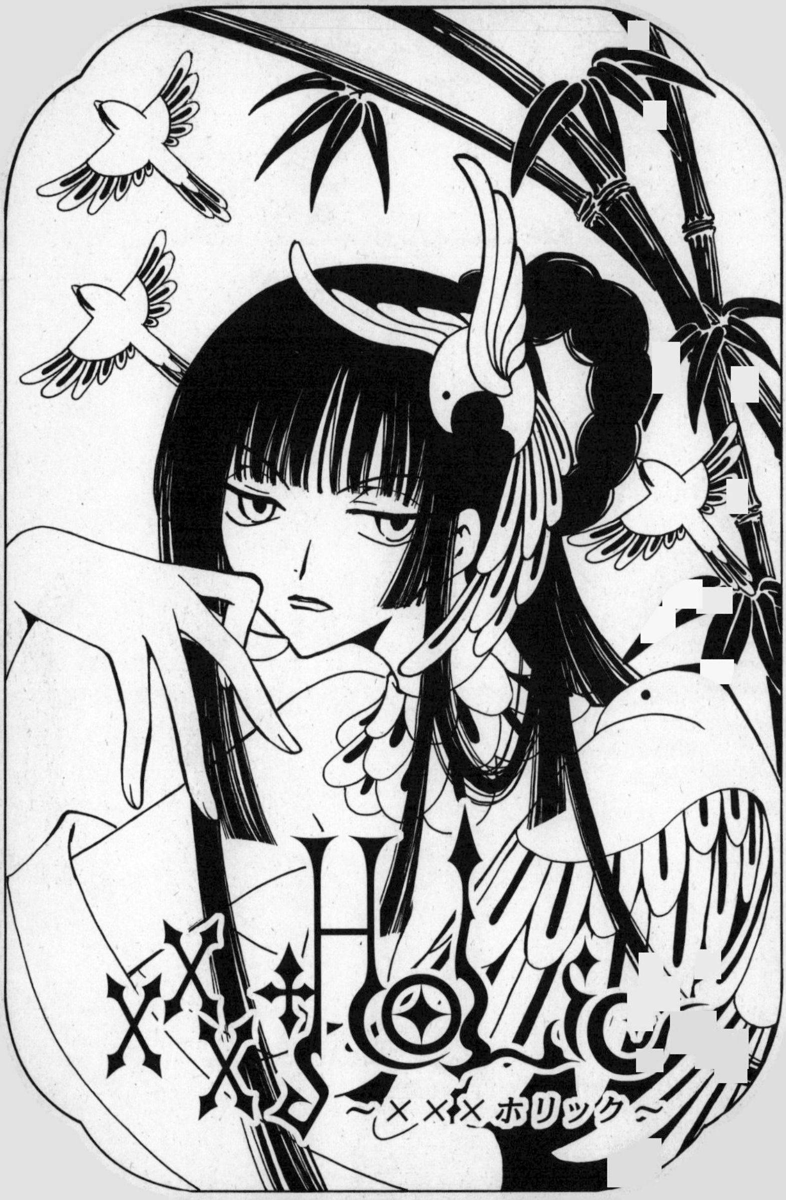
xxxHOLiC
~×××ホリック~

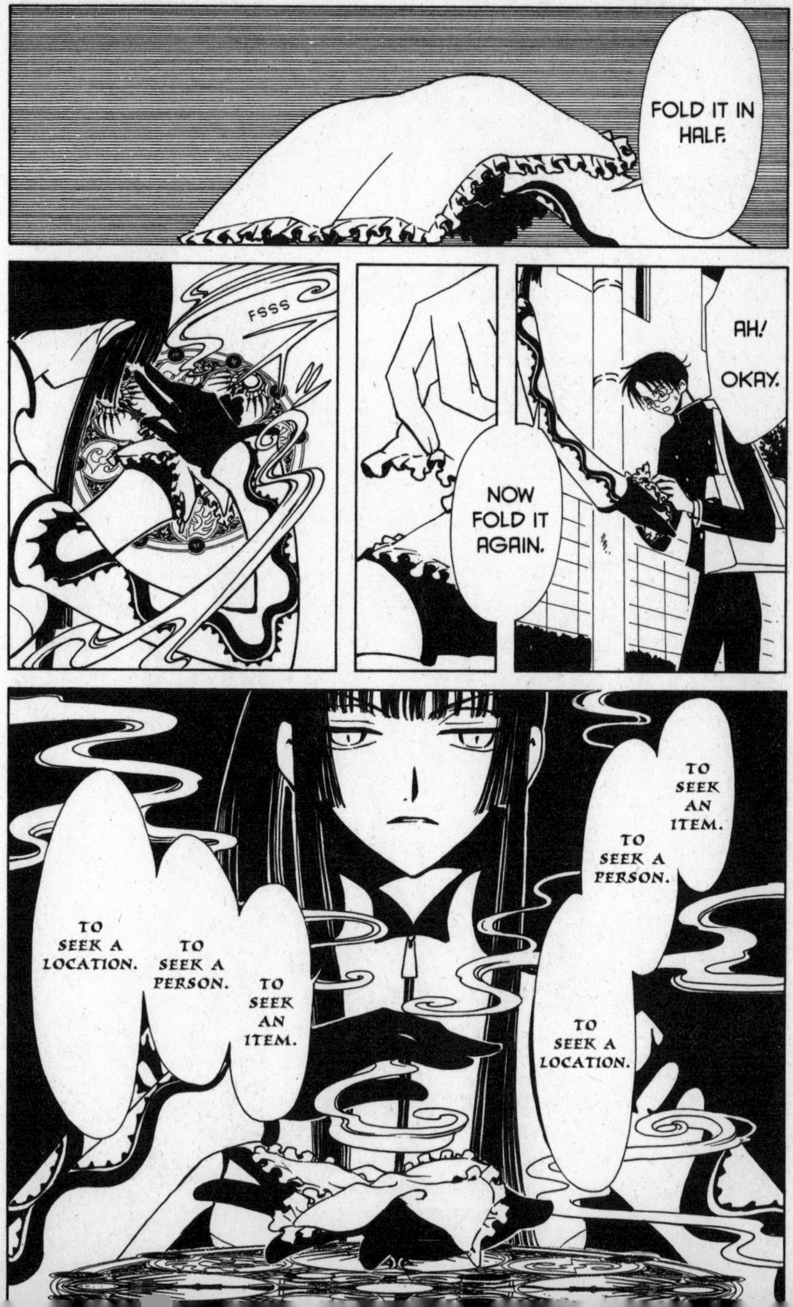
FOLD IT IN HALF.
AH!
OKAY.
NOW FOLD IT AGAIN.
FSSS
TO SEEK AN ITEM.
TO SEEK A PERSON.
TO SEEK A LOCATION.
TO SEEK A LOCATION.
TO SEEK A PERSON.
TO SEEK AN ITEM.

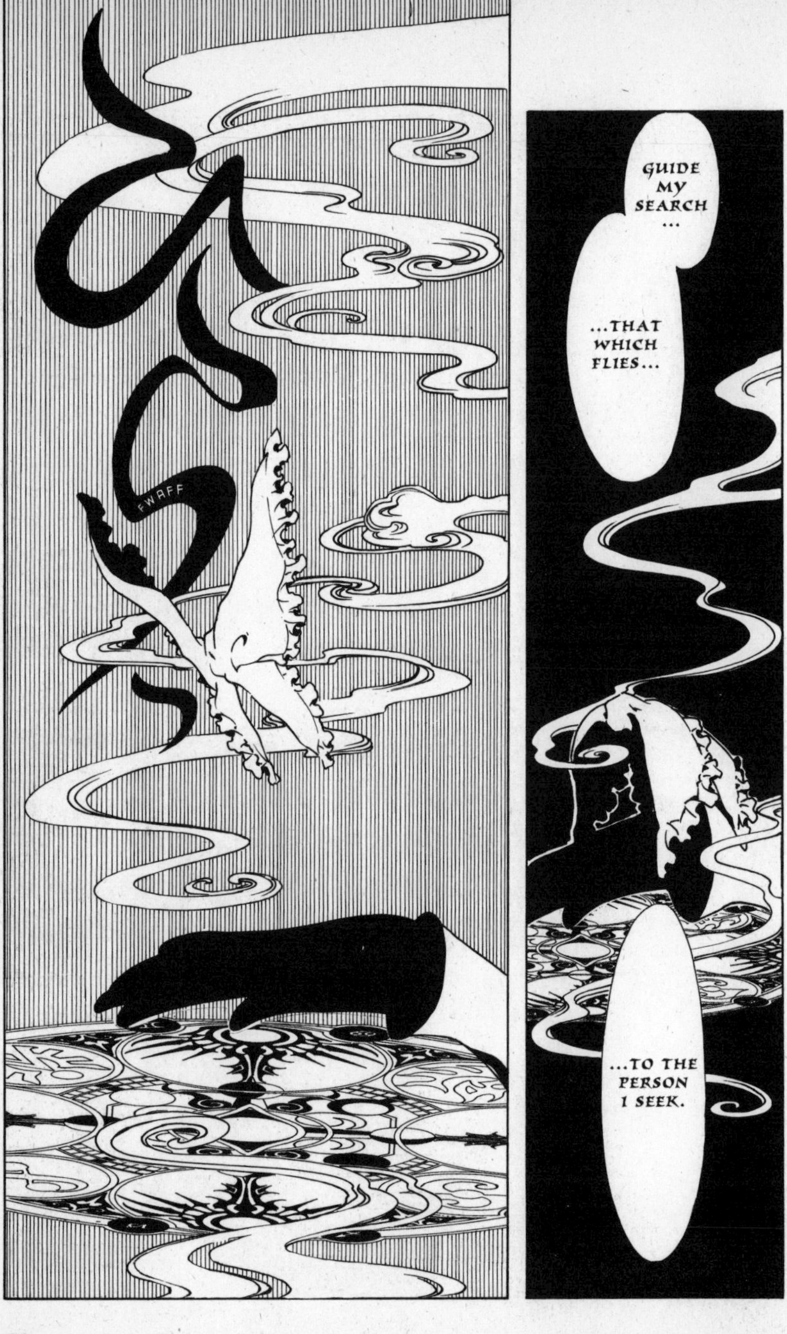
GUIDE MY SEARCH ...
...THAT WHICH FLIES...
...TO THE PERSON I SEEK.
FWAFF

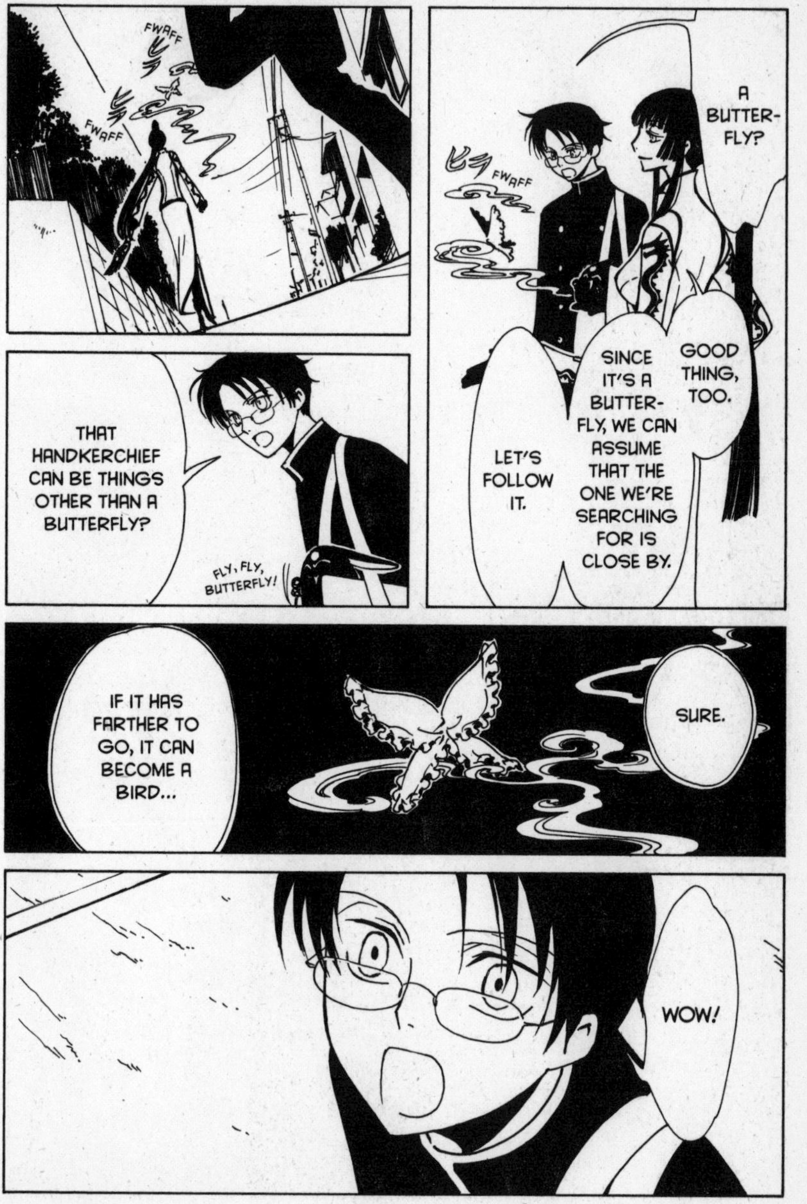
A BUTTER-FLY?
FWAFF
GOOD THING, TOO.
SINCE IT'S A BUTTER-FLY, WE CAN ASSUME THAT THE ONE WE'RE SEARCHING FOR IS CLOSE BY.
LET'S FOLLOW IT.
FWAFF
FWAFF
THAT HANDKERCHIEF CAN BE THINGS OTHER THAN A BUTTERFLY?
FLY, FLY, BUTTERFLY!
SURE.
IF IT HAS FARTHER TO GO, IT CAN BECOME A BIRD...
WOW!

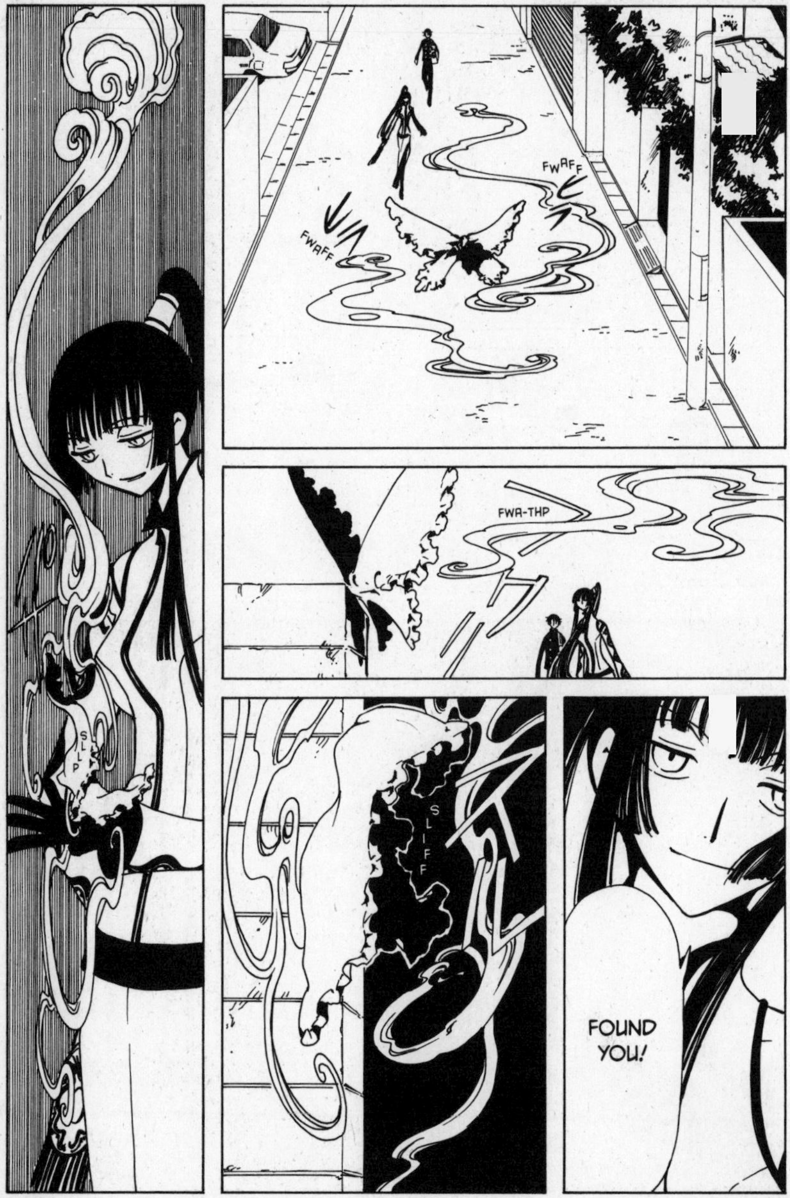
FWAFF
FWAFF
FWA-THP
FOUND YOU!
SLIFF
SLLP

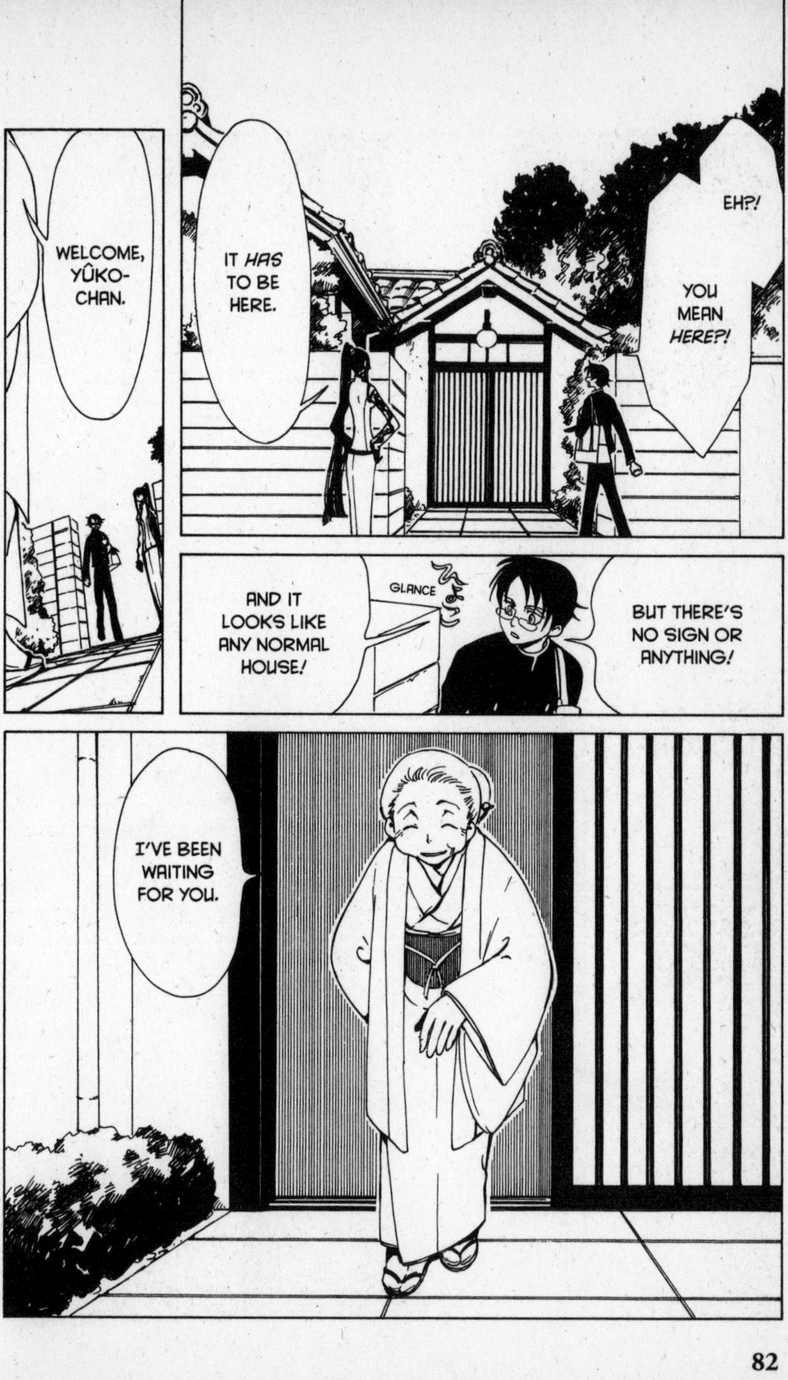
EH?!
YOU MEAN *HERE*?!
IT *HAS* TO BE HERE.
WELCOME, YÛKO-CHAN.
BUT THERE'S NO SIGN OR ANYTHING!
GLANCE
AND IT LOOKS LIKE ANY NORMAL HOUSE!
I'VE BEEN WAITING FOR YOU.

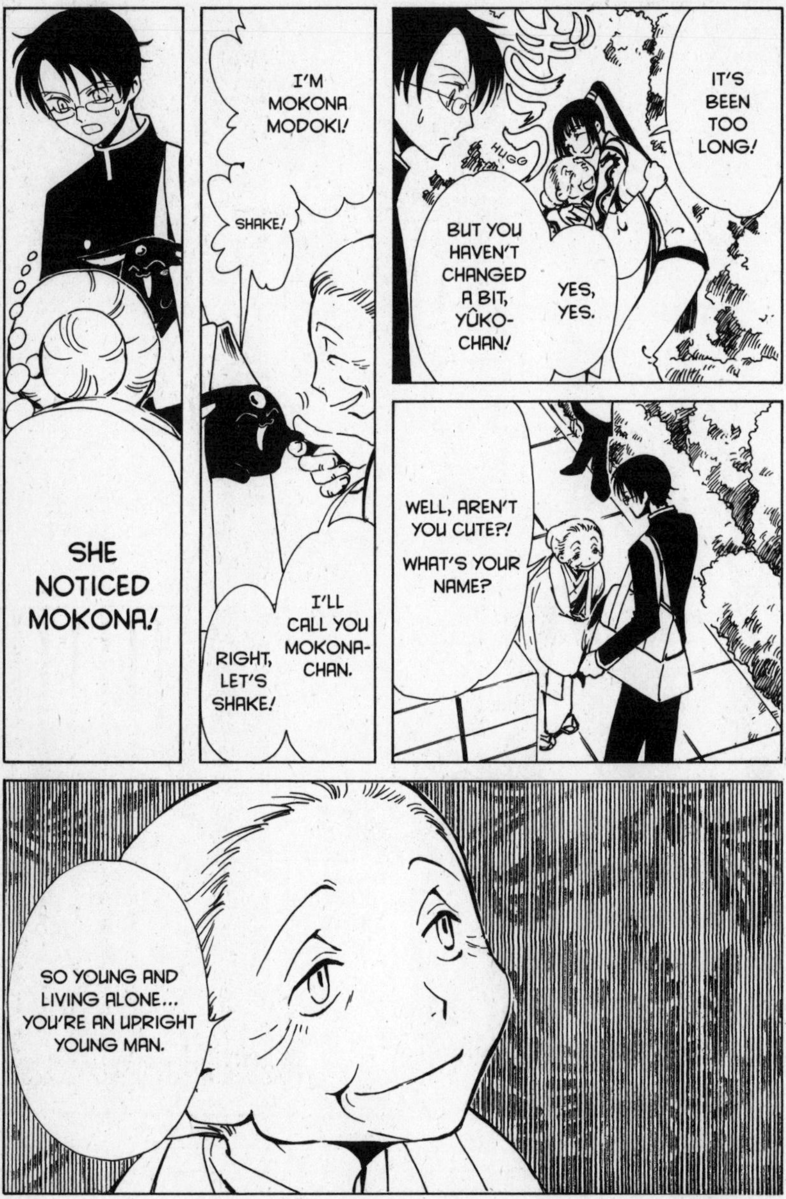
IT'S BEEN TOO LONG!
HUGG
BUT YOU HAVEN'T CHANGED A BIT, YÛKO-CHAN!
YES, YES.
WELL, AREN'T YOU CUTE?!
WHAT'S YOUR NAME?
I'M MOKONA MODOKI!
SHAKE!
I'LL CALL YOU MOKONA-CHAN.
RIGHT, LET'S SHAKE!
SHE NOTICED MOKONA!
SO YOUNG AND LIVING ALONE... YOU'RE AN UPRIGHT YOUNG MAN.

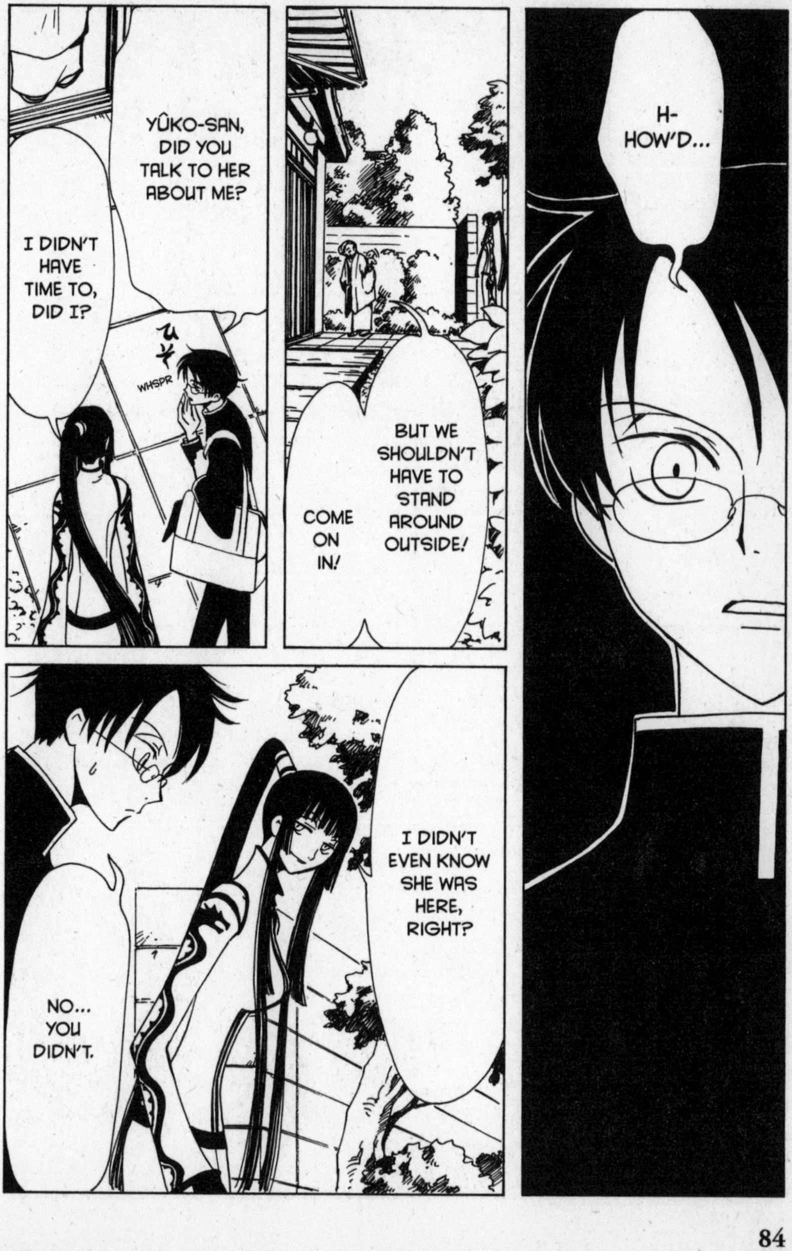
H-
HOW'D...
YÛKO-SAN, DID YOU TALK TO HER ABOUT ME?
I DIDN'T HAVE TIME TO, DID I?
WHSPR
BUT WE SHOULDN'T HAVE TO STAND AROUND OUTSIDE!
COME ON IN!
I DIDN'T EVEN KNOW SHE WAS HERE, RIGHT?
NO... YOU DIDN'T.

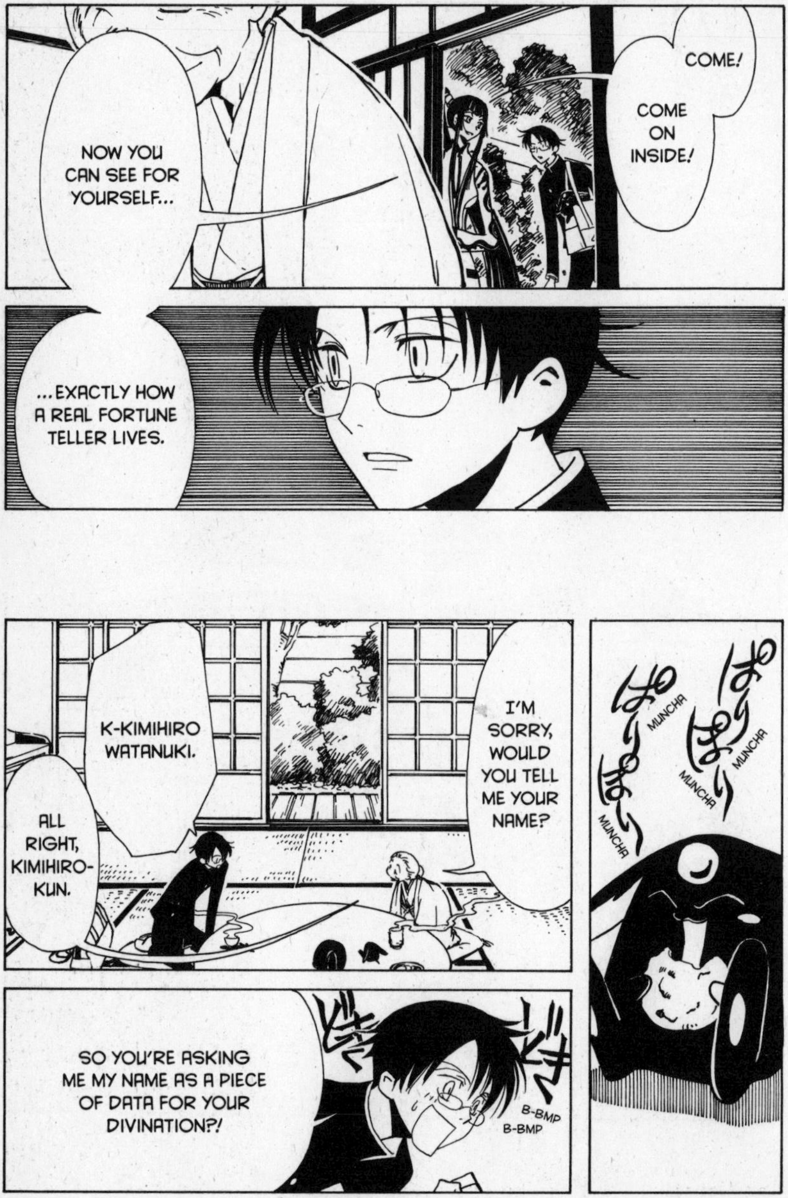
COME!
COME ON INSIDE!
NOW YOU CAN SEE FOR YOURSELF...
...EXACTLY HOW A REAL FORTUNE TELLER LIVES.
MUNCHA MUNCHA
MUNCHA MUNCHA
I'M SORRY, WOULD YOU TELL ME YOUR NAME?
K-KIMIHIRO WATANUKI.
ALL RIGHT, KIMIHIRO-KUN.
SO YOU'RE ASKING ME MY NAME AS A PIECE OF DATA FOR YOUR DIVINATION?!
B-BMP B-BMP

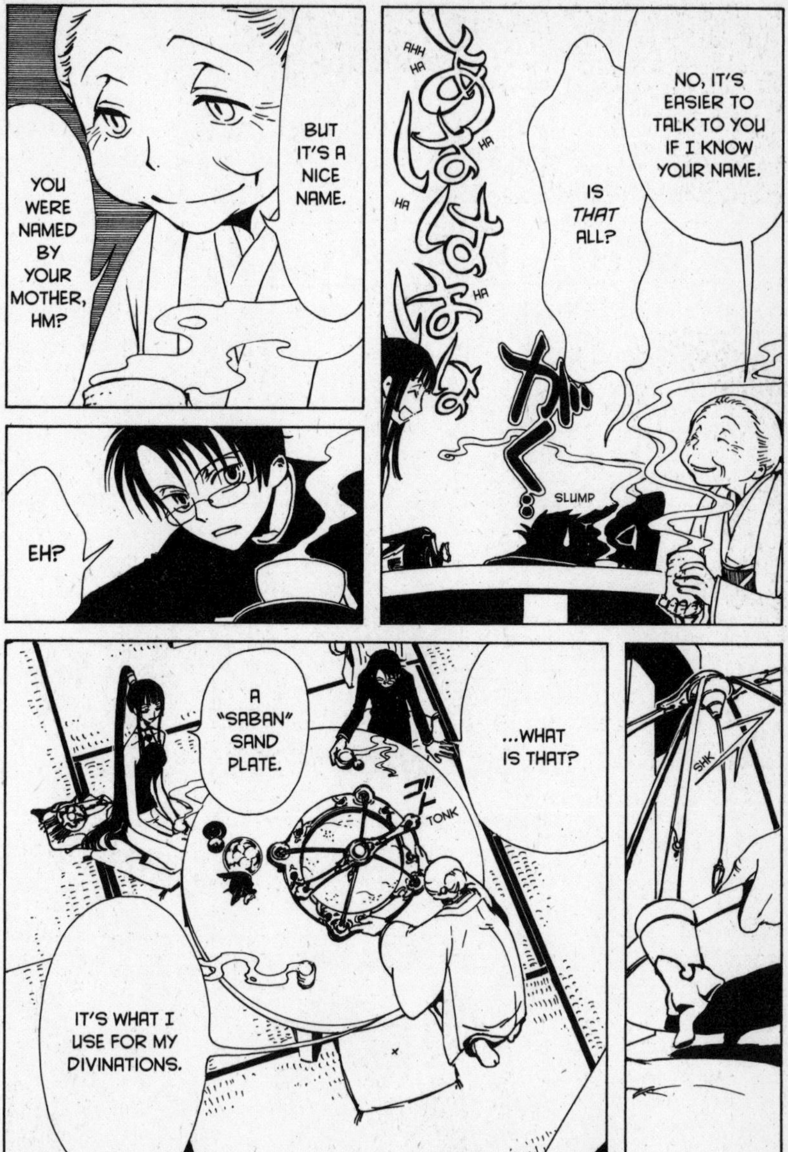
NO, IT'S EASIER TO TALK TO YOU IF I KNOW YOUR NAME.
IS THAT ALL?
AHH HA HA HA HA
SLUMP
BUT IT'S A NICE NAME.
YOU WERE NAMED BY YOUR MOTHER, HM?
EH?
SHK
...WHAT IS THAT?
TONK
A "SABAN" SAND PLATE.
IT'S WHAT I USE FOR MY DIVINATIONS.

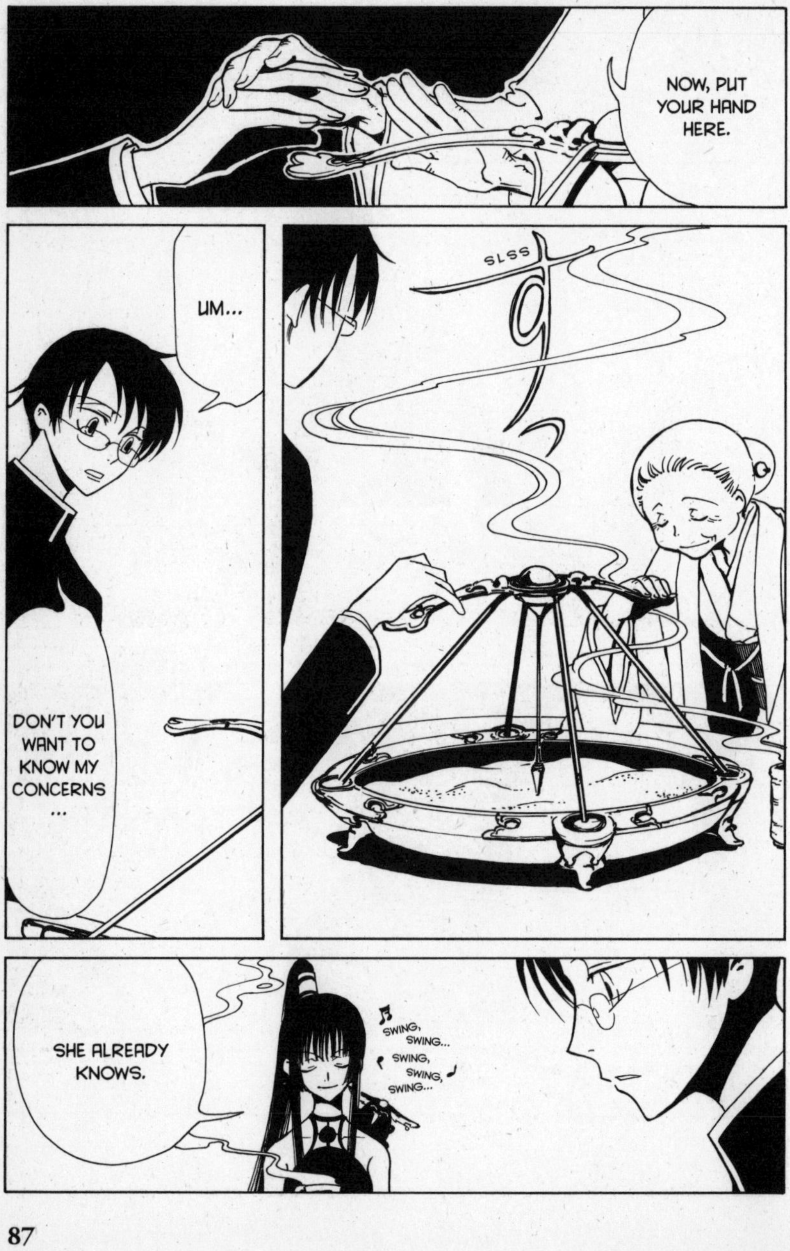
NOW, PUT YOUR HAND HERE.
SLSS
UM...
DON'T YOU WANT TO KNOW MY CONCERNS ...
SWING, SWING... SWING, SWING, SWING...
SHE ALREADY KNOWS.

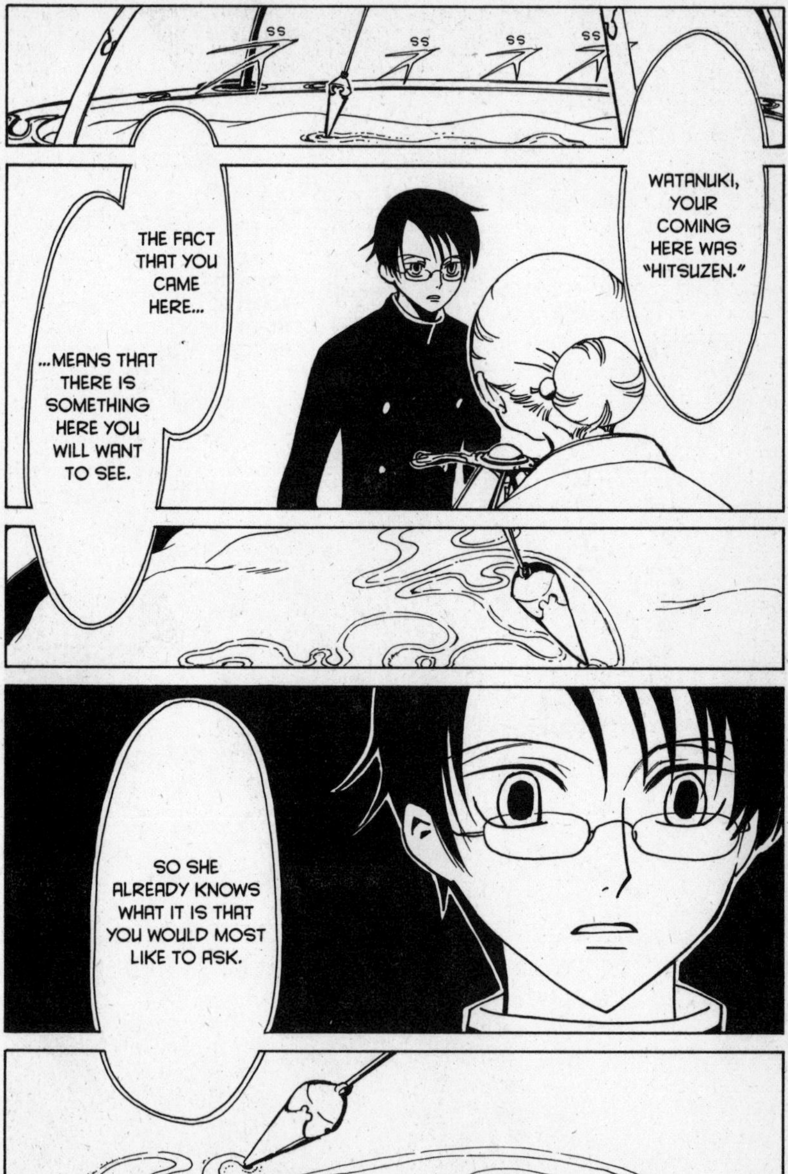
SS
SS
SS
SS
WATANUKI, YOUR COMING HERE WAS "HITSUZEN."
THE FACT THAT YOU CAME HERE...
...MEANS THAT THERE IS SOMETHING HERE YOU WILL WANT TO SEE.
SO SHE ALREADY KNOWS WHAT IT IS THAT YOU WOULD MOST LIKE TO ASK.

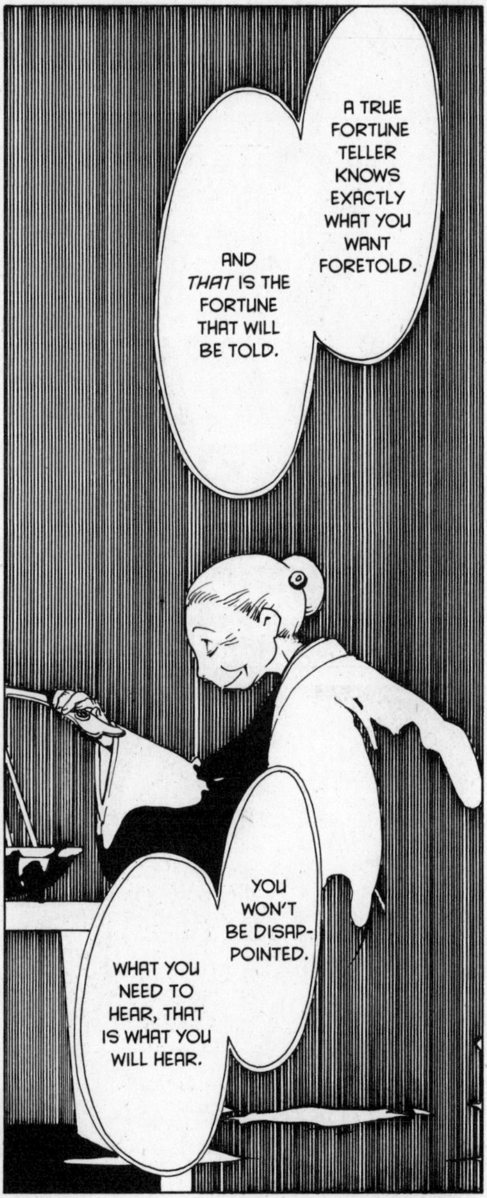
A TRUE FORTUNE TELLER KNOWS EXACTLY WHAT YOU WANT FORETOLD.
AND *THAT* IS THE FORTUNE THAT WILL BE TOLD.
YOU WON'T BE DISAP-POINTED.
WHAT YOU NEED TO HEAR, THAT IS WHAT YOU WILL HEAR.
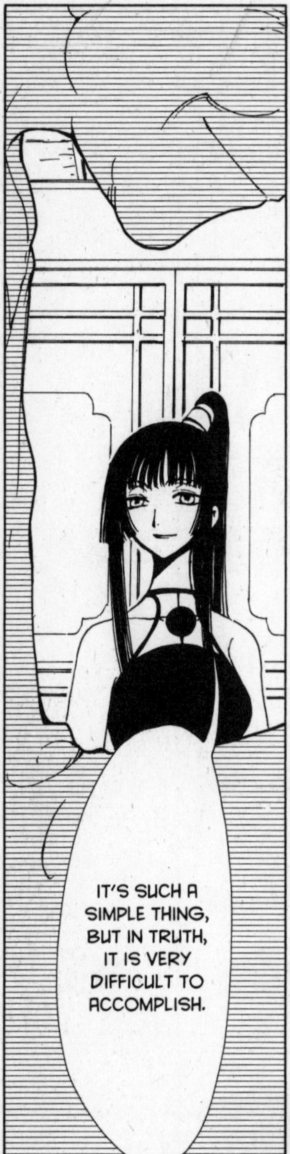
IT'S SUCH A SIMPLE THING, BUT IN TRUTH, IT IS VERY DIFFICULT TO ACCOMPLISH.

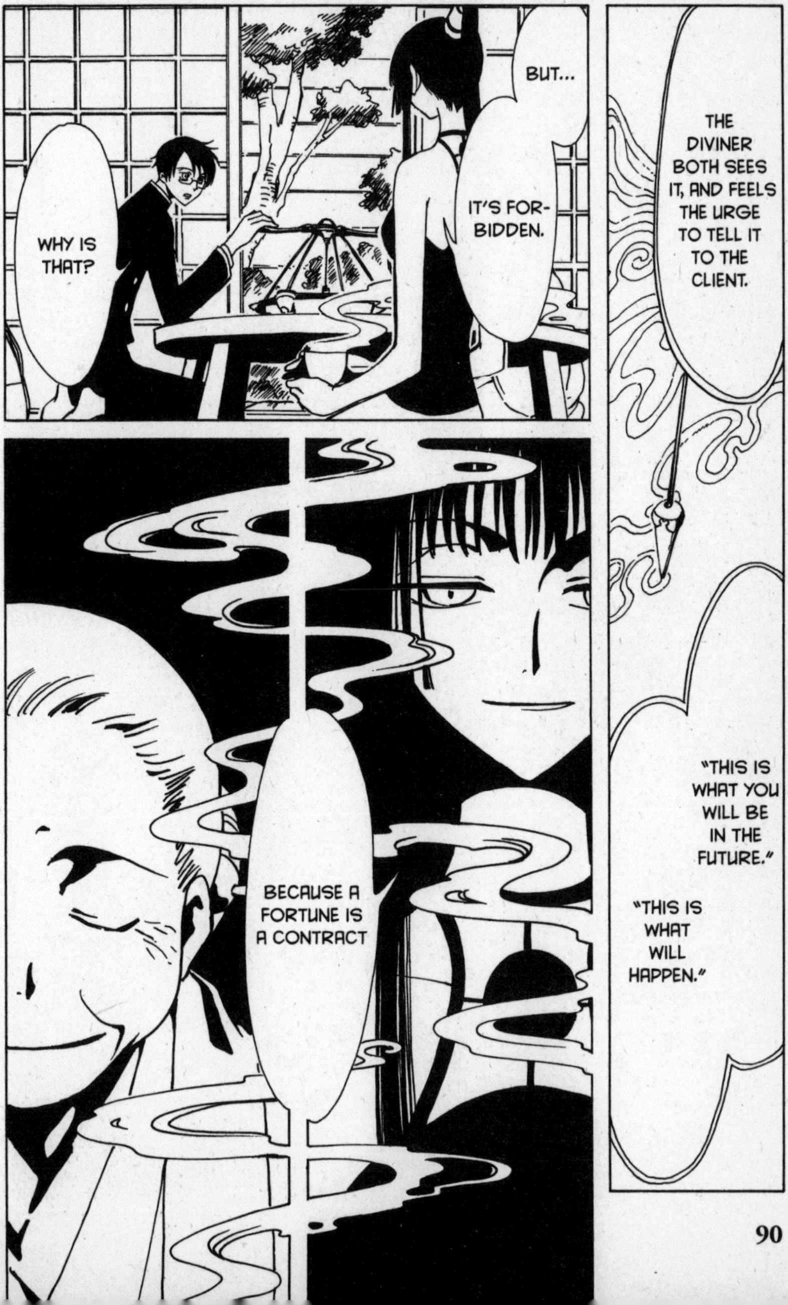
THE DIVINER BOTH SEES IT, AND FEELS THE URGE TO TELL IT TO THE CLIENT.
"THIS IS WHAT YOU WILL BE IN THE FUTURE."
"THIS IS WHAT WILL HAPPEN."
BUT...
IT'S FOR-BIDDEN.
WHY IS THAT?
BECAUSE A FORTUNE IS A CONTRACT

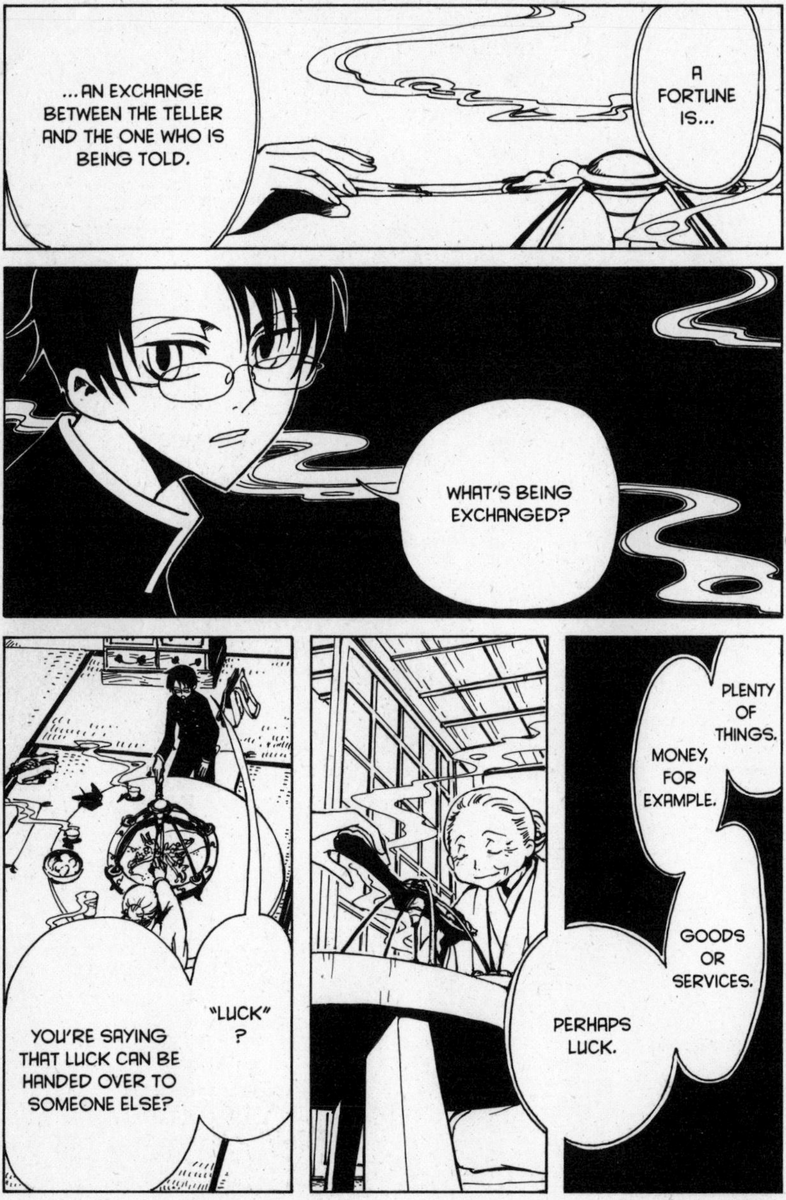
A FORTUNE IS...
...AN EXCHANGE BETWEEN THE TELLER AND THE ONE WHO IS BEING TOLD.
WHAT'S BEING EXCHANGED?
PLENTY OF THINGS.
MONEY, FOR EXAMPLE.
GOODS OR SERVICES.
PERHAPS LUCK.
"LUCK" ?
YOU'RE SAYING THAT LUCK CAN BE HANDED OVER TO SOMEONE ELSE?

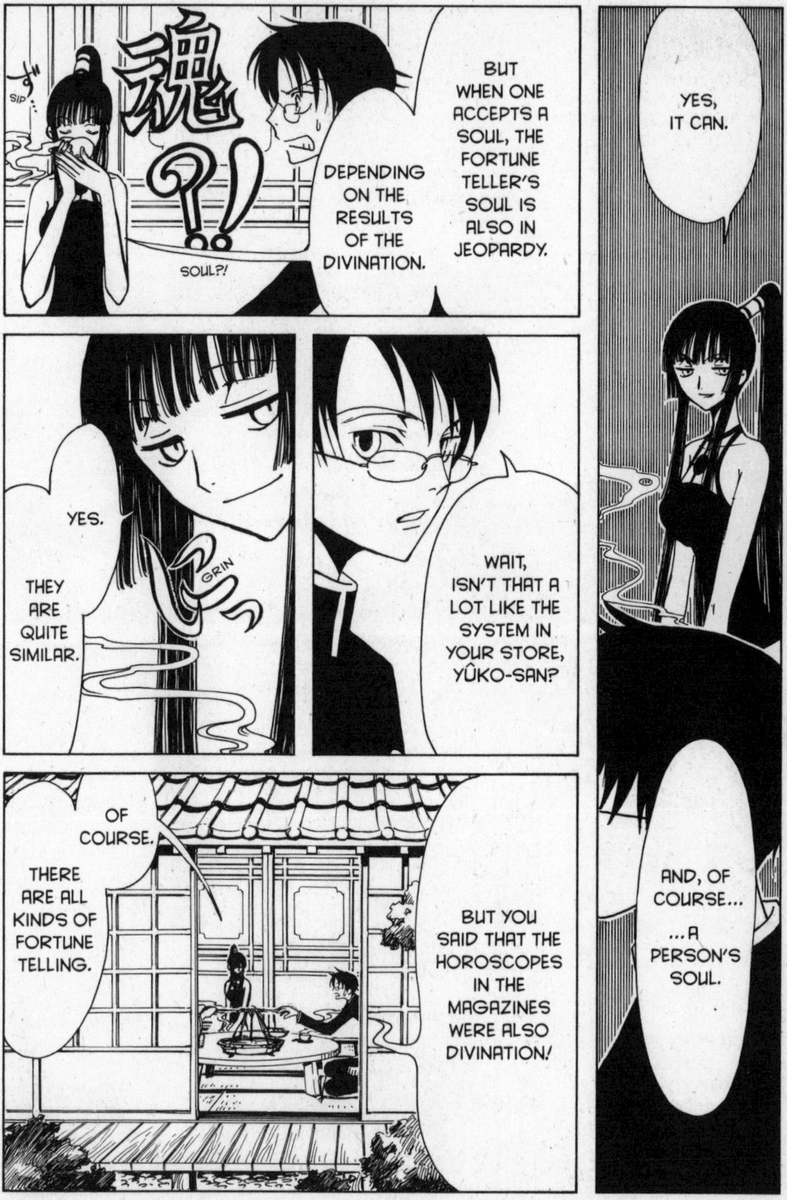
YES, IT CAN.
AND, OF COURSE...
...A PERSON'S SOUL.
ず
SIP...
魂?!
SOUL?!
BUT WHEN ONE ACCEPTS A SOUL, THE FORTUNE TELLER'S SOUL IS ALSO IN JEOPARDY.
DEPENDING ON THE RESULTS OF THE DIVINATION.
WAIT, ISN'T THAT A LOT LIKE THE SYSTEM IN YOUR STORE, YÛKO-SAN?
YES.
GRIN
THEY ARE QUITE SIMILAR.
BUT YOU SAID THAT THE HOROSCOPES IN THE MAGAZINES WERE ALSO DIVINATION!
OF COURSE.
THERE ARE ALL KINDS OF FORTUNE TELLING.

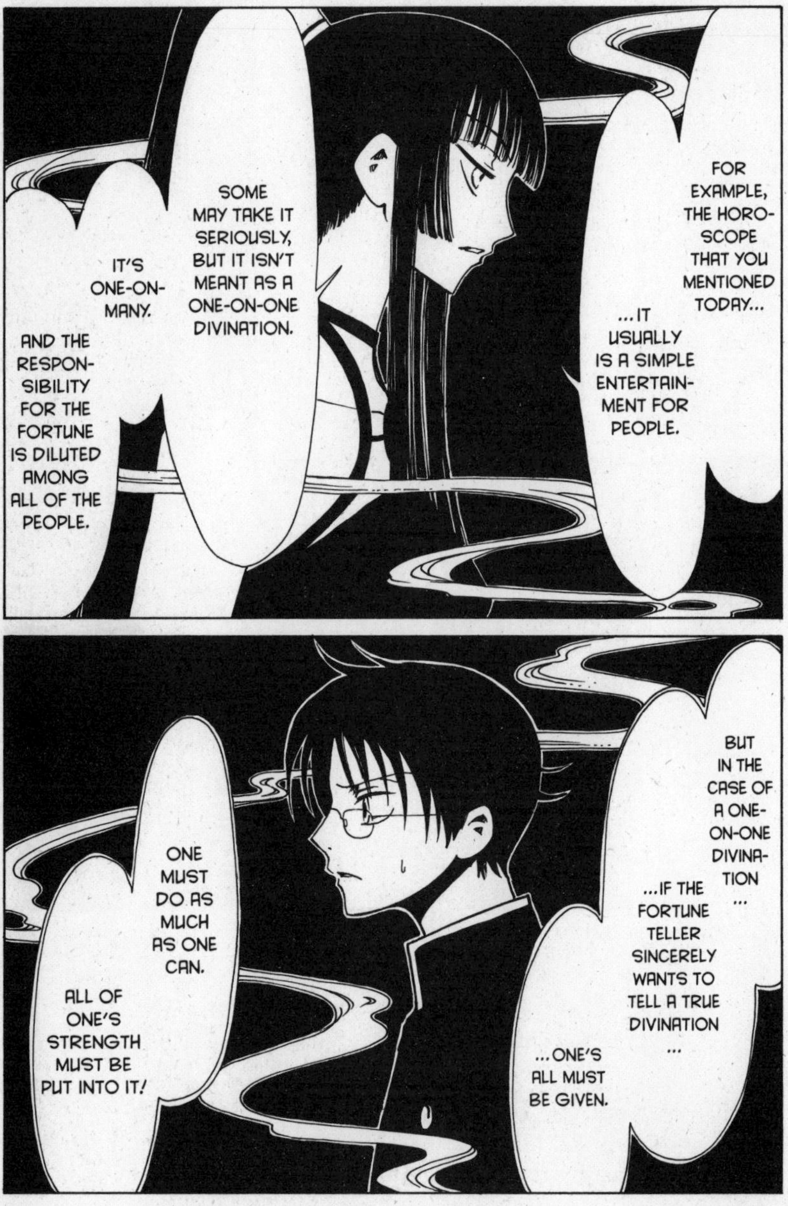
FOR EXAMPLE, THE HOROSCOPE THAT YOU MENTIONED TODAY...
...IT USUALLY IS A SIMPLE ENTERTAINMENT FOR PEOPLE.
SOME MAY TAKE IT SERIOUSLY, BUT IT ISN'T MEANT AS A ONE-ON-ONE DIVINATION.
IT'S ONE-ON-MANY.
AND THE RESPONSIBILITY FOR THE FORTUNE IS DILUTED AMONG ALL OF THE PEOPLE.
BUT IN THE CASE OF A ONE-ON-ONE DIVINATION ...
...IF THE FORTUNE TELLER SINCERELY WANTS TO TELL A TRUE DIVINATION ...
...ONE'S ALL MUST BE GIVEN.
ONE MUST DO AS MUCH AS ONE CAN.
ALL OF ONE'S STRENGTH MUST BE PUT INTO IT!

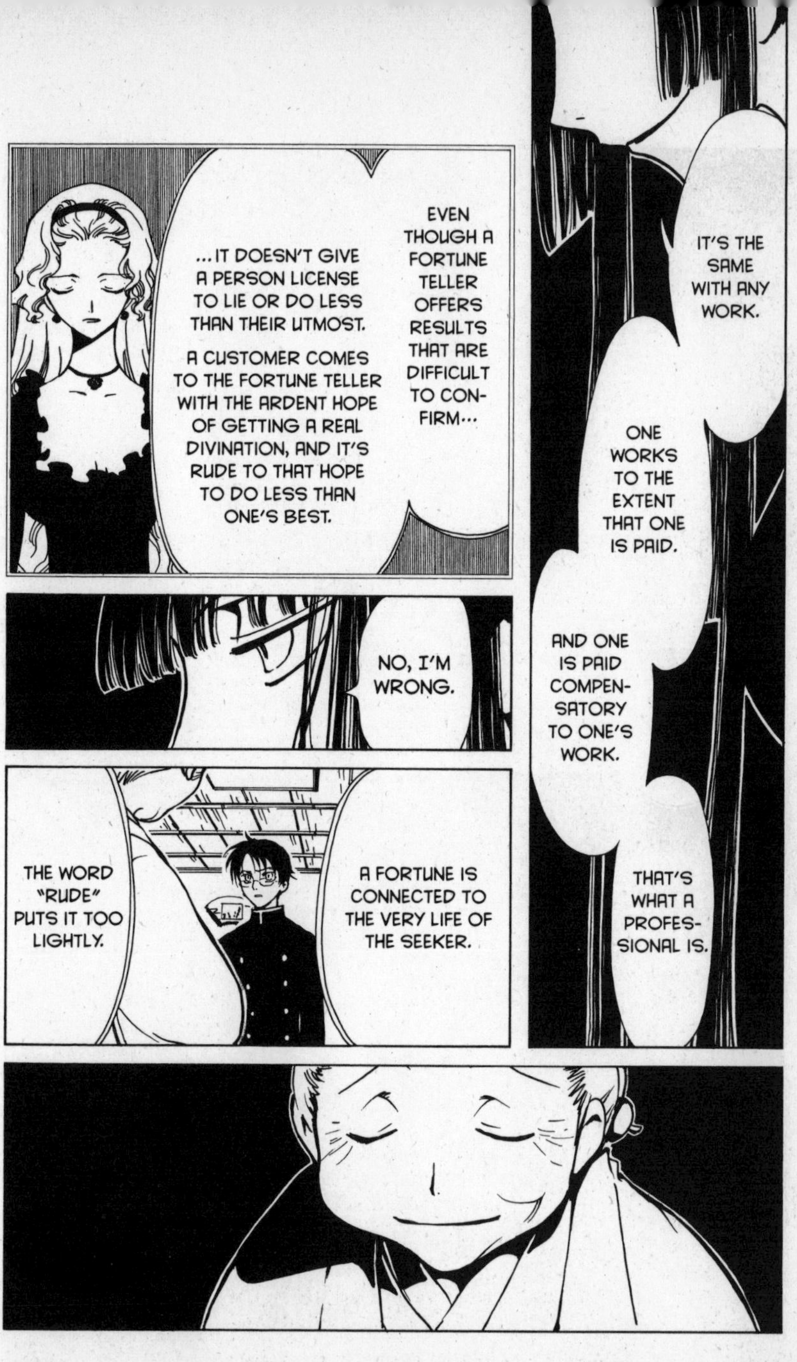
IT'S THE SAME WITH ANY WORK.
ONE WORKS TO THE EXTENT THAT ONE IS PAID.
AND ONE IS PAID COMPEN-SATORY TO ONE'S WORK.
THAT'S WHAT A PROFES-SIONAL IS.
EVEN THOUGH A FORTUNE TELLER OFFERS RESULTS THAT ARE DIFFICULT TO CON-FIRM...
...IT DOESN'T GIVE A PERSON LICENSE TO LIE OR DO LESS THAN THEIR UTMOST.
A CUSTOMER COMES TO THE FORTUNE TELLER WITH THE ARDENT HOPE OF GETTING A REAL DIVINATION, AND IT'S RUDE TO THAT HOPE TO DO LESS THAN ONE'S BEST.
NO, I'M WRONG.
A FORTUNE IS CONNECTED TO THE VERY LIFE OF THE SEEKER.
THE WORD "RUDE" PUTS IT TOO LIGHTLY.

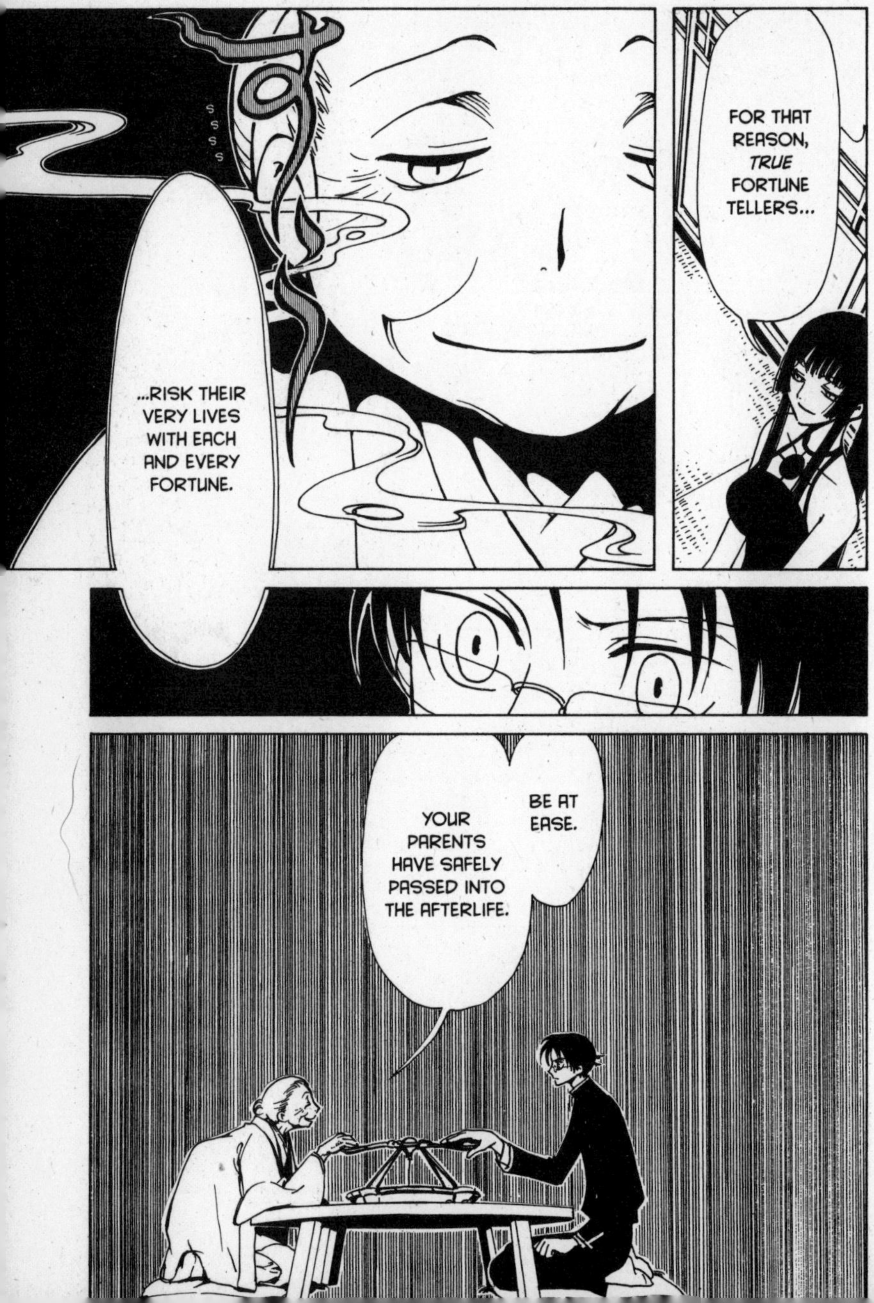
FOR THAT REASON, *TRUE* FORTUNE TELLERS...
S S S S
...RISK THEIR VERY LIVES WITH EACH AND EVERY FORTUNE.
BE AT EASE.
YOUR PARENTS HAVE SAFELY PASSED INTO THE AFTERLIFE.

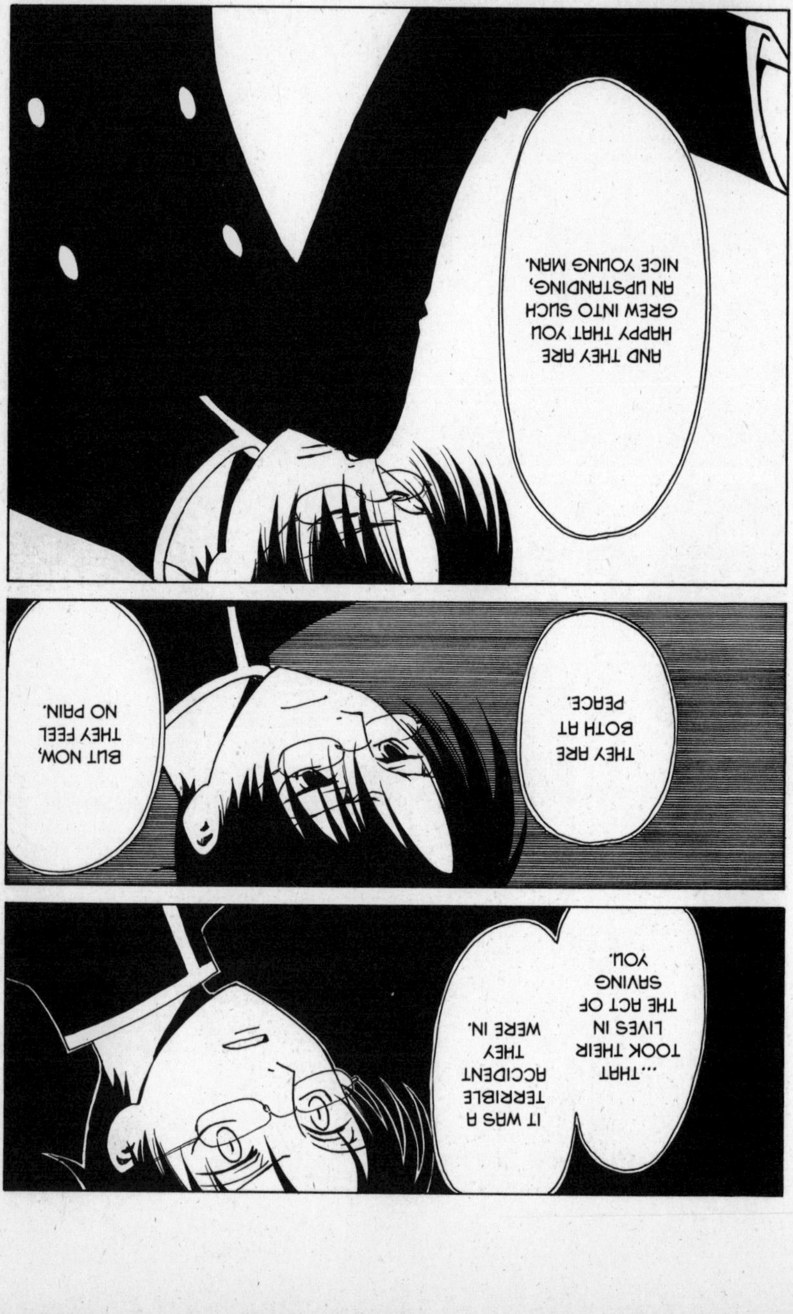
IT WAS A TERRIBLE ACCIDENT THEY WERE IN.
...THAT TOOK THEIR LIVES IN THE ACT OF SAVING YOU.
BUT NOW, THEY FEEL NO PAIN.
THEY ARE BOTH AT PEACE.
AND THEY ARE HAPPY THAT YOU GREW INTO SUCH AN UPSTANDING, NICE YOUNG MAN.

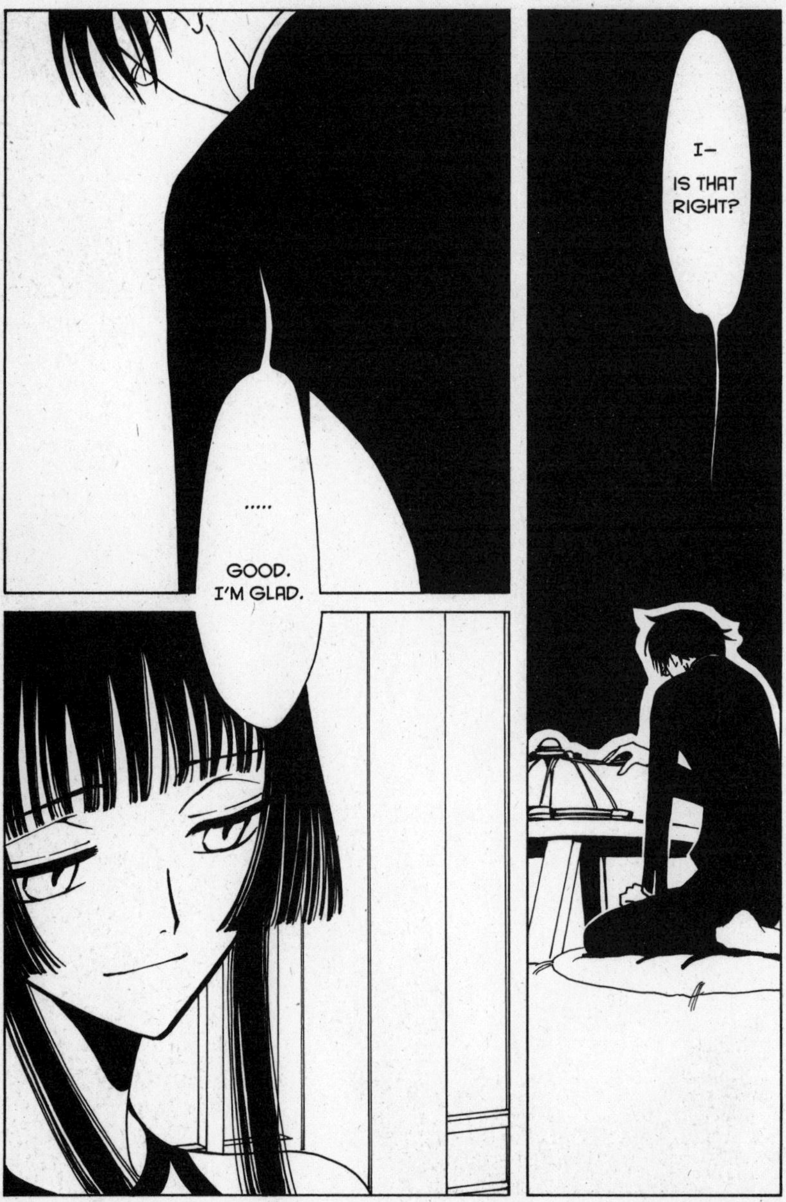
I—
IS THAT RIGHT?
.....
GOOD. I'M GLAD.

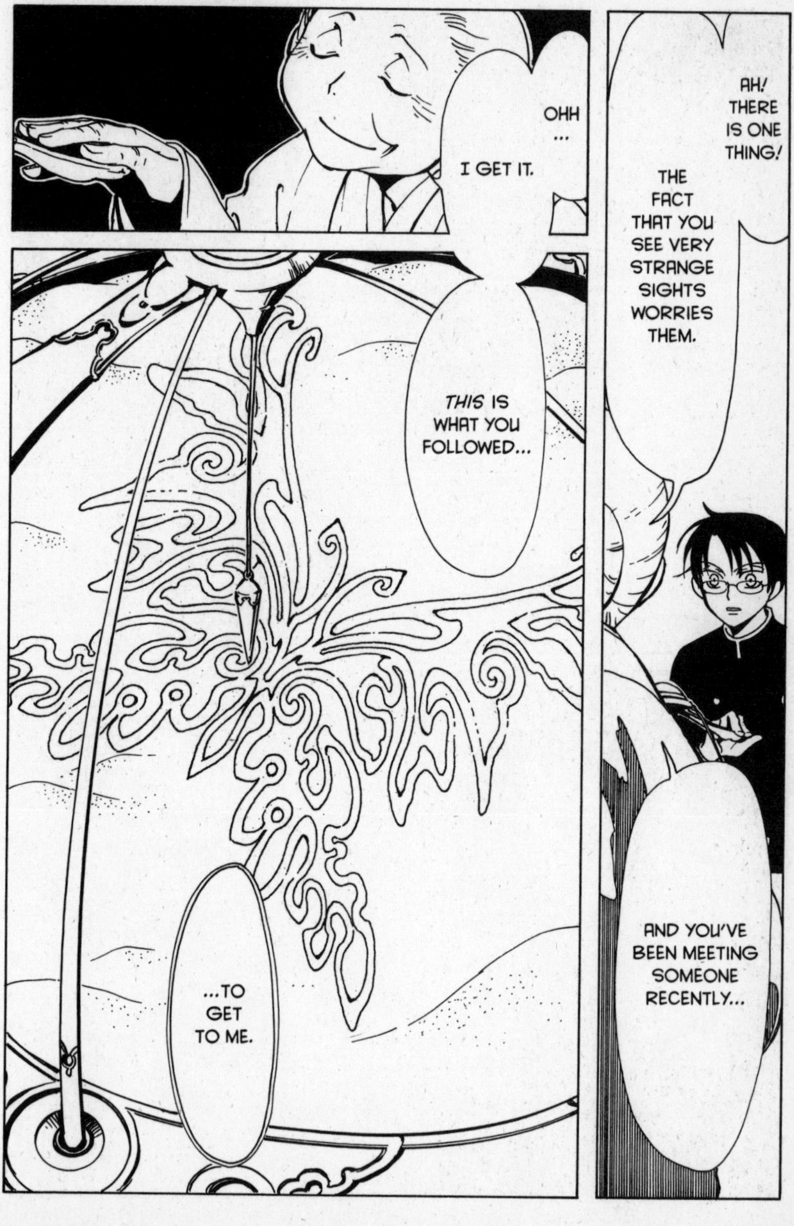
AH! THERE IS ONE THING!
THE FACT THAT YOU SEE VERY STRANGE SIGHTS WORRIES THEM.
AND YOU'VE BEEN MEETING SOMEONE RECENTLY...
OHH ...
I GET IT.
THIS IS WHAT YOU FOLLOWED...
...TO GET TO ME.

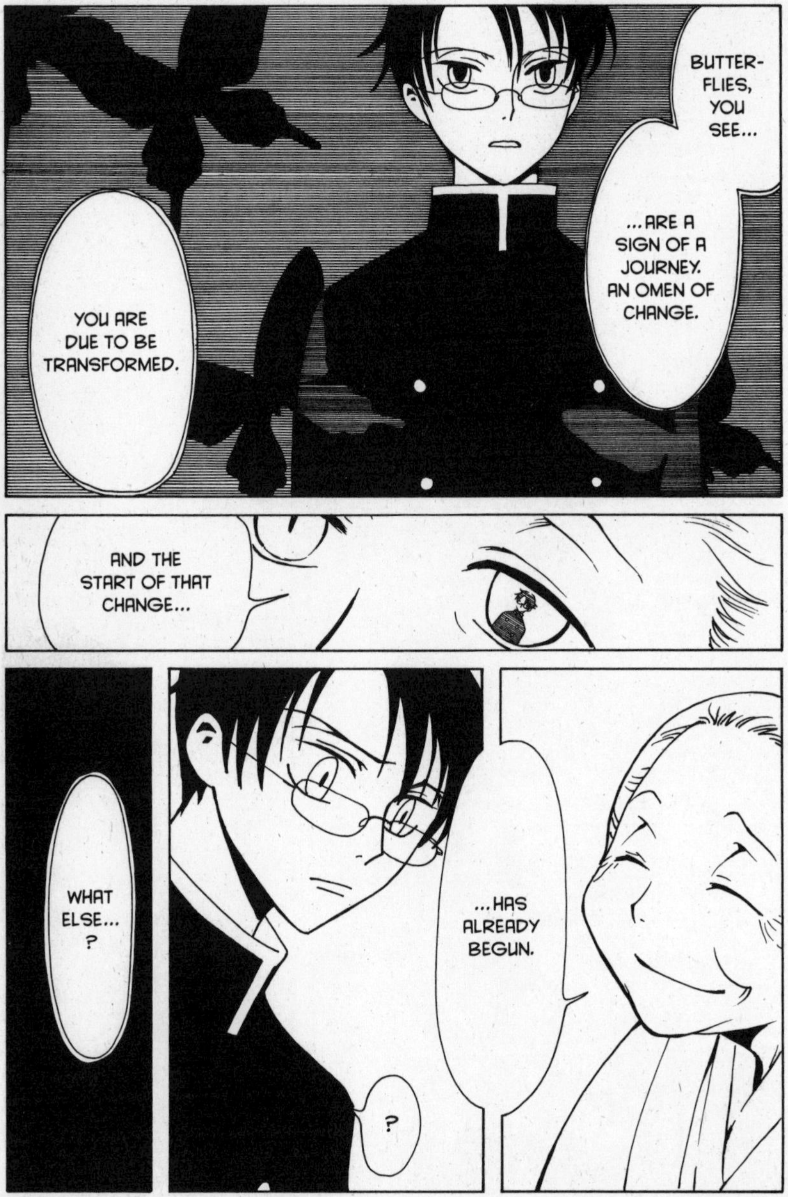
BUTTER-FLIES, YOU SEE...
...ARE A SIGN OF A JOURNEY. AN OMEN OF CHANGE.
YOU ARE DUE TO BE TRANSFORMED.
AND THE START OF THAT CHANGE...
...HAS ALREADY BEGUN.
?
WHAT ELSE... ?

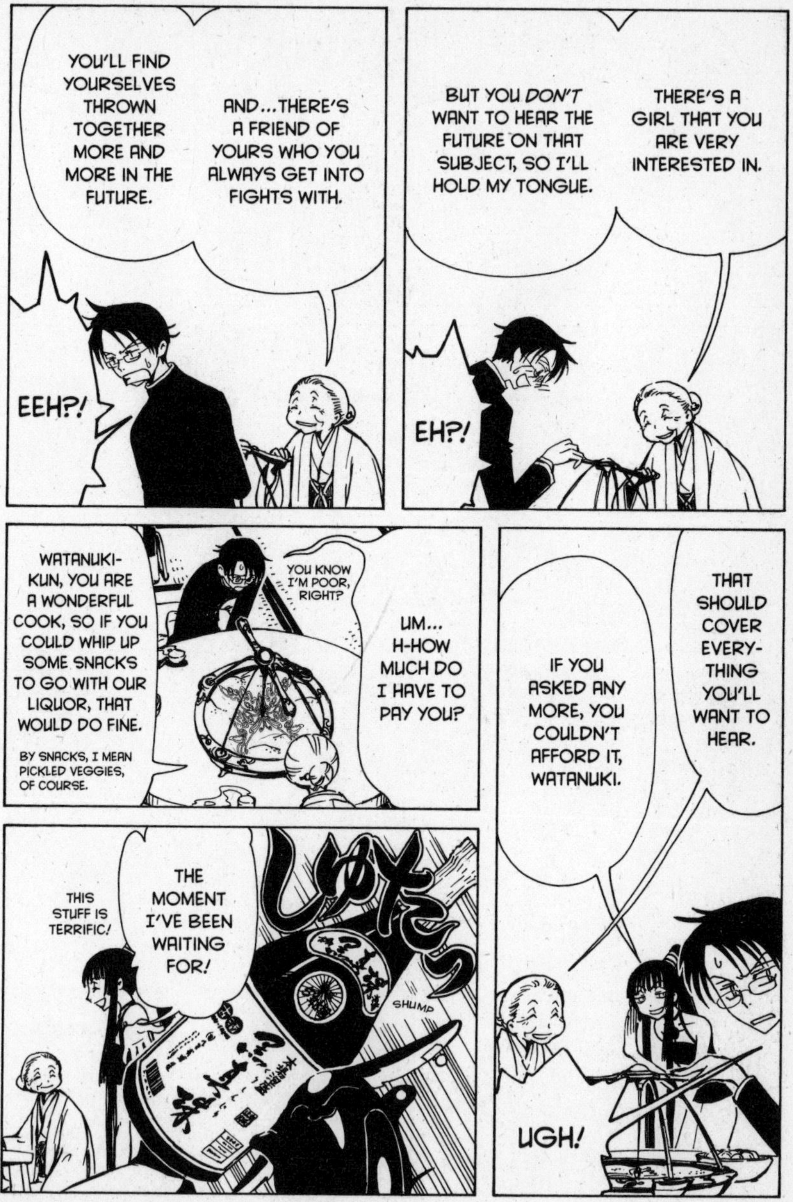
THERE'S A GIRL THAT YOU ARE VERY INTERESTED IN.
BUT YOU *DON'T* WANT TO HEAR THE FUTURE ON THAT SUBJECT, SO I'LL HOLD MY TONGUE.
EH?!
AND...THERE'S A FRIEND OF YOURS WHO YOU ALWAYS GET INTO FIGHTS WITH.
YOU'LL FIND YOURSELVES THROWN TOGETHER MORE AND MORE IN THE FUTURE.
EEH?!
THAT SHOULD COVER EVERY-THING YOU'LL WANT TO HEAR.
IF YOU ASKED ANY MORE, YOU COULDN'T AFFORD IT, WATANUKI.
UGH!
UM... H-HOW MUCH DO I HAVE TO PAY YOU?
YOU KNOW I'M POOR, RIGHT?
WATANUKI-KUN, YOU ARE A WONDERFUL COOK, SO IF YOU COULD WHIP UP SOME SNACKS TO GO WITH OUR LIQUOR, THAT WOULD DO FINE.
BY SNACKS, I MEAN PICKLED VEGGIES, OF COURSE.
THE MOMENT I'VE BEEN WAITING FOR!
THIS STUFF IS TERRIFIC!
SHUMP

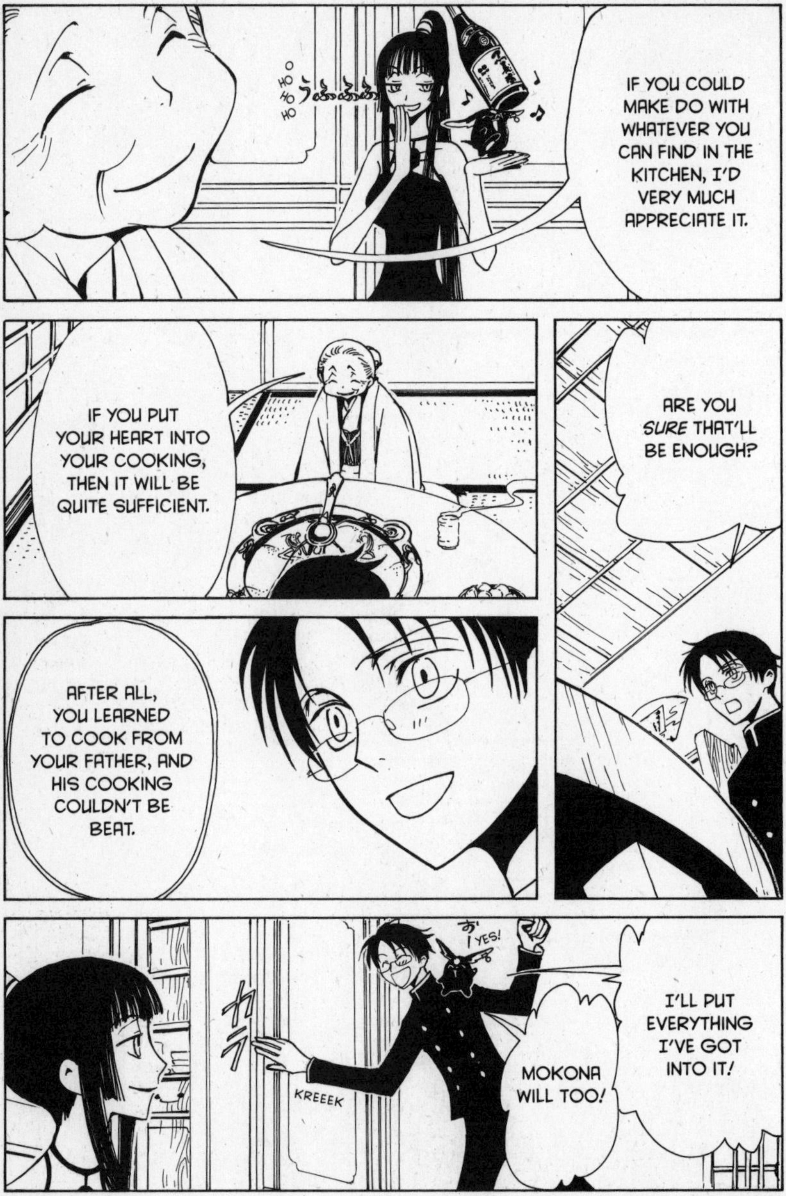
IF YOU COULD MAKE DO WITH WHATEVER YOU CAN FIND IN THE KITCHEN, I'D VERY MUCH APPRECIATE IT.
HO HO HO
ARE YOU *SURE* THAT'LL BE ENOUGH?
IF YOU PUT YOUR HEART INTO YOUR COOKING, THEN IT WILL BE QUITE SUFFICIENT.
AFTER ALL, YOU LEARNED TO COOK FROM YOUR FATHER, AND HIS COOKING COULDN'T BE BEAT.
YES!
I'LL PUT EVERYTHING I'VE GOT INTO IT!
MOKONA WILL TOO!
KREEEK

THIS WAY, RIGHT?

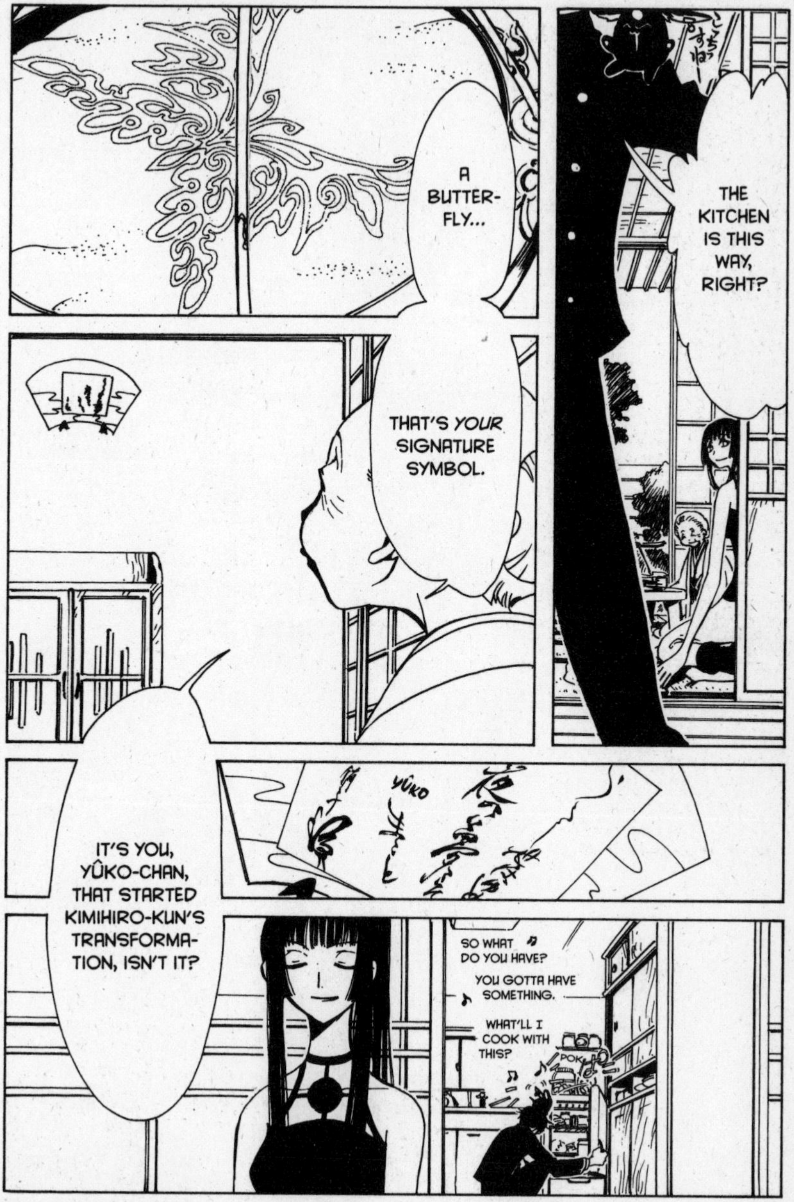
THE KITCHEN IS THIS WAY, RIGHT?
A BUTTER-FLY...
THAT'S *YOUR* SIGNATURE SYMBOL.
YÛKO
IT'S YOU, YÛKO-CHAN, THAT STARTED KIMIHIRO-KUN'S TRANSFORMA-TION, ISN'T IT?
SO WHAT DO YOU HAVE?
YOU GOTTA HAVE SOMETHING.
WHAT'LL I COOK WITH THIS?
POK

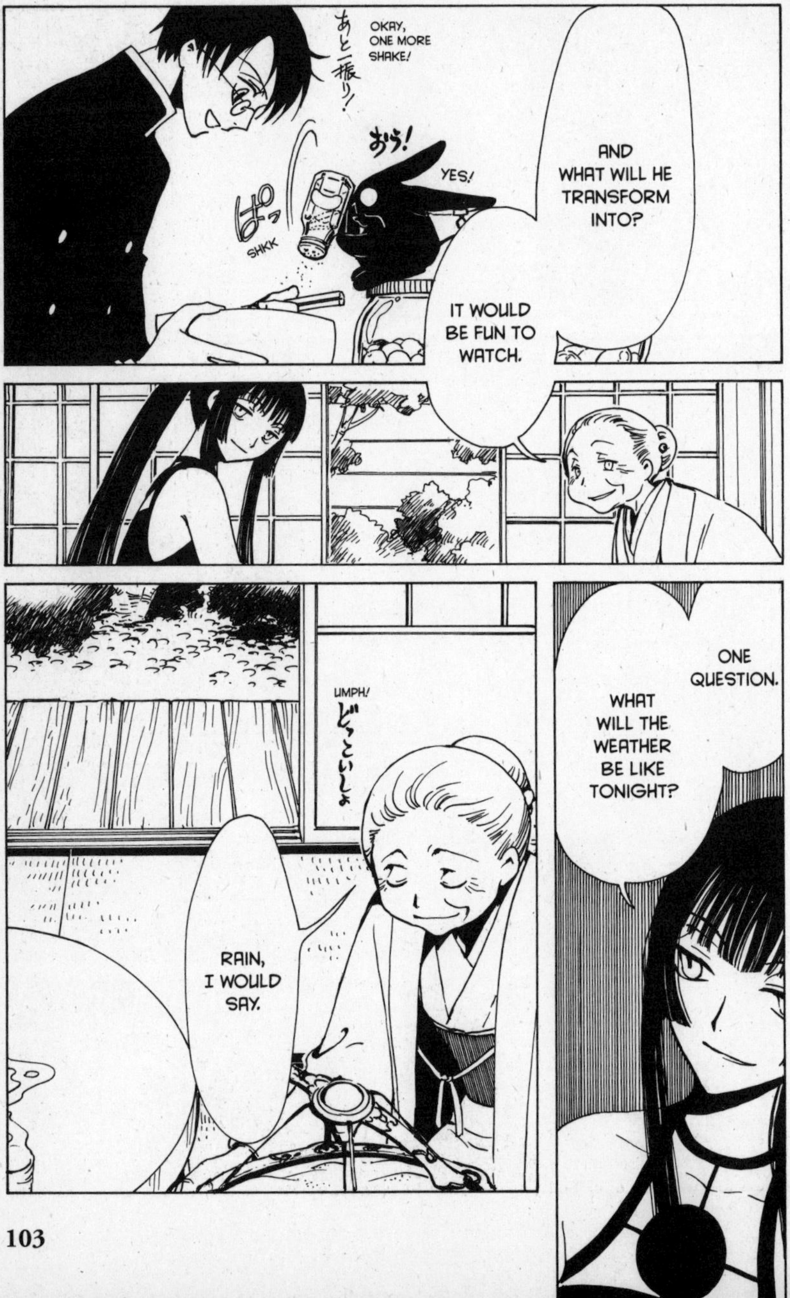
AND WHAT WILL HE TRANSFORM INTO?
OKAY, ONE MORE SHAKE!
あと一振り!
おう!
YES!
ぱっ
SHKK
IT WOULD BE FUN TO WATCH.
ONE QUESTION.
WHAT WILL THE WEATHER BE LIKE TONIGHT?
UMPH!
どっこいしょ
RAIN, I WOULD SAY.

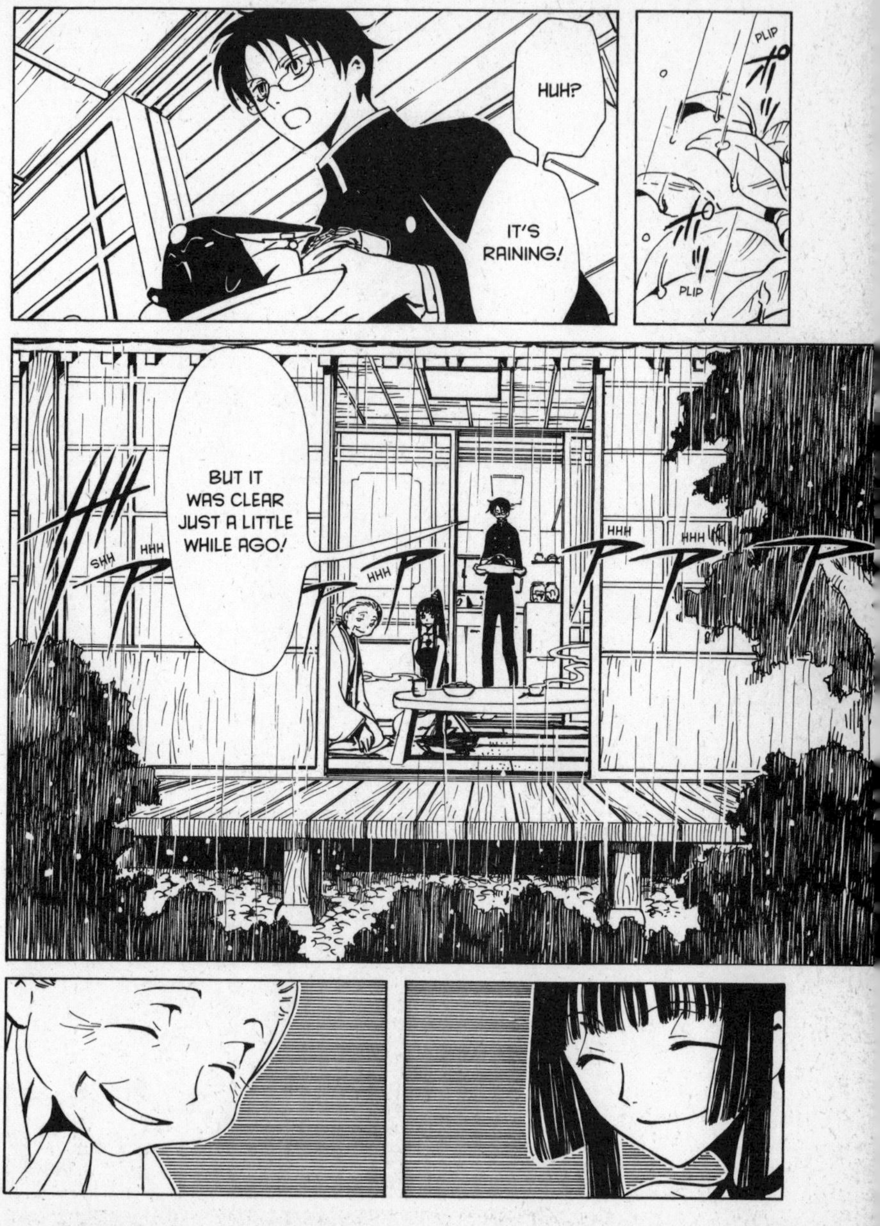
PLIP
PLIP
HUH?
IT'S RAINING!
HHH
HHH
BUT IT WAS CLEAR JUST A LITTLE WHILE AGO!
HHH
HHH
SHH

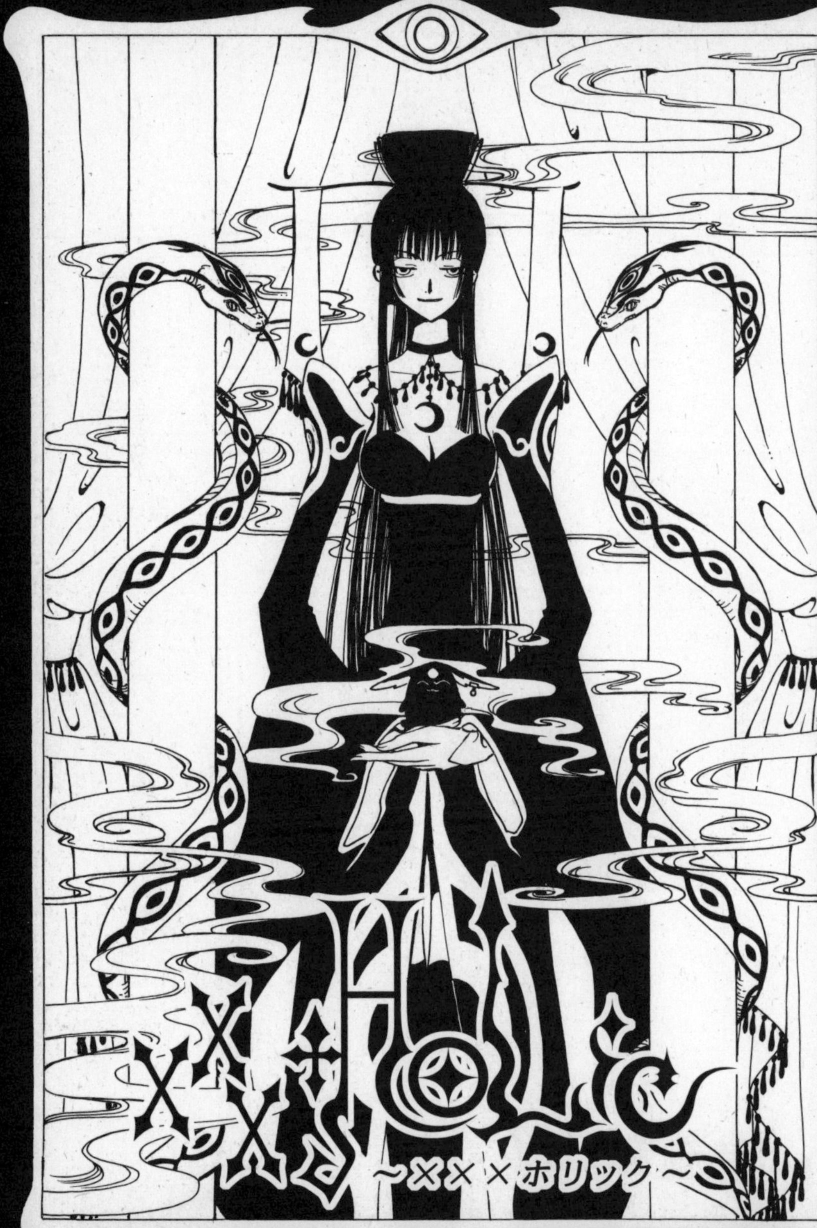
xxxHOLiC
~×××ホリック~

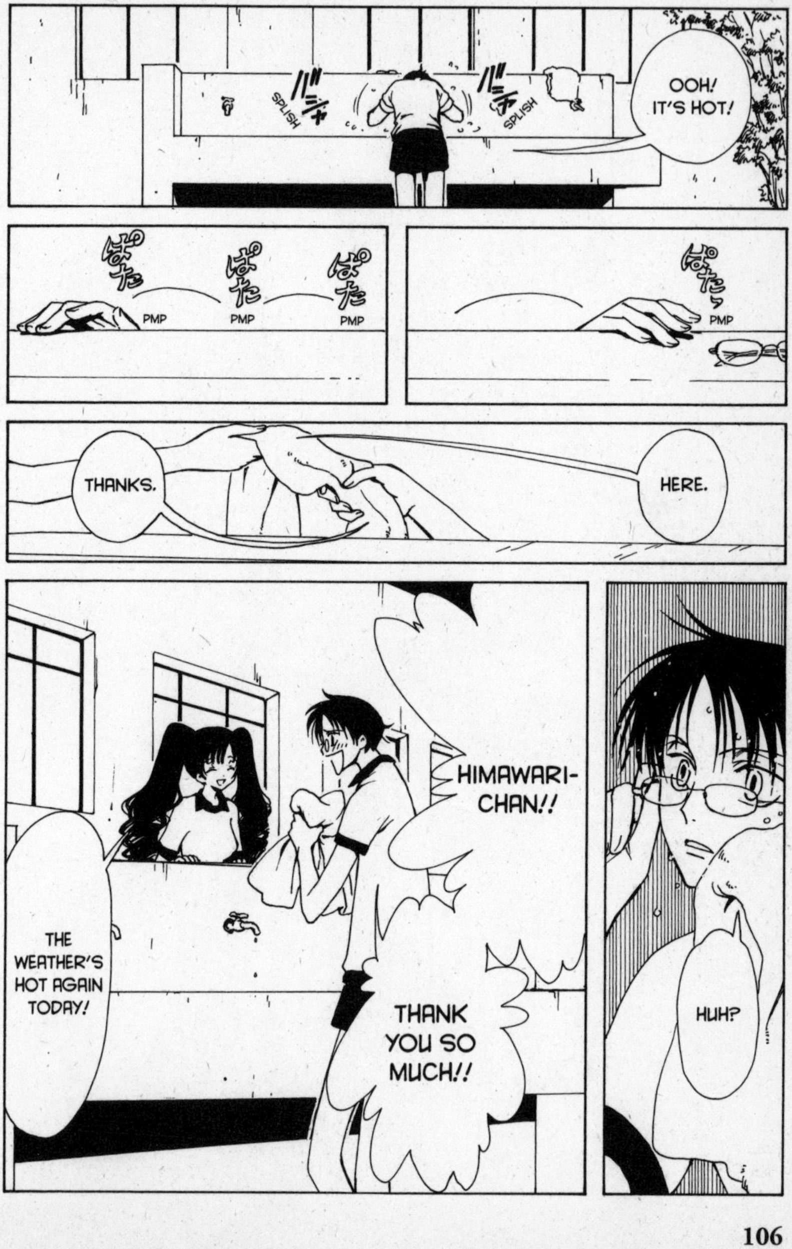
OOH! IT'S HOT!
SPLISH
SPLISH
ぱたっ
PMP
ぱた
PMP
ぱた
PMP
ぱた
PMP
HERE.
THANKS.
HUH?
HIMAWARI-CHAN!!
THANK YOU SO MUCH!!
THE WEATHER'S HOT AGAIN TODAY!

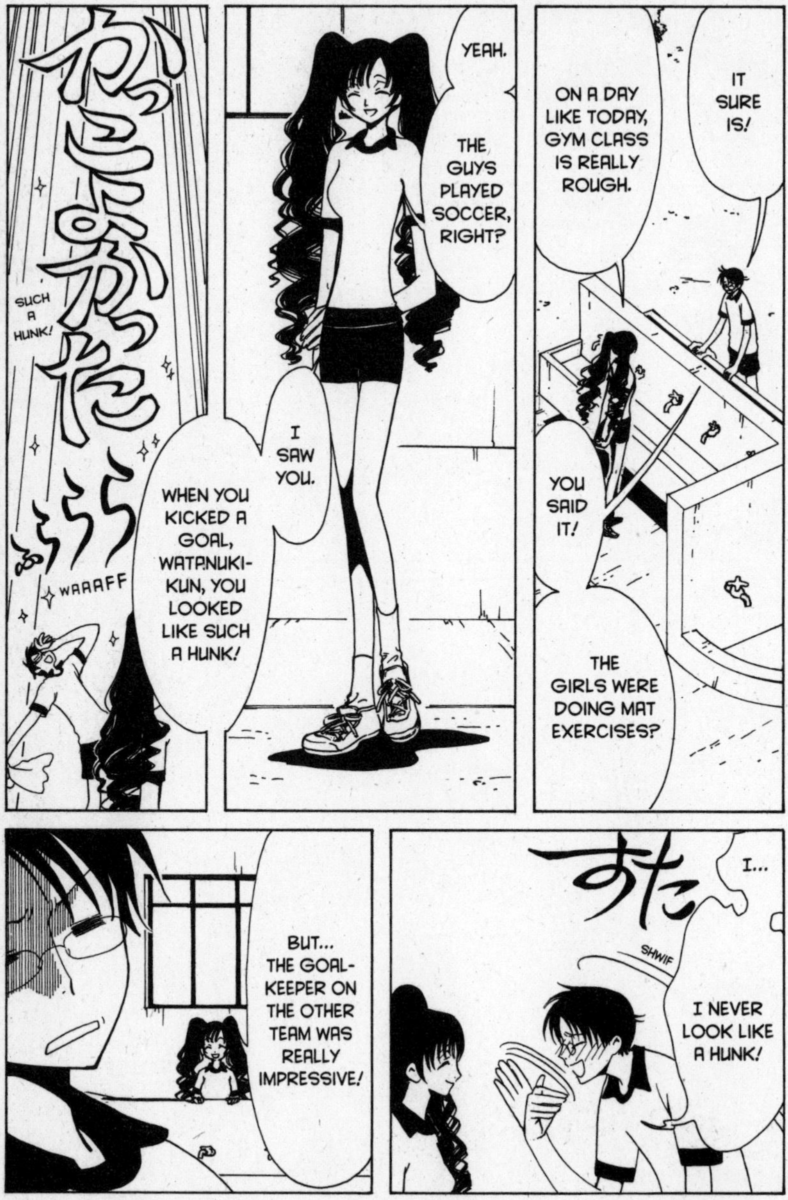
ON A DAY LIKE TODAY, GYM CLASS IS REALLY ROUGH.
IT SURE IS!
THE GIRLS WERE DOING MAT EXERCISES?
YOU SAID IT!
YEAH.
THE GUYS PLAYED SOCCER, RIGHT?
I SAW YOU.
WHEN YOU KICKED A GOAL, WATANUKI-KUN, YOU LOOKED LIKE SUCH A HUNK!
かっこよかった
SUCH A HUNK!
ふらら
WAAAFF
I...
すた
SHWIF
I NEVER LOOK LIKE A HUNK!
BUT... THE GOAL-KEEPER ON THE OTHER TEAM WAS REALLY IMPRESSIVE!

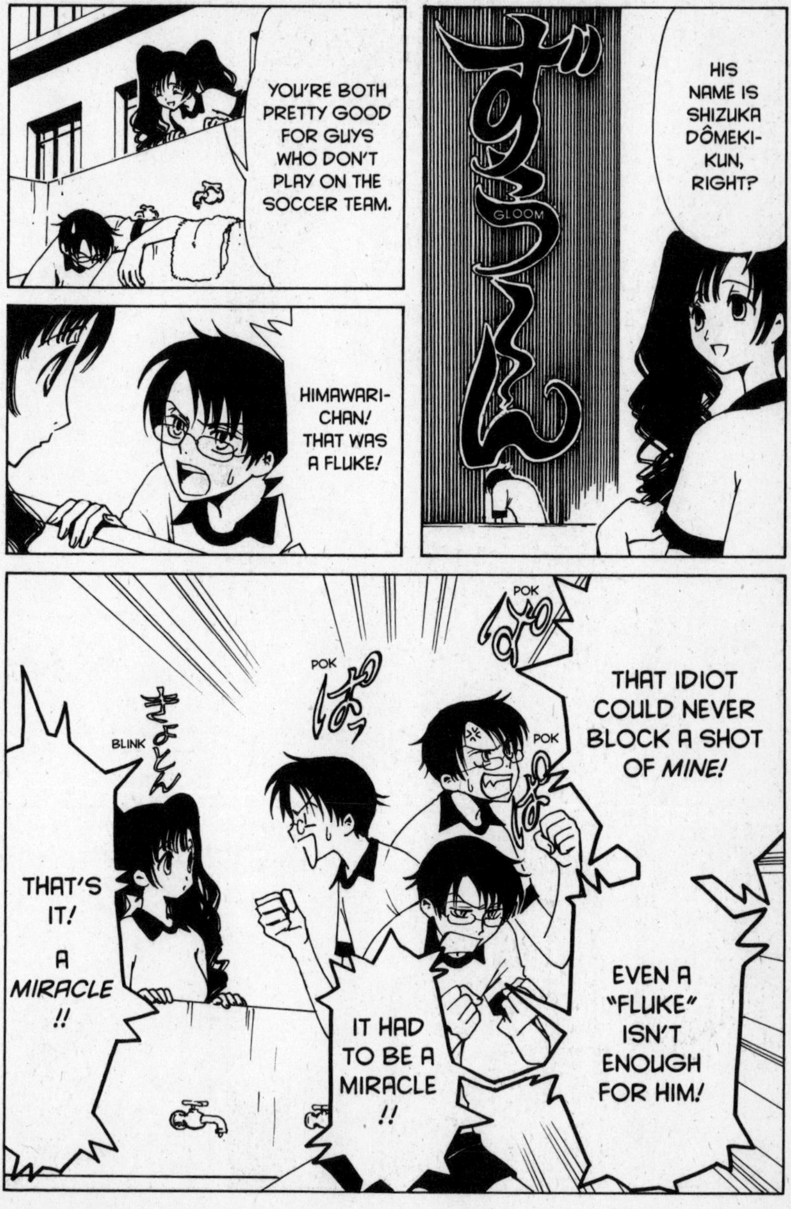
HIS NAME IS SHIZUKA DÔMEKI-KUN, RIGHT?
GLOOM
YOU'RE BOTH PRETTY GOOD FOR GUYS WHO DON'T PLAY ON THE SOCCER TEAM.
HIMAWARI-CHAN! THAT WAS A FLUKE!
POK
THAT IDIOT COULD NEVER BLOCK A SHOT OF MINE!
POK
POK
BLINK
EVEN A "FLUKE" ISN'T ENOUGH FOR HIM!
IT HAD TO BE A MIRACLE !!
THAT'S IT!
A MIRACLE !!

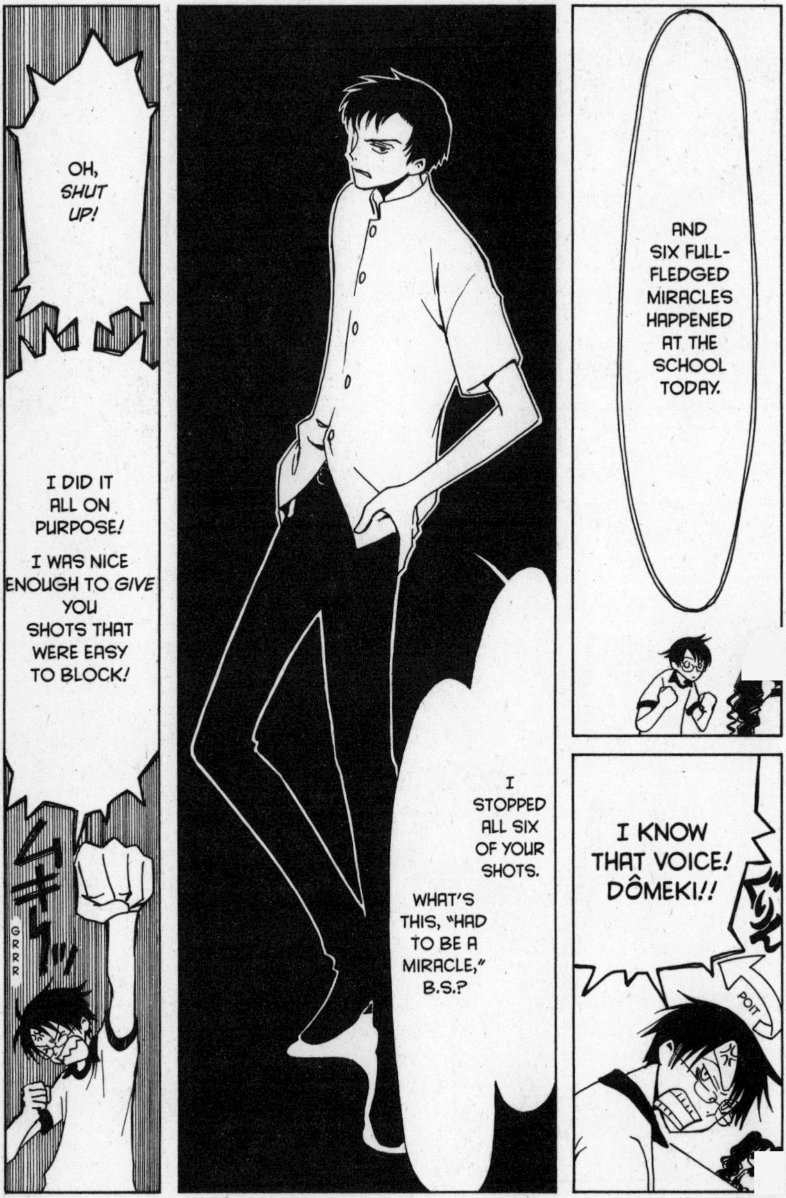
AND SIX FULL-FLEDGED MIRACLES HAPPENED AT THE SCHOOL TODAY.
I KNOW THAT VOICE! DÔMEKI!!
POIT
I STOPPED ALL SIX OF YOUR SHOTS.
WHAT'S THIS, "HAD TO BE A MIRACLE," B.S.?
OH, SHUT UP!
I DID IT ALL ON PURPOSE!
I WAS NICE ENOUGH TO GIVE YOU SHOTS THAT WERE EASY TO BLOCK!
GRRR

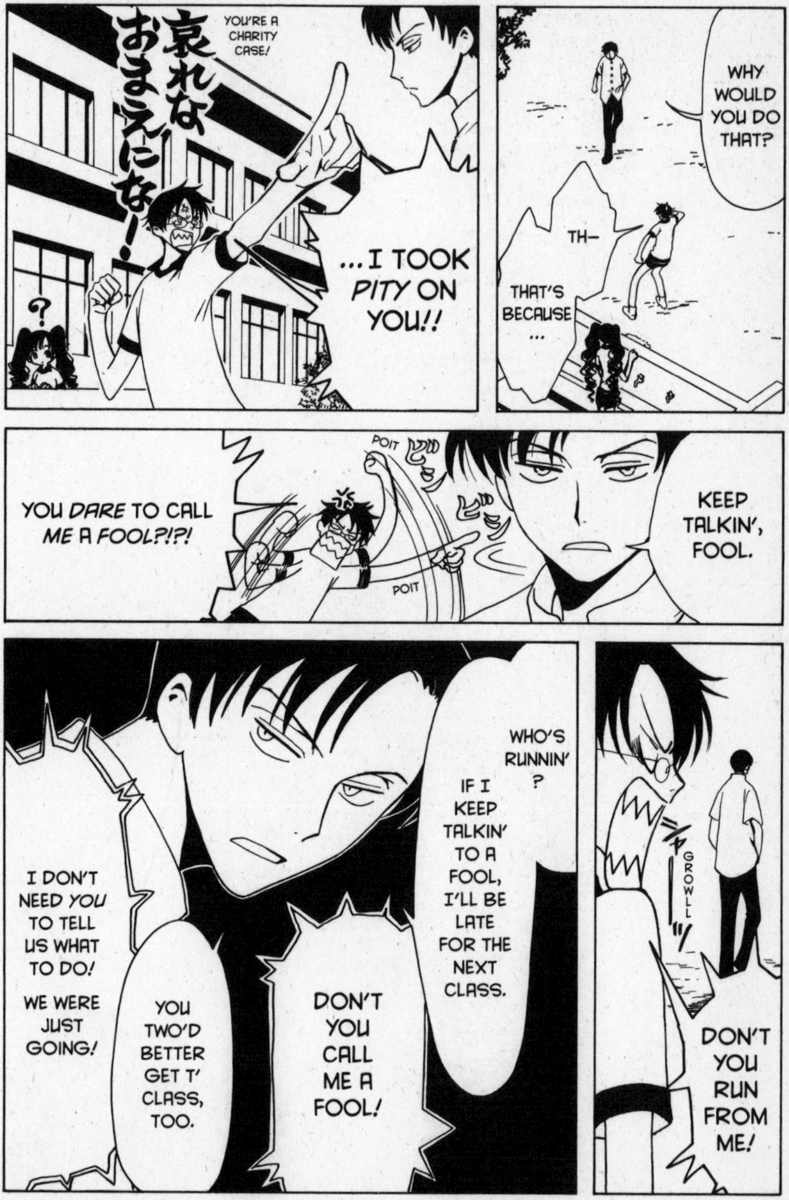
WHY WOULD YOU DO THAT?
TH—
THAT'S BECAUSE ...
...I TOOK PITY ON YOU!!
哀れなおまえにな!!
YOU'RE A CHARITY CASE!
?
KEEP TALKIN', FOOL.
POIT
POIT
YOU DARE TO CALL ME A FOOL?!?!
DON'T YOU RUN FROM ME!
GROWLL
WHO'S RUNNIN'?
IF I KEEP TALKIN' TO A FOOL, I'LL BE LATE FOR THE NEXT CLASS.
DON'T YOU CALL ME A FOOL!
YOU TWO'D BETTER GET T' CLASS, TOO.
I DON'T NEED YOU TO TELL US WHAT TO DO!
WE WERE JUST GOING!

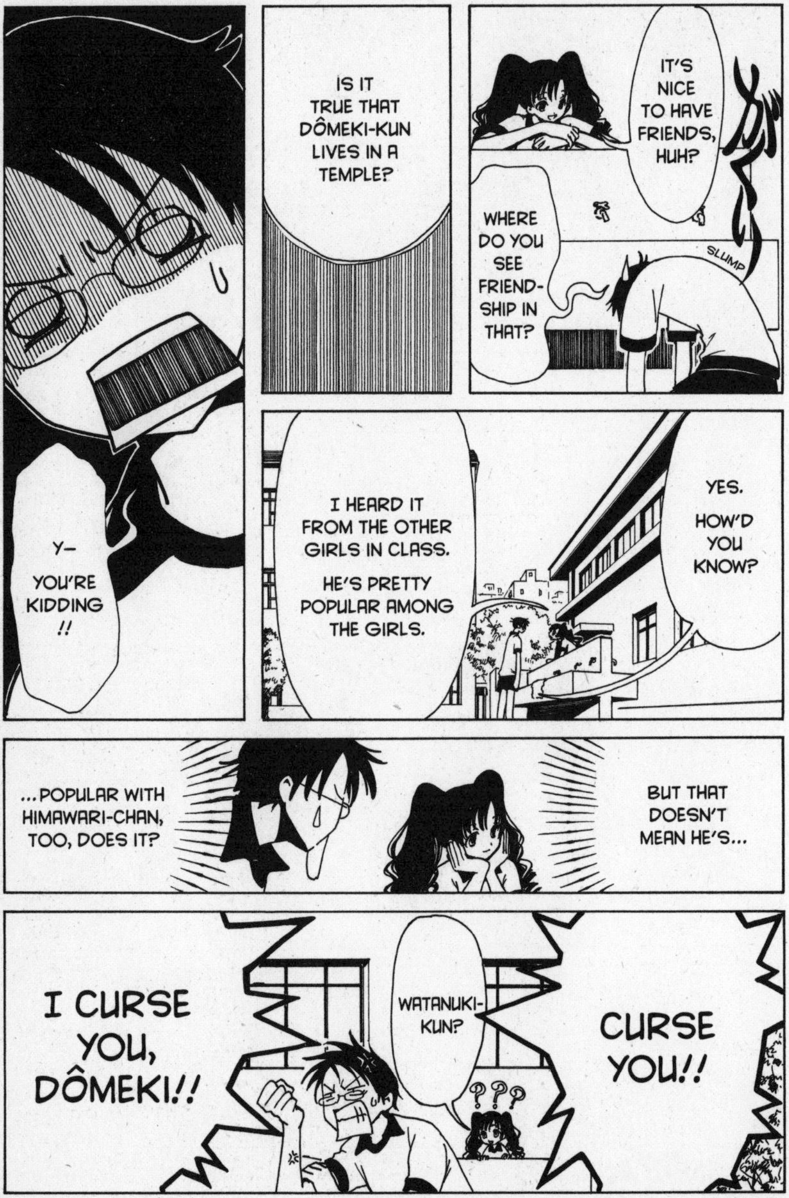
IT'S NICE TO HAVE FRIENDS, HUH?
SLUMP
WHERE DO YOU SEE FRIENDSHIP IN THAT?
IS IT TRUE THAT DÔMEKI-KUN LIVES IN A TEMPLE?
YES.
HOW'D YOU KNOW?
I HEARD IT FROM THE OTHER GIRLS IN CLASS.
HE'S PRETTY POPULAR AMONG THE GIRLS.
Y— YOU'RE KIDDING!!
BUT THAT DOESN'T MEAN HE'S...
...POPULAR WITH HIMAWARI-CHAN, TOO, DOES IT?
CURSE YOU!!
WATANUKI-KUN?
???
I CURSE YOU, DÔMEKI!!

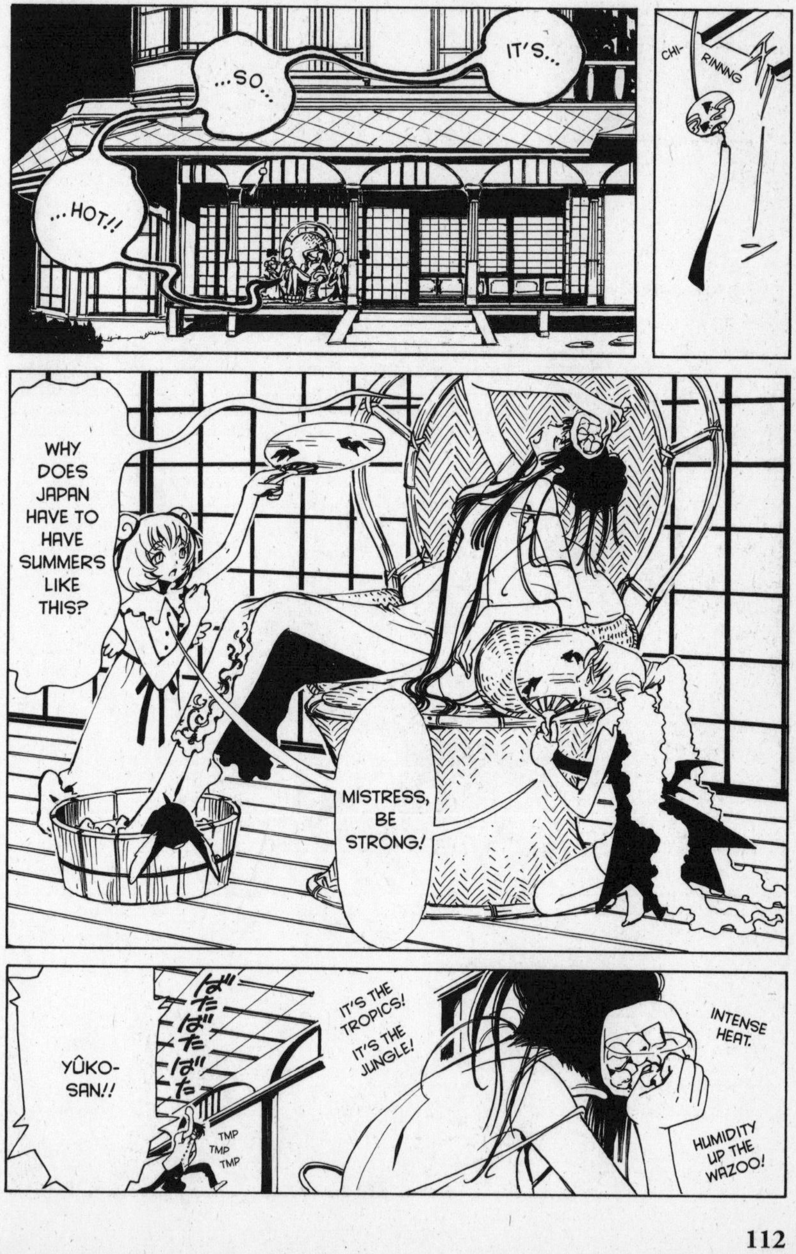
CHI-RINNNG
IT'S...
...SO...
...HOT!!
WHY DOES JAPAN HAVE TO HAVE SUMMERS LIKE THIS?
MISTRESS, BE STRONG!
INTENSE HEAT.
HUMIDITY UP THE WAZOO!
IT'S THE TROPICS!
IT'S THE JUNGLE!
ばたばたばた
TMP TMP TMP
YÛKO-SAN!!

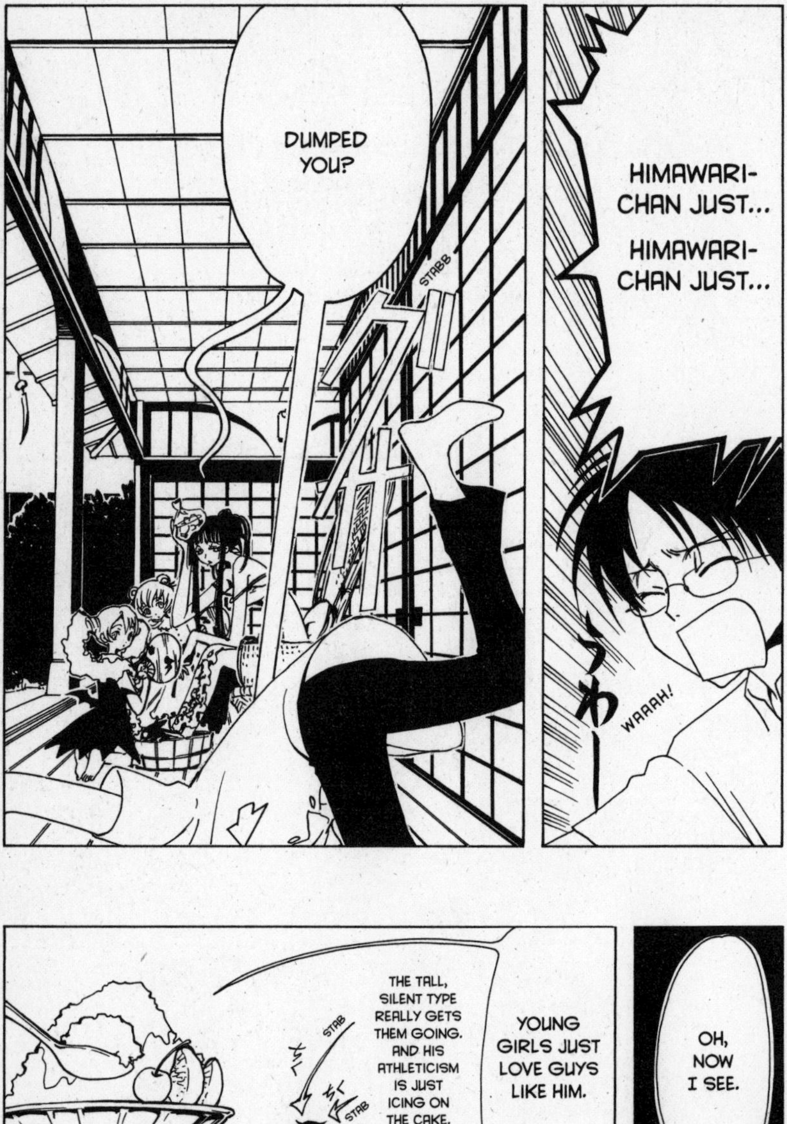
HIMAWARI-CHAN JUST...
HIMAWARI-CHAN JUST...
WAAAH!
DUMPED YOU?
STABB
OH, NOW I SEE.
YOUNG GIRLS JUST LOVE GUYS LIKE HIM.
THE TALL, SILENT TYPE REALLY GETS THEM GOING. AND HIS ATHLETICISM IS JUST ICING ON THE CAKE.
STAB
STAB

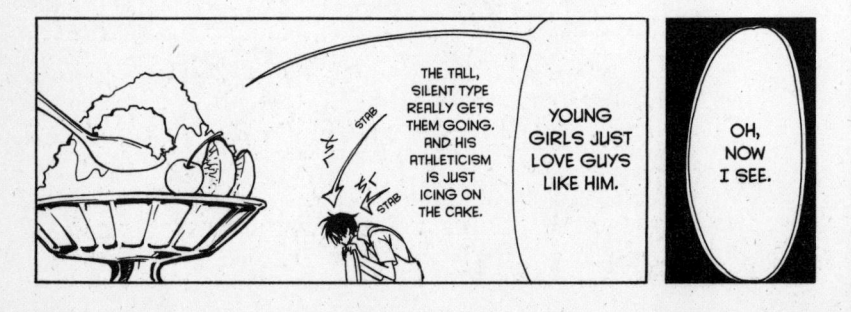

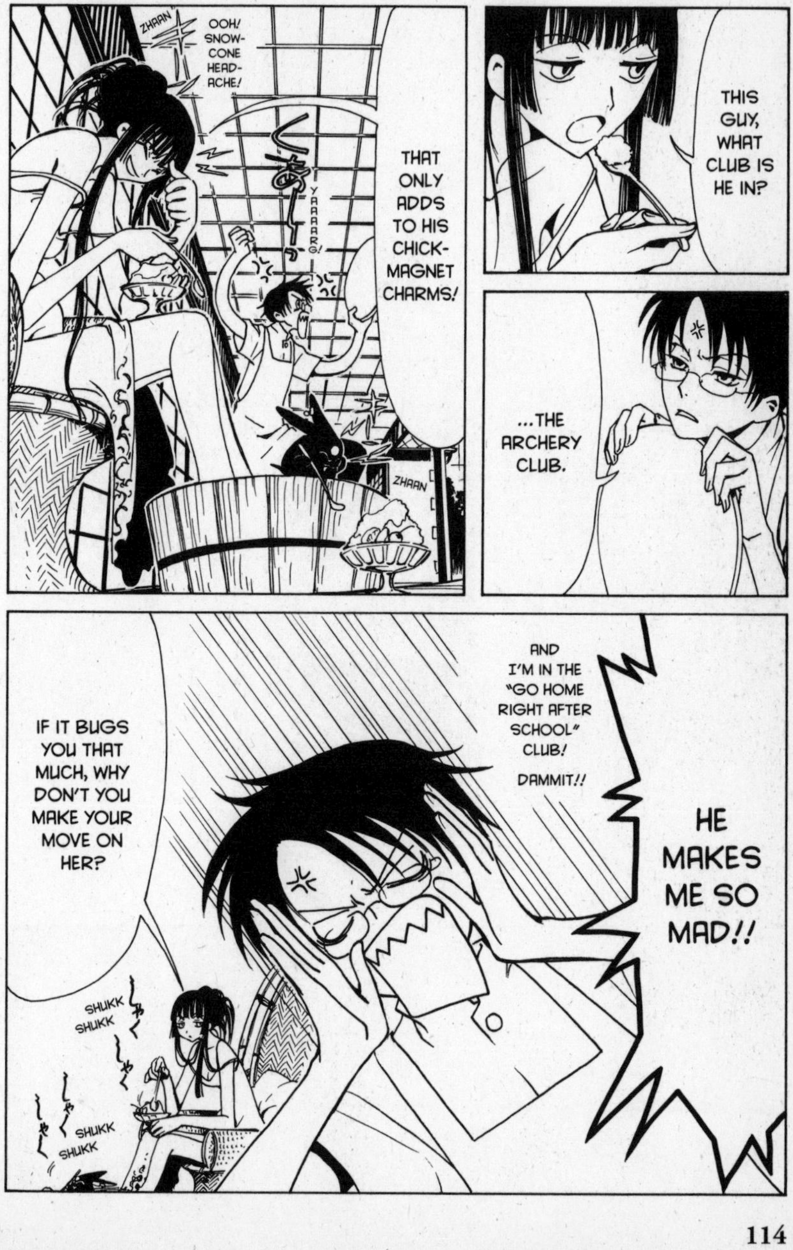
THIS GUY, WHAT CLUB IS HE IN?
...THE ARCHERY CLUB.
THAT ONLY ADDS TO HIS CHICK-MAGNET CHARMS!
OOH! SNOW-CONE HEAD-ACHE!
ZHAAN
YAAAAARG!
ZHAAN
HE MAKES ME SO MAD!!
AND I'M IN THE "GO HOME RIGHT AFTER SCHOOL" CLUB!
DAMMIT!!
IF IT BUGS YOU THAT MUCH, WHY DON'T YOU MAKE YOUR MOVE ON HER?
SHUKK SHUKK
SHUKK SHUKK

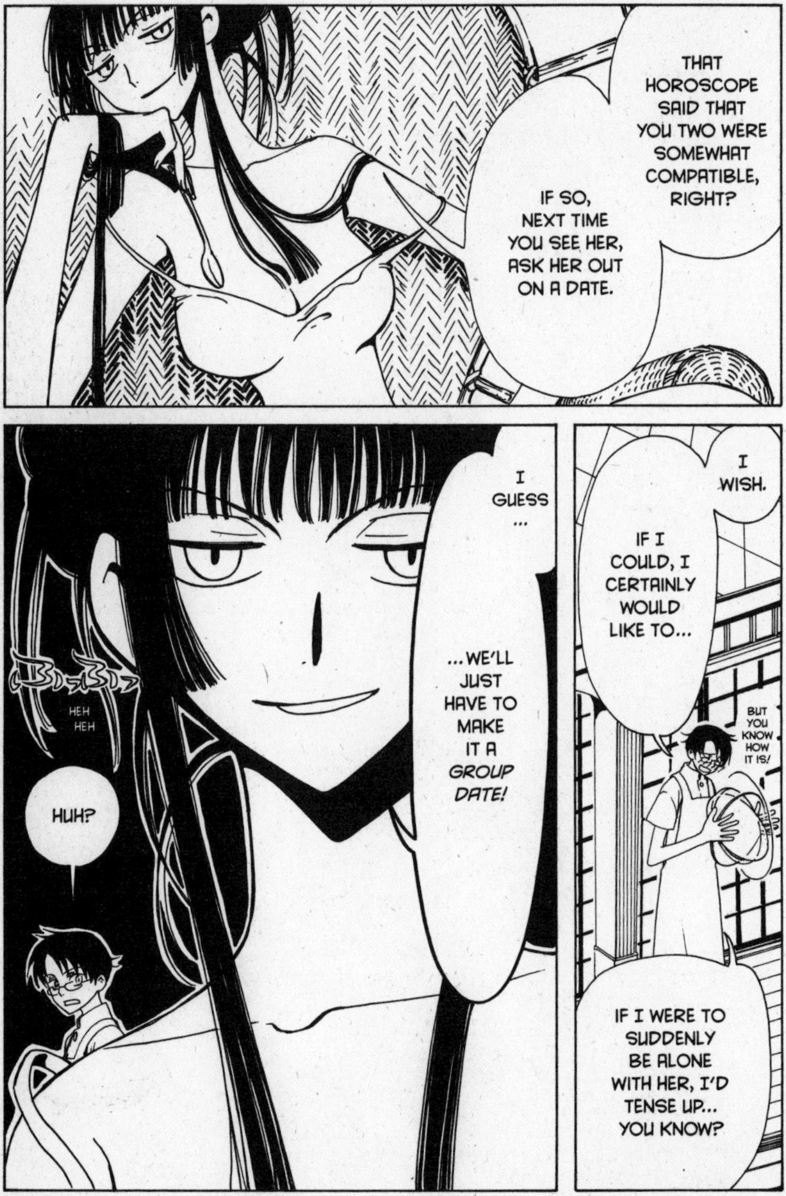
THAT HOROSCOPE SAID THAT YOU TWO WERE SOMEWHAT COMPATIBLE, RIGHT?
IF SO, NEXT TIME YOU SEE HER, ASK HER OUT ON A DATE.
I WISH.
IF I COULD, I CERTAINLY WOULD LIKE TO...
BUT YOU KNOW HOW IT IS!
IF I WERE TO SUDDENLY BE ALONE WITH HER, I'D TENSE UP... YOU KNOW?
I GUESS ...
...WE'LL JUST HAVE TO MAKE IT A GROUP DATE!
HEH HEH
HUH?

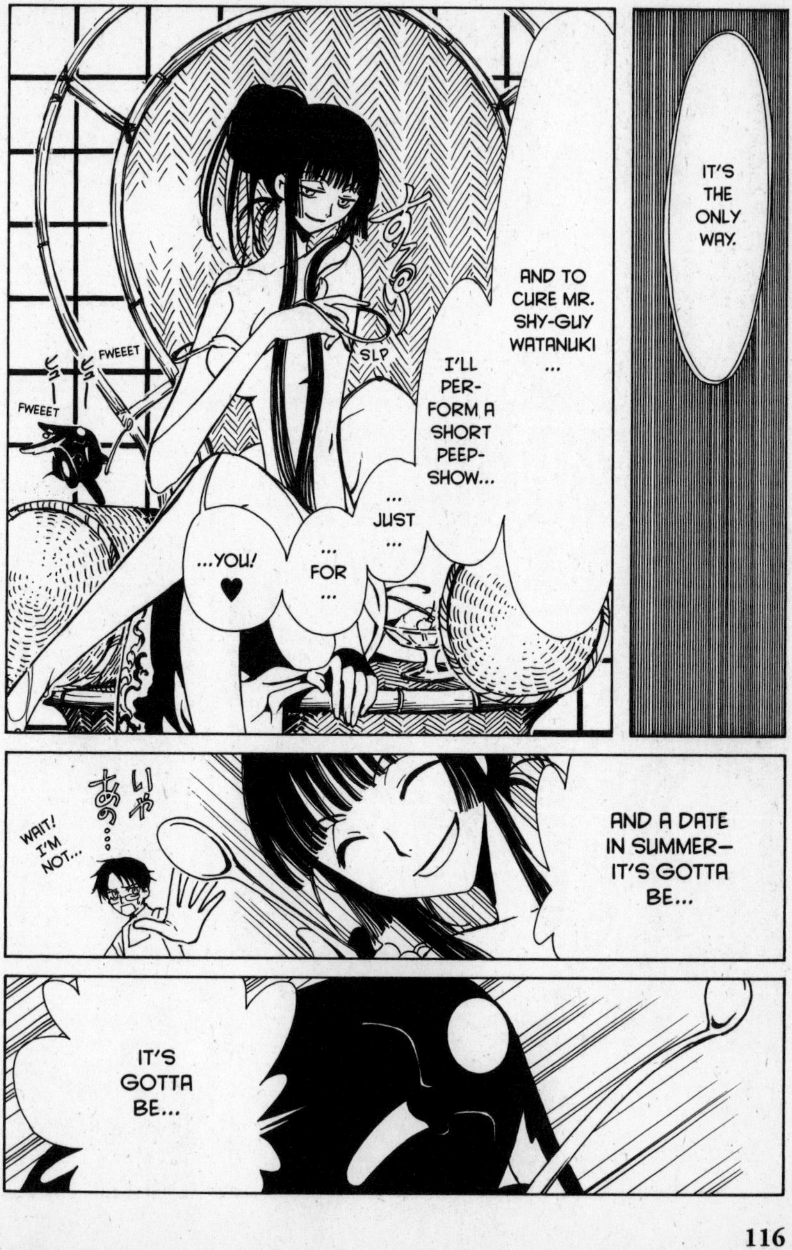
IT'S THE ONLY WAY.
AND TO CURE MR. SHY-GUY WATANUKI ...
I'LL PER-FORM A SHORT PEEP-SHOW...
SLP
... JUST ...
... FOR ...
...YOU! ♥
FWEEET
FWEEET
AND A DATE IN SUMMER— IT'S GOTTA BE...
WAIT! I'M NOT...
IT'S GOTTA BE...

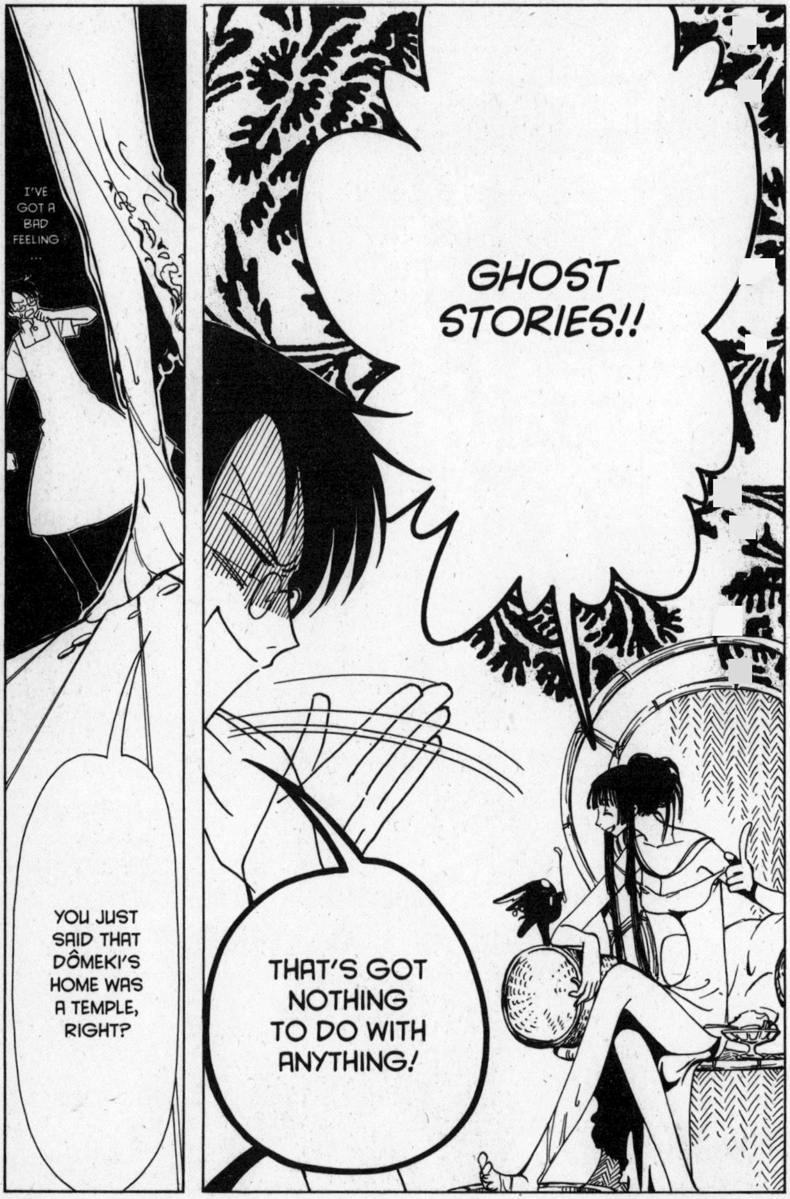
GHOST STORIES!!
THAT'S GOT NOTHING TO DO WITH ANYTHING!
I'VE GOT A BAD FEELING ...
YOU JUST SAID THAT DÔMEKI'S HOME WAS A TEMPLE, RIGHT?

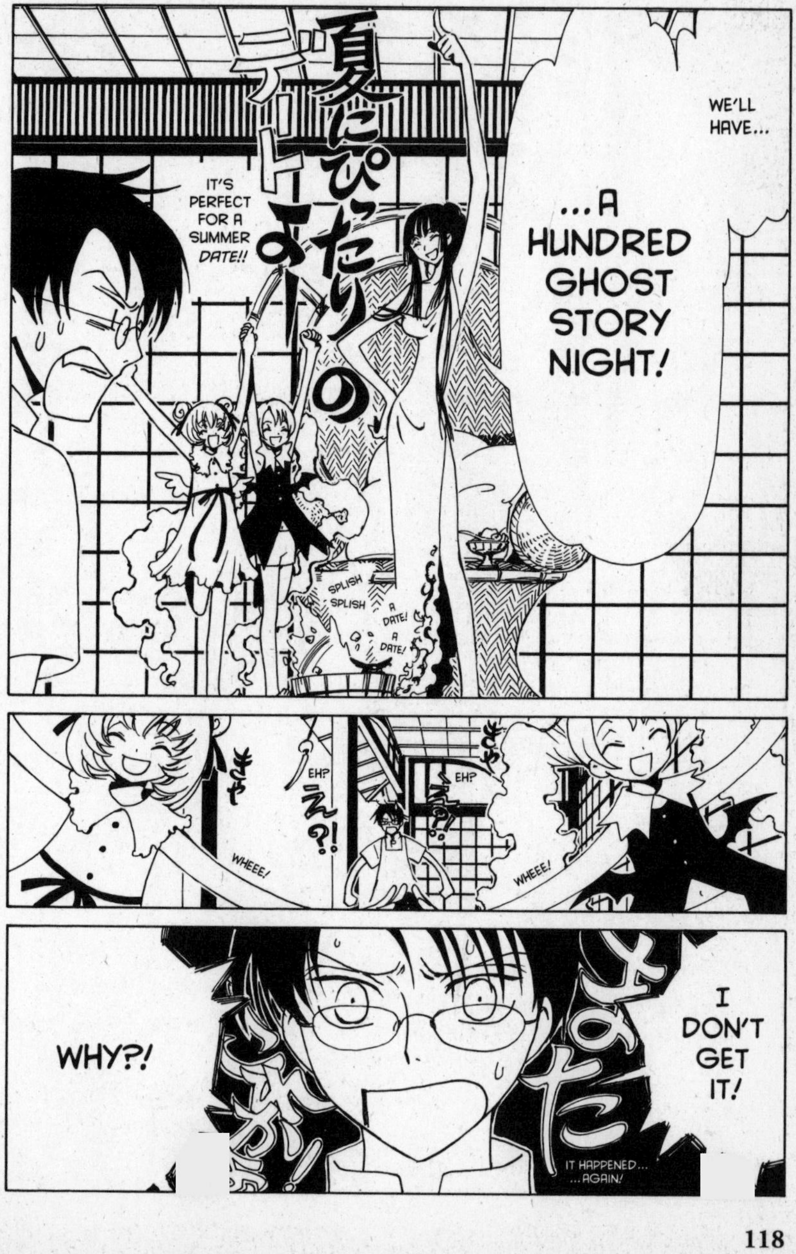
WE'LL HAVE...
...A HUNDRED GHOST STORY NIGHT!
夏にぴったりのデート
IT'S PERFECT FOR A SUMMER DATE!!
SPLISH SPLISH
A DATE! A DATE!
きゃ
WHEEE!
EH?
え?!
EH?
え?!
きゃ
WHEEE!
I DON'T GET IT!
またこれか
IT HAPPENED... ...AGAIN!
WHY?!

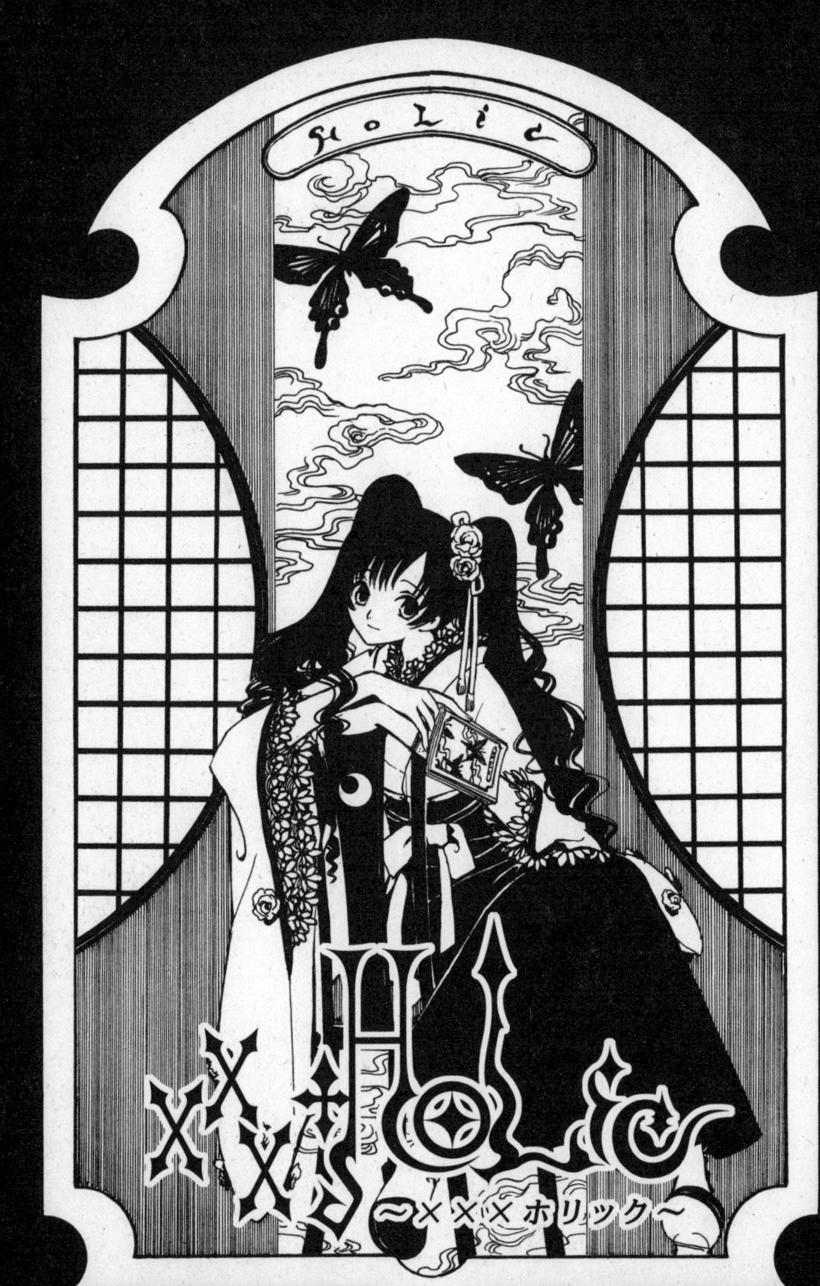
HoLic
xxxHOLiC
~×××ホリック~

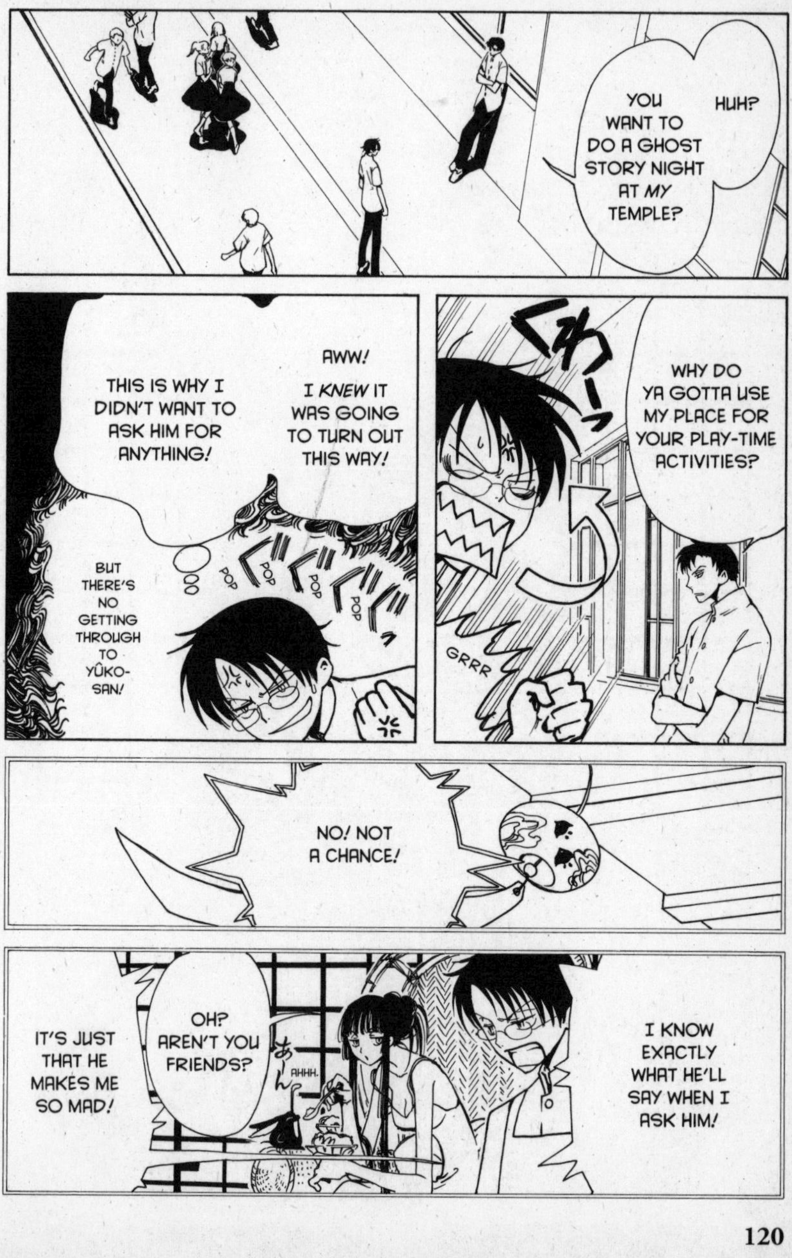
HUH?
YOU WANT TO DO A GHOST STORY NIGHT AT MY TEMPLE?
WHY DO YA GOTTA USE MY PLACE FOR YOUR PLAY-TIME ACTIVITIES?
GRRR
AWW!
I KNEW IT WAS GOING TO TURN OUT THIS WAY!
THIS IS WHY I DIDN'T WANT TO ASK HIM FOR ANYTHING!
POP
POP
POP
POP
BUT THERE'S NO GETTING THROUGH TO YÛKO-SAN!
NO! NOT A CHANCE!
I KNOW EXACTLY WHAT HE'LL SAY WHEN I ASK HIM!
AHHH.
OH? AREN'T YOU FRIENDS?
IT'S JUST THAT HE MAKES ME SO MAD!

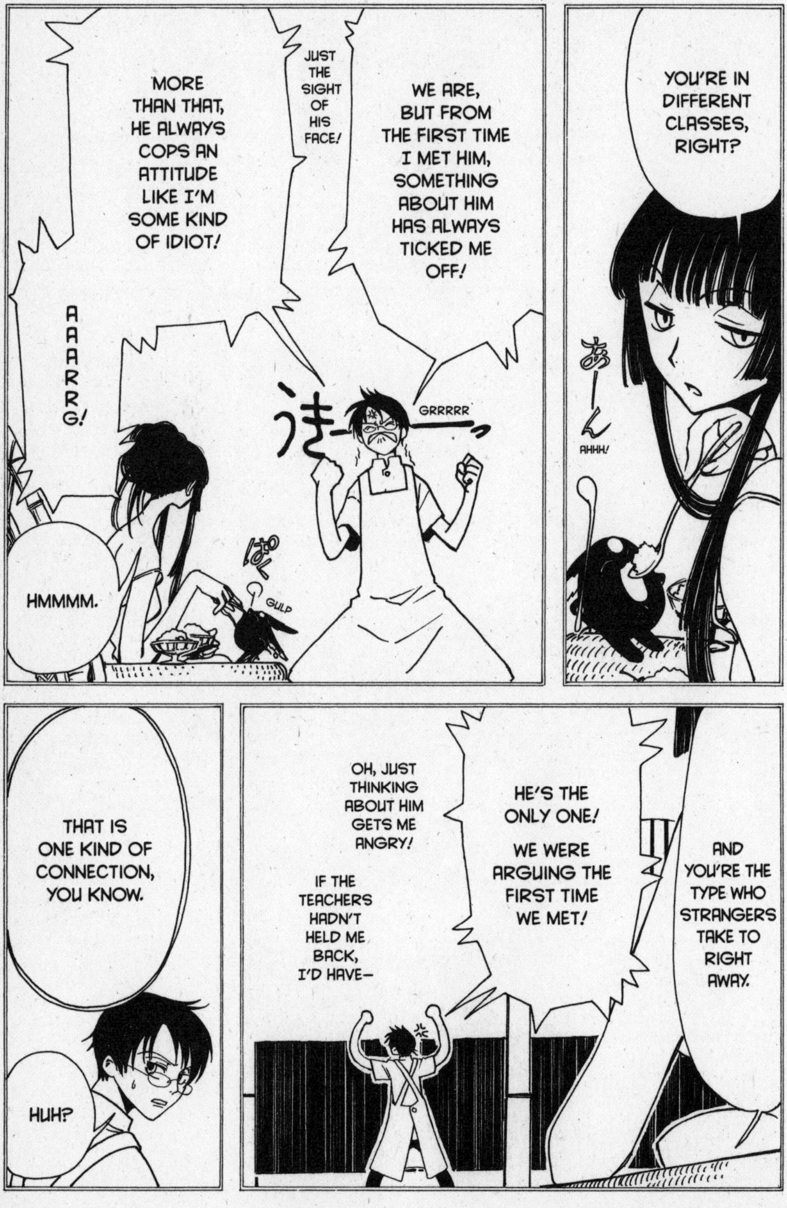
YOU'RE IN DIFFERENT CLASSES, RIGHT?
あーん
AHHH!
WE ARE, BUT FROM THE FIRST TIME I MET HIM, SOMETHING ABOUT HIM HAS ALWAYS TICKED ME OFF!
JUST THE SIGHT OF HIS FACE!
MORE THAN THAT, HE ALWAYS COPS AN ATTITUDE LIKE I'M SOME KIND OF IDIOT!
うきーっ
GRRRRR
AAAARRG!
ぱく
GULP
HMMMM.
AND YOU'RE THE TYPE WHO STRANGERS TAKE TO RIGHT AWAY.
HE'S THE ONLY ONE!
WE WERE ARGUING THE FIRST TIME WE MET!
OH, JUST THINKING ABOUT HIM GETS ME ANGRY!
IF THE TEACHERS HADN'T HELD ME BACK, I'D HAVE—
THAT IS ONE KIND OF CONNECTION, YOU KNOW.
HUH?

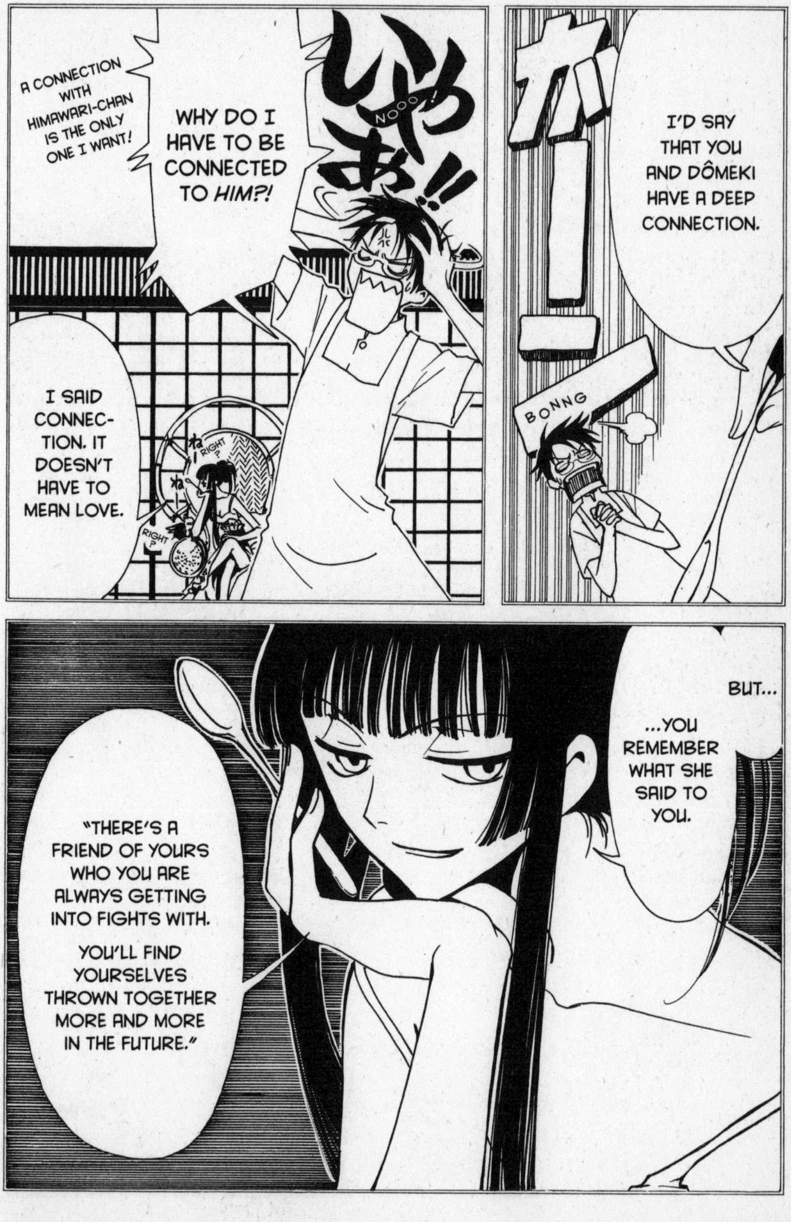
I'D SAY THAT YOU AND DÔMEKI HAVE A DEEP CONNECTION.
BONNG
WHY DO I HAVE TO BE CONNECTED TO HIM?!
A CONNECTION WITH HIMAWARI-CHAN IS THE ONLY ONE I WANT!
NOOO!
I SAID CONNECTION. IT DOESN'T HAVE TO MEAN LOVE.
RIGHT?
RIGHT?
BUT...
...YOU REMEMBER WHAT SHE SAID TO YOU.
"THERE'S A FRIEND OF YOURS WHO YOU ARE ALWAYS GETTING INTO FIGHTS WITH.
YOU'LL FIND YOURSELVES THROWN TOGETHER MORE AND MORE IN THE FUTURE."

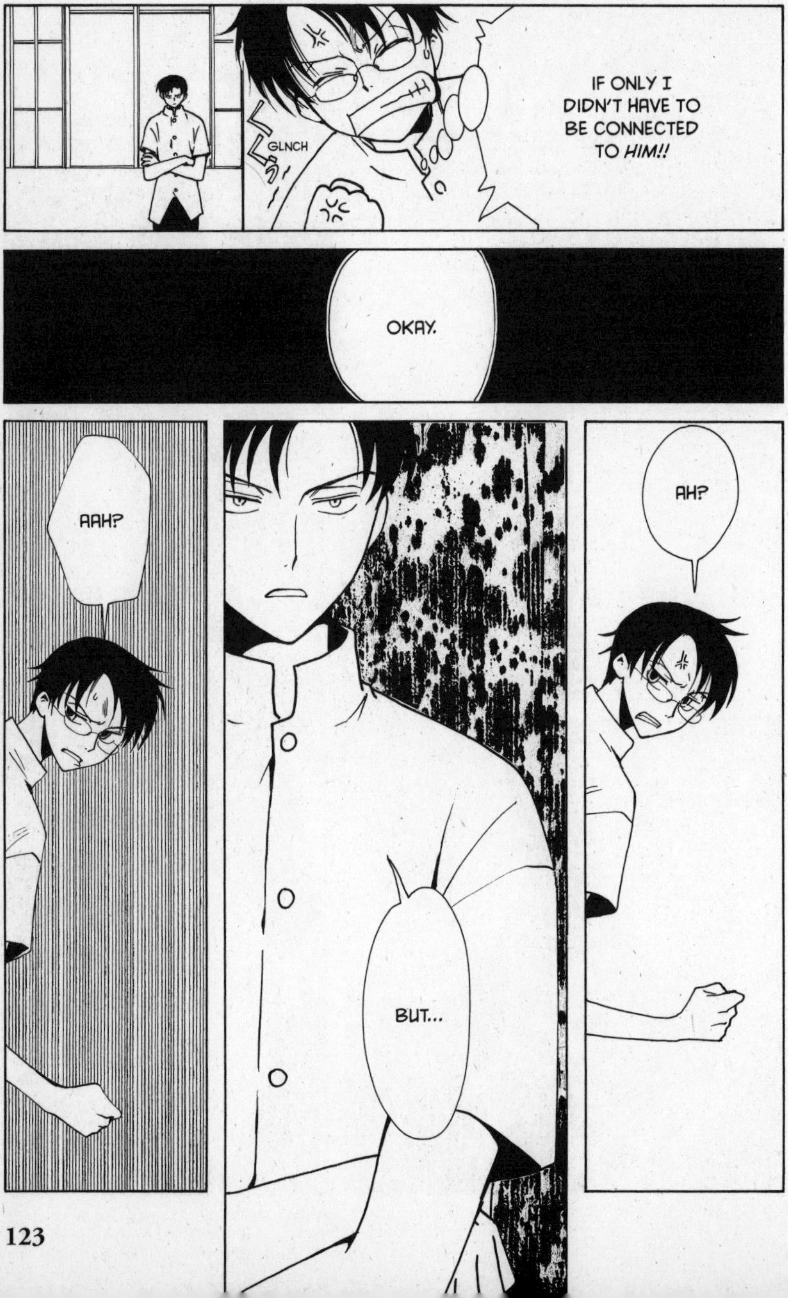
IF ONLY I DIDN'T HAVE TO BE CONNECTED TO *HIM!!*
GLNCH
OKAY.
AH?
BUT...
AAH?

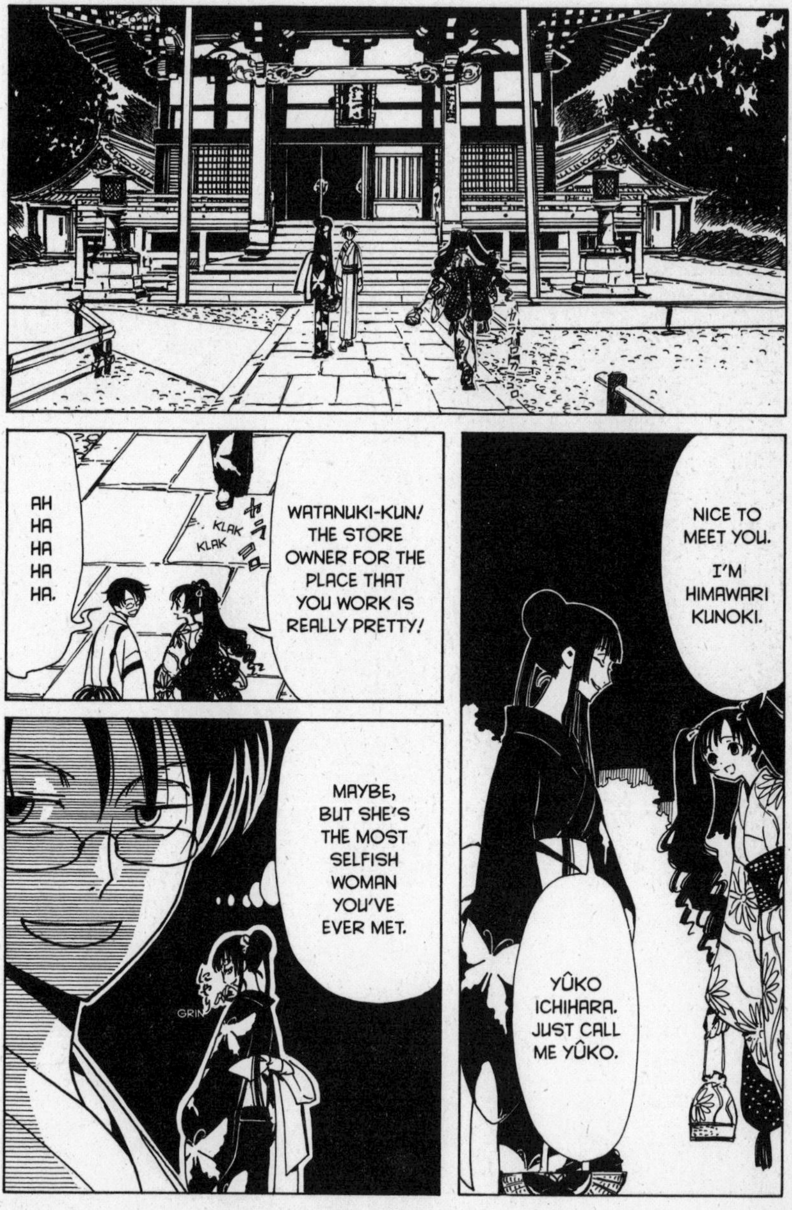
NICE TO MEET YOU.
I'M HIMAWARI KUNOKI.
YÛKO ICHIHARA. JUST CALL ME YÛKO.
WATANUKI-KUN! THE STORE OWNER FOR THE PLACE THAT YOU WORK IS REALLY PRETTY!
KLAK KLAK
AH HA HA HA HA.
MAYBE, BUT SHE'S THE MOST SELFISH WOMAN YOU'VE EVER MET.
GRIN

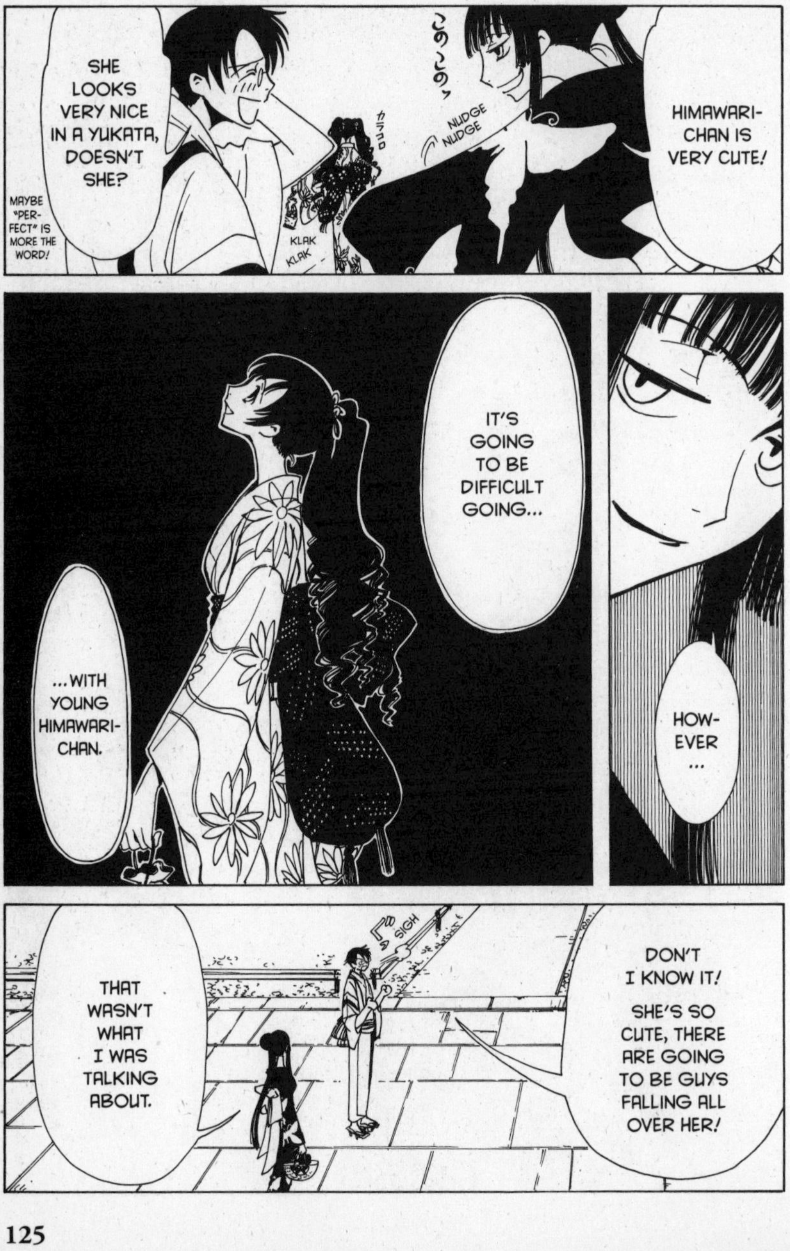
HIMAWARI-CHAN IS VERY CUTE!
NUDGE NUDGE
KLAK KLAK
SHE LOOKS VERY NICE IN A YUKATA, DOESN'T SHE?
MAYBE "PER-FECT" IS MORE THE WORD!
HOW-EVER...
IT'S GOING TO BE DIFFICULT GOING...
...WITH YOUNG HIMAWARI-CHAN.
DON'T I KNOW IT!
SHE'S SO CUTE, THERE ARE GOING TO BE GUYS FALLING ALL OVER HER!
SIGH
THAT WASN'T WHAT I WAS TALKING ABOUT.

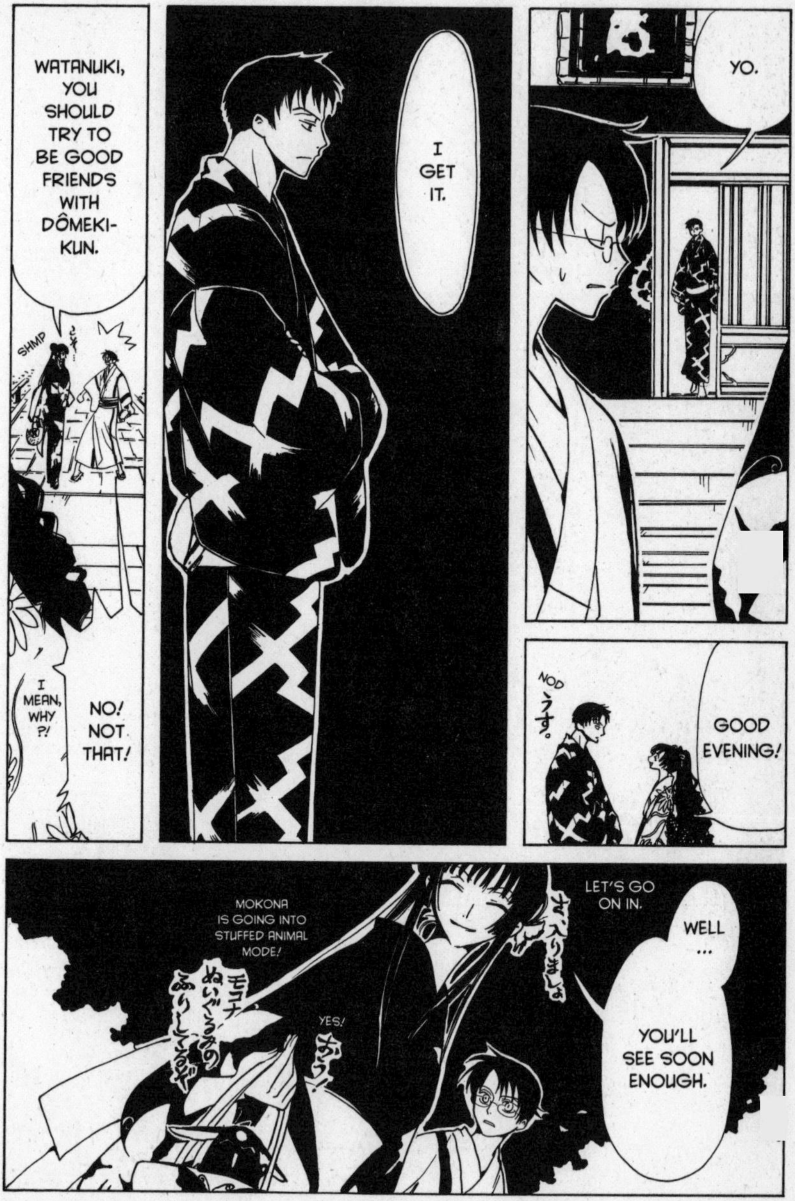
YO.
GOOD EVENING!
NOD うす。
I GET IT.
WATANUKI, YOU SHOULD TRY TO BE GOOD FRIENDS WITH DÔMEKI-KUN.
SHMP
NO! NOT THAT!
I MEAN, WHY ?!
WELL ...
YOU'LL SEE SOON ENOUGH.
LET'S GO ON IN.
さ、入りましょ
YES!
あう!
MOKONA IS GOING INTO STUFFED ANIMAL MODE!
モコナ ぬいぐるみのふりしてるぞ

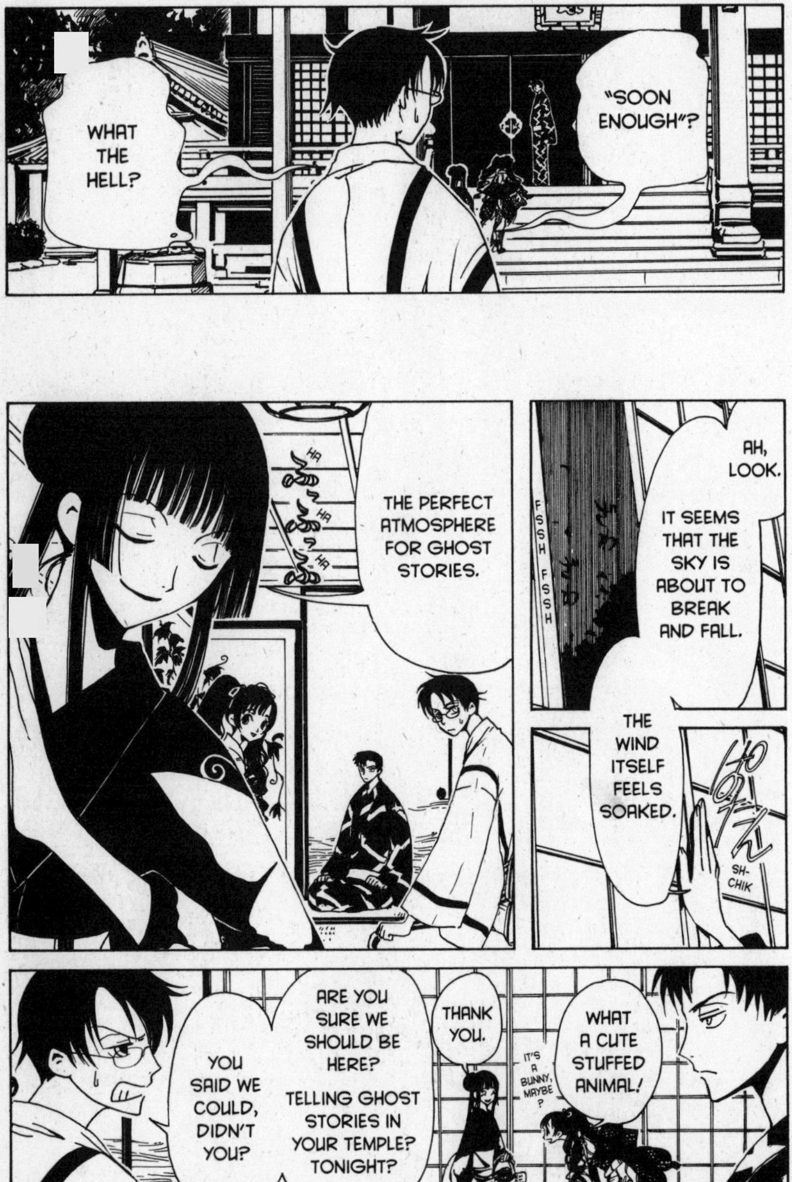
"SOON ENOUGH"?
WHAT THE HELL?
AH, LOOK.
IT SEEMS THAT THE SKY IS ABOUT TO BREAK AND FALL.
FSSH FSSH
THE WIND ITSELF FEELS SOAKED.
SH-CHIK
HA HA HA
THE PERFECT ATMOSPHERE FOR GHOST STORIES.
WHAT A CUTE STUFFED ANIMAL!
IT'S A BUNNY, MAYBE?
THANK YOU.
ARE YOU SURE WE SHOULD BE HERE?
TELLING GHOST STORIES IN YOUR TEMPLE? TONIGHT?
YOU SAID WE COULD, DIDN'T YOU?

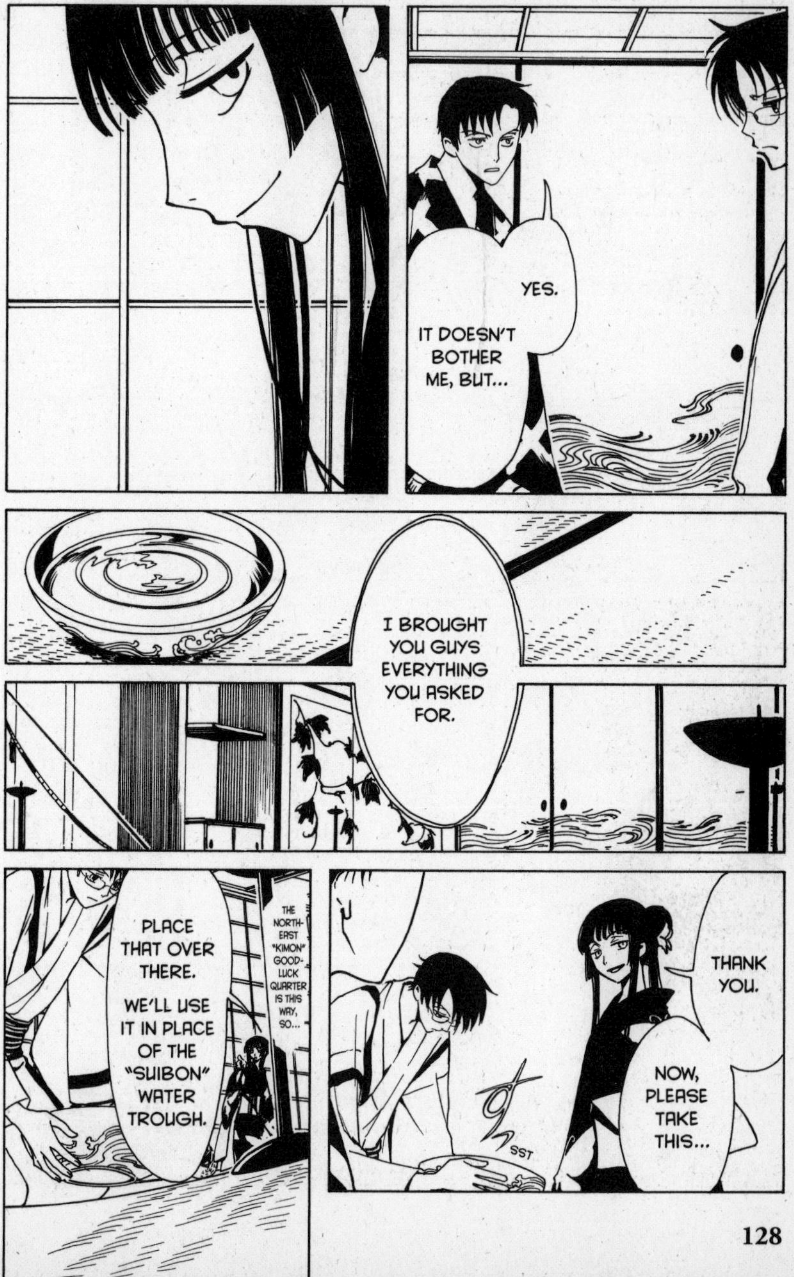
YES.
IT DOESN'T BOTHER ME, BUT...
I BROUGHT YOU GUYS EVERYTHING YOU ASKED FOR.
THANK YOU.
NOW, PLEASE TAKE THIS...
SST
THE NORTH-EAST "KIMON" GOOD-LUCK QUARTER IS THIS WAY, SO...
PLACE THAT OVER THERE.
WE'LL USE IT IN PLACE OF THE "SUIBON" WATER TROUGH.

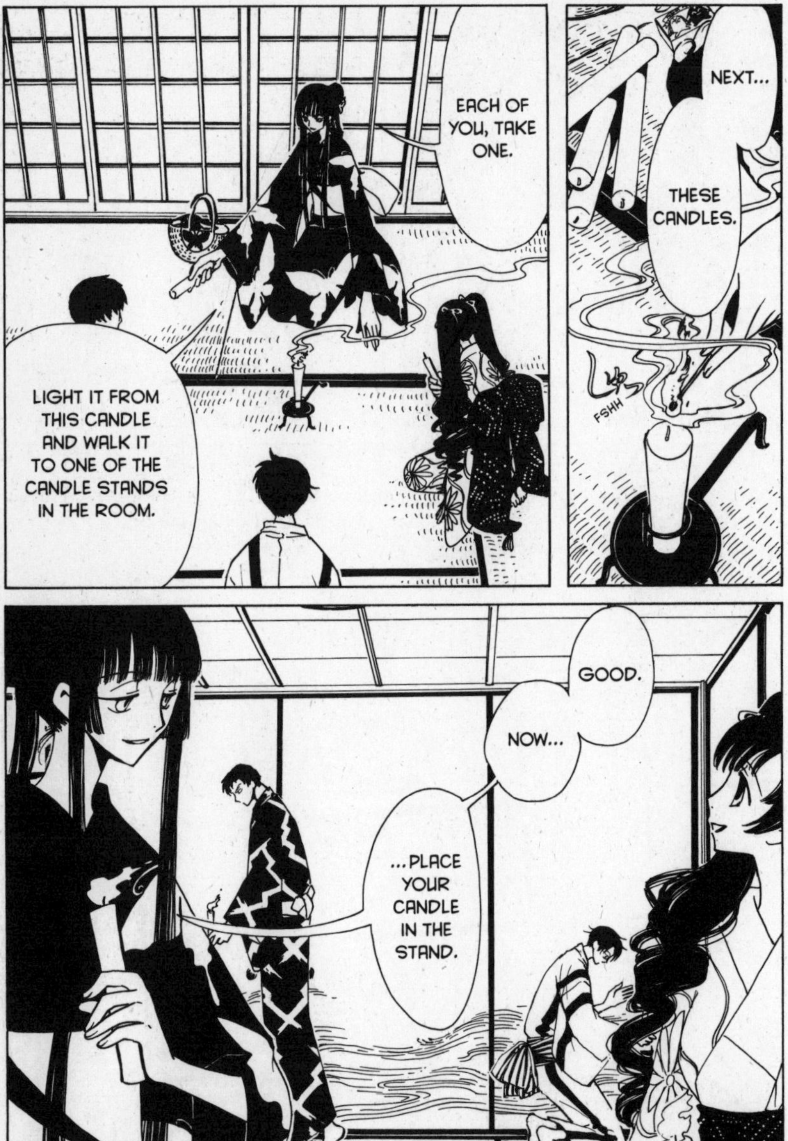
NEXT...
THESE CANDLES.
FSHH
EACH OF YOU, TAKE ONE.
LIGHT IT FROM THIS CANDLE AND WALK IT TO ONE OF THE CANDLE STANDS IN THE ROOM.
GOOD.
NOW...
...PLACE YOUR CANDLE IN THE STAND.

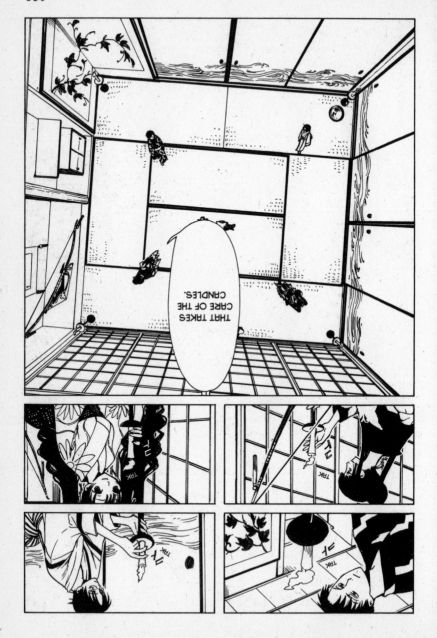

THAT TAKES
CARE OF THE
CANDLES.

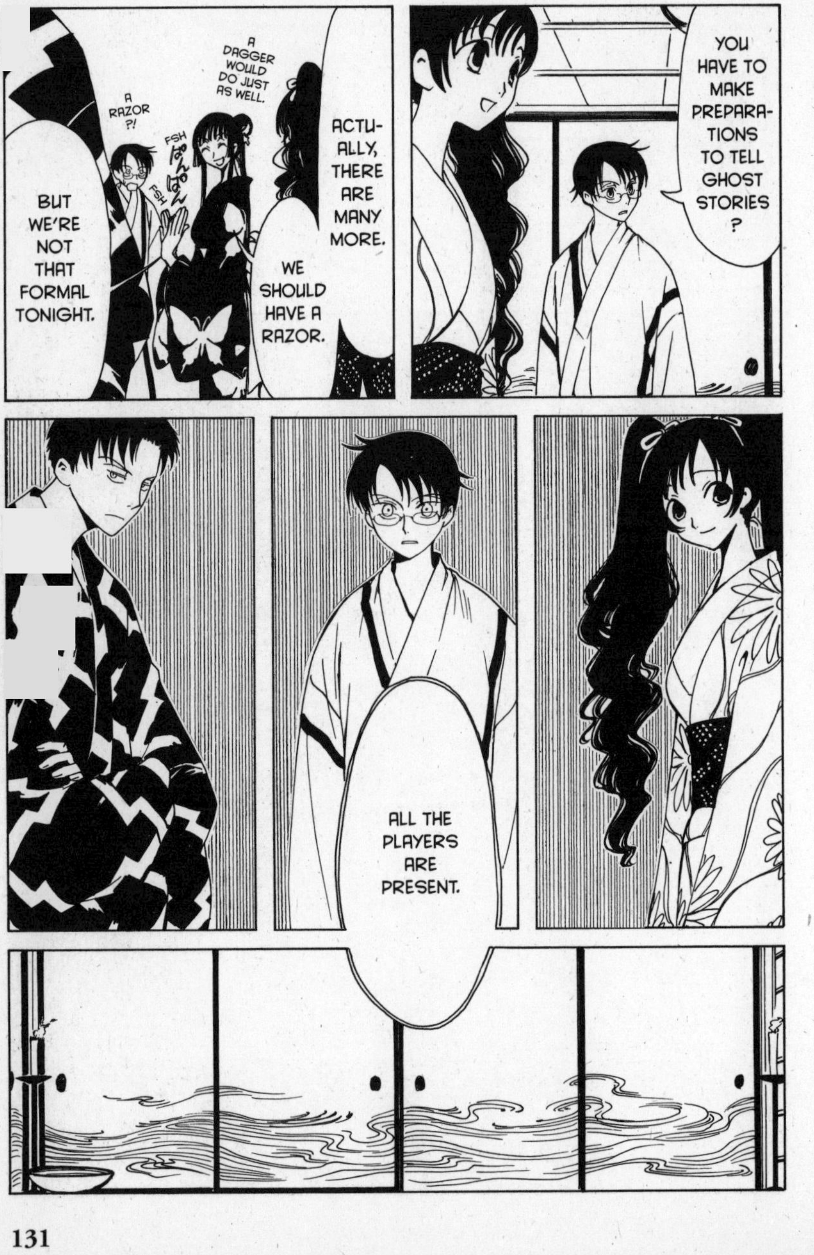
YOU HAVE TO MAKE PREPARATIONS TO TELL GHOST STORIES ?
ACTUALLY, THERE ARE MANY MORE.
WE SHOULD HAVE A RAZOR.
A DAGGER WOULD DO JUST AS WELL.
FSH
FSH
A RAZOR ?!
BUT WE'RE NOT THAT FORMAL TONIGHT.
ALL THE PLAYERS ARE PRESENT.

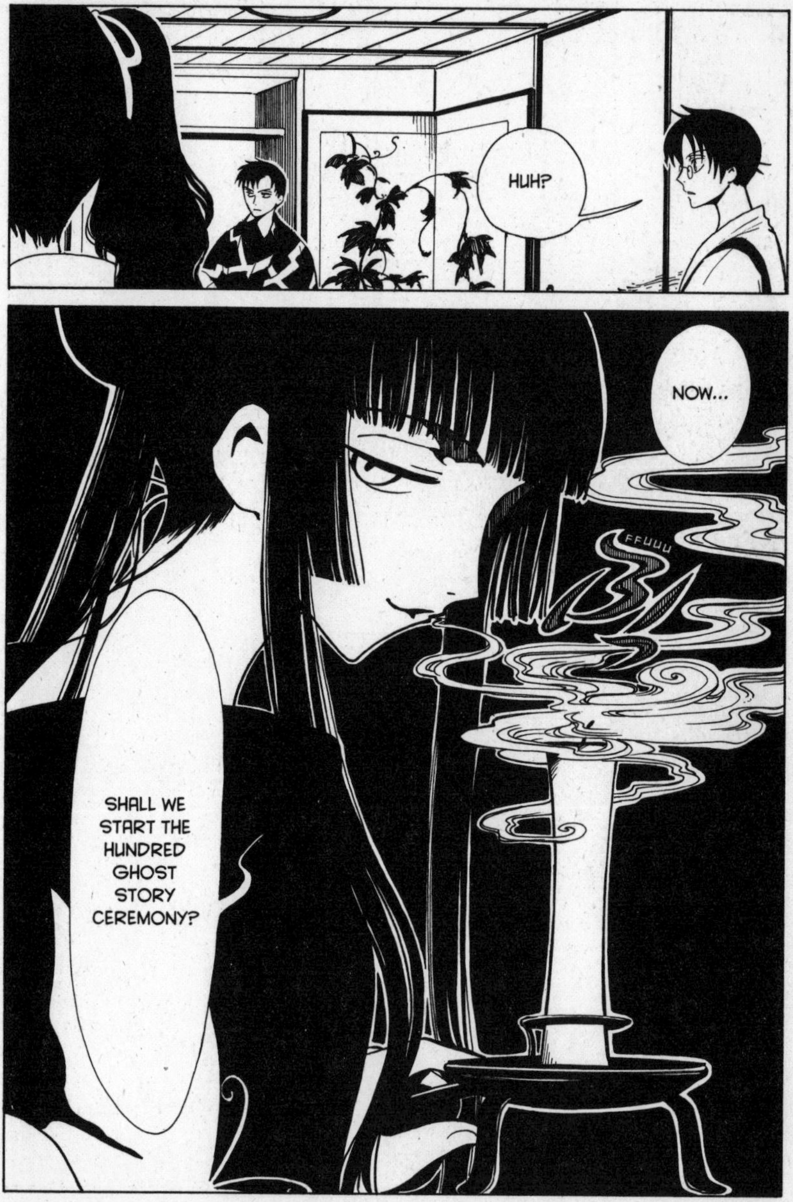
HUH?
NOW...
FFUUU
SHALL WE START THE HUNDRED GHOST STORY CEREMONY?

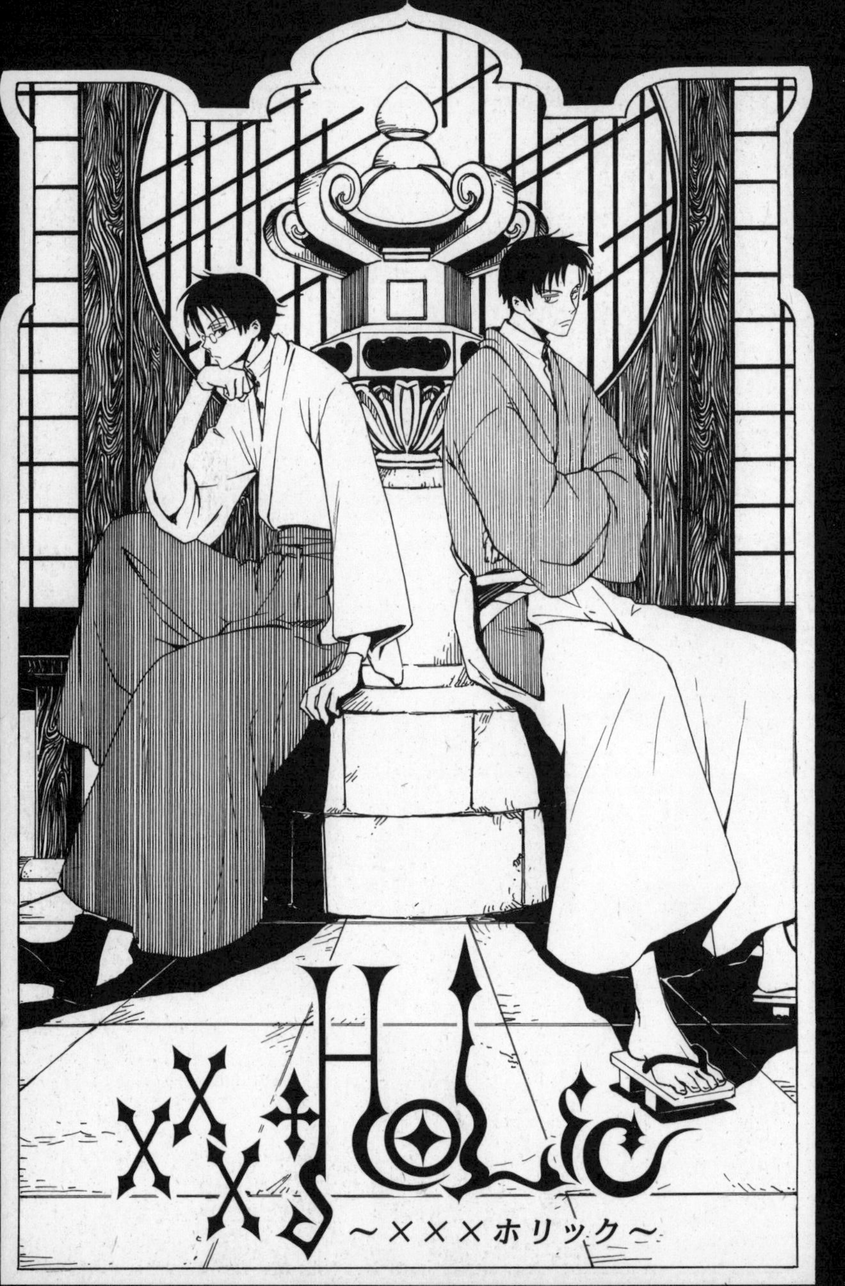
xxxHOLiC
~×××ホリック~

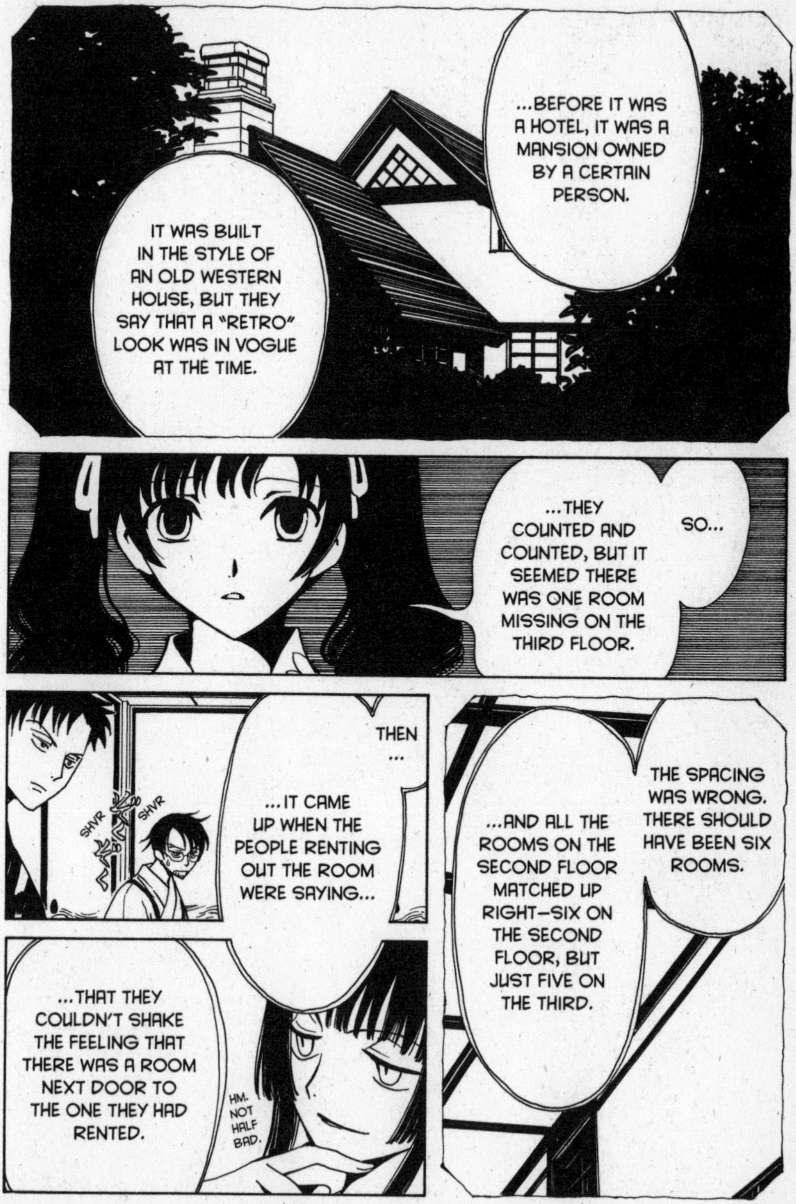
...BEFORE IT WAS A HOTEL, IT WAS A MANSION OWNED BY A CERTAIN PERSON.
IT WAS BUILT IN THE STYLE OF AN OLD WESTERN HOUSE, BUT THEY SAY THAT A "RETRO" LOOK WAS IN VOGUE AT THE TIME.
SO...
...THEY COUNTED AND COUNTED, BUT IT SEEMED THERE WAS ONE ROOM MISSING ON THE THIRD FLOOR.
THE SPACING WAS WRONG. THERE SHOULD HAVE BEEN SIX ROOMS.
...AND ALL THE ROOMS ON THE SECOND FLOOR MATCHED UP RIGHT—SIX ON THE SECOND FLOOR, BUT JUST FIVE ON THE THIRD.
THEN ...
...IT CAME UP WHEN THE PEOPLE RENTING OUT THE ROOM WERE SAYING...
SHVR
SHVR
...THAT THEY COULDN'T SHAKE THE FEELING THAT THERE WAS A ROOM NEXT DOOR TO THE ONE THEY HAD RENTED.
HM. NOT HALF BAD.

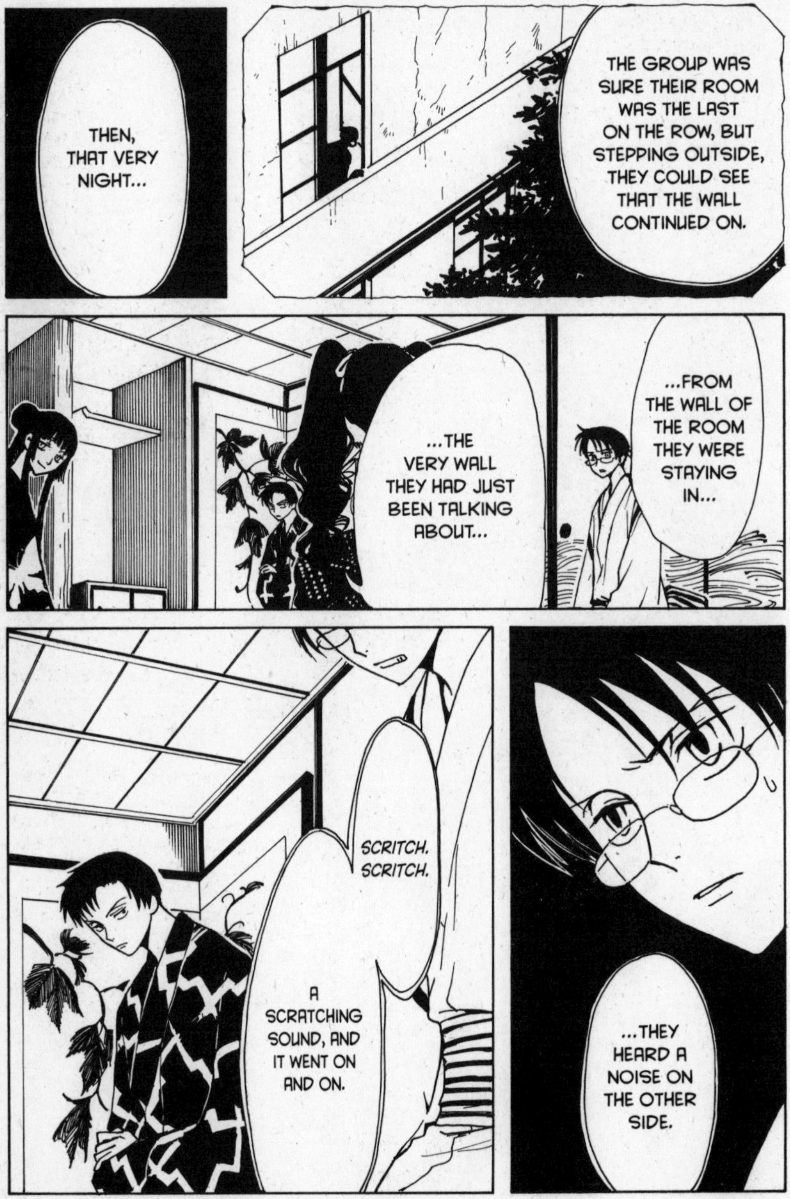
THE GROUP WAS SURE THEIR ROOM WAS THE LAST ON THE ROW, BUT STEPPING OUTSIDE, THEY COULD SEE THAT THE WALL CONTINUED ON.
THEN, THAT VERY NIGHT...
...FROM THE WALL OF THE ROOM THEY WERE STAYING IN...
...THE VERY WALL THEY HAD JUST BEEN TALKING ABOUT...
...THEY HEARD A NOISE ON THE OTHER SIDE.
SCRITCH. SCRITCH.
A SCRATCHING SOUND, AND IT WENT ON AND ON.

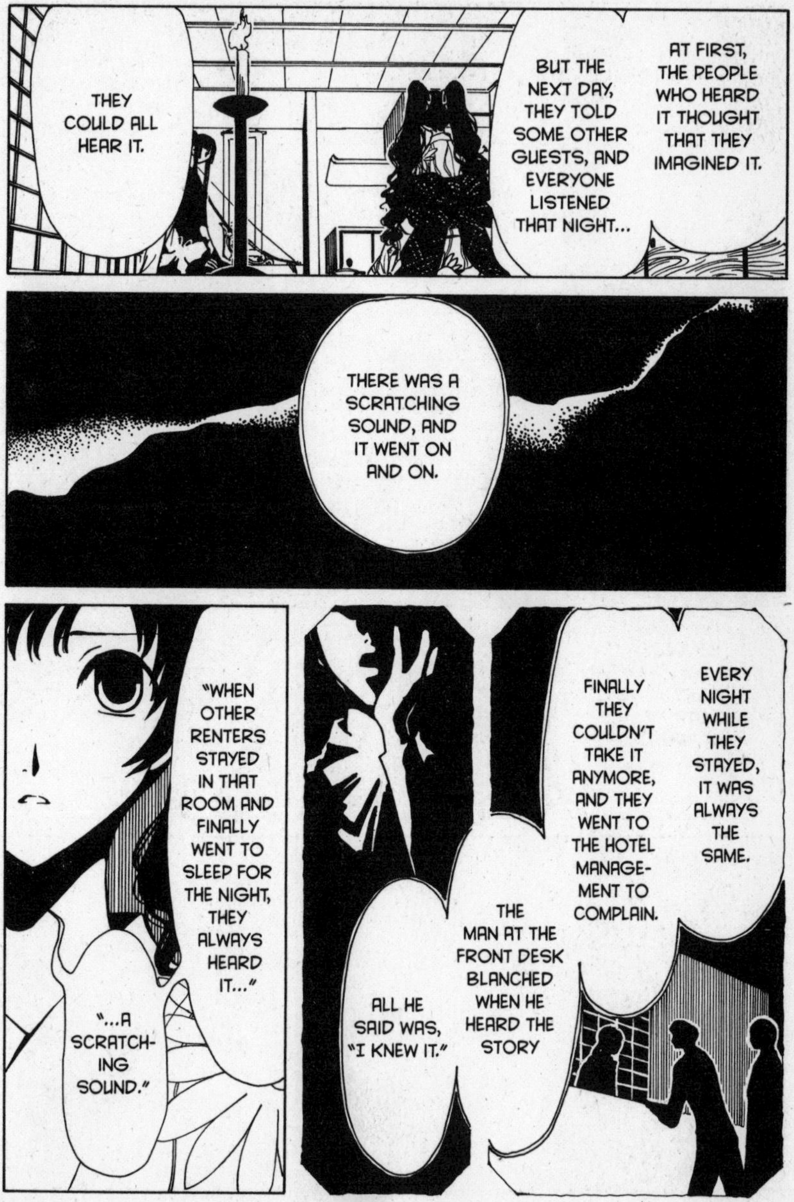
AT FIRST, THE PEOPLE WHO HEARD IT THOUGHT THAT THEY IMAGINED IT.
BUT THE NEXT DAY, THEY TOLD SOME OTHER GUESTS, AND EVERYONE LISTENED THAT NIGHT...
THEY COULD ALL HEAR IT.
THERE WAS A SCRATCHING SOUND, AND IT WENT ON AND ON.
EVERY NIGHT WHILE THEY STAYED, IT WAS ALWAYS THE SAME.
FINALLY THEY COULDN'T TAKE IT ANYMORE, AND THEY WENT TO THE HOTEL MANAGE-MENT TO COMPLAIN.
THE MAN AT THE FRONT DESK BLANCHED WHEN HE HEARD THE STORY
ALL HE SAID WAS, "I KNEW IT."
"WHEN OTHER RENTERS STAYED IN THAT ROOM AND FINALLY WENT TO SLEEP FOR THE NIGHT, THEY ALWAYS HEARD IT..."
"...A SCRATCH-ING SOUND."

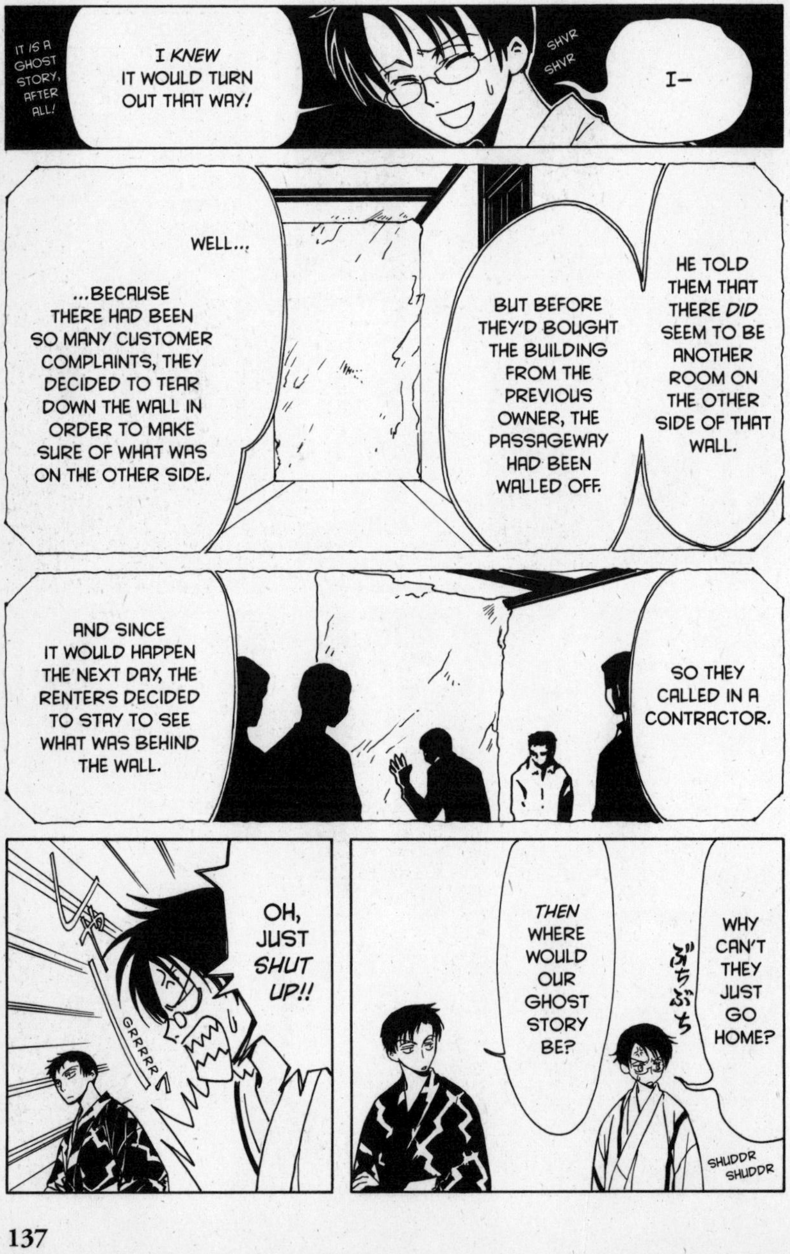
I–
SHVR SHVR
I *KNEW* IT WOULD TURN OUT THAT WAY!
IT IS A GHOST STORY, AFTER ALL!
HE TOLD THEM THAT THERE *DID* SEEM TO BE ANOTHER ROOM ON THE OTHER SIDE OF THAT WALL.
BUT BEFORE THEY'D BOUGHT THE BUILDING FROM THE PREVIOUS OWNER, THE PASSAGEWAY HAD BEEN WALLED OFF.
WELL...
...BECAUSE THERE HAD BEEN SO MANY CUSTOMER COMPLAINTS, THEY DECIDED TO TEAR DOWN THE WALL IN ORDER TO MAKE SURE OF WHAT WAS ON THE OTHER SIDE.
SO THEY CALLED IN A CONTRACTOR.
AND SINCE IT WOULD HAPPEN THE NEXT DAY, THE RENTERS DECIDED TO STAY TO SEE WHAT WAS BEHIND THE WALL.
WHY CAN'T THEY JUST GO HOME?
ぶちぶち
SHUDDR SHUDDR
THEN WHERE WOULD OUR GHOST STORY BE?
OH, JUST *SHUT UP!!*
GRRRR

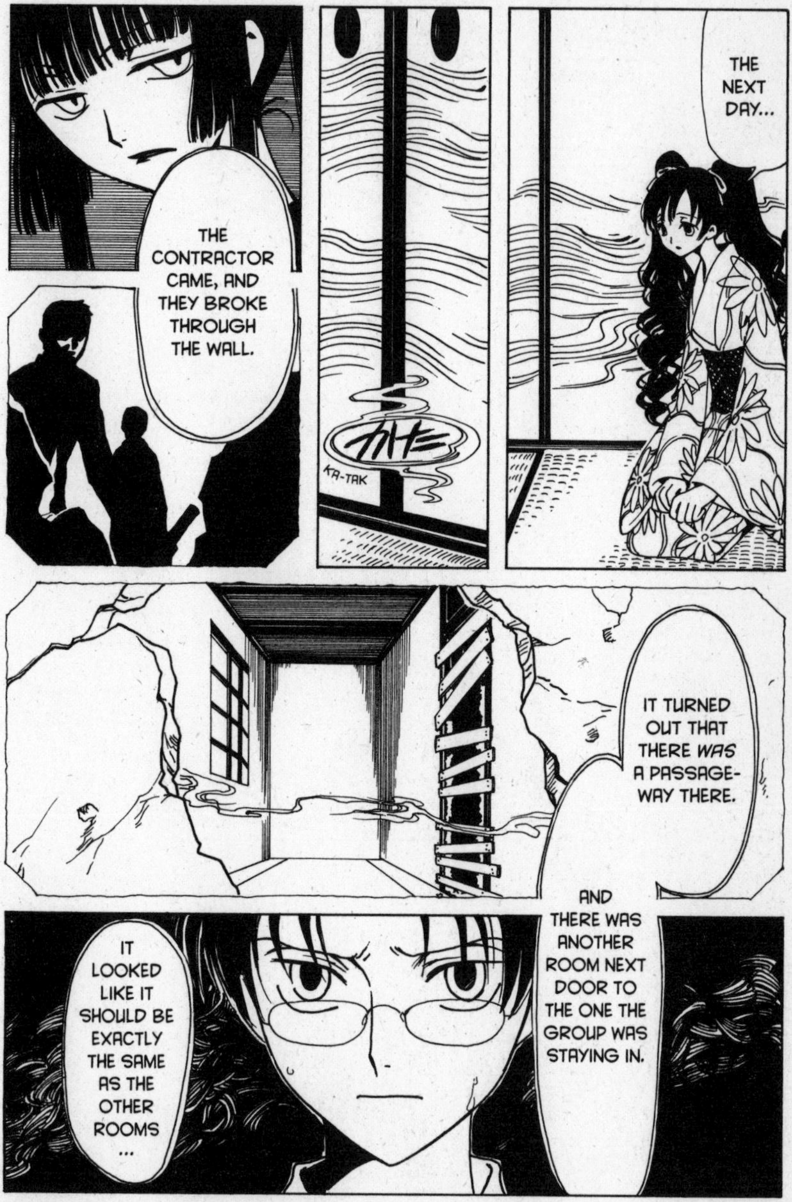
THE NEXT DAY...
カタ
KA-TAK
THE CONTRACTOR CAME, AND THEY BROKE THROUGH THE WALL.
IT TURNED OUT THAT THERE *WAS* A PASSAGE-WAY THERE.
AND THERE WAS ANOTHER ROOM NEXT DOOR TO THE ONE THE GROUP WAS STAYING IN.
IT LOOKED LIKE IT SHOULD BE EXACTLY THE SAME AS THE OTHER ROOMS ...

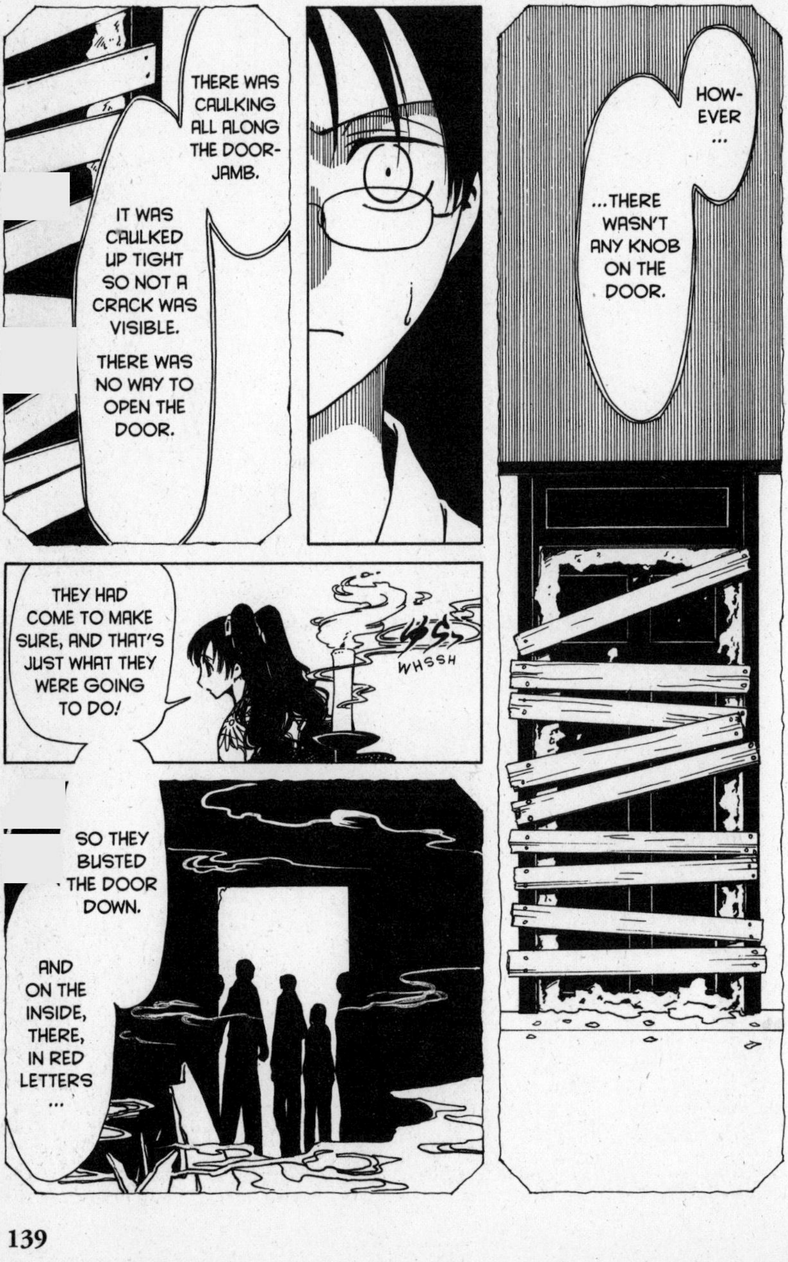
HOW-EVER ...
...THERE WASN'T ANY KNOB ON THE DOOR.
THERE WAS CAULKING ALL ALONG THE DOOR-JAMB.
IT WAS CAULKED UP TIGHT SO NOT A CRACK WAS VISIBLE.
THERE WAS NO WAY TO OPEN THE DOOR.
THEY HAD COME TO MAKE SURE, AND THAT'S JUST WHAT THEY WERE GOING TO DO!
WHSSH
SO THEY BUSTED THE DOOR DOWN.
AND ON THE INSIDE, THERE, IN RED LETTERS ...

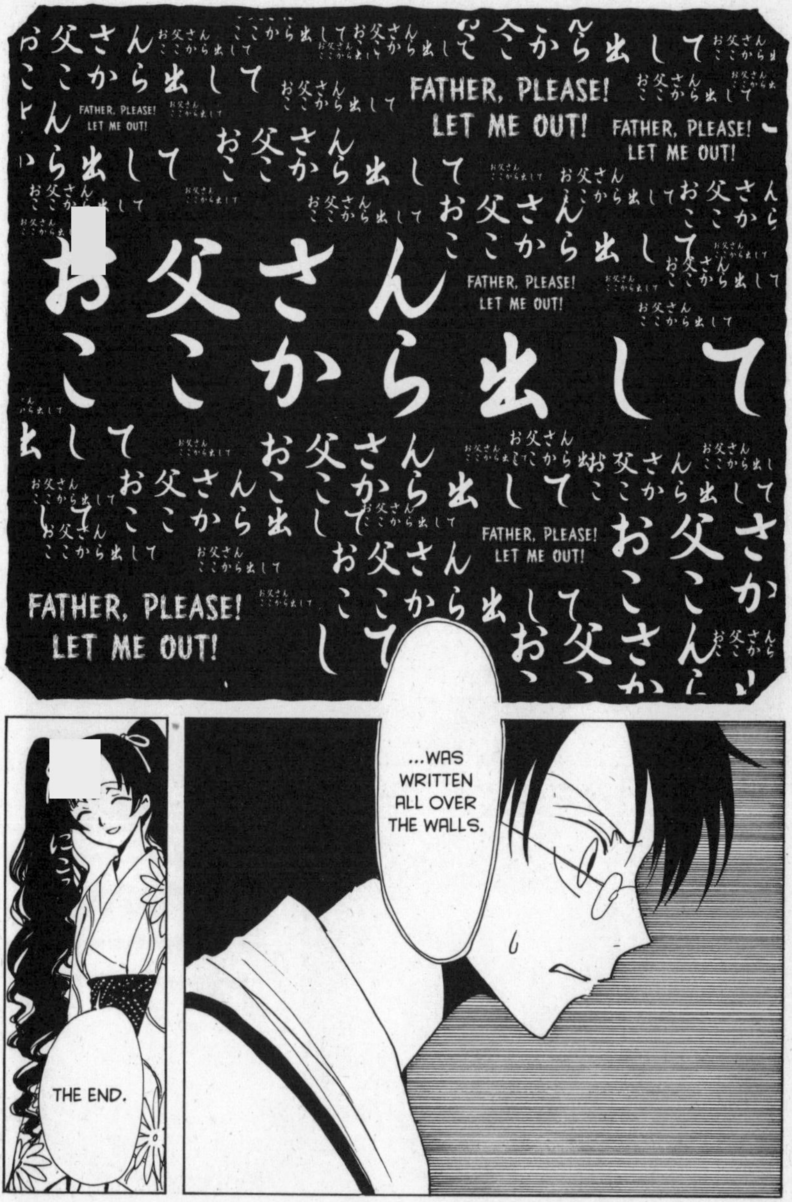
お父さん
ここから出して
FATHER, PLEASE!
LET ME OUT!
...WAS WRITTEN ALL OVER THE WALLS.
にこっ
THE END.

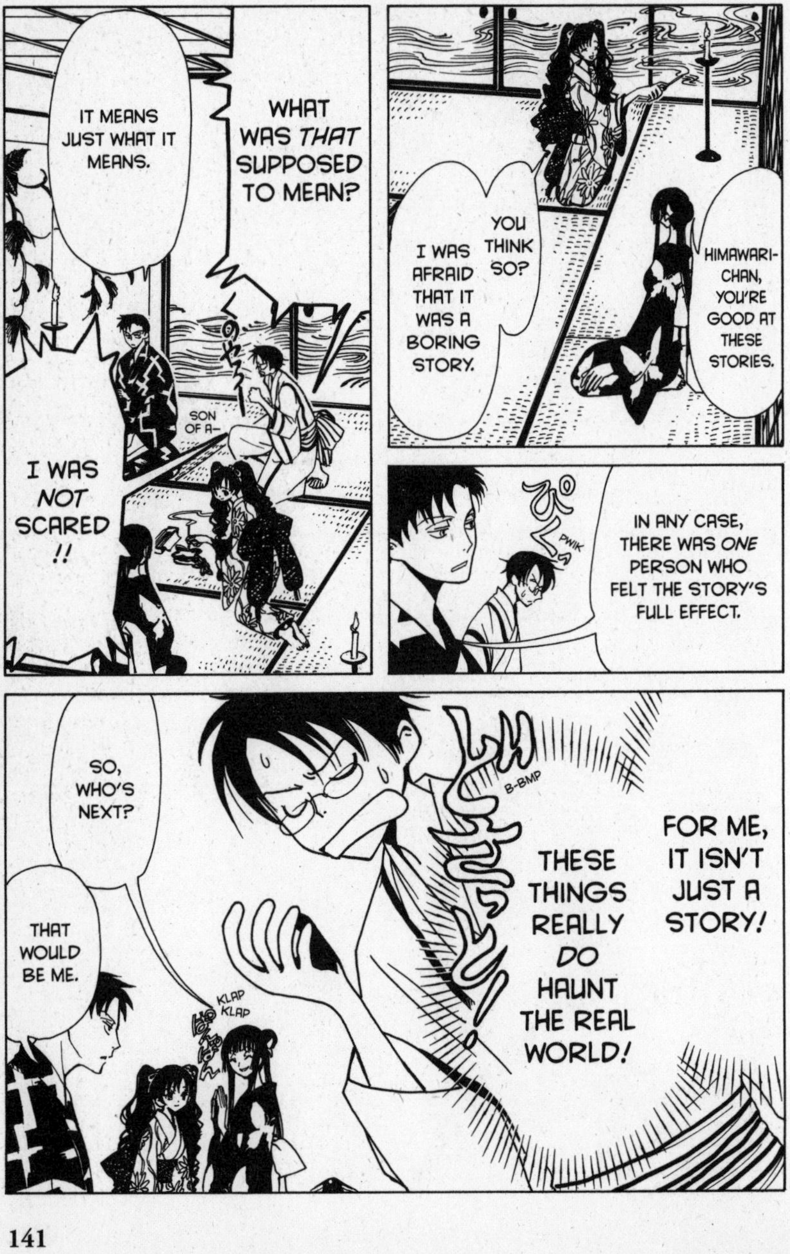
HIMAWARI-CHAN, YOU'RE GOOD AT THESE STORIES.
YOU THINK SO?
I WAS AFRAID THAT IT WAS A BORING STORY.
IN ANY CASE, THERE WAS *ONE* PERSON WHO FELT THE STORY'S FULL EFFECT.
PWIK
WHAT WAS *THAT* SUPPOSED TO MEAN?
IT MEANS JUST WHAT IT MEANS.
SON OF A—
I WAS *NOT* SCARED !!
FOR ME, IT ISN'T JUST A STORY!
THESE THINGS REALLY *DO* HAUNT THE REAL WORLD!
B-BMP
SO, WHO'S NEXT?
THAT WOULD BE ME.
KLAP KLAP

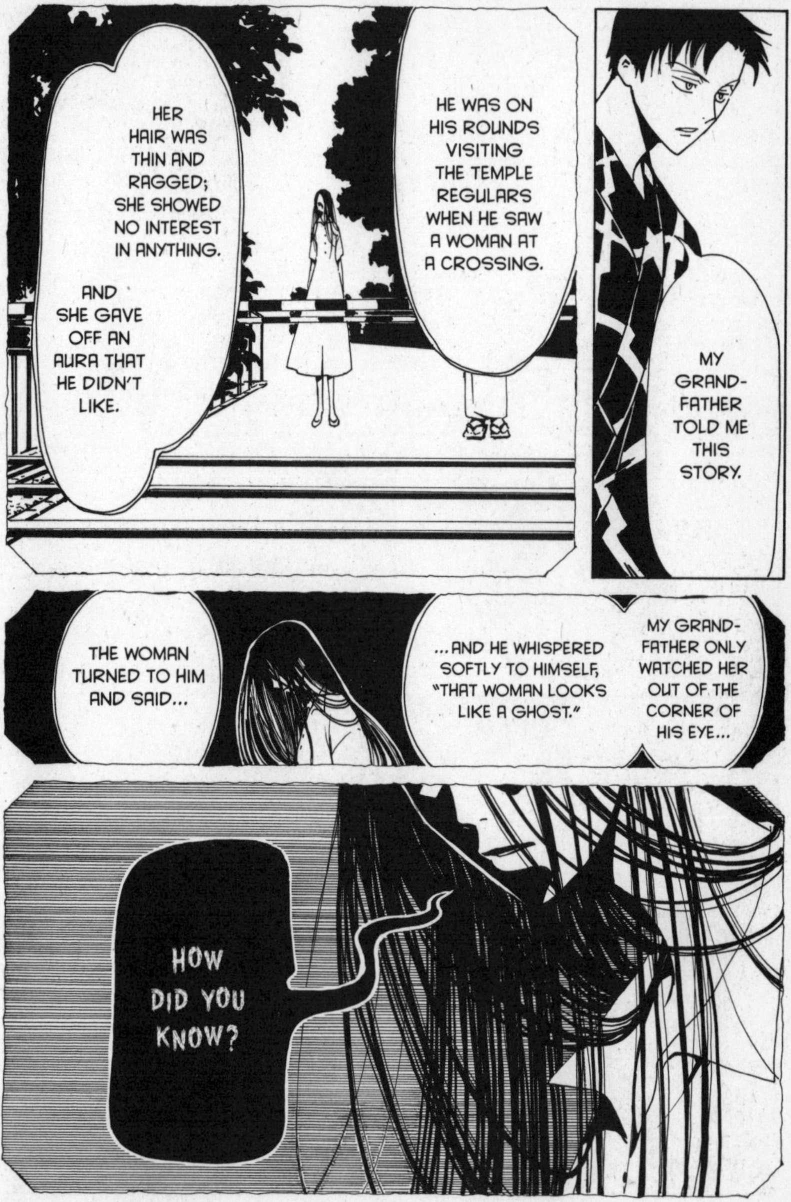
MY GRAND-FATHER TOLD ME THIS STORY.
HE WAS ON HIS ROUNDS VISITING THE TEMPLE REGULARS WHEN HE SAW A WOMAN AT A CROSSING.
HER HAIR WAS THIN AND RAGGED; SHE SHOWED NO INTEREST IN ANYTHING.
AND SHE GAVE OFF AN AURA THAT HE DIDN'T LIKE.
MY GRAND-FATHER ONLY WATCHED HER OUT OF THE CORNER OF HIS EYE...
...AND HE WHISPERED SOFTLY TO HIMSELF, "THAT WOMAN LOOKS LIKE A GHOST."
THE WOMAN TURNED TO HIM AND SAID...
HOW DID YOU KNOW?

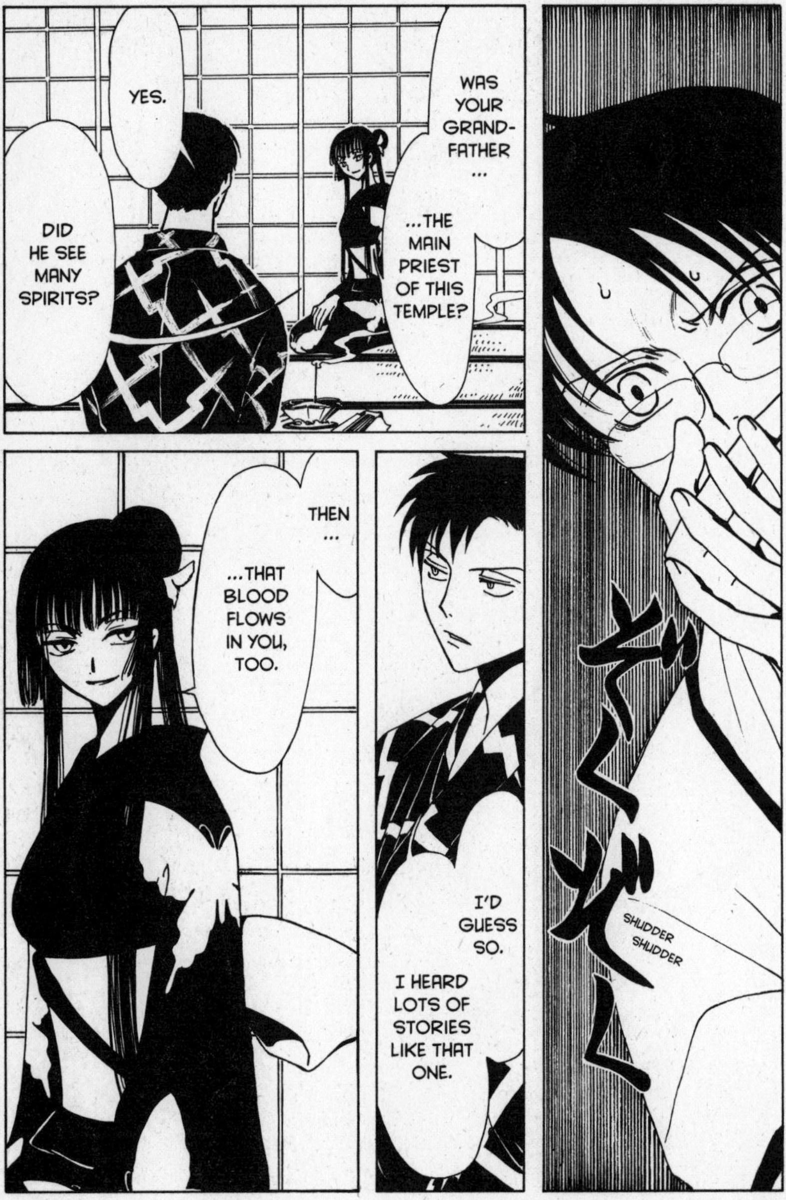

SHUDDER SHUDDER
WAS YOUR GRAND-FATHER ...
...THE MAIN PRIEST OF THIS TEMPLE?
YES.
DID HE SEE MANY SPIRITS?
I'D GUESS SO.
I HEARD LOTS OF STORIES LIKE THAT ONE.
THEN ...
...THAT BLOOD FLOWS IN YOU, TOO.

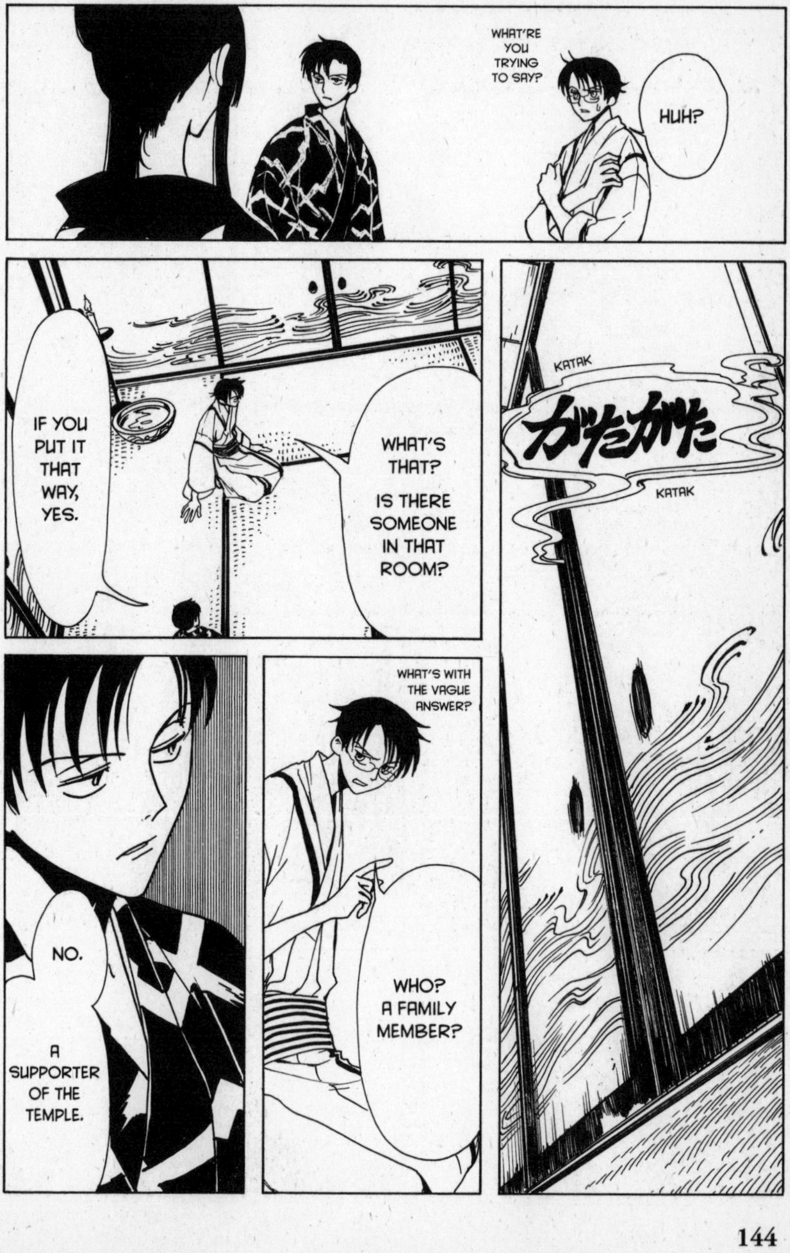
HUH?
WHAT'RE YOU TRYING TO SAY?
がたがた
KATAK KATAK
WHAT'S THAT?
IS THERE SOMEONE IN THAT ROOM?
IF YOU PUT IT THAT WAY, YES.
WHAT'S WITH THE VAGUE ANSWER?
WHO? A FAMILY MEMBER?
NO.
A SUPPORTER OF THE TEMPLE.

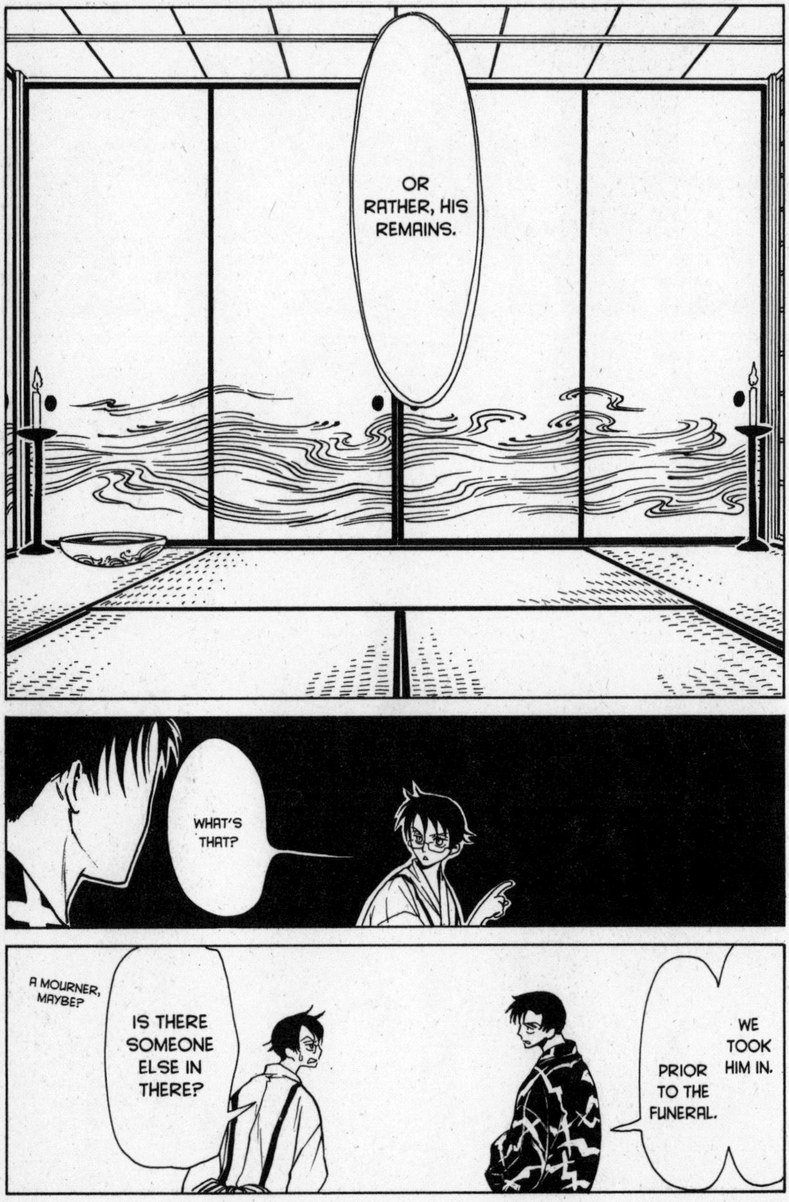
OR RATHER, HIS REMAINS.
WHAT'S THAT?
WE TOOK HIM IN.
PRIOR TO THE FUNERAL.
IS THERE SOMEONE ELSE IN THERE?
A MOURNER, MAYBE?

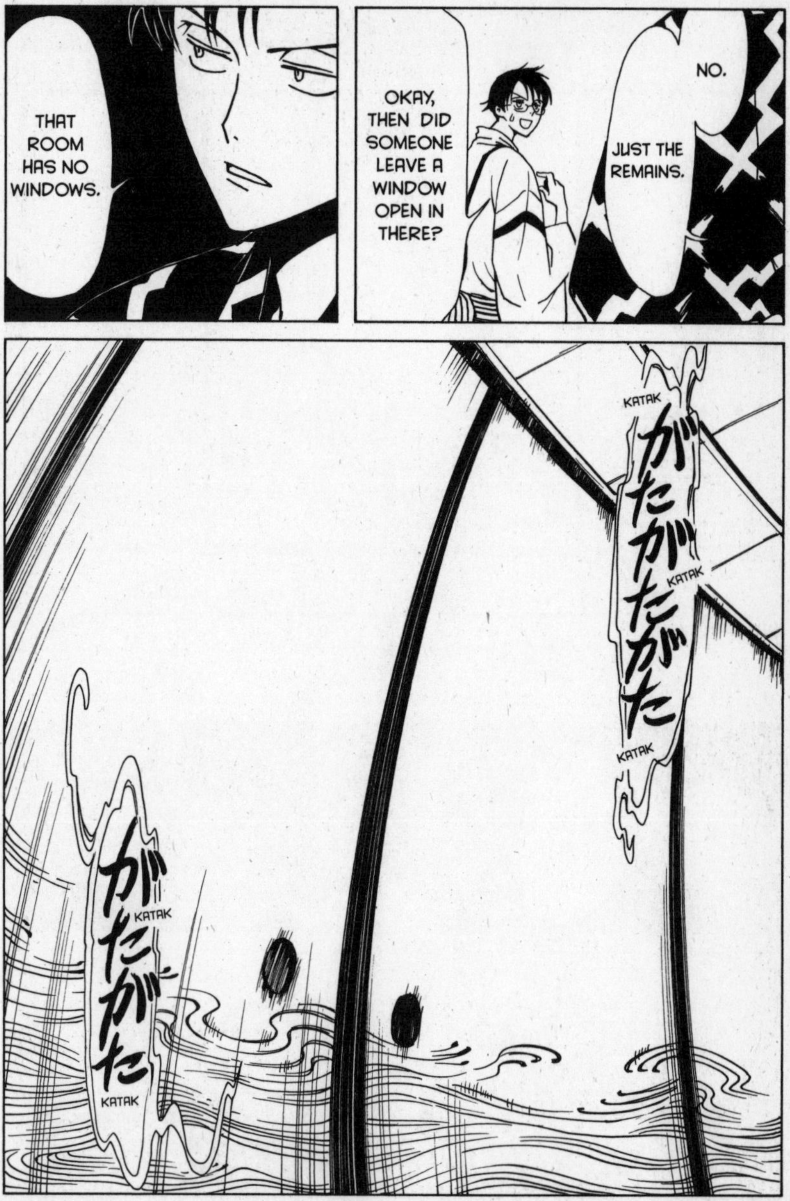
NO.
JUST THE REMAINS.
OKAY, THEN DID SOMEONE LEAVE A WINDOW OPEN IN THERE?
THAT ROOM HAS NO WINDOWS.
がたがたがたがた
KATAK
KATAK
KATAK
がたがた
KATAK
KATAK

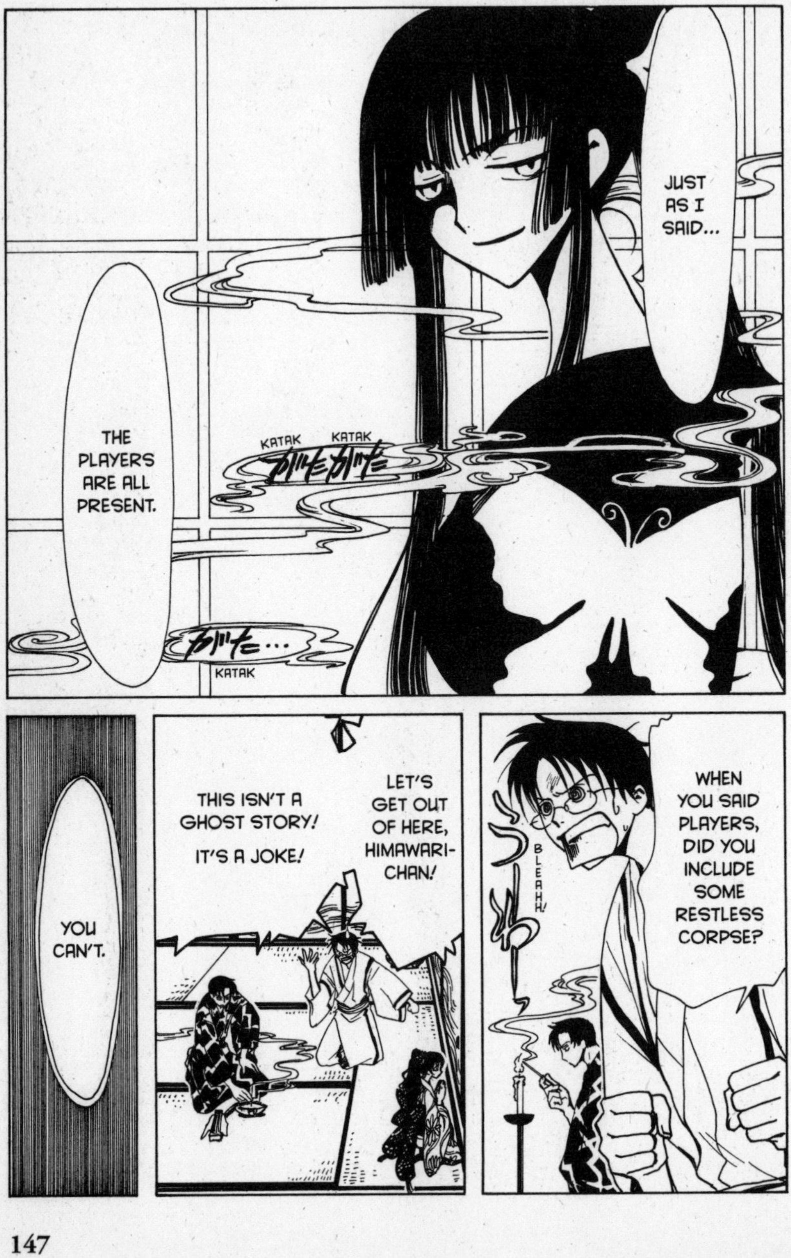
JUST AS I SAID...
KATAK KATAK
THE PLAYERS ARE ALL PRESENT.
KATAK
WHEN YOU SAID PLAYERS, DID YOU INCLUDE SOME RESTLESS CORPSE?
BLEAHH!
LET'S GET OUT OF HERE, HIMAWARI-CHAN!
THIS ISN'T A GHOST STORY!
IT'S A JOKE!
YOU CAN'T.

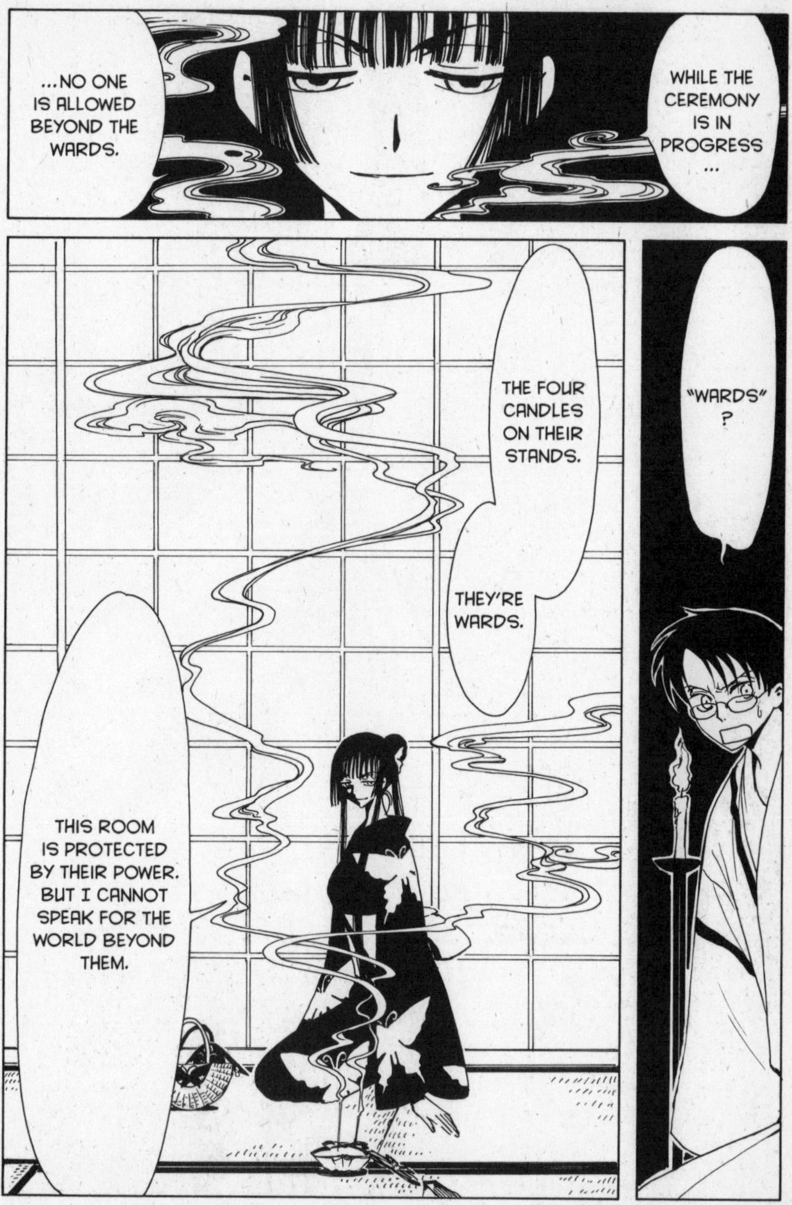
WHILE THE CEREMONY IS IN PROGRESS ...
...NO ONE IS ALLOWED BEYOND THE WARDS.
"WARDS" ?
THE FOUR CANDLES ON THEIR STANDS.
THEY'RE WARDS.
THIS ROOM IS PROTECTED BY THEIR POWER. BUT I CANNOT SPEAK FOR THE WORLD BEYOND THEM.

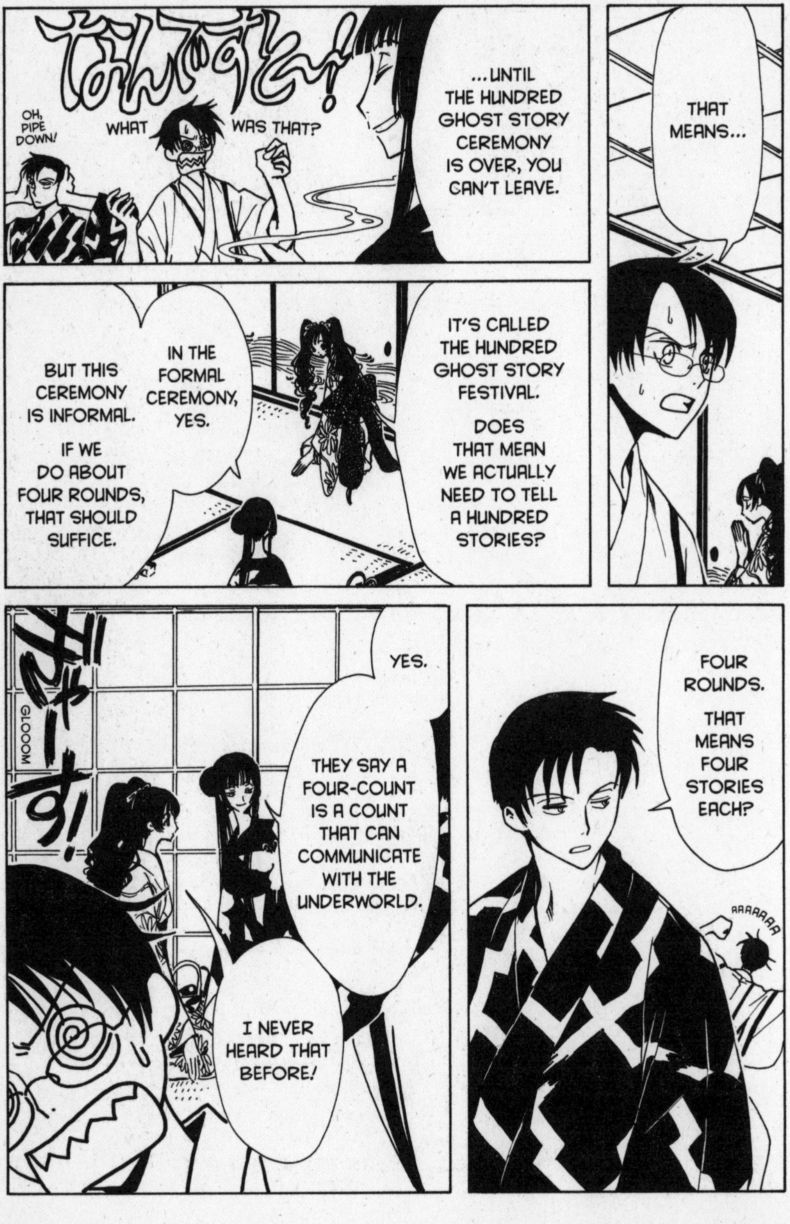
THAT MEANS...
...UNTIL THE HUNDRED GHOST STORY CEREMONY IS OVER, YOU CAN'T LEAVE.
なんですと～!
WHAT WAS THAT?
OH, PIPE DOWN!
IT'S CALLED THE HUNDRED GHOST STORY FESTIVAL.
DOES THAT MEAN WE ACTUALLY NEED TO TELL A HUNDRED STORIES?
IN THE FORMAL CEREMONY, YES.
BUT THIS CEREMONY IS INFORMAL.
IF WE DO ABOUT FOUR ROUNDS, THAT SHOULD SUFFICE.
FOUR ROUNDS.
THAT MEANS FOUR STORIES EACH?
AAAAAAA
YES.
THEY SAY A FOUR-COUNT IS A COUNT THAT CAN COMMUNICATE WITH THE UNDERWORLD.
GLOOOM
I NEVER HEARD THAT BEFORE!

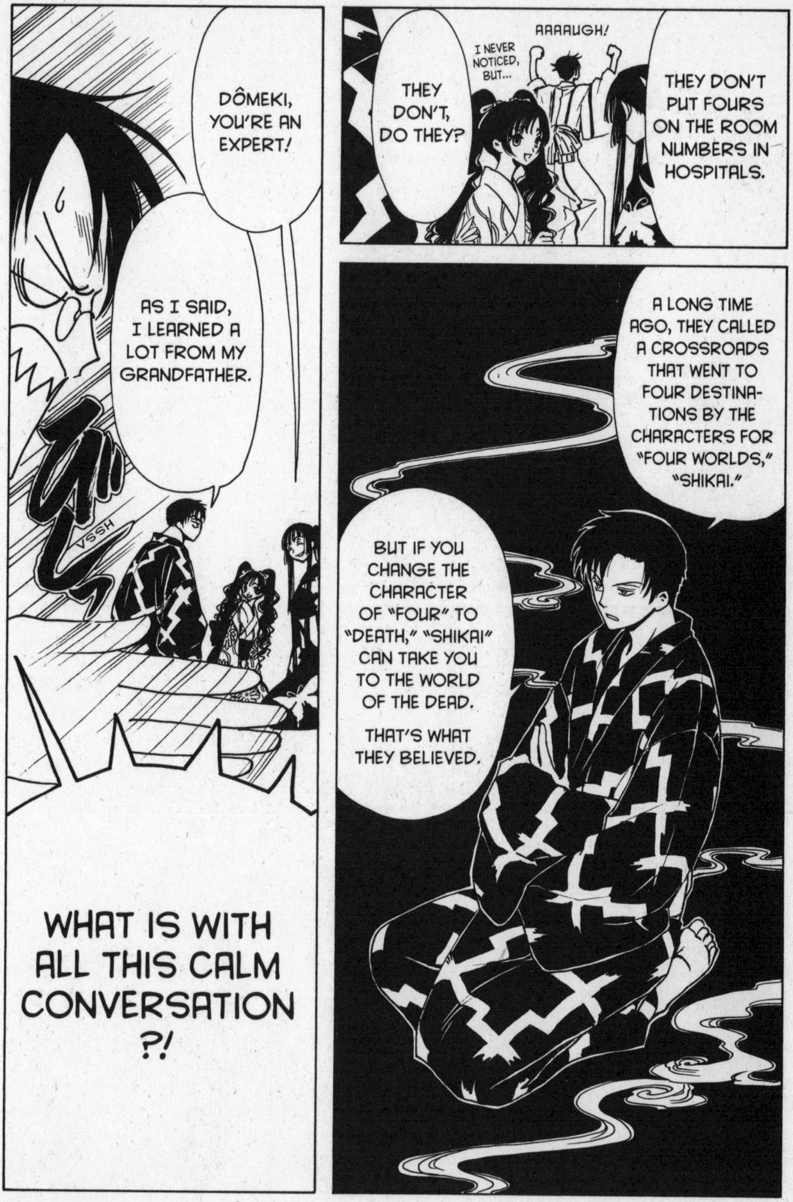
THEY DON'T PUT FOURS ON THE ROOM NUMBERS IN HOSPITALS.
AAAAAUGH!
I NEVER NOTICED, BUT...
THEY DON'T, DO THEY?
A LONG TIME AGO, THEY CALLED A CROSSROADS THAT WENT TO FOUR DESTINA-TIONS BY THE CHARACTERS FOR "FOUR WORLDS," "SHIKAI."
BUT IF YOU CHANGE THE CHARACTER OF "FOUR" TO "DEATH," "SHIKAI" CAN TAKE YOU TO THE WORLD OF THE DEAD.
THAT'S WHAT THEY BELIEVED.
DÔMEKI, YOU'RE AN EXPERT!
AS I SAID, I LEARNED A LOT FROM MY GRANDFATHER.
VSSH
WHAT IS WITH ALL THIS CALM CONVERSATION ?!

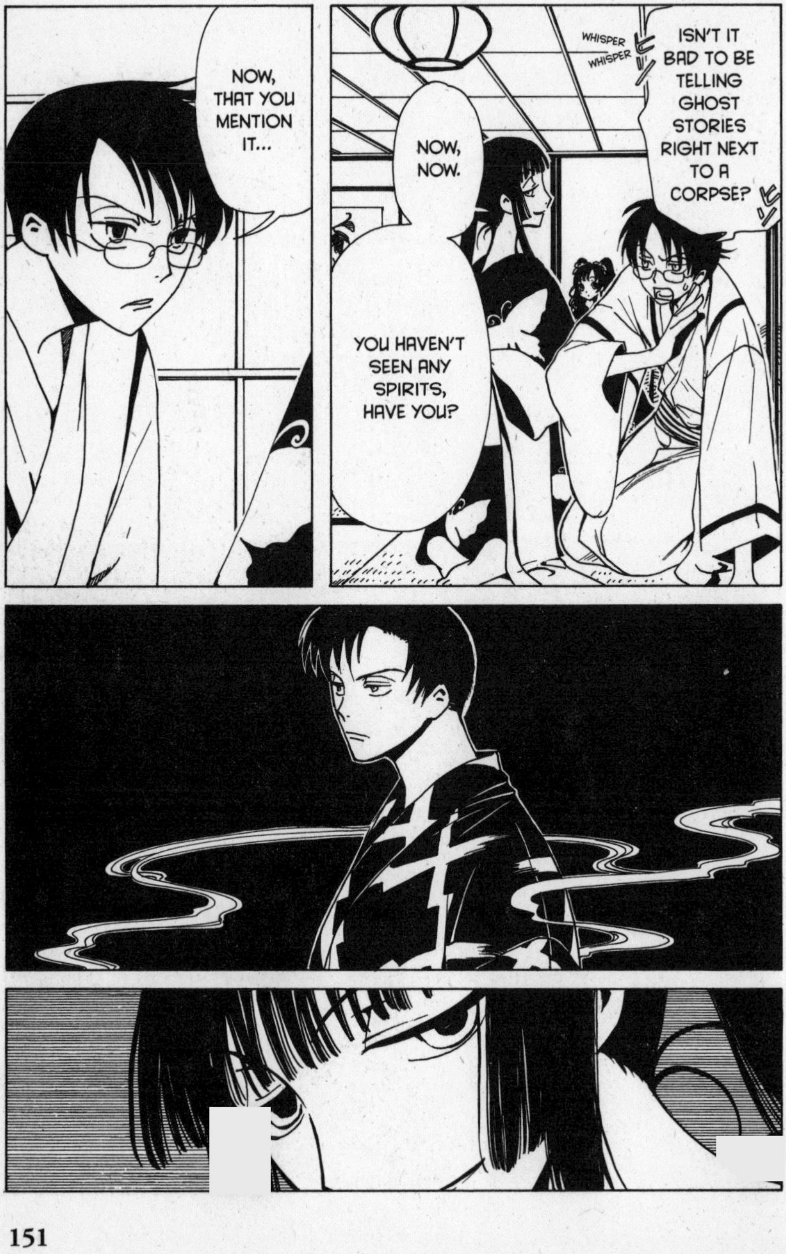
WHISPER
WHISPER
ISN'T IT BAD TO BE TELLING GHOST STORIES RIGHT NEXT TO A CORPSE?
NOW, NOW.
YOU HAVEN'T SEEN ANY SPIRITS, HAVE YOU?
NOW, THAT YOU MENTION IT...

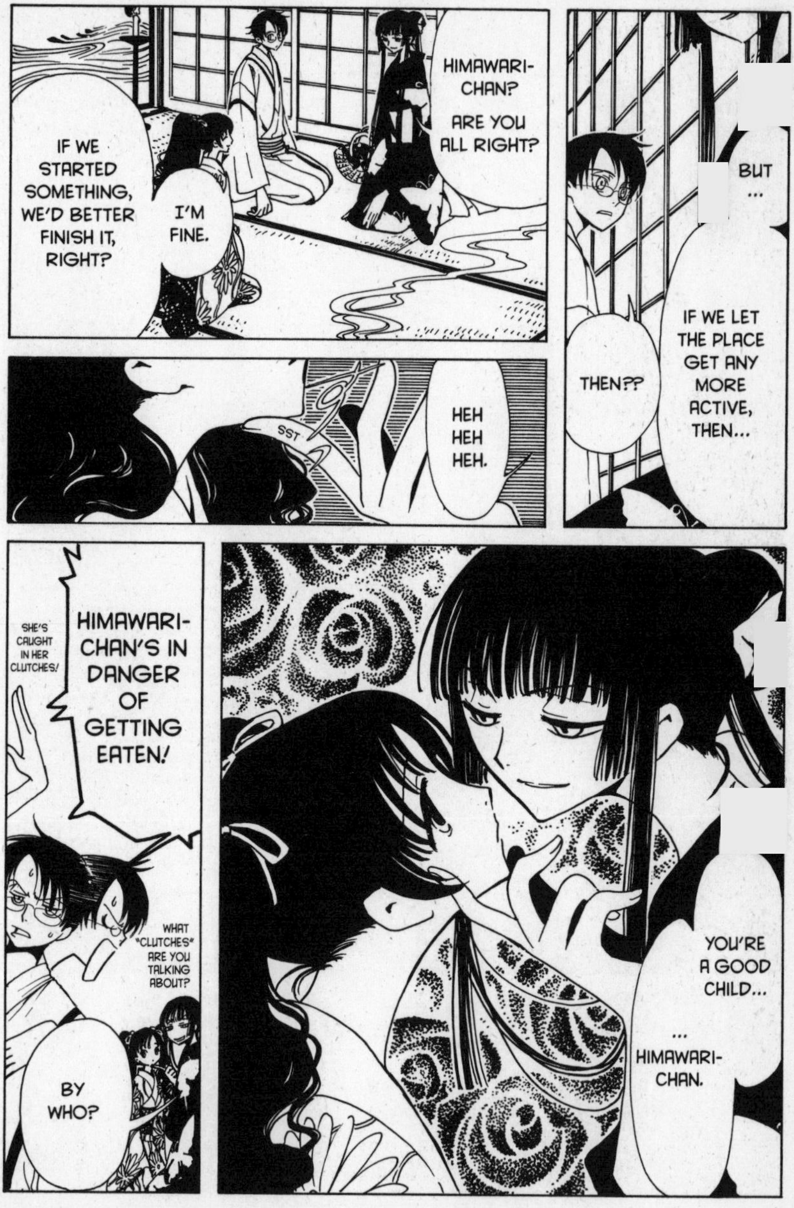
BUT ...
IF WE LET THE PLACE GET ANY MORE ACTIVE, THEN...
THEN??
HIMAWARI-CHAN?
ARE YOU ALL RIGHT?
I'M FINE.
IF WE STARTED SOMETHING, WE'D BETTER FINISH IT, RIGHT?
HEH HEH HEH.
SST
YOU'RE A GOOD CHILD...
... HIMAWARI-CHAN.
HIMAWARI-CHAN'S IN DANGER OF GETTING EATEN!
SHE'S CAUGHT IN HER CLUTCHES!
WHAT "CLUTCHES" ARE YOU TALKING ABOUT?
BY WHO?

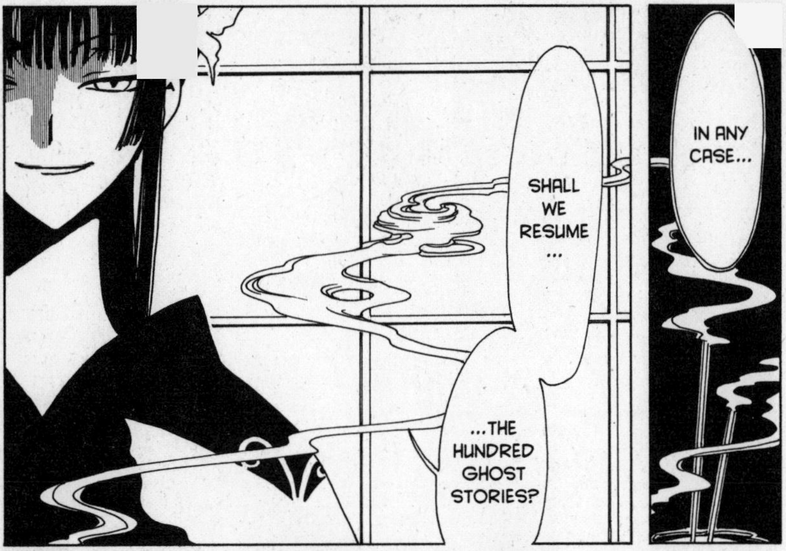
IN ANY CASE...
SHALL WE RESUME ...
...THE HUNDRED GHOST STORIES?

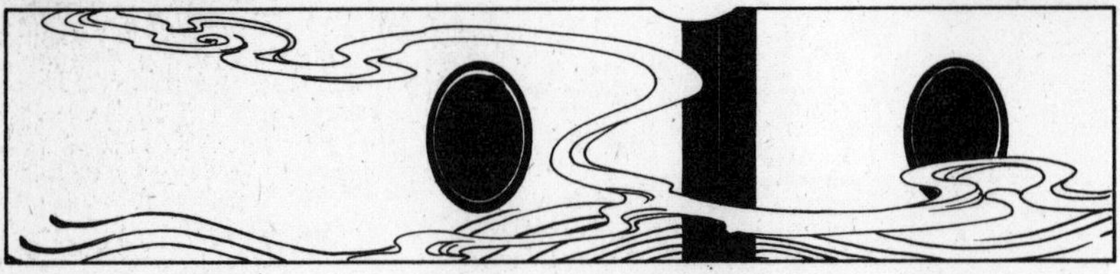

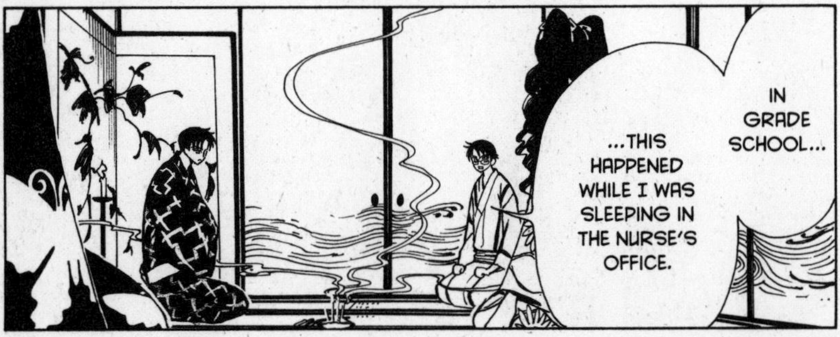
IN GRADE SCHOOL...
...THIS HAPPENED WHILE I WAS SLEEPING IN THE NURSE'S OFFICE.

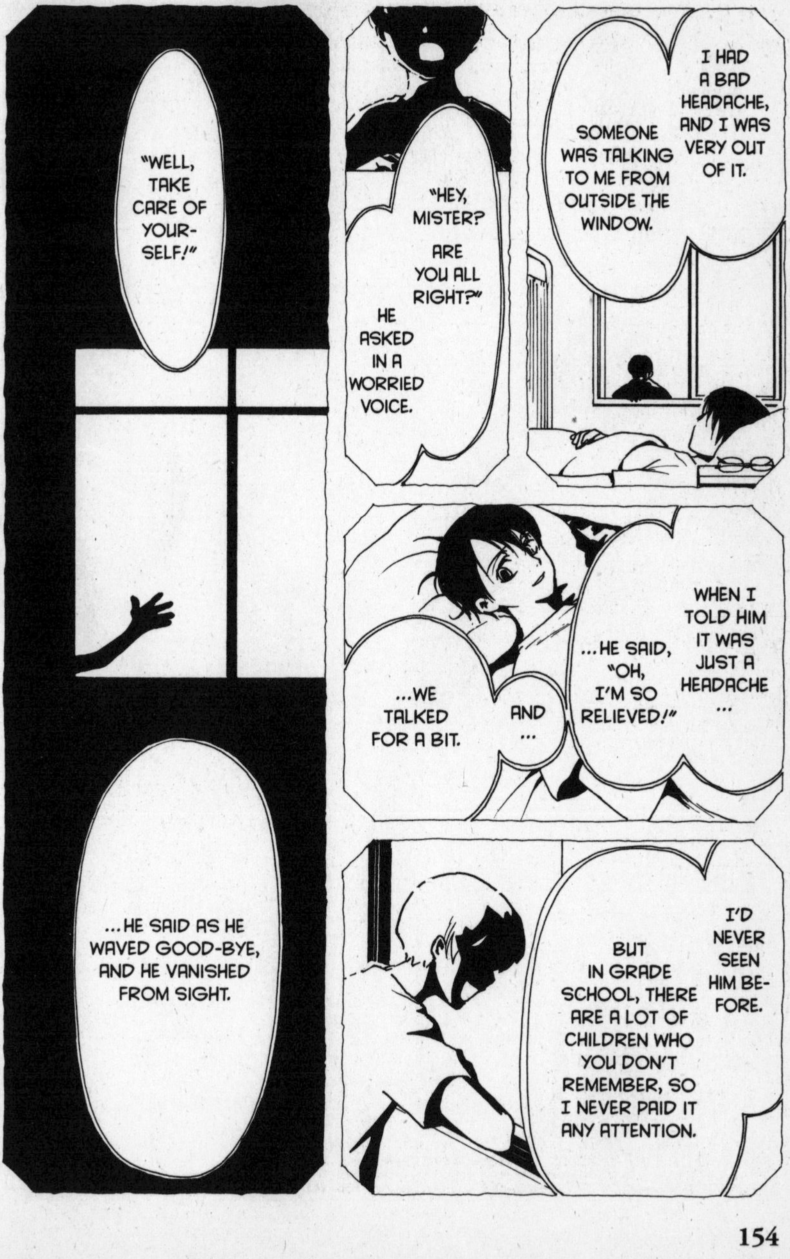
I HAD A BAD HEADACHE, AND I WAS VERY OUT OF IT.
SOMEONE WAS TALKING TO ME FROM OUTSIDE THE WINDOW.
"HEY, MISTER?
ARE YOU ALL RIGHT?"
HE ASKED IN A WORRIED VOICE.
WHEN I TOLD HIM IT WAS JUST A HEADACHE ...
...HE SAID, "OH, I'M SO RELIEVED!"
AND ...
...WE TALKED FOR A BIT.
I'D NEVER SEEN HIM BE-FORE.
BUT IN GRADE SCHOOL, THERE ARE A LOT OF CHILDREN WHO YOU DON'T REMEMBER, SO I NEVER PAID IT ANY ATTENTION.
"WELL, TAKE CARE OF YOUR-SELF!"
...HE SAID AS HE WAVED GOOD-BYE, AND HE VANISHED FROM SIGHT.

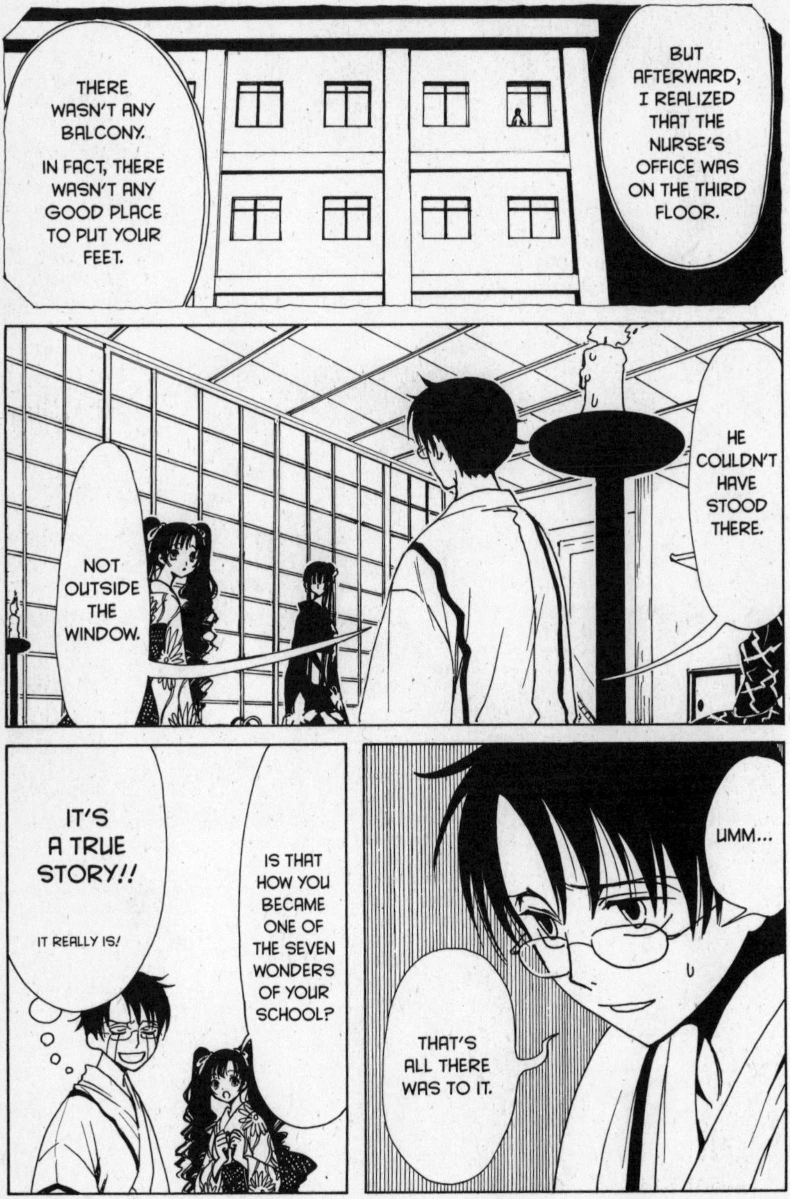
BUT AFTERWARD, I REALIZED THAT THE NURSE'S OFFICE WAS ON THE THIRD FLOOR.
THERE WASN'T ANY BALCONY.
IN FACT, THERE WASN'T ANY GOOD PLACE TO PUT YOUR FEET.
HE COULDN'T HAVE STOOD THERE.
NOT OUTSIDE THE WINDOW.
UMM...
THAT'S ALL THERE WAS TO IT.
IS THAT HOW YOU BECAME ONE OF THE SEVEN WONDERS OF YOUR SCHOOL?
IT'S A TRUE STORY!!
IT REALLY IS!

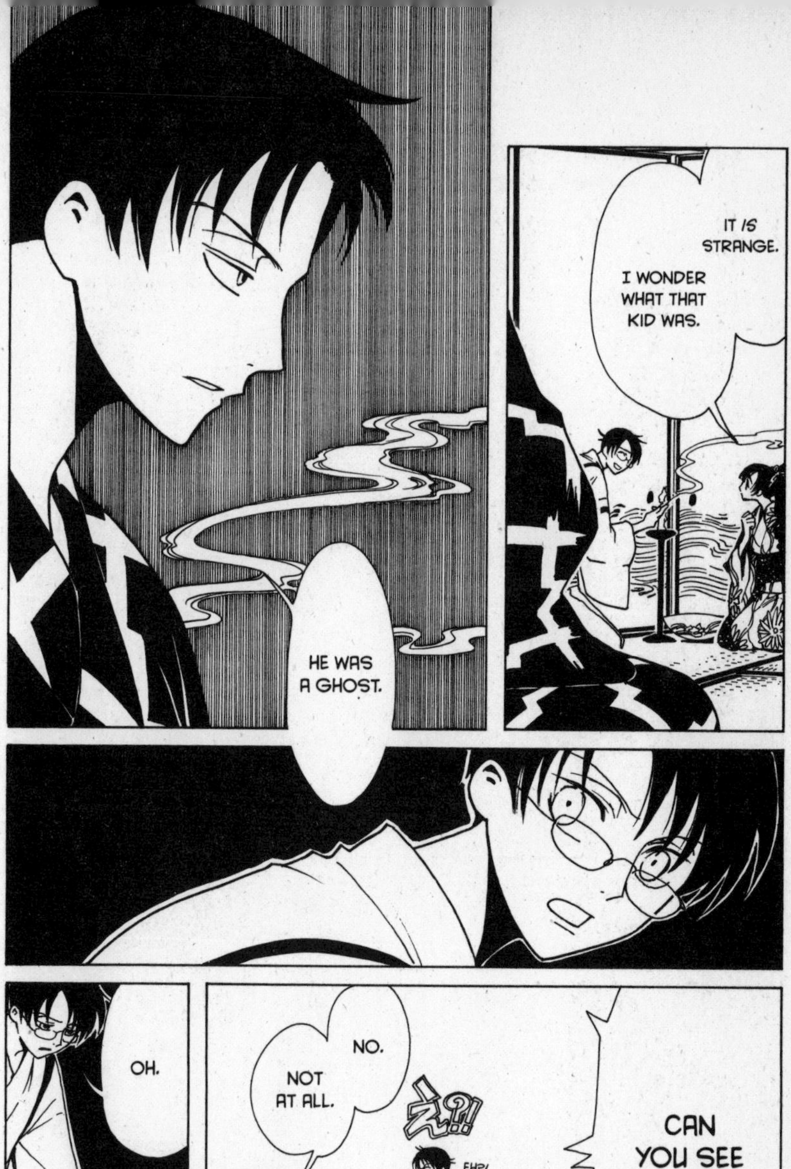
IT IS STRANGE.
I WONDER WHAT THAT KID WAS.
HE WAS A GHOST.
CAN YOU SEE SPIRITS?
え?!!
EH?!
NO.
NOT AT ALL.
OH.

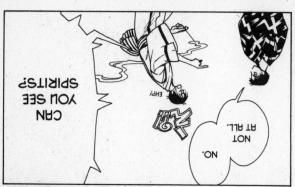

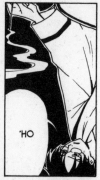

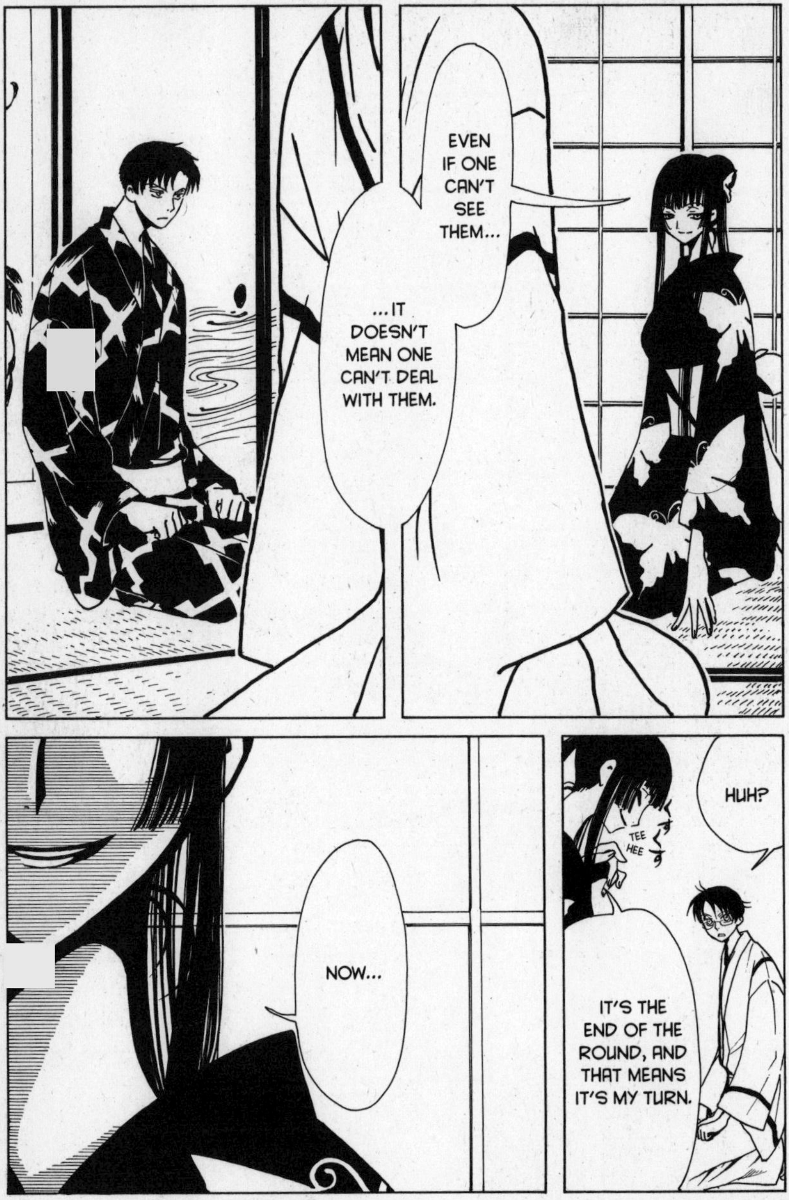
EVEN IF ONE CAN'T SEE THEM...
...IT DOESN'T MEAN ONE CAN'T DEAL WITH THEM.
HUH?
TEE HEE
IT'S THE END OF THE ROUND, AND THAT MEANS IT'S MY TURN.
NOW...

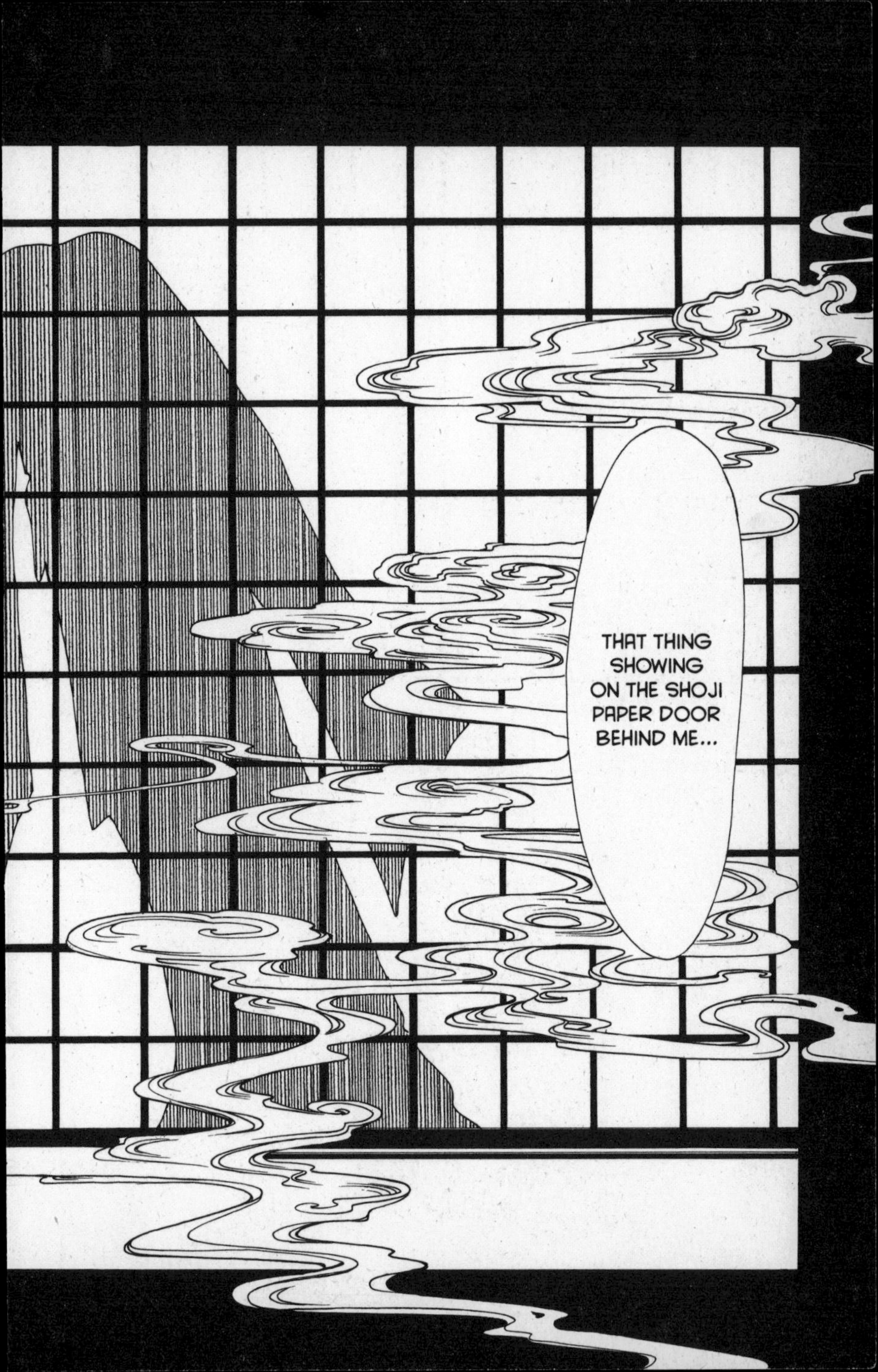
THAT THING SHOWING ON THE SHOJI PAPER DOOR BEHIND ME...

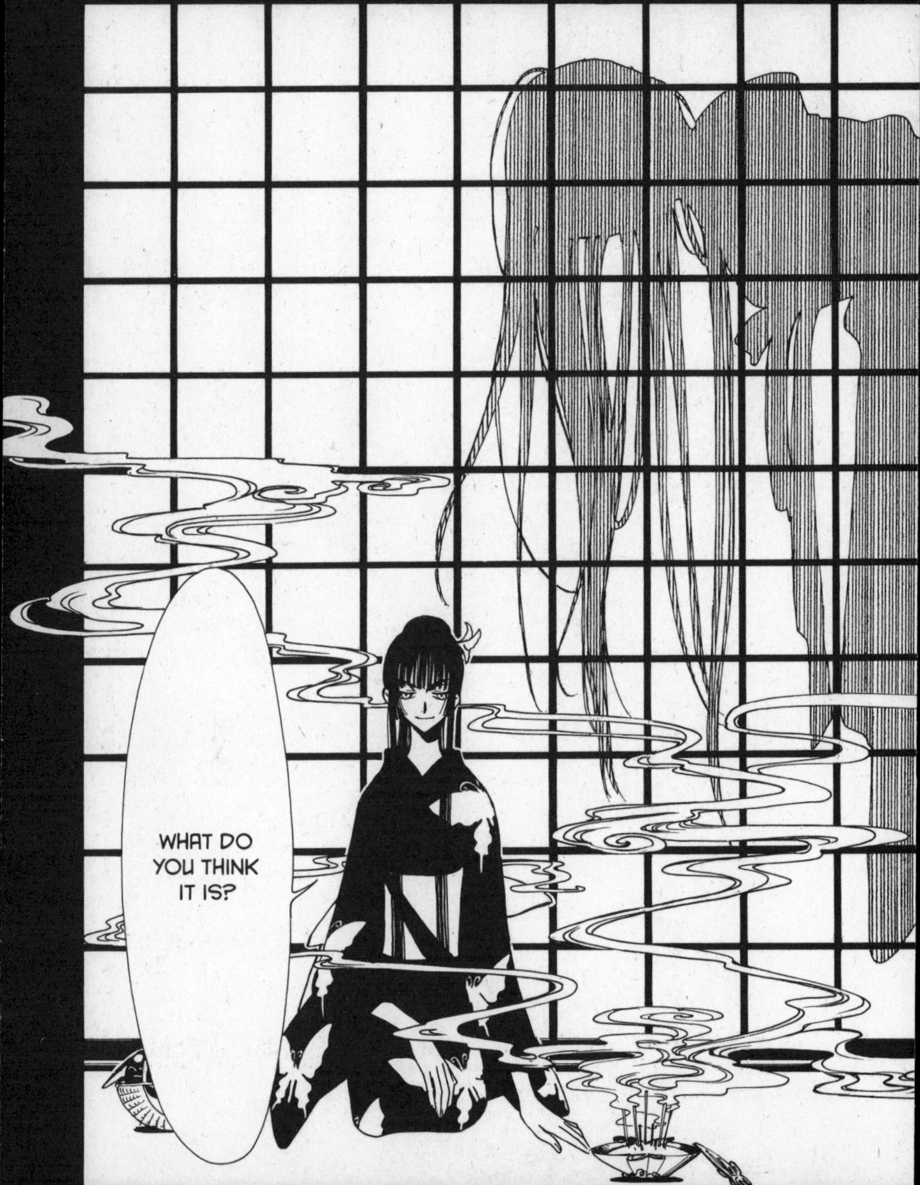
WHAT DO YOU THINK IT IS?

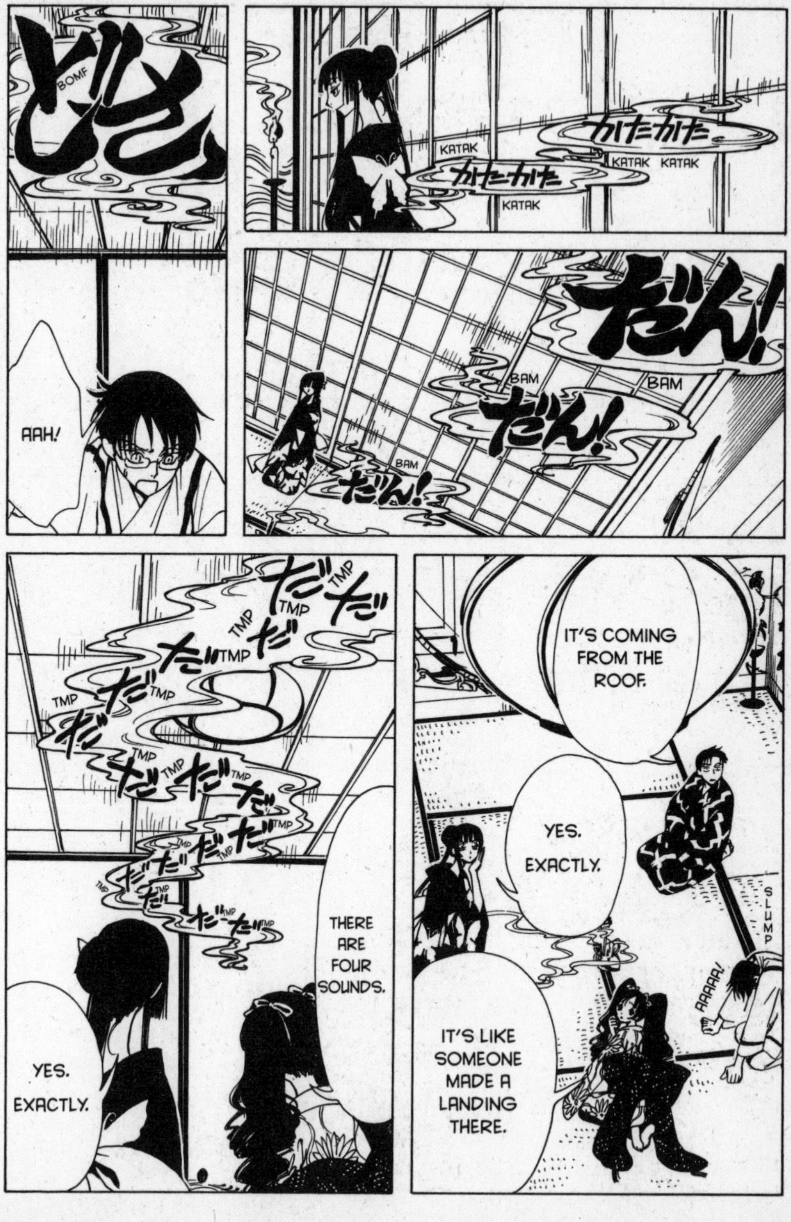

かたかた KATAK KATAK
かたかた KATAK KATAK
どさ BOMF
だん! BAM
だん! BAM
だん! BAM
AAH!
IT'S COMING FROM THE ROOF.
YES. EXACTLY.
SLUMP
AAAAA!
IT'S LIKE SOMEONE MADE A LANDING THERE.
だだだだだだだだだだだだ TMP
THERE ARE FOUR SOUNDS.
YES. EXACTLY.

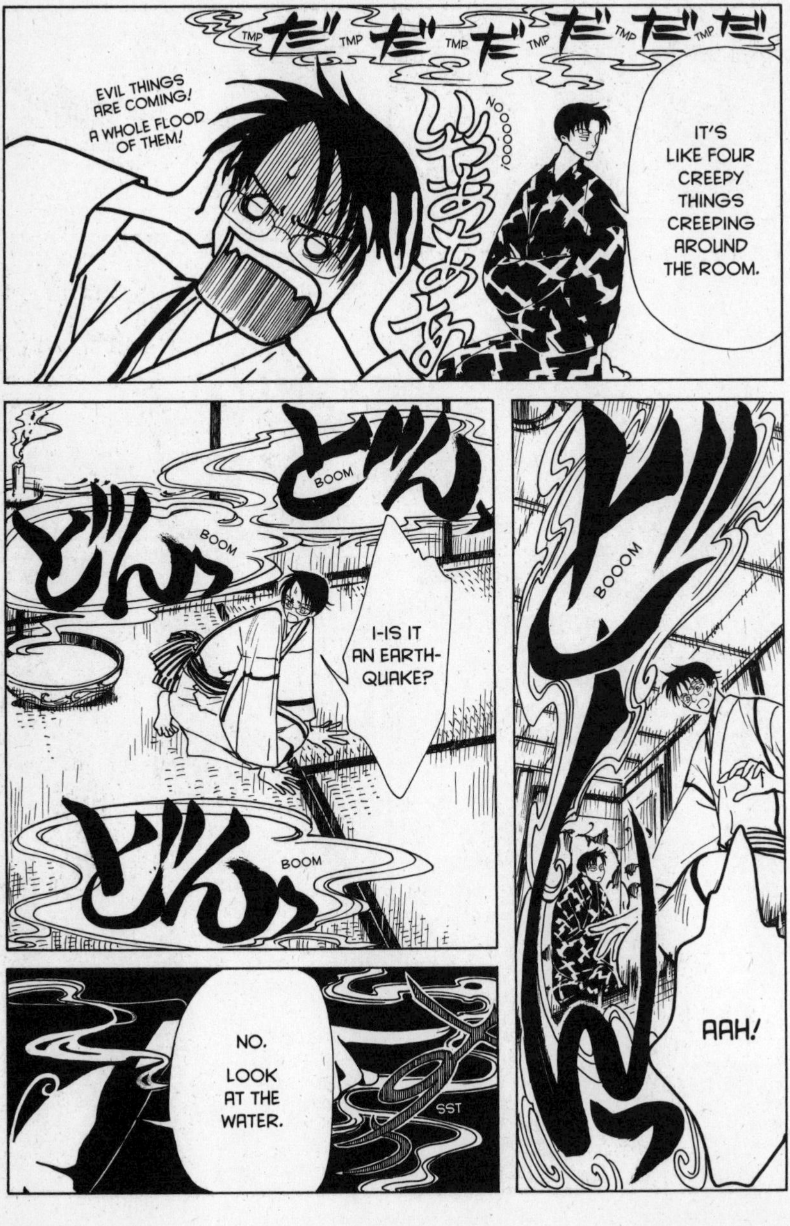

TMP TMP TMP TMP TMP TMP
IT'S LIKE FOUR CREEPY THINGS CREEPING AROUND THE ROOM.
EVIL THINGS ARE COMING! A WHOLE FLOOD OF THEM!
NOOOOOO!
BOOOM
AAH!
BOOM
BOOM
I-IS IT AN EARTH-QUAKE?
BOOM
NO.
LOOK AT THE WATER.
SST

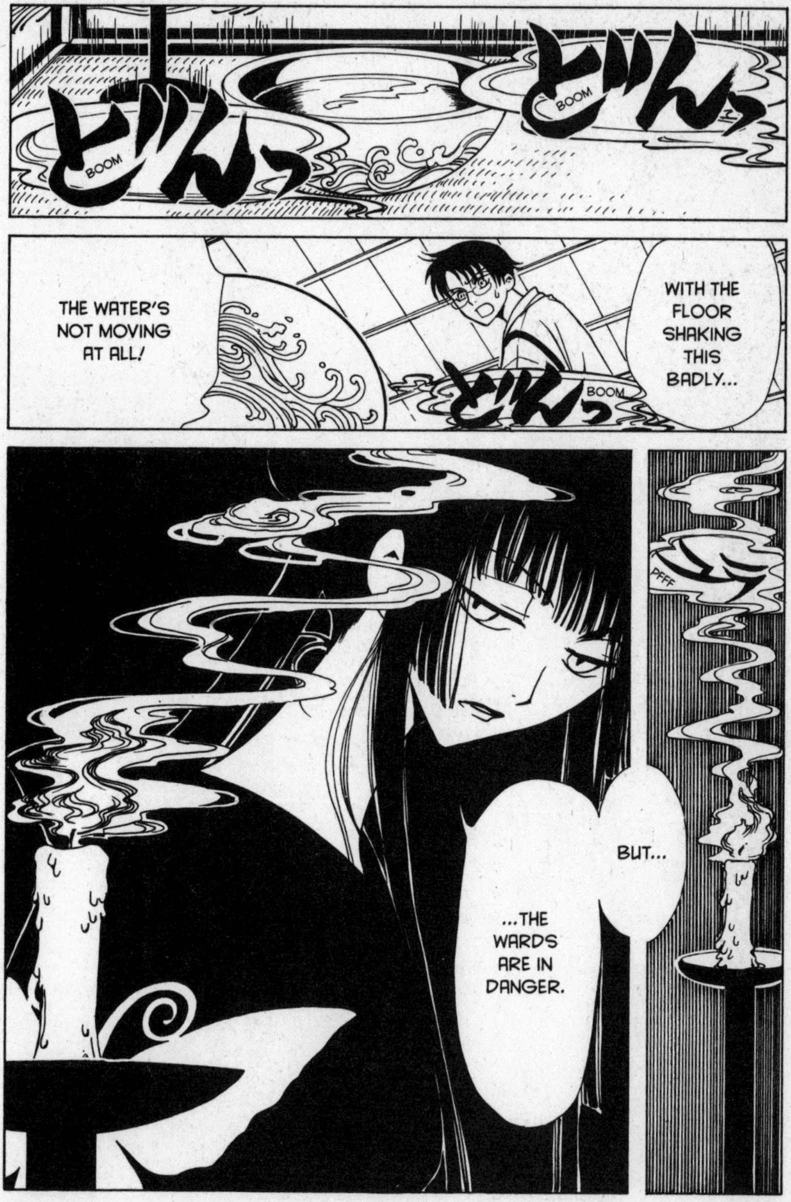
BOOM
BOOM
WITH THE FLOOR SHAKING THIS BADLY...
BOOM
THE WATER'S NOT MOVING AT ALL!
PFFF
BUT...
...THE WARDS ARE IN DANGER.

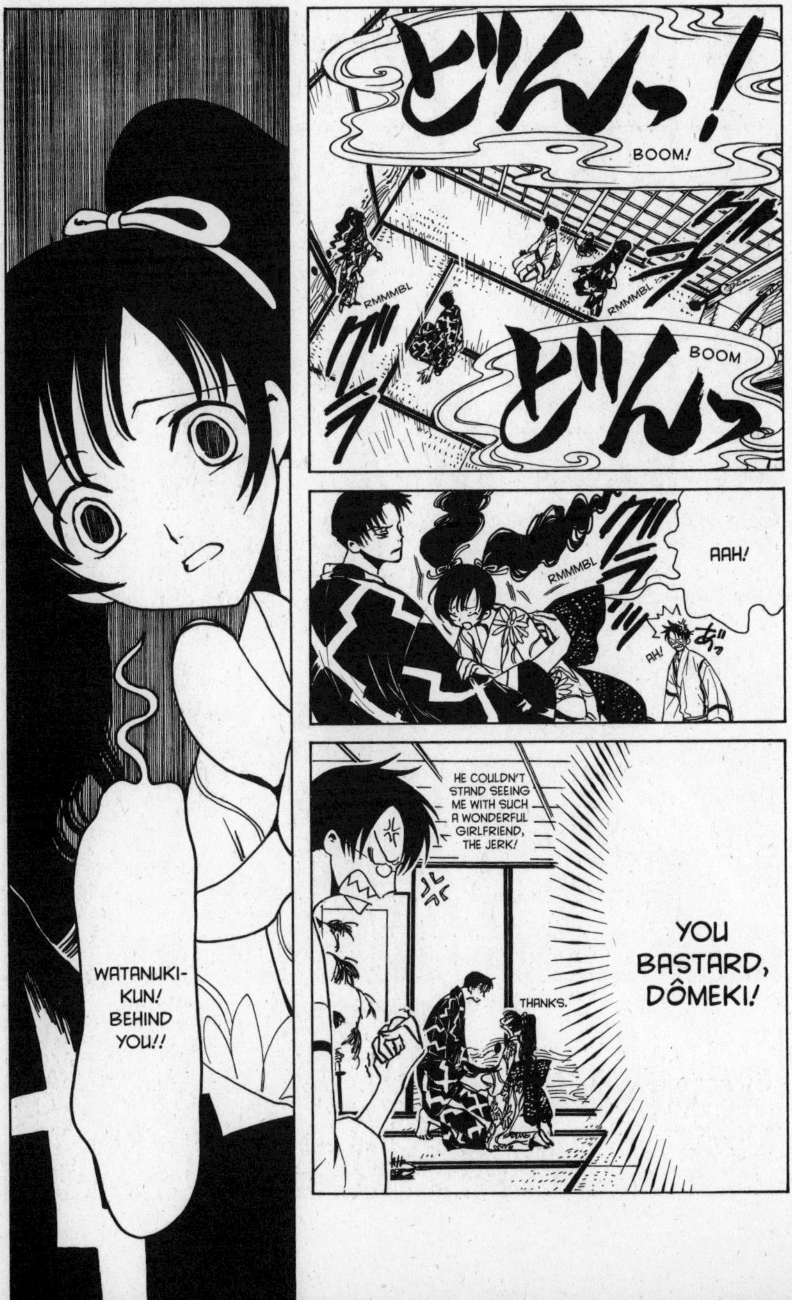
どんっ!
BOOM!
RMMMBL
RMMMBL
どんっ
BOOM
AAH!
RMMMBL
あっ
AH!
YOU BASTARD, DÔMEKI!
HE COULDN'T STAND SEEING ME WITH SUCH A WONDERFUL GIRLFRIEND, THE JERK!
THANKS.
WATANUKI-KUN! BEHIND YOU!!

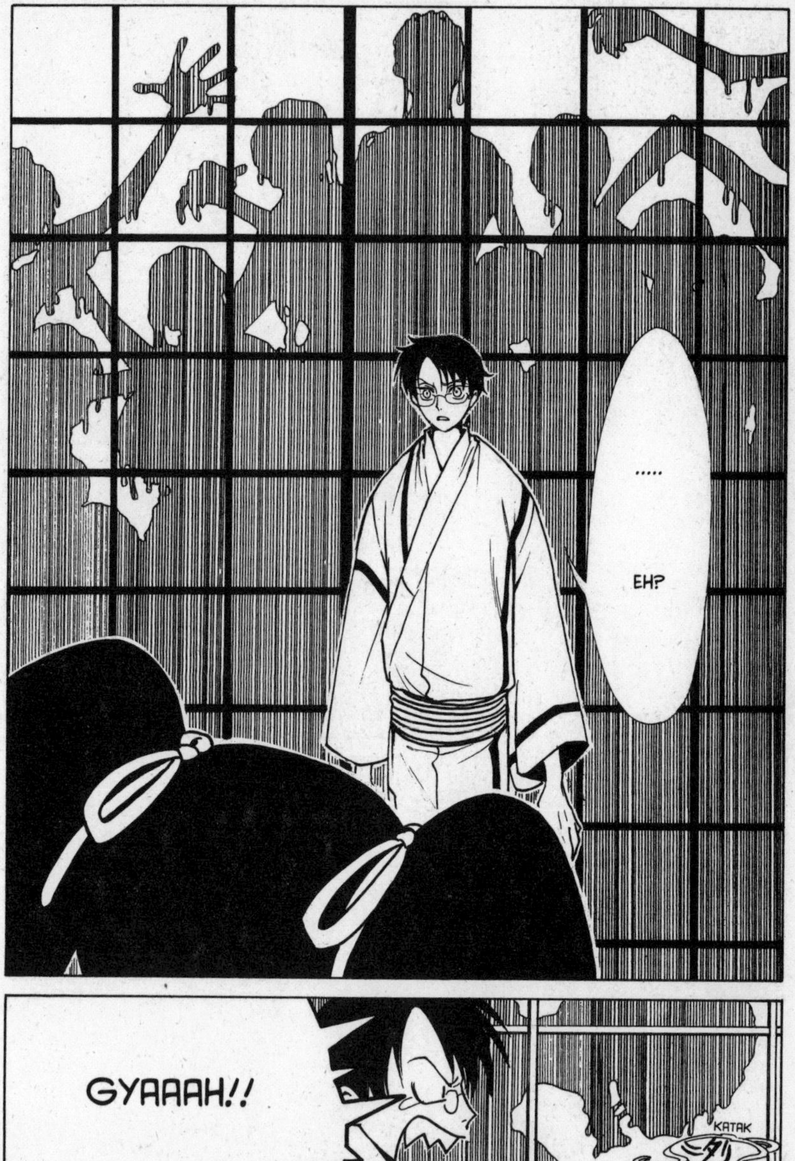
.....
EH?

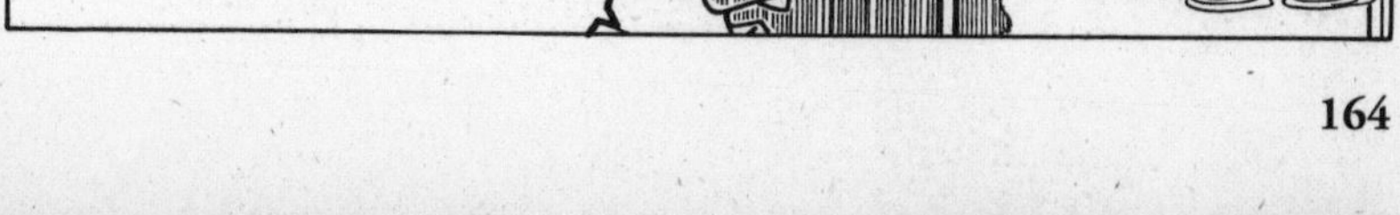
KATAK
GYAAAH!!

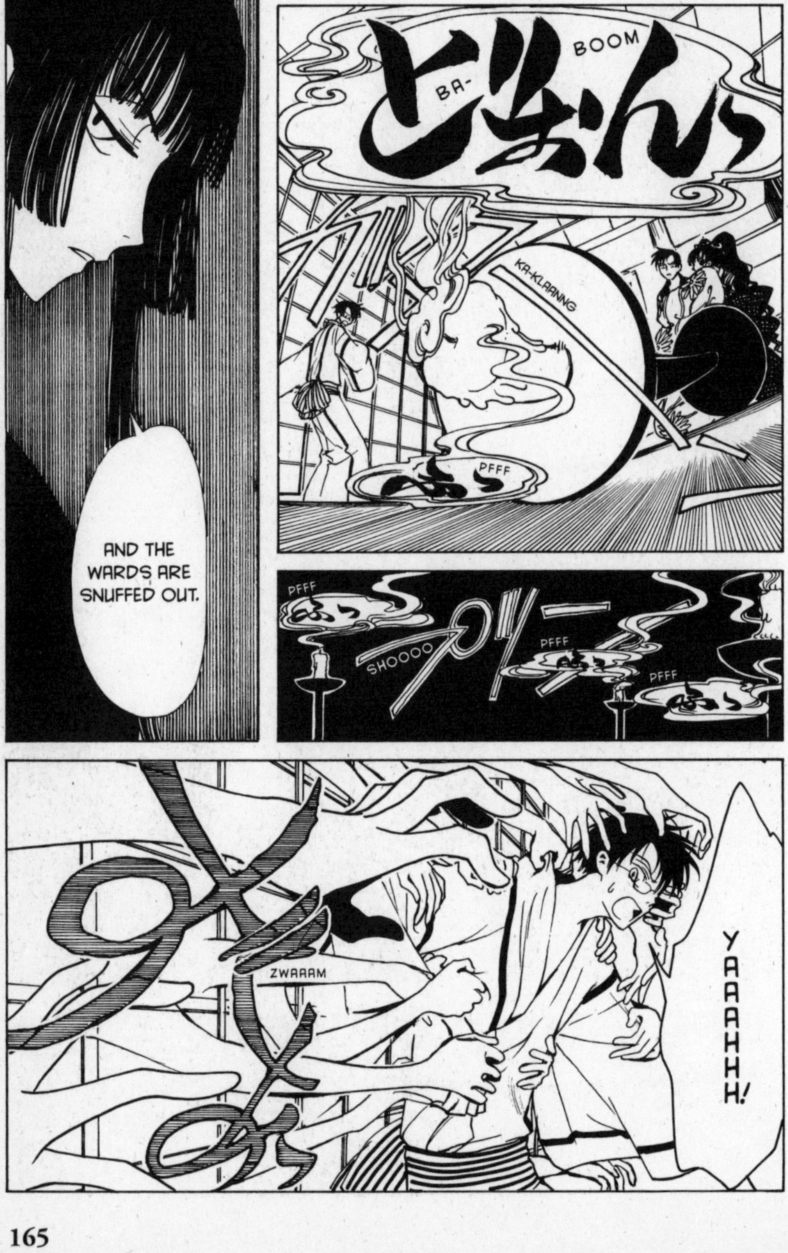
BA-BOOM
KA-KLAANNG
PFFF
PFFF
PFFF
SHOOOO
PFFF
AND THE WARDS ARE SNUFFED OUT.
YAAAHHH!
ZWAAAM

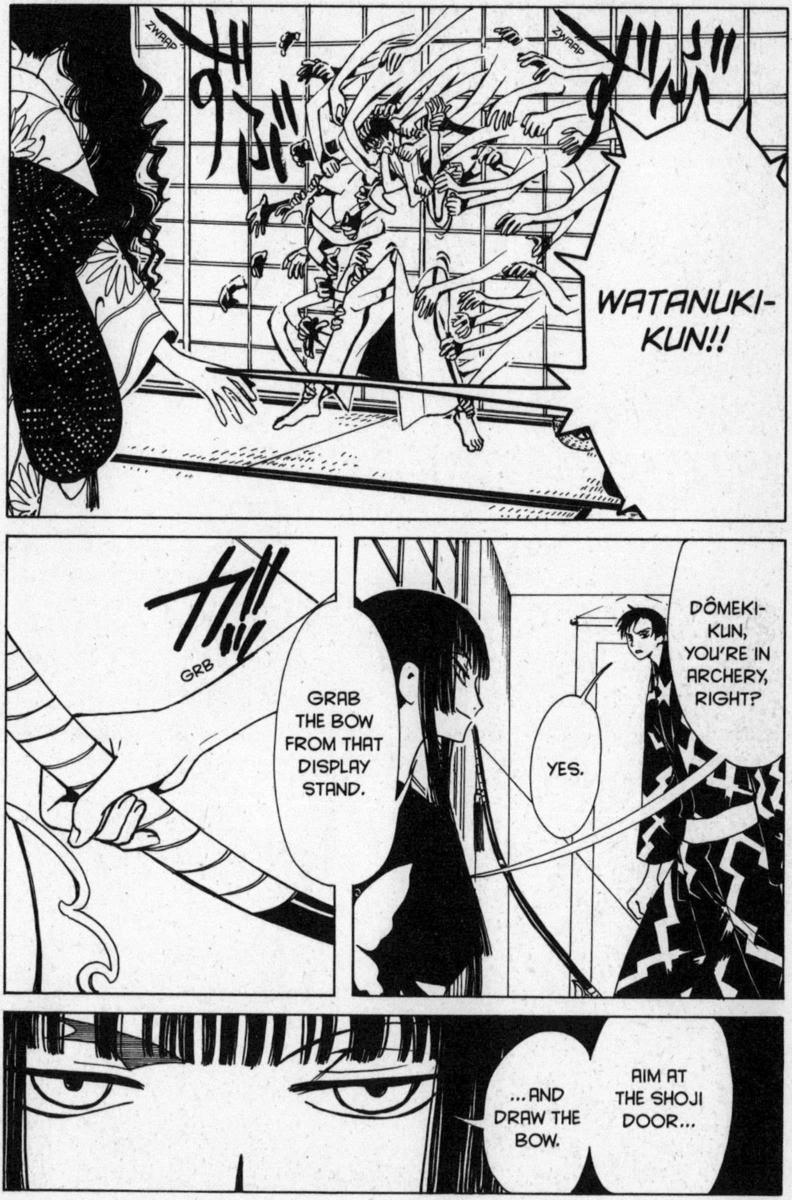
ZWAAP
ZWAAP
WATANUKI-KUN!!
DÔMEKI-KUN, YOU'RE IN ARCHERY, RIGHT?
YES.
GRAB THE BOW FROM THAT DISPLAY STAND.
GRB
AIM AT THE SHOJI DOOR...
...AND DRAW THE BOW.

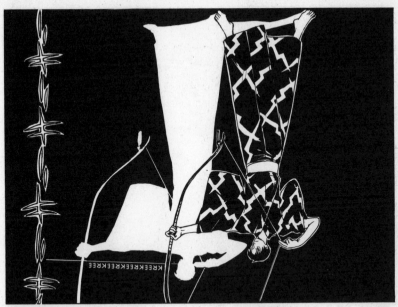

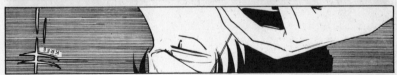

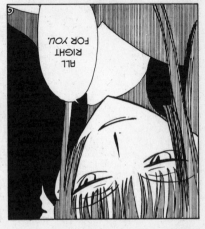

BUT I DON'T HAVE ANY ARROWS.
IT'S ALL RIGHT.
ALL RIGHT FOR *YOU*.
KREE
KREEKREEKREEKREE

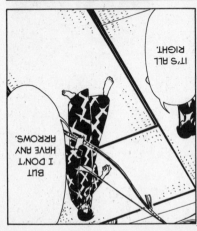

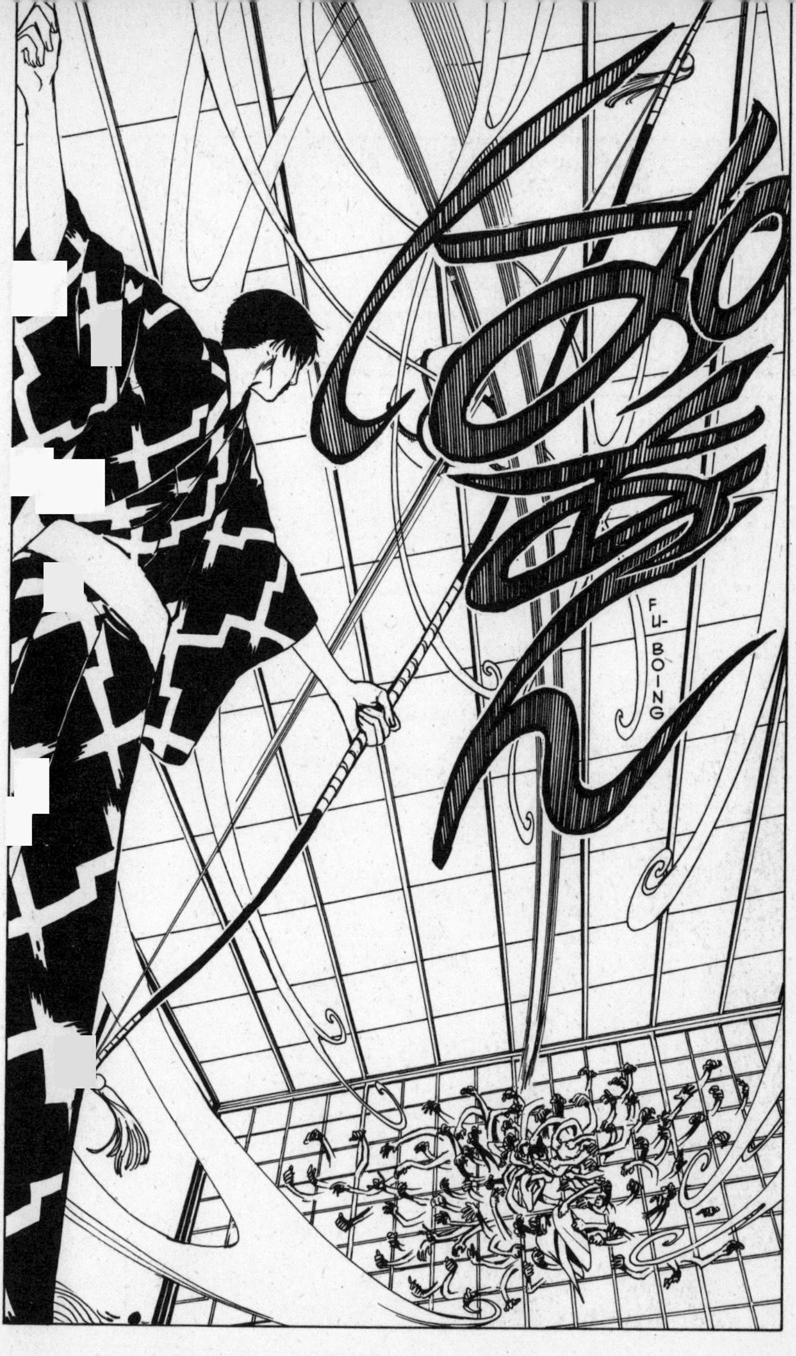
FU-BOING

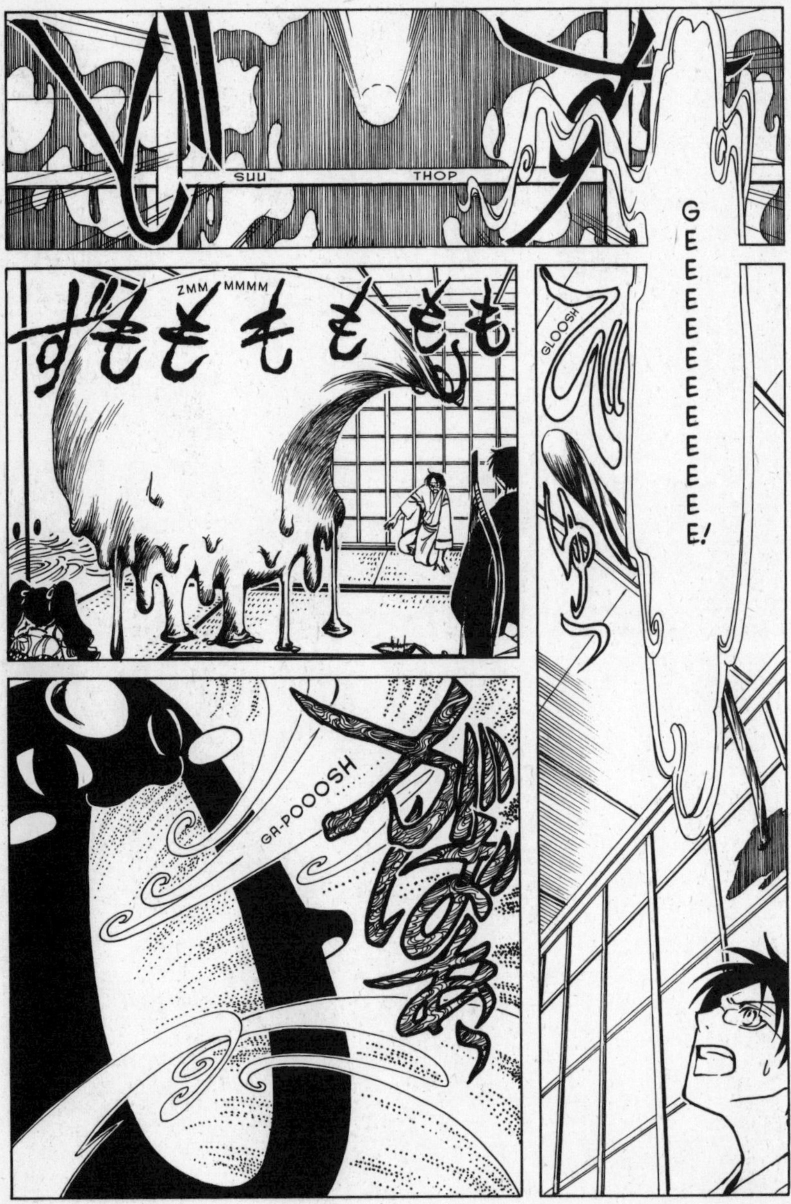
THOP
SUU
GEEEEEEEEEEEEE!
GLOOSH
ZMM MMMM
GR-POOOSH

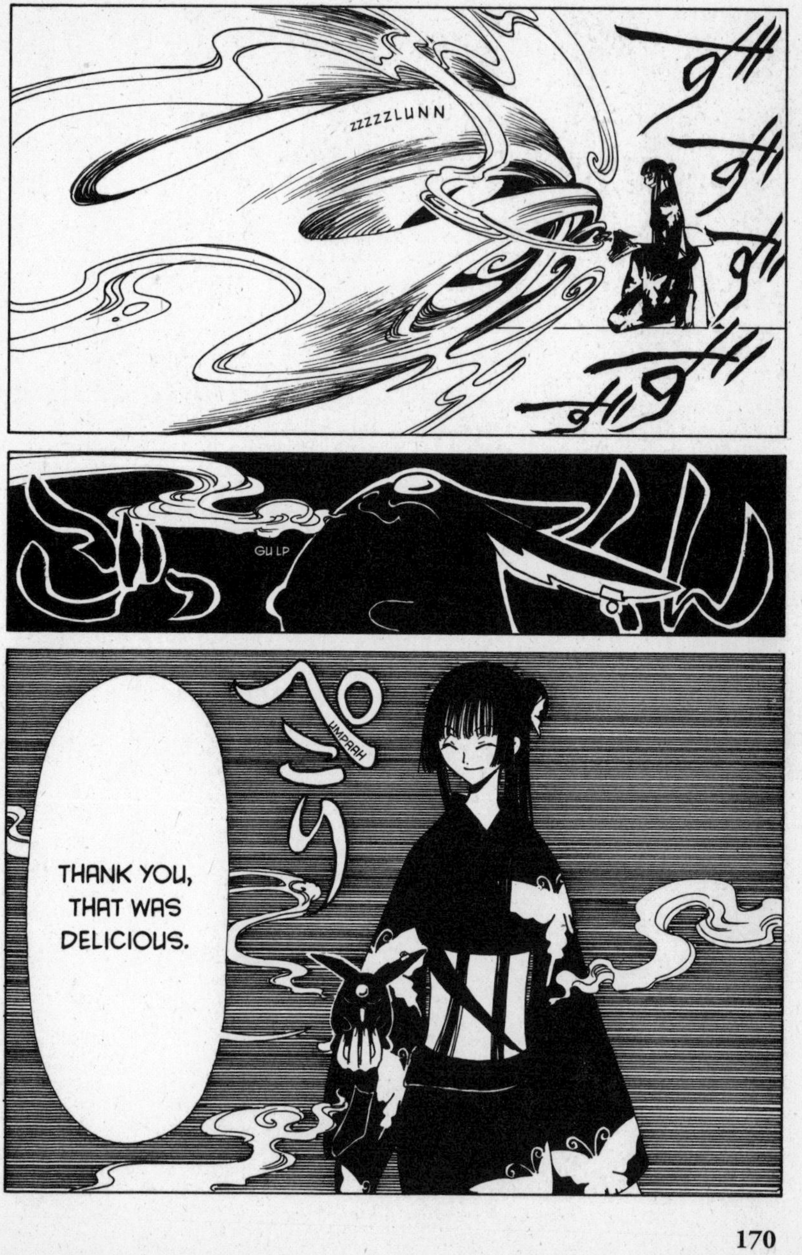
ZZZZZLUNN
GULP
HMPAAH
THANK YOU, THAT WAS DELICIOUS.

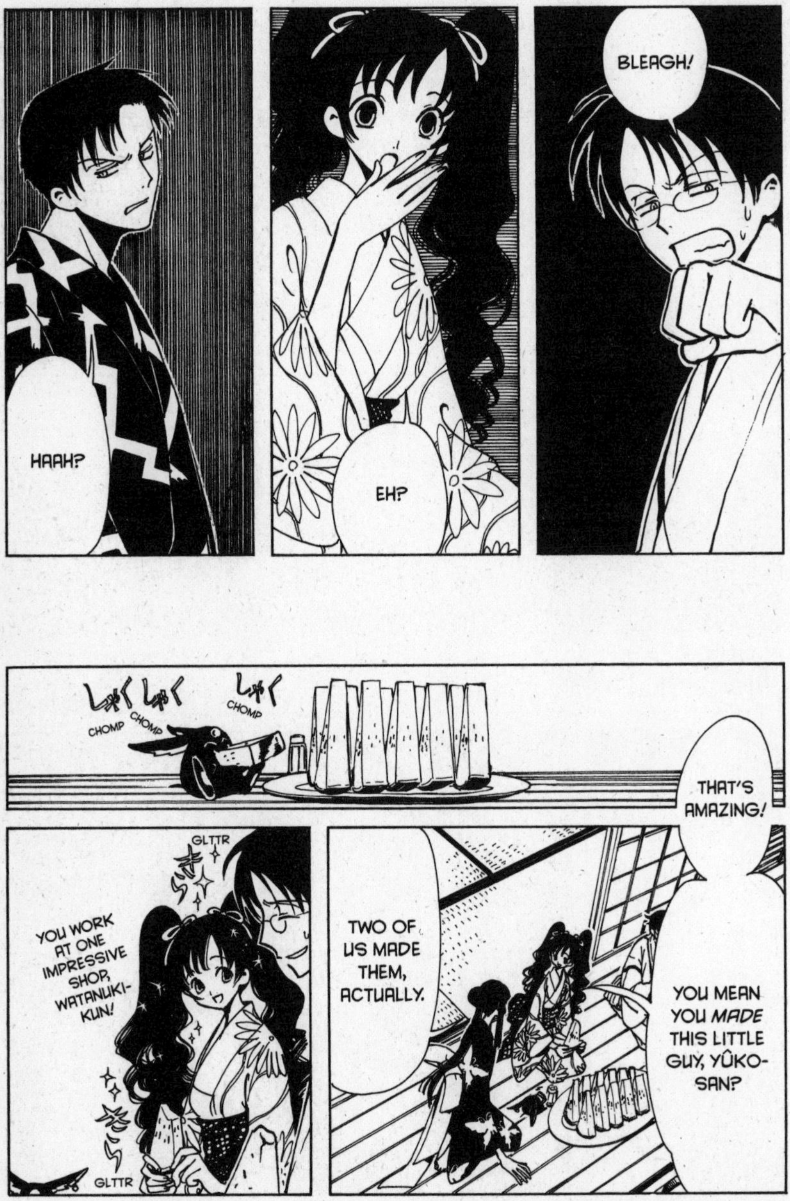
BLEAGH!
EH?
HAAH?
THAT'S AMAZING!
しゃくしゃく しゃく
CHOMP CHOMP CHOMP
YOU MEAN YOU MADE THIS LITTLE GUY, YÛKO-SAN?
TWO OF US MADE THEM, ACTUALLY.
GLTTR
YOU WORK AT ONE IMPRESSIVE SHOP, WATANUKI-KUN!
GLTTR

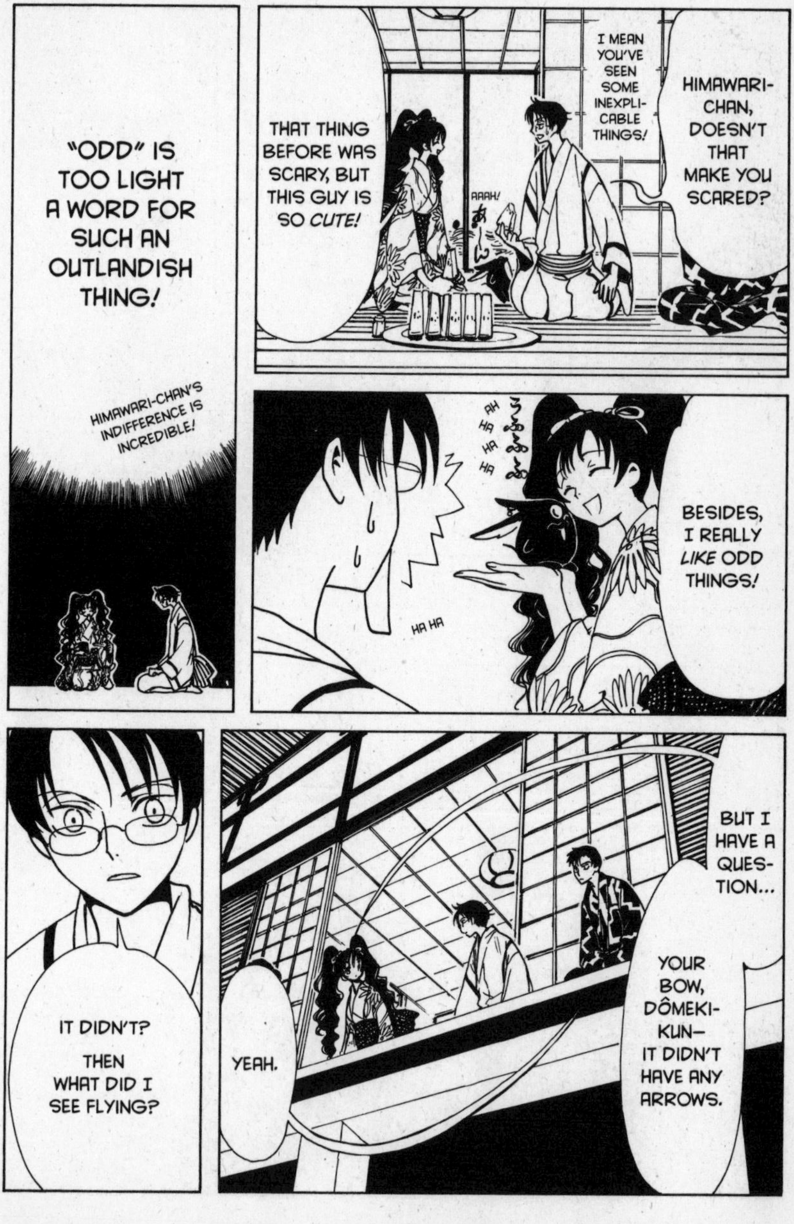

HIMAWARI-CHAN, DOESN'T THAT MAKE YOU SCARED?
I MEAN YOU'VE SEEN SOME INEXPLICABLE THINGS!
THAT THING BEFORE WAS SCARY, BUT THIS GUY IS SO *CUTE!*
AAAH!
BESIDES, I REALLY *LIKE* ODD THINGS!
AH HA HA HA
HA HA
"ODD" IS TOO LIGHT A WORD FOR SUCH AN OUTLANDISH THING!
HIMAWARI-CHAN'S INDIFFERENCE IS INCREDIBLE!
BUT I HAVE A QUESTION...
YOUR BOW, DÔMEKI-KUN— IT DIDN'T HAVE ANY ARROWS.
YEAH.
IT DIDN'T?
THEN WHAT DID I SEE FLYING?

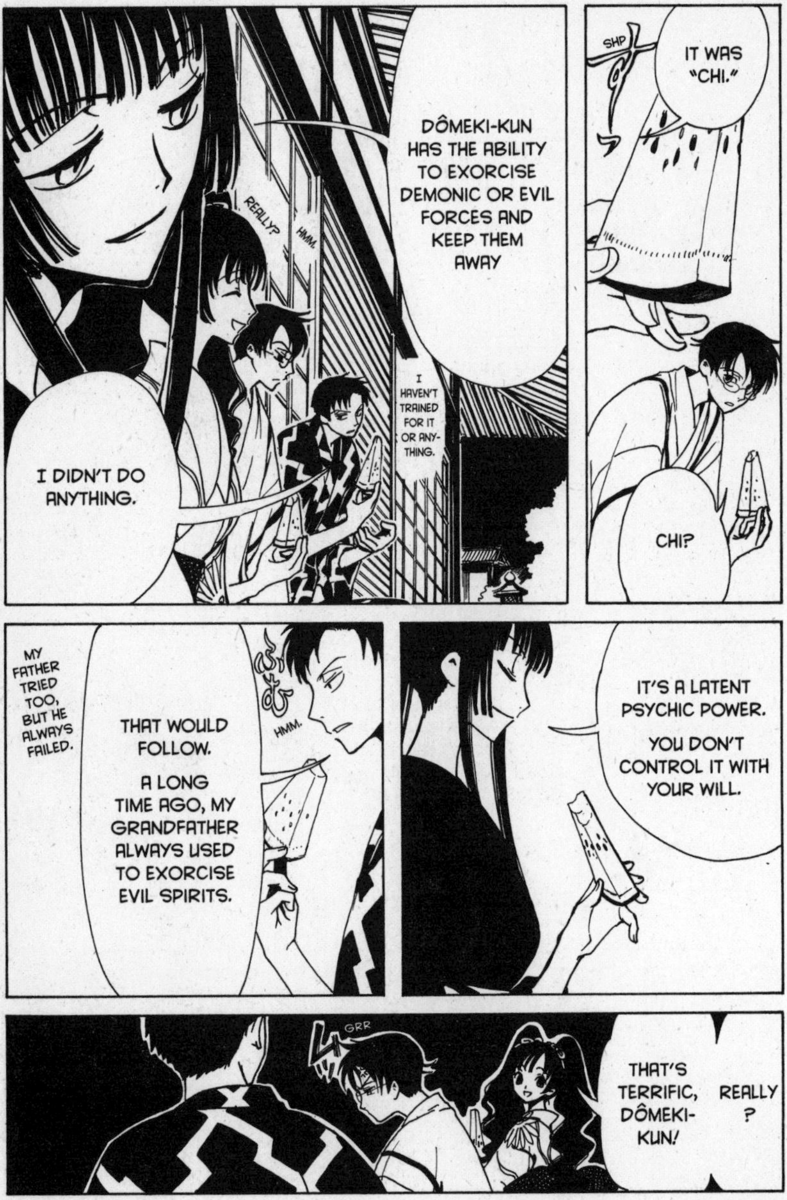
IT WAS "CHI."
SHP
CHI?
DÔMEKI-KUN HAS THE ABILITY TO EXORCISE DEMONIC OR EVIL FORCES AND KEEP THEM AWAY
REALLY?
HMM.
I HAVEN'T TRAINED FOR IT OR ANYTHING.
I DIDN'T DO ANYTHING.
IT'S A LATENT PSYCHIC POWER.
YOU DON'T CONTROL IT WITH YOUR WILL.
HMM.
THAT WOULD FOLLOW.
A LONG TIME AGO, MY GRANDFATHER ALWAYS USED TO EXORCISE EVIL SPIRITS.
MY FATHER TRIED TOO, BUT HE ALWAYS FAILED.
REALLY ?
THAT'S TERRIFIC, DÔMEKI-KUN!
GRR

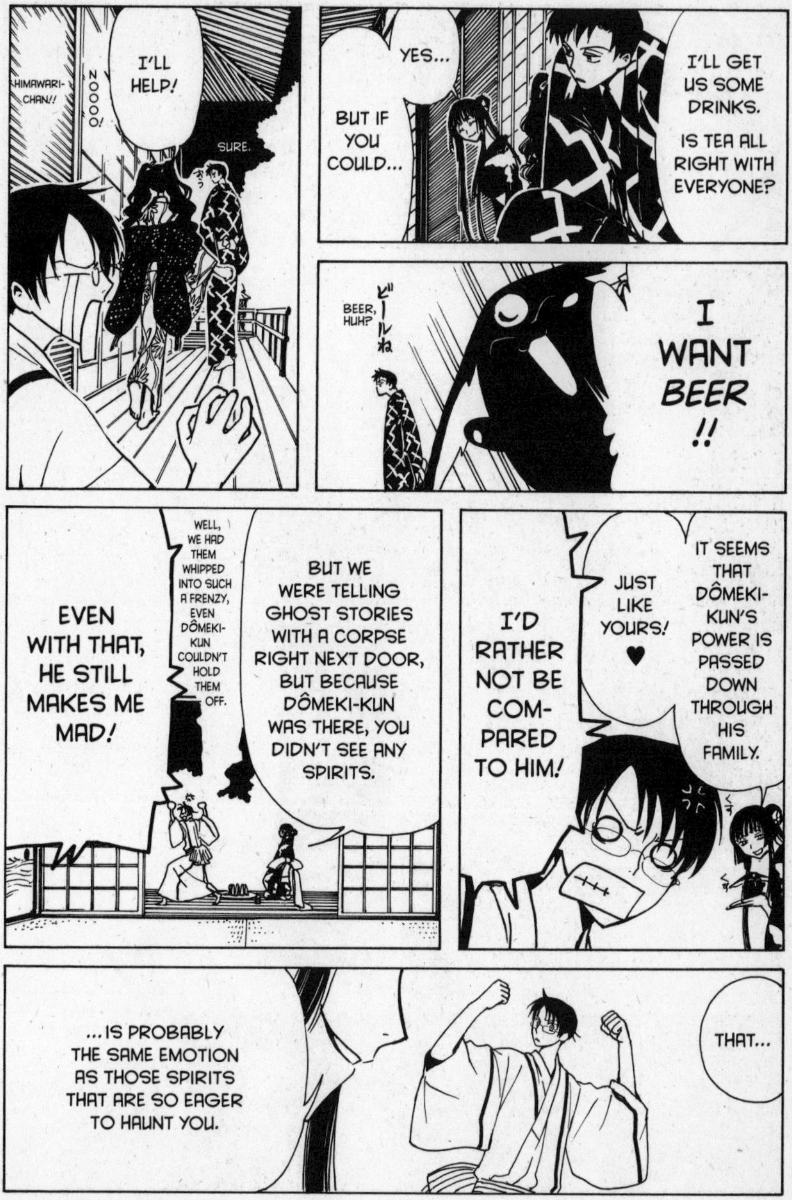

I'LL GET US SOME DRINKS.
IS TEA ALL RIGHT WITH EVERYONE?
YES...
BUT IF YOU COULD...
I WANT BEER !!
BEER, HUH?
ビールね
I'LL HELP!
NOOOO!
HIMAWARI-CHAN!!
SURE.
IT SEEMS THAT DÔMEKI-KUN'S POWER IS PASSED DOWN THROUGH HIS FAMILY.
JUST LIKE YOURS! ♥
I'D RATHER NOT BE COM-PARED TO HIM!
BUT WE WERE TELLING GHOST STORIES WITH A CORPSE RIGHT NEXT DOOR, BUT BECAUSE DÔMEKI-KUN WAS THERE, YOU DIDN'T SEE ANY SPIRITS.
WELL, WE HAD THEM WHIPPED INTO SUCH A FRENZY, EVEN DÔMEKI-KUN COULDN'T HOLD THEM OFF.
EVEN WITH THAT, HE STILL MAKES ME MAD!
THAT...
...IS PROBABLY THE SAME EMOTION AS THOSE SPIRITS THAT ARE SO EAGER TO HAUNT YOU.

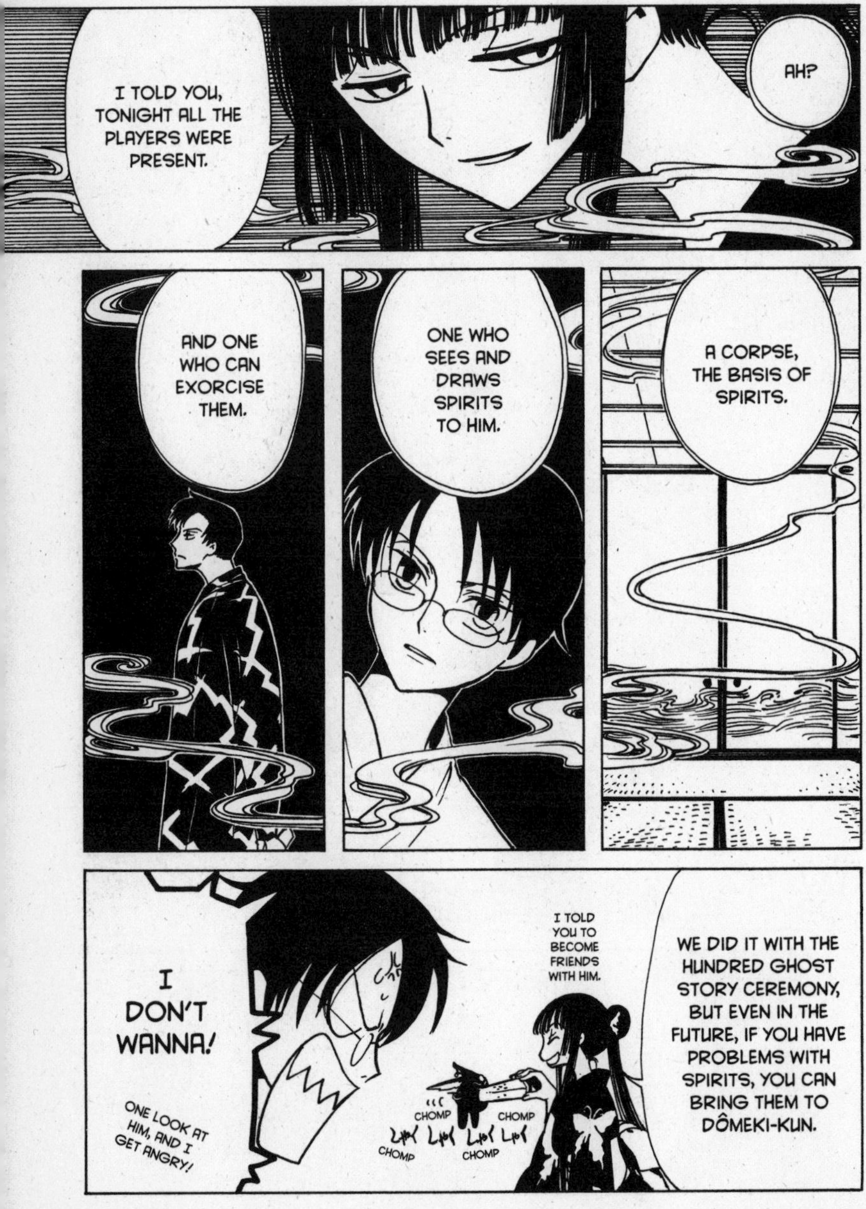
AH?
I TOLD YOU, TONIGHT ALL THE PLAYERS WERE PRESENT.
A CORPSE, THE BASIS OF SPIRITS.
ONE WHO SEES AND DRAWS SPIRITS TO HIM.
AND ONE WHO CAN EXORCISE THEM.
WE DID IT WITH THE HUNDRED GHOST STORY CEREMONY, BUT EVEN IN THE FUTURE, IF YOU HAVE PROBLEMS WITH SPIRITS, YOU CAN BRING THEM TO DÔMEKI-KUN.
I TOLD YOU TO BECOME FRIENDS WITH HIM.
CHOMP CHOMP CHOMP CHOMP
I DON'T WANNA!
ONE LOOK AT HIM, AND I GET ANGRY!

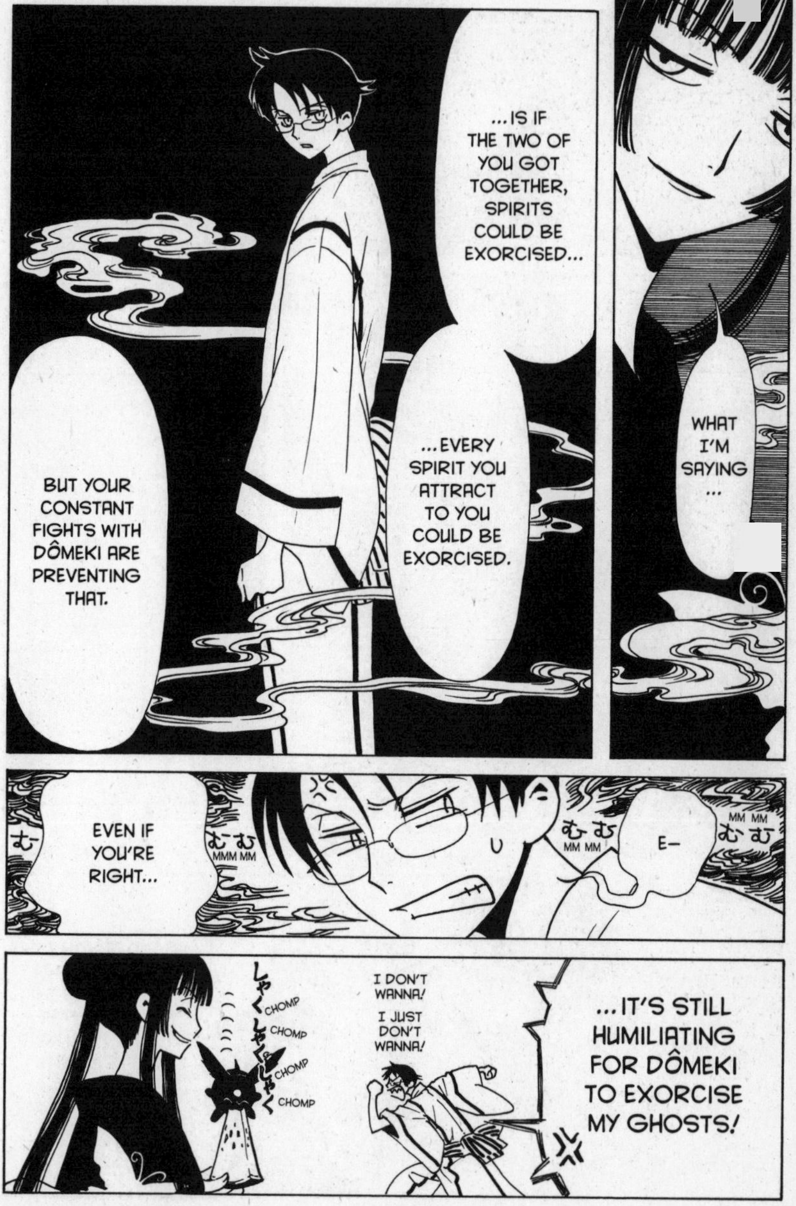
WHAT I'M SAYING ...
...IS IF THE TWO OF YOU GOT TOGETHER, SPIRITS COULD BE EXORCISED...
...EVERY SPIRIT YOU ATTRACT TO YOU COULD BE EXORCISED.
BUT YOUR CONSTANT FIGHTS WITH DÔMEKI ARE PREVENTING THAT.
MM MM
E–
MM MM
MMM MM
EVEN IF YOU'RE RIGHT...
...IT'S STILL HUMILIATING FOR DÔMEKI TO EXORCISE MY GHOSTS!
I DON'T WANNA!
I JUST DON'T WANNA!
CHOMP
CHOMP
CHOMP
CHOMP

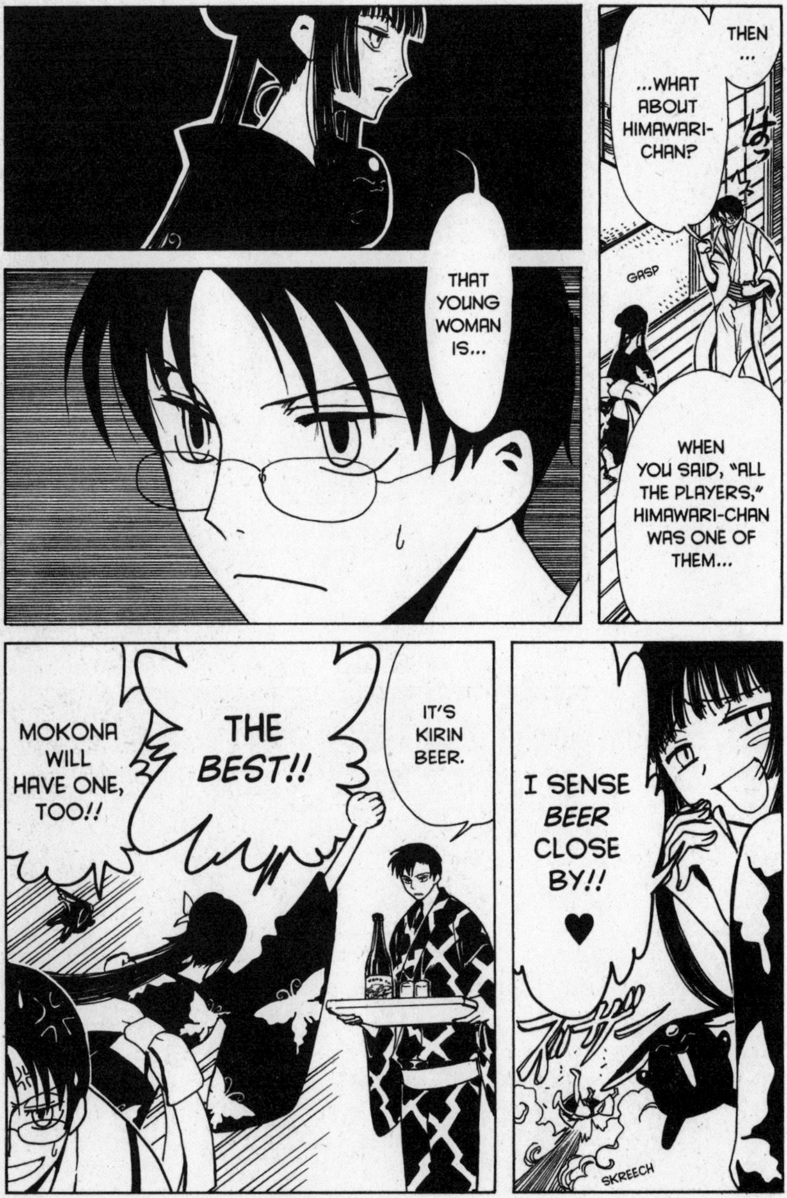
THEN ...
...WHAT ABOUT HIMAWARI-CHAN?
GASP
WHEN YOU SAID, "ALL THE PLAYERS," HIMAWARI-CHAN WAS ONE OF THEM...
THAT YOUNG WOMAN IS...
I SENSE BEER CLOSE BY!! ♥
SKREECH
IT'S KIRIN BEER.
THE BEST!!
MOKONA WILL HAVE ONE, TOO!!

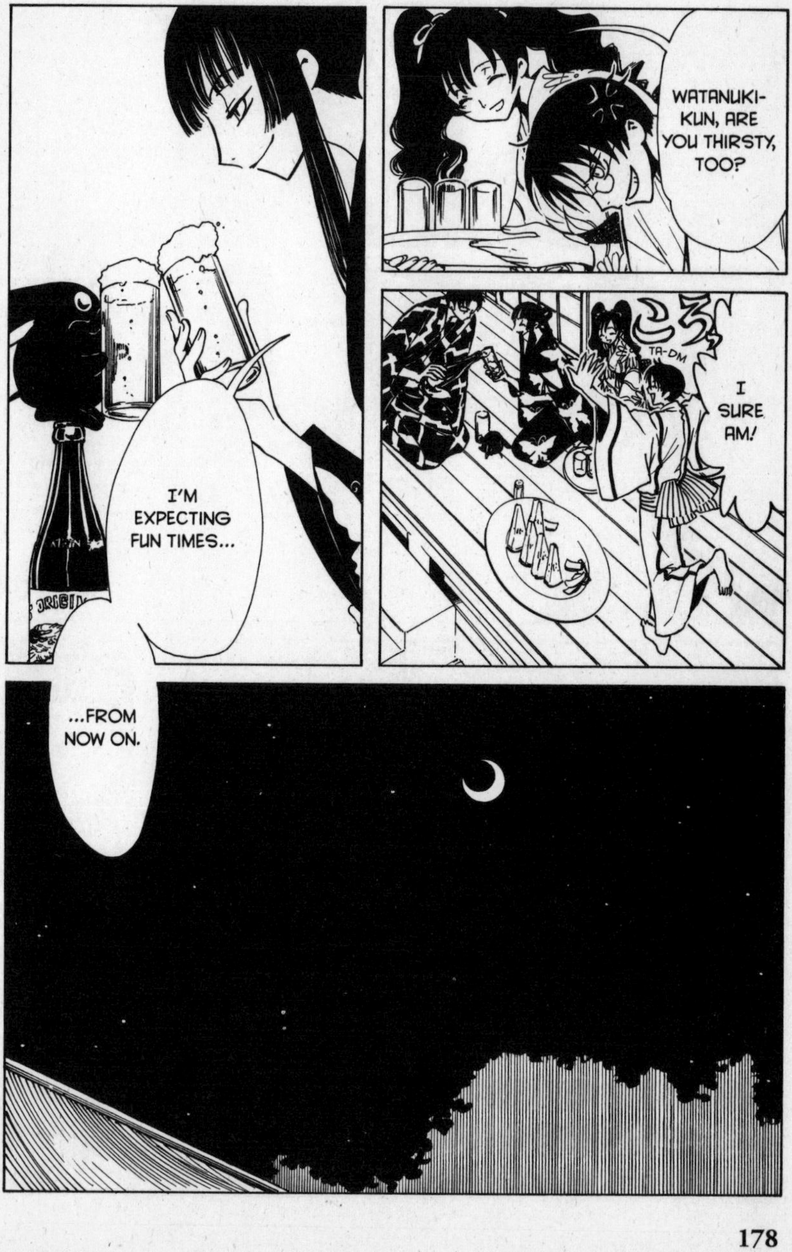
WATANUKI-KUN, ARE YOU THIRSTY, TOO?
TA-DM
I SURE AM!
I'M EXPECTING FUN TIMES...
...FROM NOW ON.

⇥ Continued ⇤

in *Tsubasa* Volume 2 and *xxxHolic* Volume 3

About the Creators

CLAMP is a group of four women who have become the most popular manga artists in America—Ageha Ohkawa, Mokona, Satsuki Igarashi, and Tsubaki Nekoi. They started out as doujinshi (fan comics) creators, but their skill and craft brought them to the attention of publishers very quickly. Their first work from a major publisher was *RG Veda*, but their first mass success was with *Magic Knight Rayearth*. From there, they went on to write many series, including *Cardcaptor Sakura* and *Chobits*, two of the most popular manga in the United States. Like many Japanese manga artists, they prefer to avoid the spotlight, and little is known about them personally.

CLAMP is currently publishing three series in Japan: *Tsubasa* and *xxxHOLiC* with Kodansha and *Gohou Drug* with Kadokawa.

Past Works

CLAMP have created many series. Here is a brief overview of one of them.

Magic Knight Rayearth

Hikaru, Umi, and Fuu never dreamed their field trip would end up in another dimension, but that's exactly what happens to the trio of middle school students from different schools. After hearing a voice calling to them in the Tokyo Tower, the three are shocked as the floor mysteriously opens up—and sucks them into the magical land called Cephiro. The girls learn they are its last line of defense against an evil priest, Zagato, seeking to enslave and reshape the land in his image.

Hikaru, Umi, and Fuu were summoned by the imprisoned Princess Emeraude, Cephiro's Pillar, who has kept their land peaceful. They are told by the mysterious Clef that the world was shaped by Emeraude's vision and thoughts, but since she's been trapped a darkness threatens the land. The trio are told the only way to return to Earth is to become the Magic Knights of legend and help save this universe.

After being given Mokona as an apparent mascot, each gets a portion of power from an elemental. Hikaru is one with fire, Umi has a link to water, and Fuu has ties to the wind. As the girls learn more and use their newfound powers, they will grow stronger. The trio are now on a quest to find the other elements necessary to aid in the rescue of Emeraude, but it's not an easy journey. There are evil forces seeking to destroy the potential Knights. Against almost impossible odds and facing bodily harm and danger, the freshman Knights attempt to save Cephiro and return home to the lives each left behind.

Artifacts and Miscellany

Over in *Tsubasa* you'll find a lot of characters from a variety of CLAMP manga making an appearance. Here in the second volume of *xxxHOLiC*, you'll find a few artifacts and other appearances that might be a bit hard to understand if you haven't read all of CLAMP's work. Don't read this section if you haven't read this volume yet—there's a reason we put this information at the end of the book!

Kero

The one *Cardcaptor Sakura* character most conspicuously absent from *Tsubasa* is Kero, the plush animal-like Guardian Beast that advises the CS Sakura. This stuffed animal in the back room of Yûko's shop looks suspiciously like Kero. Is it just a pleasant surprise for the reader, or is it a hint at what's to come?

Clow Reed

Referenced in *xxxHOLiC* Volume 1, Clow Reed makes his first (partial) appearance in *xxxHOLiC* Volume 2. Clow Reed was the creator of the Clow Cards, the Cardcaptor wand, and of the guardians Kero/Cerberus and Yue. In conjunction with Yûko, Clow Reed also created the Mokonas.

Kurogane

You can learn a lot more about Kurogane over in *Tsubasa,* but here's the thumbnail version: A warrior ninja who fights in the service of Princess Tomoyo, Kurogane is quick-tempered, violent, arrogant, and unrestrained. In an effort to teach him humility and, perhaps, empathy, Tomoyo has sent him to visit Yûko, the space-time witch. Like Fai and Syaoran, Kurogane has a wish: to return home.

Fai D. Florite

Again, you'll learn a lot more about Fai by reading his story in *Tsubasa.* Fai is himself a wizard in his land of Celes. When we first meet him in *Tsubasa,* he appears to have just completed a battle with Prince Ashura. Whether he won or lost that battle is unclear. Leaving his beloved creation Chi behind to guard against Ashura's return, Fai seeks Yûko to grant a wish directly opposite to Kurogane's: to journey without being forced to return home.

The Apple

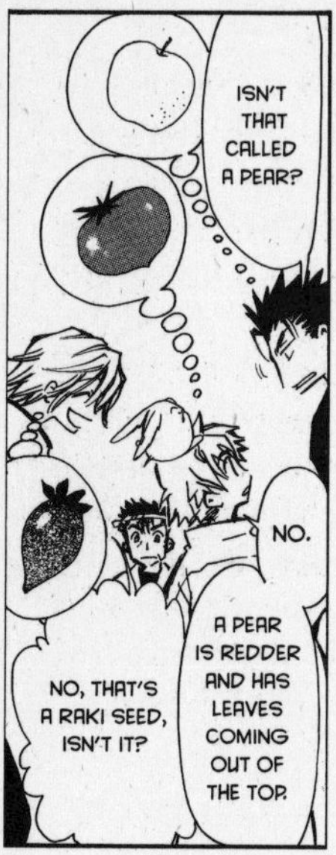
ISN'T THAT CALLED A PEAR?
NO.
A PEAR IS REDDER AND HAS LEAVES COMING OUT OF THE TOP.
NO, THAT'S A RAKI SEED, ISN'T IT?

Ah, now here's where it starts to get fun. Over in *Tsubasa,* Syaoran and his traveling companions are exploring the world of Hanshin. In the marketplace, they find an apple. Since each person comes from a different dimension, each has a different expectation of what an apple should look like. Mokona insists that they buy the apple, and that would seem to be the end of it.

But if you're paying close attention, you'll notice Mokona-White gulping the apple down . . .

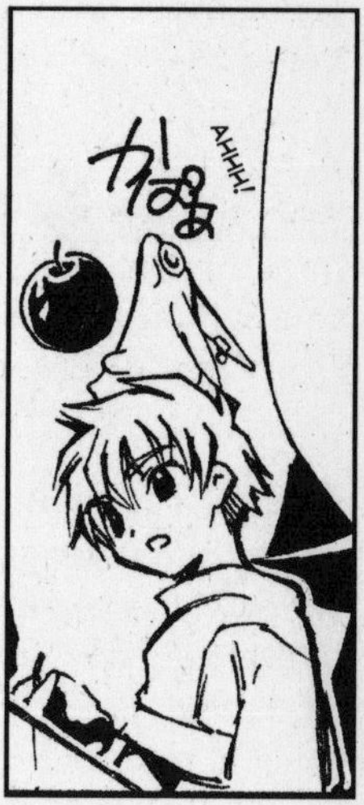
AHHH!

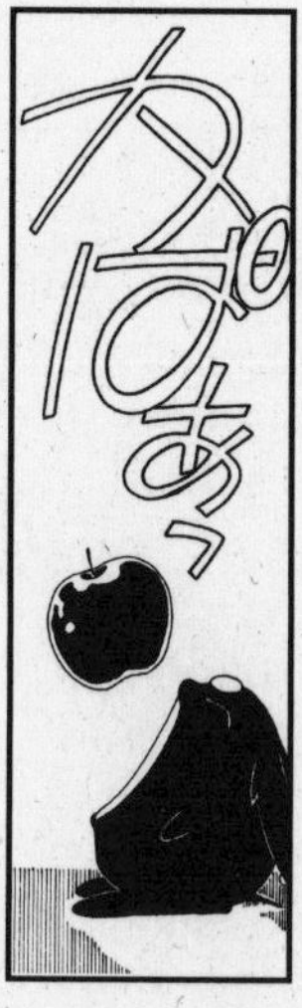

. . . and Mokona-Black choking it right back up! A little disgusting, perhaps, but fun nonetheless.

Uranai: Fortune-telling in Japan

On almost every street in Japan there are signs for one form or another of fortune-telling—they're as common as McDonald's signs are in Western circles. The Japanese believe fortune-telling is a very important part of daily life, and the general term for fortune-telling in Japan is *uranai*. In modern American society, fortune-telling usually consists of a few major areas: psychic reading, palmistry, zodiac astrology, and tarot. There are other areas, but those four categories comprise probably 85% or more of the paid fortune-telling in America. Japanese *uranai* makes use of those four, but the variety of other styles is much, much wider. Throw in Chinese astrology, the Tantric-based 27-constellation astrology, blood-type analysis, various versions of numerology, and *uranai* based on the *kanji* characters in your name, and that's only scratching the surface. Japan also embraces *uranai* more than America—walk down any downtown street in Tokyo and you will find some woman with a table and a sign in a darkened corner of the sidewalk. If she's good, she'll have customers lining up all night long.

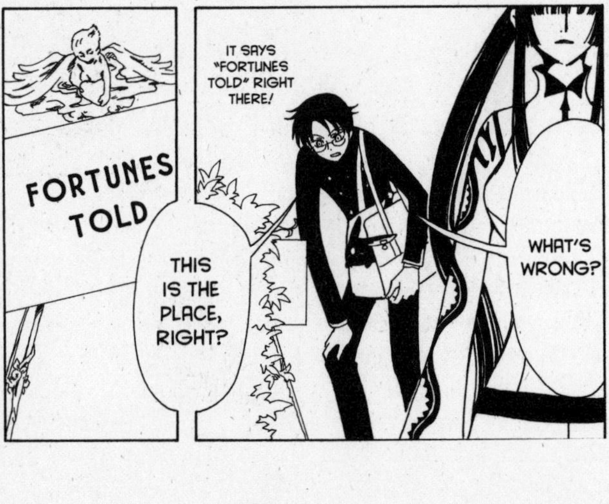
IT SAYS "FORTUNES TOLD" RIGHT THERE!
WHAT'S WRONG?
FORTUNES TOLD
THIS IS THE PLACE, RIGHT?

Some people won't even make any important decisions without first consulting some type of fortune-teller. There are three main types practiced in Japan: Omikuji, Seimeihandan, and Teso.

Omikuji is arguably the most popular. It's comparable to the use of Chinese fortune cookies. Many people go to shrines to purchase Omikuji to learn about the upcoming year. You get Omikuji by picking a piece of wood with a number on it. The number is exchanged for the slip of paper containing either good or bad luck. If it's good luck, the next year looks great! If it's bad luck, you can dispel it by visiting a shrine and tying the slip of paper to a tree there.

Seimeihandan means divination. It's the practice of using a person's name to determine his or her future, and it was used by Yûko to determine Watanuki's future in *xxxHOLiC* Volume 1. Many Japanese believe a person's name will decide what type of life he or she has. Fortune-tellers count the strokes in the kanji of a client's name and use that information to give advice and news.

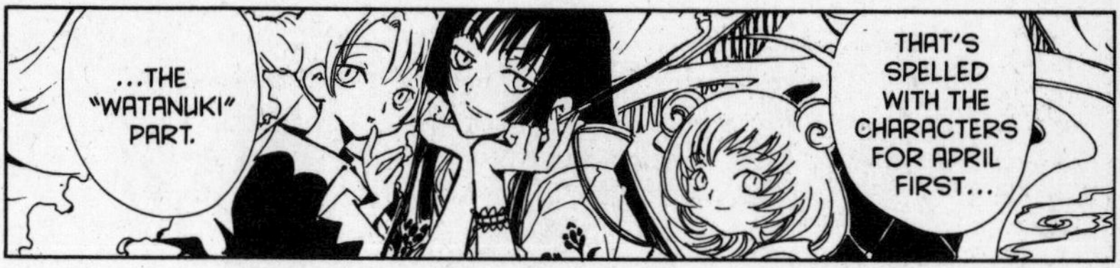
THAT'S SPELLED WITH THE CHARACTERS FOR APRIL FIRST...
...THE "WATANUKI" PART.

Teso is the common palm-reading that most Western people are familiar with. A fortune-teller will examine the lines on a person's palm and use that as a basis for determining personality and the future. Everyone has unique lines, and each one has a different significance such as the love line, the life line, the heart line, etc. By examining all the lines together a lot can be learned.

Translation Notes

For your edification and reading pleasure, here are notes to help you understand some of the cultural and story references from our translation of *xxxHOLiC*.

It's . . . so . . . hot!

In Japan, summer is the time for the dead (see below), a time for catching colds, and a time for complaining about how hot and sticky Tokyo is. With temperatures in the nineties and humidity nearing 100%, they have every right to complain. Some would say that with the technological advancements that come out of Japan, one should expect more air conditioners. But traditional-style homes are not built for this luxury, and the ever-traditional Yûko both swelters in her traditional home and, as per tradition, complains up a storm.

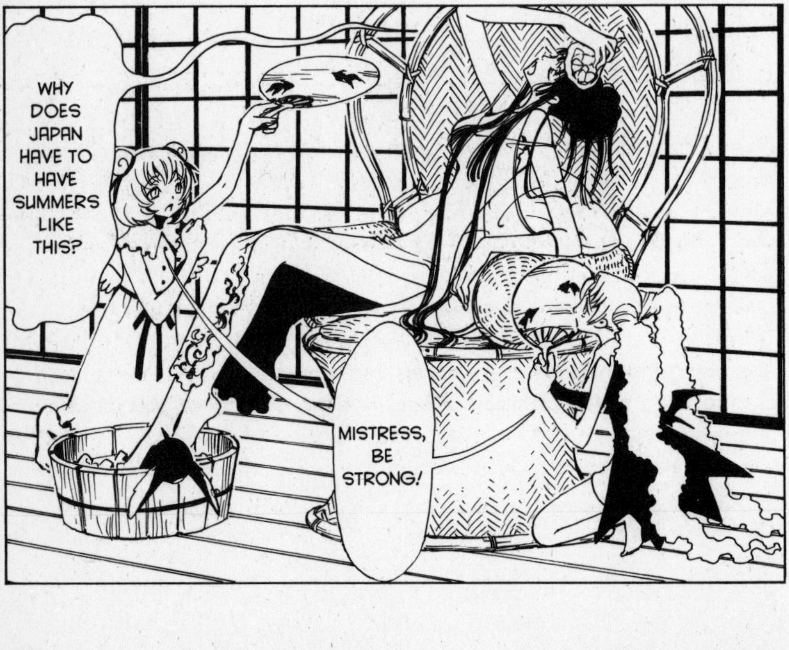
MISTRESS, BE STRONG!
WHY DOES JAPAN HAVE TO HAVE SUMMERS LIKE THIS?

The "Go Home Right After School Club"

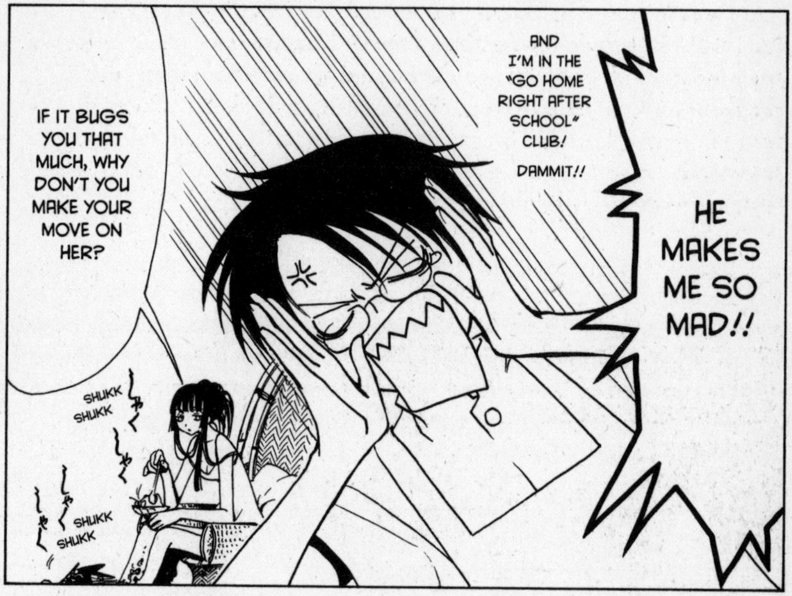
HE MAKES ME SO MAD!!
AND I'M IN THE "GO HOME RIGHT AFTER SCHOOL" CLUB!
DAMMIT!!
IF IT BUGS YOU THAT MUCH, WHY DON'T YOU MAKE YOUR MOVE ON HER?
SHUKK SHUKK
SHUKK SHUKK

As you probably guessed, there is no official club called the "Go Home Right After School Club." It's just a name for the students who haven't joined clubs. But most Japanese students do belong to a club of some sort—mostly sports clubs or hobby clubs. The clubs are not only a way to explore a student's interests, but also provide a social group, contacts, and moral or psychological support for the student. Dômeki's Archery Club is considered one of the more elite clubs of any high school because of the skill and concentration needed. Of course, the most popular clubs for guys are the soccer and baseball clubs.

Ghost Stories in the Summer

America centers its ghost season around Halloween, and so the harvest has become connected, in North American minds, with ghosts and ghouls. In Japan, *O-bon,* the annual festival celebrating one's ancestors which usually takes place in August (the date can differ from temple to temple), has become the gateway for the dead—or at least frightening stories about them. After long centuries of *O-bon* tradition, high summer has become the season for ghosts.

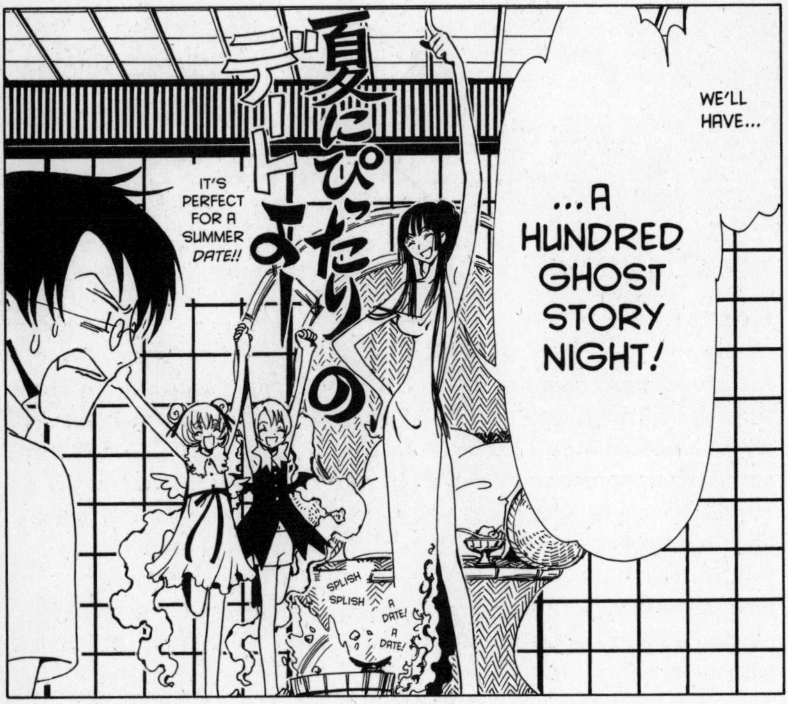

WE'LL HAVE...
...A HUNDRED GHOST STORY NIGHT!
夏にぴったりのデート
IT'S PERFECT FOR A SUMMER DATE!!
SPLISH SPLISH
A DATE!
A DATE!

Yukata

Tokyo, in the summer, is hot and sticky (see above), and one of the practical and beautiful innovations that Japan developed for this very purpose is a light cotton kimono called a *yukata*. Inexpensive and exquisitely decorated with prints or embroidery, women's *yukata* are a delightful addition to festivals and ceremonies.

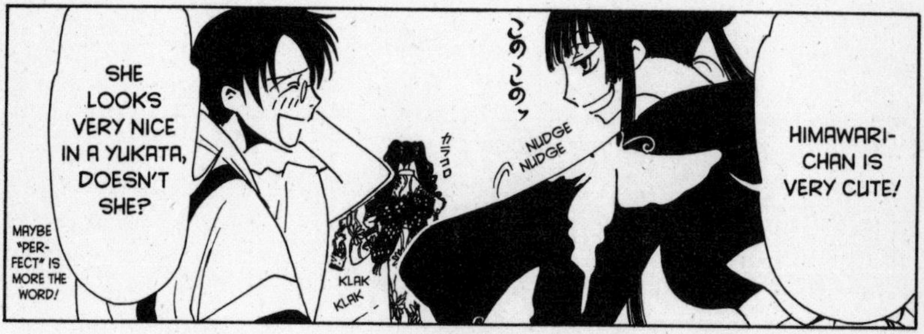
HIMAWARI-CHAN IS VERY CUTE!
NUDGE NUDGE
KLAK KLAK
SHE LOOKS VERY NICE IN A YUKATA, DOESN'T SHE?
MAYBE "PER-FECT" IS MORE THE WORD!

Hotel Room

American hotels tend to have rooms on both sides of the hall. Older-style Japanese hotels and apartment blocks tend to have a hallway against one exterior wall, and all of the rooms lined up like blocks along it. That's why there was only one room off of the walled-off hallway in Himawari-chan's story.

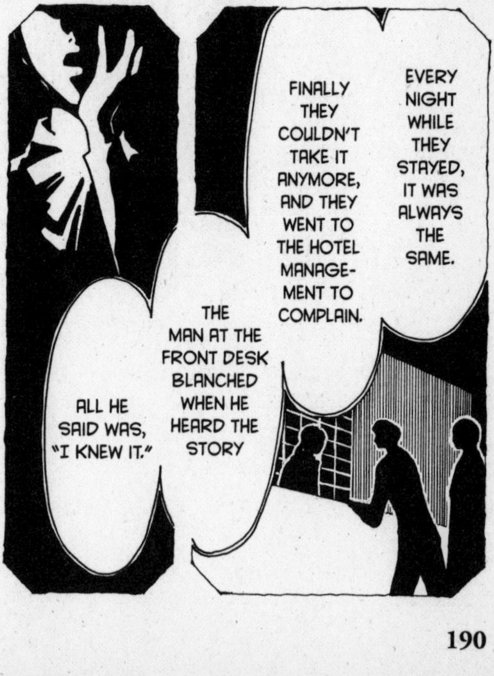
EVERY NIGHT WHILE THEY STAYED, IT WAS ALWAYS THE SAME.
FINALLY THEY COULDN'T TAKE IT ANYMORE, AND THEY WENT TO THE HOTEL MANAGE-MENT TO COMPLAIN.
THE MAN AT THE FRONT DESK BLANCHED WHEN HE HEARD THE STORY
ALL HE SAID WAS, "I KNEW IT."

Preview of Volume 3

Here is an excerpt from Volume 3, on sale in English now.

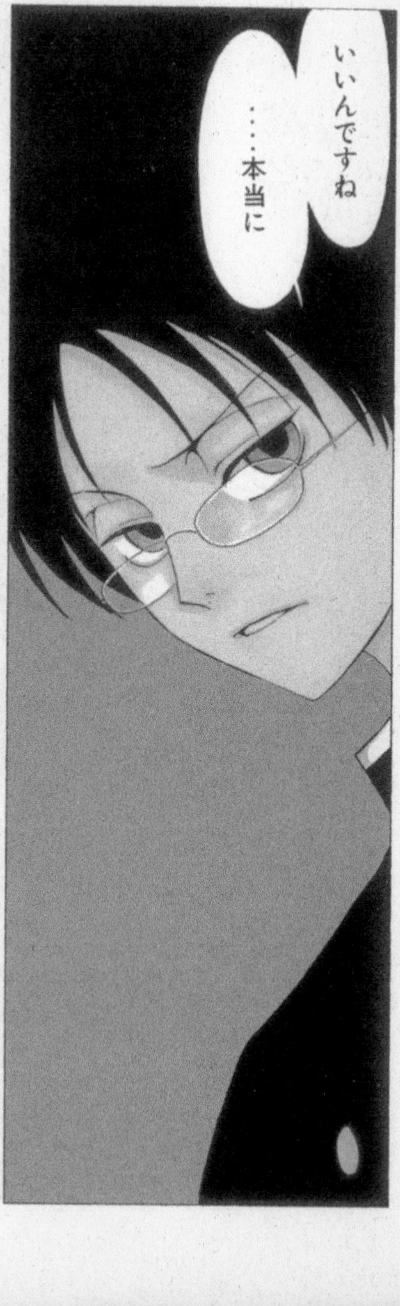
いいんですね
……本当に

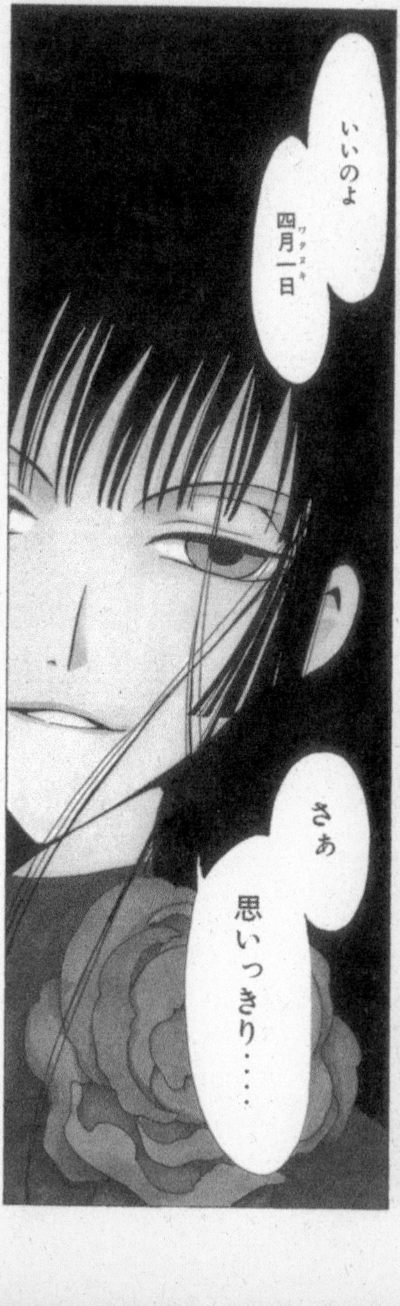
いいのよ
四月一日
さぁ
思いっきり……

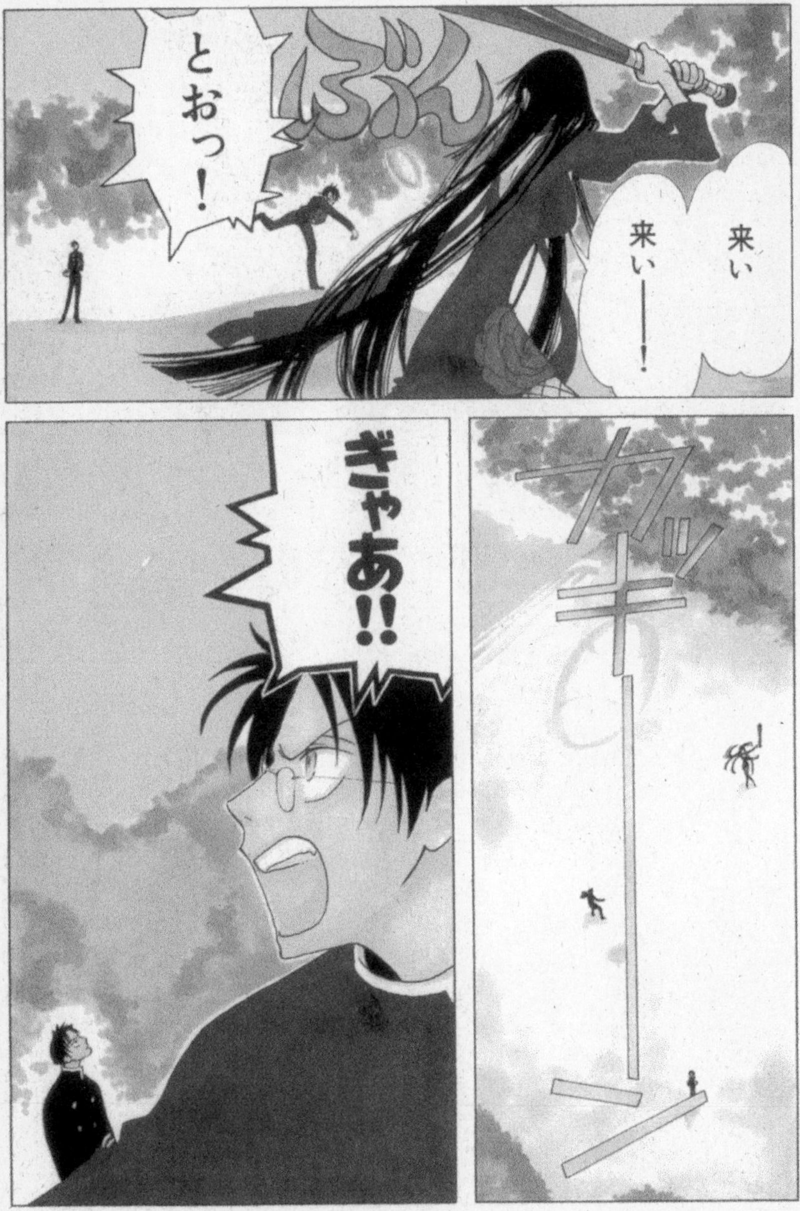
来い来い――!
ぶん
とおっ!
カッキーン
ぎゃあ!!

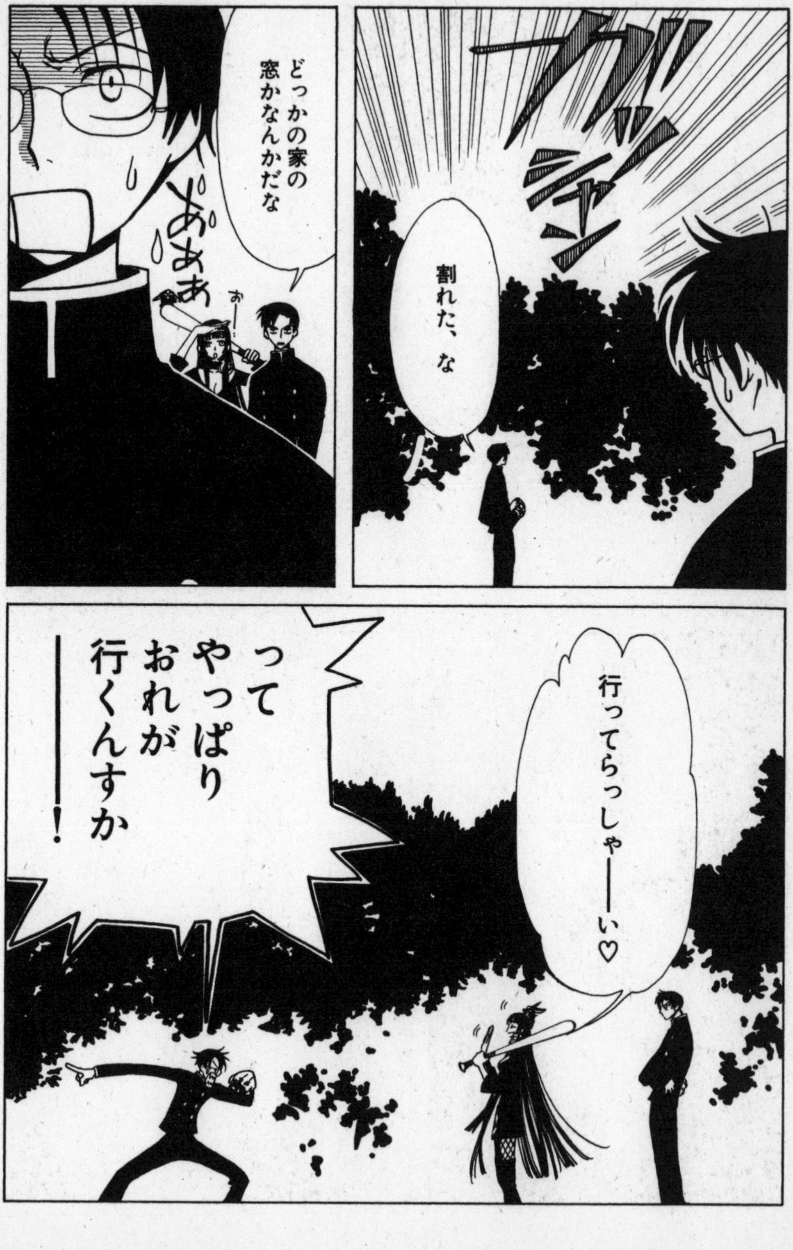
ガシャン
割れた、な
どっかの家の窓かなんかだな
ああ
おー…
行ってらっしゃ――い♡
ってやっぱりおれが行くんすか――！

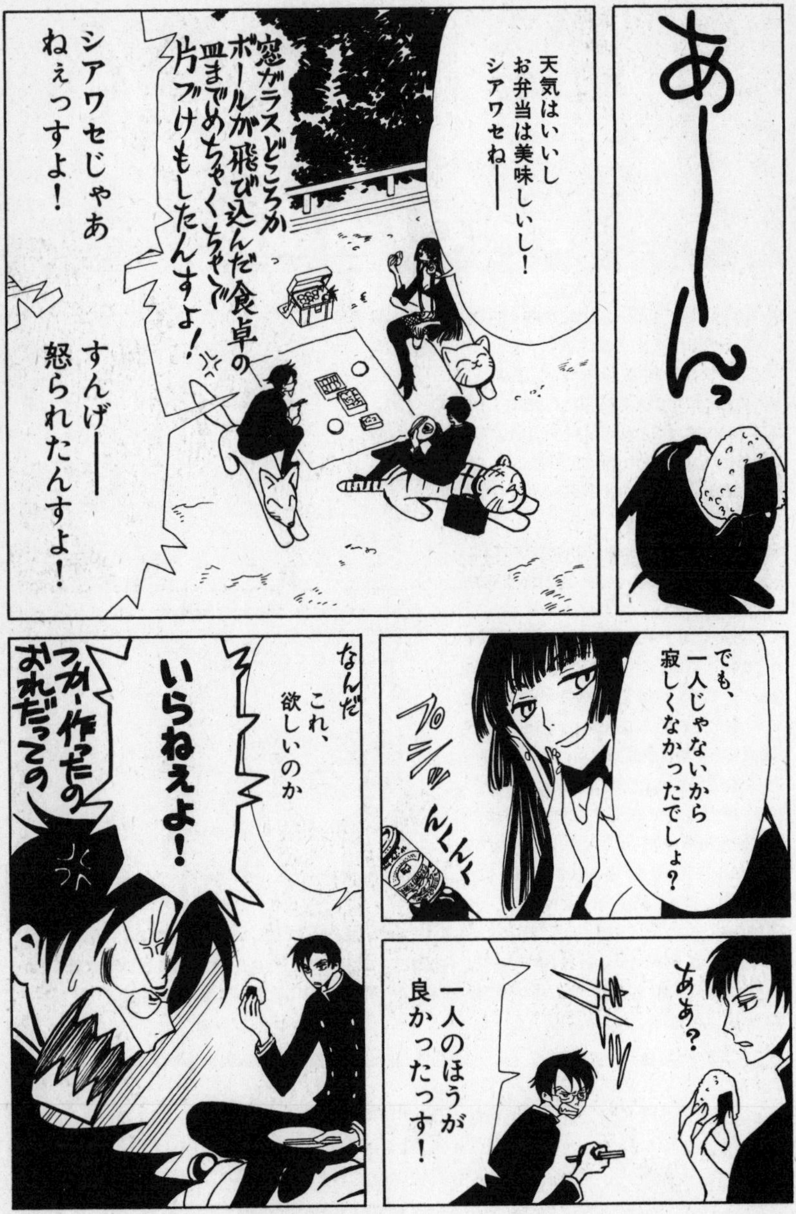
あーんっ
天気はいいし
お弁当は美味しいし！
シアワセねー
窓ガラスどころか
ボールが飛び込んだ食卓の
皿までめちゃくちゃで
片づけもしたんすよ！
シアワセじゃあ
ねぇっすよ！
すんげー
怒られたんすよ！
でも、
一人じゃないから
寂しくなかったでしょ？
プシュ
んくんく
ああ？
一人のほうが
良かったっす！
なんだ
これ、
欲しいのか
いらねえよ！
つか、作ったの
おれだってての

NEGIMA! ™

BY KEN AKAMATSU

Negi Springfield is a ten-year-old wizard teaching English at an all-girls Japanese school. He dreams of becoming a master wizard like his legendary father, the Thousand Master. At first his biggest concern was concealing his magic powers, because if he's ever caught using them publicly, he thinks he'll be turned into an ermine! But in a world that gets stranger every day, it turns out that the strangest people of all are Negi's students! From a librarian with a magic book to a centuries-old vampire, from a robot to a ninja, Negi will risk his own life to protect the girls in his care!

Ages: 16 +

Special extras in each volume! Read them all!

VISIT WWW.DELREYMANGA.COM TO:
- View release date calendars for upcoming volumes
- Sign up for Del Rey's free manga e-newsletter
- Find out the latest about new Del Rey Manga series

ART BY MASATSUGU IWASE
ORIGINAL STORY BY HAJIME YATATE
AND YOSHIYUKI TOMINO

In the world of the Cosmic Era, a war is under way between the genetically enhanced humans known as Coordinators and those who remain unmodified, called Naturals. The Natural-dominated Earth Alliance, struggling to catch up with the Coordinators' superior technology, has secretly developed its own Gundam mobile suits at a neutral space colony. But through a twist of fate, a young Coordinator named Kira Yamato becomes the pilot of the Alliance's prototype Strike Gundam, and finds himself forced to fight his own people in order to protect his friends. Featuring all the best elements of the legendary Gundam saga, this thrilling series reimagines the gripping story of men, women, and magnificent fighting machines in epic conflict.

Ages: 13 +

Special extras in each volume! Read them all!

VISIT WWW.DELREYMANGA.COM TO:
- View release date calendars for upcoming volumes
- Sign up for Del Rey's free manga e-newsletter
- Find out the latest about new Del Rey Manga series

Del Rey *Imagine*™

Four new titles in our exciting program of classic
fantasy and science fiction, carefully selected and
newly repackaged to appeal to a new generation
of readers ages 12 and up!

BLACK HORSES FOR THE KING by Anne McCaffrey
The tale of a boy whose skill with horses helps build the
army King Arthur needs to save all Britain—by the author of
the bestselling Dragonriders of Pern novels.
On sale now

PAWN OF PROPHECY: *The Belgariad, Book 1*
by David Eddings
Selected as a 2003 Popular Paperback for Young Adults by
the Young Adult Library Services Association (YALSA).
Young Garian must face a master of the darkest magic, if his
home and all the West are to be saved!
On sale now

THE OATHBOUND WIZARD by Christopher Stasheff
Student Matt Mandrell never imagined that his research into
music would lead him to a strange scrap of parchment that
would forever change his life. . . .
On sale now

THE SECRET OF THE UNICORN QUEEN:
Volume 1: SWEPT AWAY and SUN BLIND
by Josepha Sherman and Gwen Hansen
Long out of print and in high demand, an omnibus volume
of the first two books about young Sheila McCarthy's
adventures after being swept away into a fantasy world.
On sale now

Published by Del Rey
Available wherever books are sold